Praise for the novels of

WILBUR
SMITH

'Read on, adventure fans.'
NEW YORK TIMES

'A rich, compelling look back in time [to]
when history and myth intermingled.'
SAN FRANCISCO CHRONICLE

'Only a handful of 20th century writers tantalize
our senses as well as Smith. A rare author who
wields a razor-sharp sword of craftsmanship.'
TULSA WORLD

'He paces his tale as swiftly as he can with
swordplay aplenty and killing strokes that come
like lightning out of a sunny blue sky.'
KIRKUS REVIEWS

'Best Historical Novelist – I say Wilbur Smith, with his
swashbuckling novels of Africa. The bodices rip and the
blood flows. You can get lost in Wilbur Smith and
misplace all of August.'
STEPHEN KING

'Action is the name of Wilbur Smith's game
and he is the master.'
WASHINGTON POST

Wilbur Smith was born in Central Africa in 1933. He became a full-time writer in 1964 following the success of *When the Lion Feeds*, and has since published over forty global bestsellers, including the Courtney Series, the Ballantyne Series, the Egyptian Series, the Hector Cross Series and many successful standalone novels, all meticulously researched on his numerous expeditions worldwide. A worldwide phenomenon, his readership built up over fifty-five years of writing, establishing him as one of the most successful and impressive brand authors in the world.

The establishment of the Wilbur & Niso Smith Foundation in 2015 cemented Wilbur's passion for empowering writers, promoting literacy and advancing adventure writing as a genre. The foundation's flagship program is the Wilbur Smith Adventure Writing Prize.

Wilbur Smith died peacefully at home in 2021 with his wife, Niso, by his side, leaving behind him a rich treasure-trove of novels and stories that will delight readers for years to come. For all the latest information on Wilbur Smith's writing visit www.wilbursmithbooks.com or facebook.com/WilburSmith

WILBUR SMITH

STORM TIDE

WITH TOM HARPER

ZAFFRE

All rights reserved, including the right of reproduction in whole or in part in any form.
First published in the United States of America in 2022 by Zaffre,
an imprint of Bonnier Books UK

Typeset by IDSUK (Data Connection) Ltd
Printed in the USA

10 9 8 7 6 5 4 3 2 1

Hardcover ISBN: 978–1–8387–7886–6
Canadian paperback ISBN: 978–1–8387–7887–3
Digital ISBN: 978–1–8387–7888–0

For information, contact
251 Park Avenue South, Floor 12, New York, New York 10010
www.bonnierbooks.co.uk

SUSTAINABLE
FORESTRY
INITIATIVE

Certified Sourcing

www.forests.org
SFI-01984

This book is for my wife
MOKHINISO
who is the best thing that has ever happened to me

THE COURTNEY FAMILY
IN STORM TIDE

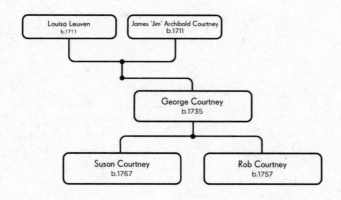

Louisa Leuven
b.1711

James 'Jim' Archibald Courtney
b.1711

George Courtney
b.1735

Susan Courtney
b.1767

Rob Courtney
b.1757

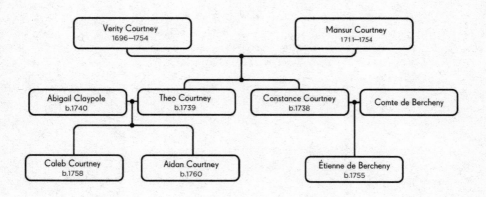

Verity Courtney
1696—1754

Mansur Courtney
1711—1754

Abigail Claypole
b.1740

Theo Courtney
b.1739

Constance Courtney
b.1738

Comte de Bercheny

Caleb Courtney
b.1758

Aidan Courtney
b.1760

Étienne de Bercheny
b.1755

Find out more about the Courtneys and see the Courtney family tree in full at

www.wilbursmithbooks.com/courtney-family-tree

EAST COAST OF AFRICA, 1774

Robert Courtney stalked his prey.

He hardly made a ripple as he waded through the crystal waters of the lagoon. At seventeen years old, he was already over six feet tall and still growing. His skin was tanned deep brown from a life spent under the African sun, his muscles strongly defined by work in the fields and long swims in the ocean. The fishing spear he held over his shoulder was as light as an arrow in his hands.

Above him, a great promontory rose steeply over Nativity Bay, while to his left the water disappeared in a tangle of mangrove swamps. A balmy breeze blew in from the sea, so soft it barely tickled the hairs on the back of his neck.

He stared into the water, tensing the arm that gripped the fishing spear. He ignored the small fish darting between his legs. He was after larger prey. Big kob and rock cod sometimes found their way into the bay to bask in the warm shallows. To spear them as they shimmered like mirages took speed and skill, but Rob had been playing in this bay since before he could walk. He could whip the spear down without a splash, instinctively adjusting his angle for the water's distortion.

Even so, it needed an element of luck to make the kill.

He had seen a movement by the rocks on the south side of the bay. He approached slowly, gliding through the water so as not to alert his quarry. The water grew deeper. Now he could no longer wade, but floated on his stomach, pushing forwards with little kicks that barely broke the surface.

A shadow caught his eye, dark against the white sandy bottom. It was too big to be a crab, too perfectly round to be a stone. He was intrigued. Forgetting the fish for a moment, he dropped his spear, letting it float on its wooden shaft. He duck-dived down. Tiny fish scurried out of his path as two strong kicks propelled him to the seabed. He reached for the object one-handed and was surprised when it didn't come away. Even with both arms, it took all his strength to lift it from the sand.

He broke the surface again and held his prize aloft, treading water. The moment he cupped it in his hands, he knew what it must be. Far heavier than you would expect for its size, with traces of its smooth iron surface still visible under the barnacles that encrusted it.

It was a cannonball.

He knew there had once been a battle in this bay. His grand-father, Jim, and his great-grandfather Tom had fought in it almost forty years ago. Rob had heard the stories so often he could recite them by heart. How the Caliph of Oman had brought his fleet to punish the Courtneys, and how Tom had lured those ships into the bay only to burn them to the water-line with heated shot. For years the skeletons of the sunken fleet had lurked in the bay like ancient monsters. But storms and tides had done their work, and the timbers had slipped out to sea or been washed ashore to be burned as firewood. The battle was disappearing from memory. When his grandparents died, it would be no more than a legend.

Rob wondered at the shifting currents and tides that had revealed the cannonball now. It was a long time since any gun had been fired in anger in Nativity Bay.

He was so busy staring at the relic he almost missed the movement in the water. The powerful thrust, the ripple of a fin piercing the surface. He looked up to see an enormous fish surging towards him.

Not a fish. A shark. A tiger shark.

It was so close, he could see every detail. The dark stripes down its flank, the open jaws, the yellow teeth pointing side-ways like the blade of a saw. From a boat, Rob had once seen a tiger shark bite clean through a turtle's shell. This one was a juvenile, but it was already bigger than Rob. It must have swum in to hunt in the shallow waters of the bay.

Rob had no time to escape. The shark was the hunter, and the ocean was its element. His spear had drifted out of reach.

The jaws stretched wider. Rob could see its two eyes, dark and malevolent, homing in on him. He had one chance.

He lifted the cannonball with both arms and brought it down with all his force. It struck the shark a glancing blow on the nose, inches from Rob's exposed stomach. The shark recoiled madly, slapping Rob viciously with its tail as it whipped around.

The impact knocked the cannonball from Rob's hands. The shark turned again to make another attack.

Rob lunged for his spear, kicking out with all his strength. His splashing drew the shark towards him. It pressed forwards with great thrusts of its tail, as keen as a bullet through the water. Its jaws opened to swallow his leg.

Desperately, Rob threw out his arm and grabbed the shaft of the spear. He jackknifed his body, snatching his legs from the shark's mouth as it snapped shut, teeth grazing his flesh. Blood clouded the water, driving the shark into a frenzy. It collided into him – a whirling mass of abrasive skin and fins – with such fury that Rob almost lost his hold on the spear.

His feet touched firm sand. Only for a second, but it gave Rob enough balance to hurl the spear around in a savage arc, just as the shark attacked again. The tip punctured its rubbery flesh and sank deep into its body.

The beast convulsed and writhed, churning the water red as its blood spilled out. A killer to the last, even in its dying moments the taste of its own blood drove it mad with hunger. Rob swam a distance away, watching and breathing hard. He felt no sympathy for the beast. His little sister often came to swim in this bay. Rob shuddered to think of her delicate body caught in those jaws.

Eventually the shark stopped moving. It rose to the surface and floated belly-up in the sea. Rob thrust the spear deeper into its flesh, then looped the rope over his shoulder to drag it to the beach. They would eat shark meat that night.

At that moment, the thunderous explosion of a cannon echoed across the water. Rob looked up and saw the prow of a ship sailing around the cape into the channel at the mouth of the bay. Quickly, he let go of the shark and kicked towards the sheltering rocks at the edge of the lagoon. Few captains knew the hidden entrance, and fewer still would risk their vessels through the treacherous passage without a pilot. But there was always the worry that one day a pirate or a slaver might chance upon it.

This ship was none of those. Rob gave a whoop of delight as he recognised the bare-breasted figurehead arcing forwards under the bowsprit. He clambered onto the rocks to watch her pass, shouting and waving at the crew.

She was a handsome vessel, a trim schooner with gunports picked out in black on white-painted planking. Her patched canvas told of the rigours of her ocean voyage, but her heavy-laden hull said she had done good business. Any deeper, and she would have grounded herself on the bar that guarded the mouth of the channel, but her captain steered her expertly past the hazards. Her topmen reefed the sails, while a gun crew on her foredeck secured the bow chaser which had fired the salute. As her stern swung around, Rob saw the name '*Dunstanburgh Castle*' across her transom.

Rob loved ships. They had fascinated him all his life. How many times had he climbed to the top of the bluffs with his father's spyglass to watch a distant sail scudding past? He had made his father tell him all the names until he knew them in his sleep: proud Indiamen and stout brigantines, Arab dhows from Zanzibar, and Bermuda sloops with their triangular sails. Most of all, he loved the men of war, the frigates and line-of-battle ships he occasionally saw beating up the coast from Cape Town, the red ensigns streaming from their sterns. Once – the most thrilling moment of his life – he had witnessed two frigates trade broadsides for nearly three hours, just a few miles off the coast. He had never forgotten the sight of the guns running out like rows of teeth, or the wall of flame as they fired in perfect unison.

The *Dunstanburgh Castle* was smaller than those warships, with only four guns on either side to discourage pirates. But even before her anchor touched the sandy bottom, Rob had swum over to the vessel, swarmed up her ladder and was peering through the gangway.

'Permission to come aboard,' he said.

'Who on God's earth are you?' A balding man with a flushed red face strode towards him across the deck. He had drawn a long, vicious knife. 'Damn me!' he swore. 'Is there no corner of this coast that is safe from pirates and savages?'

He stared at Rob, ready to gut him in an instant. With his skin tanned as brown as a walnut, dripping wet, smeared with shark's blood and naked as Adam, Rob looked like some kind of hideous sea sprite.

The man's anger slowly dissipated as memory came into focus. He returned his knife to its sheath, clapped his arms around the boy and embraced him.

'Robert Courtney. You have grown so big I barely recognised you. It is good to see you.'

'And you too, Captain Cornish.'

'Call me Tawny. Your grandfather always does.' He stepped back to get a better look at Rob. 'What is that blood on your leg?'

Rob looked down. The shark's teeth had left a row of red cuts from his knee to his ankle. If he had hesitated for a split second longer he would have lost the leg.

He gestured over the side, where the shark was floating towards shore.

'I caught us some dinner.'

He said it casually, but Tawny could see the effort it had taken.

'You have become a man,' he said gruffly. Then: 'You look a true pirate.'

'All I need is a ship.'

Rob hadn't stopped grinning since he came aboard. Even at anchor, he loved to feel the rhythm of the ship. The creak of the rigging; the gentle sway of the deck beneath his feet; the boatswain's shouts; the smell of tar and rum: the sensations were intoxicating.

Cornish studied him. He could read the look on the boy's face, the same yearning he had felt himself at that age.

'I could use some extra hands. Perhaps I will speak to your father.'

Rob's grin spread into a beaming smile. 'Would you?'

'I will. Now get your drawers on, and let us go ashore to see your family.'

B y the time the pinnace reached the beach, a party had gathered to meet them. Robert's father and grandmother had turned up, with his little sister Susan running between them, her golden braids flapping. Servants and workers crowded around them, for the Courtneys employed many of the local tribespeople on their estate. Most had served the family for decades and were treated more like family than staff.

Rob's father, George, gave Cornish a stiff handshake. His grandmother, Louisa, was less formal: she flung her arms around him and gave him a great kiss on the cheek.

'It is so good to see you,' she exclaimed. She brushed a strand of grey hair from his temple. 'What is this? It seems like only yesterday it was your father standing on this beach, after we had defeated that monster Zayn al-Din.'

Cornish doffed his hat. 'We are all older, ma'am. But you look as beautiful as ever.'

Louisa tutted and brushed the flattery aside. But there was truth in the captain's compliment. Though nearly sixty, she had lost none of her looks. Her creamy skin was supple, with only the faintest lines betraying her age. Her long blond hair had faded to white, but was still as fine as Chinese silk. And the blue eyes that smiled at Cornish were flawless, the colour of the deep ocean on a summer's day.

They narrowed with concern when she looked at Rob.

'What has happened to you?'

Cornish had had his surgeon salve and bandage the shark bite on Rob's leg, and given Rob a pair of canvas trousers to cover it.

'Do not tell my father,' Rob had begged him. But now when he looked down, he saw a dribble of blood had escaped and was trickling down his ankle onto his foot.

'It is only a graze,' he muttered.

In fact, there was a throbbing ache in his leg, and he felt light-headed. It took considerable effort to stay upright. But he gritted his teeth, and tried to stay on his feet.

Louisa's eyes missed nothing. She glanced at the shark, which the servants had pulled in and begun to butcher on the beach, then back at Rob. Three dark spots were spreading across the leg of his trousers like an outbreak of measles, where blood had seeped through the bandages into the cloth.

'Did you fight that shark?'

'Yes,' Rob admitted, unable to keep the pride from his voice.

His father scowled. Though twenty years younger than Louisa, he seemed older. His face was grey, his hair white. His back was bent forwards from years leaning on his stick, which he needed because his left leg was made of wood below the knee. He seldom smiled.

'You were supposed to be seeing to the cattle herd out at Dutchman's Creek, not playing at the seaside.'

Rob felt a flash of anger. A ship had arrived, and all his father cared about was farm chores. Rob bit his tongue. He knew if he tried to defend himself, it would provoke another quarrel. In his father's eyes he was still a boy to be ordered about, not a youth on the cusp of manhood.

'The boy is growing up,' said Cornish. George's scowl deepened; Cornish hastily changed the subject. 'Where is Jim?'

A shadow crossed Louisa's face. 'He is waiting for you at the house. He is not as strong as he was. But it will do him a world of good to see you.'

Cornish gave her his arm, and walked her up the beach. Rob's father fell in behind them, struggling to keep up as his wooden leg sank into the sand. Rob followed, wincing with every step but too proud to show it.

At the top of the beach, the shore opened out into flatland between hills and jungle. A river wound through it towards the sea, and on its bend stood the Courtney family compound. It had been built by Rob's great-grandfather, Tom. He had been running for his life when he reached Nativity Bay, and the home he built reflected his needs. It had been constructed like a fort, with the river for a moat and gun emplacements covering every approach. A glacis and a stockade wall completed the defences, and they had been enough to repel his enemies.

But that was forty years ago. The wooden stockade still ran around the perimeter, but now it was more to keep the cattle and goats from eating the flowers in the gardens Louisa had planted. The raised earth gun platforms at the corners had been turned into vegetable patches, while the only cannons to be seen were sunk upright into the ground to form gateposts. The buildings were white and unsullied, sparkling with the seashells that had been crushed into the lime.

It was a peaceful place, now: the only home that Rob had ever known.

His grandfather, Jim, was waiting for them on the veranda of the big house. His broad frame was stooped from a lifetime of working the land. His hair had turned white and he leaned on a cane. But the strength in his green eyes was undimmed, and it was an ageless smile that lit up his face when he saw Louisa approaching with Cornish.

He kissed Louisa and clapped his arms around Cornish.

'It seems a long time since our fathers fought Zayn al-Din and Uncle Guy in this bay,' he said.

'It is a long time,' Cornish agreed. 'God rest their souls.'

Tom Courtney had died ten years before, at the great age of ninety-one. His wife, Sarah, had survived him by a day and then she, too, had passed away. They were buried together on the headland at the top of the bluffs, in the red earth of the continent they had made their home.

'I will pay my respects before I go,' said Cornish. 'But life is for the living, and we are not done yet. Let me show you what I have profited on my latest voyage.'

Cornish told them tales of his travels, while they dined on the shark that Rob had killed. He was returning from India, and he had brought gifts for everyone: a bolt of fine silk for Susan, a jewelled box for Louisa, a painted miniature for George and a curved dagger for Rob. As he spoke of the great trading cities he had visited – Calcutta, Madras and Bombay – the pictures he conjured made Rob's eyes go wide with excitement. Jim leaned forwards, tapping his cane with delight to hear of Cornish's adventures.

'Did you ever go to India, grandfather?' Rob asked.

Jim shook his head. 'My father went often on his trading voyages, as did my cousin Mansur. But I have always preferred the plains of Africa to the open ocean.'

'Mansur settled in Madras, did he not?' Cornish asked Jim.

The light in Jim's eyes dulled. 'He did, after he and my father quarrelled. Some years ago, I heard that he had died when the French attacked the city. I sent letters to Madras to find out what had happened to his children, Constance and Theo, but all I heard was that they were living with a relative in Calcutta. I never learned what became of them afterwards.'

'It broke our hearts,' said Louisa softly. 'Mansur and Jim were like brothers.'

'And what of the rest of the world?' said Rob. As exciting as his family history had been, he had heard the stories so often they could not help but become dulled. He did not want to live in the past. 'What wars and battles and great contests now do they talk about in the coffee houses of London?'

Cornish puffed on his pipe. 'You forget it is almost two years since I left England. So far as I know, the country is at peace. But I cannot think it will last long. The colonists in America are making an almighty fuss about their liberty. I guess they mean to fight for it.'

'What is wrong with that?' Rob asked. 'All men deserve their liberty.'

'If you saw the blacks toiling in their fields,' said Cornish, 'you would wonder how deep their love of liberty runs.'

Rob didn't understand. 'We have blacks working in our fields.'

'And you pay them for it, and at the end of the day they go back to their homes and families, and if they do not like the work they go elsewhere.'

'It is different in America,' Louisa explained. 'They work as slaves.'

'I was moored in Cape Town harbour next to a Yankee slaver once,' Cornish said. 'All I heard was chains and wailing. And as for the stench – Hell itself could not smell so terrible. In the mornings, we used to watch the crew dump the bodies of those who had died in the night. Many were children no older than your Susan. They tossed them overboard and left them for the sharks.'

A distant look had come into Louisa's eyes; she was haunted by pain and sorrow.

'I came to Africa on a ship like that. We were convicts, not slaves, but they treated us the same.' She shivered. 'No human being should ever have to suffer that.'

Cornish nodded. 'The Yankees complain that King George treats them as slaves because he asks them to pay their taxes, but they'll beat a man to death for not working hard enough. That is how much they love *liberty* for any but themselves.'

'It will come to nothing,' said George confidently.

He hated talk of conflict, of anything that might intrude on the peace of Nativity Bay. In that, as in so much else, he was the mirror opposite of his son. Rob loved tales of war, battle and adventure. Many times, George had found Rob sitting at his grandfather's knee, listening to stories of the great exploits of the Courtneys of old. 'Why aren't you brave and strong like the other Courtneys?' Rob had asked once, speaking plainly as only a child could. He had grown up since then and learned tact, but the question always lingered unanswered, an unbridgeable chasm between father and son.

'Britain has the mightiest army and navy in the world,' George said. 'A few thousand colonists will not dare to defy them.'

'Maybe so,' Cornish allowed. 'But France has not forgotten how Britain bloodied her nose a few years back. France lost an empire in North America, and she would dearly love to get it back. If the colonists fight, the French may join them. And then King George will have a fantastic war on his hands.'

George shrugged. 'We are well out of it here.'

Rob was unable to check his emotions. He had glimpsed another world, and he was hungry for more of it.

'How can you say that, Pa? If there is to be a war, I would want to fight in it.'

George was about to make a sharp retort, but Jim spoke first.

'I remember how it was when I was your age. To fight for a cause, for a family or your honour, is a noble purpose. But perhaps when you have seen something of war, you will understand why your elders are less eager to embrace it.'

'It is a waste of time,' said George harshly.

Rob knew his father had been adventurous in his youth. He had heard the stories from his grandparents. He had dim memories of being a small boy, sitting on the tip of the cape searching the ocean for the first sight of his father's sail return-ing. He remembered the sand between his toes as he ran down the beach to meet the jollyboat rowing his father ashore. He was so excited he could not wait on the shore but waded out, until his father reached over the side of the boat and scooped him out of the water. They would go up to the big house, and Rob would sit on his father's knee while the family gathered around to hear the stories of his latest voyage.

Nothing was the same after George lost his leg. It had been a minor incident, a scuffle with pirates off the coast of Madagascar. The Courtneys had chased them off easily, and the musket ball that had ricocheted into George's calf barely seemed to have broken the skin. But the wound festered. The rot spread, and soon the only way to save his life was to amputate the limb. Rob would never forget sitting outside the house, listening to the screams as Jim sawed off his own son's leg. Neither man had recovered fully from the experience. George had never gone to sea again.

Cornish saw the look on Rob's face. 'Your son is grown up,' he said to George. 'It is time he made his way in the world.'

'Maybe,' said George. 'In a few years, perhaps.'

Rob could not keep his news to himself any longer.

'Captain Cornish has offered me a berth on his ship,' he burst out.

George's face darkened. 'Then I am sorry he has misled you. He had no right to make that offer.'

'I want to go,' said Rob.

'I cannot allow it. I need you here, Rob. There is much work to do on the farm. And if any danger threatened, who would defend your sister and your grandmother?'

'All the local tribes are loyal to us,' Rob protested. 'If there were any troubles, they would protect you.'

'If you will not think of me, at least think of your grandfather. Will you break an old man's heart to go off on some foolish adventure?'

Jim stirred. In his old age, he fell asleep in his chair so often the others sometimes forgot he was there. But now he rose, gripping his cane with iron determination.

'You know nothing,' he said to George. 'The only thing that would break my heart is seeing my grandson kept here against his will. He must go out, explore the world and make his own fortune. As you did, once.'

George tapped his wooden leg bitterly. 'Look what it got me. Do you want the same for Robert?'

'I want him to live.'

'So do I.'

'No! You want him to stay alive – and that is very different.'

They glared at each other. Rob looked between them, the two men he loved most in the world. His father, and the grand-father who had been almost a second father to him. He hated being the cause of a quarrel between them. But above all – and the feeling was growing stronger – he hated these two old men telling him what to do.

'Did you ever think I should have some say in my own life?' he shouted.

Before either man could reply, he stormed out of the house.

George glowered after him. Jim made to follow, but Louisa put her hand on his arm.

'Let him be,' she counselled. 'He needs time to cool down.'

Tawny Cornish stood awkwardly. 'I should return to my ship.'

'I will walk you down,' said George.

After they had gone, Jim and Louisa sat on the steps outside the house, as they had done so many times, looking at the sky and picking out the constellations. The bright band of the Milky Way lit up the heavens, while around them fireflies glimmered among the bushes.

'If we had not conceived George in a thousand miles of uninhabited wilderness, I would start to worry you had been unfaithful,' said Jim gruffly. 'How can he be a son of mine?'

Louisa put her head on Jim's shoulder. 'Do you remember when he was a boy? Always on his feet, always prying into everything. Every stick he picked up was a sword or a gun.'

'When did he become such a coward?'

Louisa stiffened. 'Do not say that. You do not have to prove yourself in battle to be brave.'

'I sometimes think when I amputated his leg, I accidentally cut off his balls as well.'

Louisa had never heard him speak like this. She supposed that as Jim's strength waned, he felt his own impotence more keenly.

'George was as adventurous as you ever were,' she said. 'When he quit the sea, he did it for Rob and Susan. He did not want to risk making them orphans.'

Jim was silent. He knew she was right, though his pride would not let him admit it. He remembered the screams as he wielded the saw.

'In any event, he should not stand in Rob's way. It is time the boy took charge of his own destiny.'

'Of course,' said Louisa. 'And George will realise that in time. Having you shouting in his face will only make it harder. He is stubborn, like all you Courtneys.'

Jim's expression softened. 'You are a Courtney, too, my love. You became one the day you married me.'

'And did you wait for your father's say-so before you whisked me away from Cape Town?'

'As I recall, we were too busy galloping away from the whole Dutch garrison to ask his approval.' Jim's voice was hoarse, but his eyes were bright with the memory. 'You did not complain at the time.'

'And I have never regretted it.' Louisa stood and helped Jim to his feet. 'But we cannot control what our children do, still less our grandchildren. We must trust to God.'

'I would rather trust to a good horse and a gun in my hand.'

Louisa kissed him. 'Jim Courtney,' she murmured, 'you will never change.'

Cornish stayed a week. In happier times he would have remained longer, but he could see that his presence only deepened the rift between Rob and George. Father and son barely spoke to each other, and if they did it always ended in shouts and slammed doors. When Cornish announced he would leave, he could almost feel his hosts' relief.

The Courtneys walked down to the beach with Cornish – all except Jim, who complained of a headache. Rob felt as if he was following his own funeral. At the shore, Cornish clasped Rob's hand, and looked at him with pity in his eyes.

'Perhaps next time I call, lad,' he said gruffly. 'It is a hard life on this continent. You must not grudge your father for wanting you by his side.'

There was nothing Rob could say. He watched the pinnace row out to the *Dunstanburgh Castle*, the topmen running along the yards to loosen the sails. He imagined how the world would look from that height, balanced on a thin spar with nothing except a hundred feet of air between him and the ocean. The crew fitted the spokes to the capstan and began hauling up the anchor. As the ship prepared for departure, it seemed as if his whole future was about to sail away.

Rob refused to look at his father.

A howling rose from the compound behind them. For a moment, Rob thought it was the dogs. Then he realised it was their African servants, wailing in melancholy. It must be a song of farewell for Cornish and his crew, yet it sounded so heart-rending it made Rob's pain seem small by comparison.

One of the servants came running down the track from the house. He came to a halt and dropped to his knees on the sand. The look on his face told Rob it was something much worse than Cornish's departure.

'Massa Jim is dead.'

Without a doctor present, no one knew what had caused Jim's death. Perhaps it was a sudden heart attack, an instant extinguishing of life. Rob hoped he hadn't suffered, that death came quickly, like a candle being snuffed. It was all so mysterious and troubling. They buried him on the headland, in a simple grave beside his mother and father. Cornish, who had returned from his ship, said the funeral service; George delivered a short eulogy. Rob did not know what to say. He had been almost too young to remember his mother's death. Since then, he had lived a blessed life. The only loss he had known was when his dog, Samson, had been killed by a snake bite. Now, grief was a new and terrible experience for him. He did not know why he felt such despair. He had to fight back the tears that threatened to flood his cheeks, for he knew his father would not approve.

The day after the funeral, Rob visited the grave. Freshly turned soil rimmed the stone slab they had placed over the coffin, the inscription still dusty white from the marks of the chisel.

James Courtney
1711 – 1774

Rob's father stood at the grave, his head bowed. He looked different: shrunken somehow, as if the loss of his father had removed an essential part of his soul. He was diminishing; first there was his physical injury, and now his spirit was eroding. Rob sensed the changes, as if day was turning to night. He saw him not as an omnipotent authority figure but as a lonely, frail, greying man.

Rob moved to his father's side in silence. He could not think of anything to say. He wanted to throw his arms around him, to bear some of the burden of his sorrow. But he could feel the pride and solitude radiating from George like the heat of a fire, and he did not dare move.

At last he could not stand the silence any longer.

'I will never forget the story of how he rescued Grandmother Louisa from a convict ship as it was dashed to pieces on the shore.' He had heard the tale a thousand times, and it still sounded incredible.

George said nothing.

'He was a true hero,' Rob continued.

It was hard to imagine the twinkle-eyed old man he had known as the amazing adventurer he had heard about.

George shot him a sideways glance. Suspicion twisted his face.

'And I am not, I suppose?'

Rob started. 'I did not mean that.'

'I have seen how you look at me.' George tapped his wooden leg. 'Your father the cripple, the stay-at-home. Could not hold a candle to the great Jim Courtney.'

George had always possessed an acerbic streak. But Rob had never seen him as bitter as this.

'How can you stand at his grave, with him not one day buried, and say that?' Rob said. 'Your own father.'

George stared at his son. 'When you are older you will understand.'

'I am going to leave home,' said Rob suddenly. He did not know where the words came from. He had not meant to broach the subject so soon after Jim's death, but as soon as he said it, he felt a great burden had been lifted.

'We discussed this before,' said George. 'You cannot leave. I forbid it.'

'No,' said Rob. 'If any good can come from Grandfather's death, it has given me a second chance to leave with Captain Cornish. You said you needed me to look after your father. Now that burden is lifted.'

'And now I say I need you to work the land.'

'And I say that even if every field was harvested, and all our cattle fat, you would still find an excuse to make me stay.' Rob turned away. 'I am going, Father, whether you say aye or no.'

'You will do as you're damn well told.'

George's hand landed heavily on Rob's shoulder. He spun his son around. Before Rob could react, George hit him hard across his cheek.

Tears pricked Rob's eyes, though not from the pain. As a boy, George had beaten him just like any father – but not for many years. Beyond the anger of the moment and the bruise rising on his cheek, what hurt most of all was the underlying message of the blow: *You are no more than a child.*

Rob hit back.

He was not a child. He had grown to manhood, his body lean and prime. The punch he threw had a power behind it, charged with youth and fury. His fist struck his father's chin so hard it lifted him off the ground and deposited him on his backside three feet away. The wooden leg caught awkwardly in a crack. Bent backwards, it snapped in two.

Rob stood over his father. George lay on his back like an overturned beetle, the stump of his wooden leg sticking in the air. His lip was bleeding, his face was white with astonishment.

'You will pay for that,' he gasped.

'No.' Rob looked down at his father. He felt sick, though he couldn't tell if it was guilt or contempt. 'You are not my master. You are nothing but an old man.'

A tear escaped his eye. Rob wiped it away. Blood pumped in his ears, making a sound like the most violent ocean storm. Before his father could see him cry, he turned and ran down the path.

Rob did not go to dinner that evening. He stayed in his room.

At nine o'clock, he heard Louisa's soft knock on his door. He didn't answer, although when he opened the door some time later he found she'd left him a tray of food. He devoured it hungrily.

At ten o'clock, he heard the familiar rhythm of his father's wooden leg tapping down the hall as he went to bed, tentative and unsure. He'd had to splint the leg together to repair it, and he did not know if he could trust his weight to it. Rob waited for George to pass by.

The tapping stopped outside Rob's room.

Rob could see his father's shadow through the crack below the door. He waited for it to open, holding his breath. He saw the handle turn. He wondered what he would say to his father. Had he come to apologise, or to shout at Rob again?

He would never know. The handle was released, the shadow moved on. George walked away up the corridor. *Tap. Tap. Tap.* Rob heard the creak of his father's bedroom door, then silence.

Rob breathed again. There was an ache in his chest, though he couldn't tell if it was relief or disappointment.

At eleven o'clock, the light under the door went out as the servants extinguished the lamps and retired to their quarters. The only sound was the insects chirping outside, and the call of an eagle owl in a tree nearby. Rob lay on his bed, fully dressed, staring at the ceiling and fighting his last-minute doubts. Could he do this?

He rubbed his face and felt the bruise his father had left. Did he want to stay here all his life and end up like his father: bitter and shrunken? He climbed off the bed. He had packed his clothes, his knife, the necklace he had made out of the shark's tooth and a few other belongings in a canvas bag. He dropped it out of the window and clambered after it. The night air was cool, the moon so bright it dimmed the stars. It refreshed him. He was doing the right thing.

He crept away from the house, through the stockade fence and down the path to the beach. His head was brim-full of thoughts of the adventure ahead; he didn't think to take a last look back until the house had disappeared behind him.

Down in the bay, the *Dunstanburgh Castle* sat at anchor, ready to sail on the morning tide. The calm water around her gleamed like a mirror. There was a small dugout canoe drawn up above the tidemark. Rob dragged it to the water's edge and stowed his bag. He was about to get in, when suddenly a voice behind him said:

'Where do you think you are going, Robert Courtney?'

Rob spun around, to see his grandmother emerging from the shadows of a kapok tree. Her silver hair was luminous, her white dress like a shaft of moonlight.

'I thought the fish might be rising in the bay,' Rob lied.

'And what do you expect to catch without a rod or a spear?'

Rob was glad she could not see him blush in the dark.

'I was running away,' he mumbled. Then, finding his courage. 'I *am* running away. To join Captain Cornish's ship.'

To his surprise, she didn't argue. 'Of course you are.'

He stared at her. 'You will not try to stop me?'

'Would you listen?'

She moved towards him. He noticed she was carrying two bundles: a small round bag tied at the neck, and a long, thin parcel wrapped in a sheet.

'I know you cannot stay here. I have seen the way you look at the sea, and the ships that call. You gaze at that blue horizon and long to discover what is beyond it.'

Rob had never heard her talk like this before. For the first time in what seemed like his whole life, he felt that he was speaking to someone who truly understood him.

'But be careful,' Louisa warned him. 'Before Tom came to Nativity Bay, not one of the Courtney men lived out their full years. Tom's father, his grandfather, his three brothers . . . they all met violent, untimely ends. Fort Auspice has been a paradise for us, a place where the family can live in peace. I fear what will happen to you if you leave it.'

Rob saw the concern in her face. He heard the anguish in her voice. But he was seventeen, and immortal as all young men think they are, and he did not believe her.

'I must do this,' he told her.

She wiped a tear from the corner of her eye. 'I knew you would say that. Jim would have said the same.'

She handed the bag she carried to Rob. It was only small, but her thin arms struggled with the weight. When he took it, he heard the clink of coins.

'Consider it your inheritance from Jim,' she said. 'Wherever you go, it will ease your path. And if you are a true Courtney, you will make it grow tenfold before you come home.'

Rob took the bag with amazement. He had never held so much money before, had never even thought of it.

'Also, I want you to have this.'

Louisa took the second bundle and unwrapped it. Rob gasped. He had seen it before, many times.

'Uncle Jim's Neptune sword.'

'It was presented to our family by Sir Francis Drake himself,' said Louisa, though Rob knew all the stories by heart. 'Every man in the Courtney line has carried it into battle.'

Moonlight gleamed on the blue Toledo steel. Rob thumbed the blade. Jim had not used it in anger for years, yet the blade was as sharp as the day it was forged. He turned it in his hands, thrilling to feel the perfect balance of the weapon.

He craved it with all his soul. But–

'I cannot take this.' He pushed it back into Louisa's hands. 'It should go to my father.'

'Your father is a good man. He is my son, and I love him, but he is forged from a different metal than the other Courtneys. He will never use this sword again. It was not meant to be kept sheathed, gathering dust in a forgotten corner of an unknown continent. Jim wanted you to have it – and so do I.'

She put it in his hand and closed his fingers around it. Rob's arm trembled as he took it. For the first time, he felt the heavy finality of his decision.

'Will I see you again?' For a moment his voice sounded like a child's again.

'Of course you will,' said Louisa briskly. 'I am not so terribly old, and the tides will always bring you home. Come back wealthy and strong, and with a beautiful young bride on your arm and a brood of great-grandchildren for me to spoil.'

'I promise,' said Rob.

'Now go. Cornish needs a full tide to get his ship over the bar, and he will not delay.'

They embraced. Rob's strong arms almost crushed Louisa's thin body with the strength of his emotion. For a moment she feared he might never let her go.

But the lure of the sea was irresistible. He released her, kissed her on the cheek, and loaded the sword and the money into the waiting canoe. Louisa pushed him off, wading into the water in her nightdress until he was clear. He paddled out to the ship with strong, confident strokes.

'Farewell!' he called back.

The moonlight made a silver path on the bay, straight towards the anchored ship and out into the open ocean. Soon Rob was nothing more than a shadow against the bright water. Louisa touched the cross she wore around her neck.

'God speed,' she whispered, though not without a tremor in her heart. She put her hand on her breast. There was a lump there, invisible beneath the skin. She had told no one, not even Jim, but she had felt it, growing inside her with malignant power.

There was no point trying to fight it. Her life had had its share of sorrows, but it had also given her many joys. She was content.

But she knew she would never see Rob again.

Rob hid himself in the hold, which was thick with the aromatic spices of Cornish's Indian cargo. He meant to wait two days, so there could be no chance of Cornish sending him back. In the end, he needed to relieve himself so badly he emerged, blinking and shamefaced, just as the ship's bell struck noon. The great whale-backed summit of the cape was still clearly visible behind them.

Tawny Cornish surveyed him sternly. 'A stowaway, eh?'

'Please,' Rob begged. 'Do not take me back.'

'I cannot take the responsibility. If any harm came to you . . .'

Cornish was torn. It was late in the season to catch the trade winds, and he would count the cost in lost profits of every day's delay reaching London. But he could not in good conscience take the boy from his family.

'What would I tell Louisa?'

'It was Grandmother who helped me stow away. She gave me this.'

The Neptune sword sang in the morning sunlight as he pulled it out.

'Put that away,' said Cornish hurriedly. 'That is a weapon that should not be drawn lightly.'

Rob obeyed. 'You said yourself I should make my own way in the world.'

The breeze snapped the masthead pennant. Cornish made his decision.

'I will sign you on as a fo'c's'le hand. But you will have to earn your keep,' he warned Rob. 'No loitering or shirking.'

Rob's grin was so wide his jaw ached. 'Thank you, sir. I promise you will not regret it.'

Cornish assigned Rob a mess and a watch, and ordered one of the mates to show him the ropes. Rob was a quick learner, and an eager student. His mind and body moulded naturally to his tasks. Soon, he could run aloft as fast as any of the topmen, balancing on the yards like a cat as the ship rolled beneath. He could splice a line, reef a sail and tie a knot all while a hundred feet in the air. His young body, already strong, grew harder. Cornish was a firm taskmaster, but he could hardly hide his pride. Even when Rob returned from shore leave in Cape Town sporting a hangover and a livid tattoo on his arm, the captain barely raised an eyebrow.

He had caroused hard in Cape Town, determined to prove himself a rough, tough, but loyal mate. His gang of sailors drank and sang, Rob's voice growing hoarse as he poured his heart and soul into the melodies. As one of the youngest he could reach the top notes, which he would sustain until his breath ran out, and everyone in the room clapped and yelled encouragement, standing him drink after drink. He was free, this was a new life, and he felt a surge of pent-up life force urging him on to ever more devilish pranks and laughter. He wanted to mark himself as one of the crew, so he bit his lip and looked away as the tattooist carved intricately into the skin of his upper arm, the pain as nothing compared to the joy of camaraderie. Imprinted for a lifetime was a bold anchor entwined in muscular rope. Arms around shoulders, bonded by blood and unshakeable brotherly love, the gang stumbled from tavern to tavern and into the night.

The boy was growing up.

'You are like a wild colt that has jumped the paddock fence,' Cornish told Rob. 'Just like your grandfather, Jim.'

Rob glowed with pride. He knew there was no higher compliment Cornish could give, nor one that Rob would cherish more.

The *Dunstanburgh Castle* rounded the Cape of Good Hope and ploughed into the great rollers of the Atlantic Ocean. Soon afterwards, the coast of Africa slipped below the horizon. Rob, working at the masthead, was the last man on the ship to see the continent before it vanished. The only home he had ever known.

But that was the past. He turned his back on it, and set his face towards the north-west, to the new horizons and new continents that awaited him.

On the far side of the ocean, nearly eight thousand miles away in the colony of Massachusetts, Theo Courtney was in a towering fury.

'What is this?' he demanded, waving two scraps of paper. They had been a single sheet, until he had torn it apart in his anger. 'I found it in your bedroom.'

Caleb Courtney stood in the farmhouse kitchen and stared his father down. There was no doubting their relationship: both had the same strong frame, thick red hair and piercing green eyes. Theo's face was tanned from long hours overseeing his farms, while Caleb's was still speckled with youthful freckles. Otherwise, there was little difference between them.

'It is a pamphlet,' said Cal coolly. 'And you should not have been spying in my bedroom.'

'It is treason,' Theo spluttered. 'It says that our colony should break with Britain and declare for independence.'

'You call it treason. I call it common sense.' And then, because Cal was of an age when he could not resist provocation: 'King George is a tyrant who means to make slaves of us all.'

'I risked my life in the King's armies!' Theo shouted. 'While you and your hothead friends were sucking your mothers' teats, I was fighting to keep the colonies safe from the French. And now that menace has gone, and the King of England has the *temerity* to ask the colonies to pay for their own deliverance, you call it slavery?'

'We do not vote for the Parliament in London. Why then should we submit to their demands? Only the legislatures of the colonies have the right to levy taxes.'

Theo's face flushed so red he looked as if he might explode.

'We are Englishmen. If Parliament cannot make our laws, it is anarchy.'

'He doesn't mean it, Pa,' said a voice from the doorway. It was Theo's second son Aidan, smaller and darker than his older brother. He had listened to the argument unnoticed. 'Just 'cause he read it doesn't mean he thinks it.'

'Keep out, Aidan,' said Cal. 'This is not your business.'

'I live here, too. If there's to be a war—'

'There will be no war,' said Theo, in a voice that brooked no argument. He crumpled the two scraps of paper into a ball and threw it into the fire. He glared at Cal, defying him to protest. 'And if I hear any more of this treason, you will find you are not yet old enough that I cannot give you a thrashing.'

'Nothing compared to the thrashing we will give King George,' muttered Cal. He skipped out of the kitchen, avoiding the pewter mug Theo had thrown at his ear.

He went to the stables and saddled up his horse, Maverick. He needed to ride.

The horse's presence soothed him. Maverick had been a birthday present from his father, a fearsome stallion with a coat as glossy and black as wet tar. He was named after Samuel Maverick, the apprentice who had been shot dead by the British in the Boston Massacre a few years earlier and had become a martyr to the cause of liberty. Maverick had been part of a crowd confronting British soldiers. When the soldiers raised their muskets to scare off the mob, Maverick called out, 'Fire away, you damned lobsterbacks!' – which they did, killing Maverick and four others.

Theo thought Cal had named the horse for his fearsome temper, and Cal had not told him the truth. He did not want his father to think he was ungrateful.

He stroked Maverick's nose and combed a knot from his mane. He buckled the girth, and was about to step up into the stirrups when a shadow fell across the stable doorway.

'You're not running away, are you?' said Aidan, in a fearful voice.

'I'll be back for supper,' said Cal curtly.

Ever since Aidan could walk, he had followed his big brother like a shadow, desperate not to be left behind. When Cal learned to ride, Aidan had dislocated his collarbone trying to clamber onto the horse. When Cal started boxing with his friends, Aidan had come home with a broken arm. Sometimes, Cal appreciated the adoration. For most of the past fourteen years, he had found it intensely annoying.

'Where are you going?' said Aidan.

'Over to the Hartwell farm.'

'Why?'

Cal didn't answer.

'You've been there five times in the last week. Are you sweet on Liza Hartwell?'

'Of course not,' said Cal.

'Then why?'

Cal hesitated. Seeing he had an opening, Aidan played his trump card.

'If you don't say, I'll tell Pa you've been spooning Liza Hartwell in her barn. He'll forbid you to ever go again.'

'I'd punch the daylights out of you if you did that.'

'I'd still tell.'

Cal glared at his younger brother. He did not trust Aidan to keep a secret, but he did not want his father asking questions about his visits to the Hartwell farm. And he badly wanted to tell someone his news.

'Promise you won't tell a soul.'

'I swear,' said Aidan solemnly.

'Blood brothers?'

Aidan put up his hand. A thin scar showed on the palm where he had cut it open six years earlier. A childish oath, but they both took it as solemnly as if they'd sworn on the Bible. Cal raised his own hand and pressed it against his brother's.

He lowered his voice. 'We've formed a group. It's called the Army of the Blood of Liberty.'

Aidan squinted. 'The what?'

'The Army of the Blood of Liberty.' Cal tried to invest the name with gravitas and majesty, though he knew it was a mouthful. The name was a compromise. Half the boys had insisted they should be the Army of Liberty, the others were adamant they should be the Blood of Liberty. After hours of heated debate, they had settled on both.

'Who's in it?' asked Aidan.

'Boys from the farms. Sam Hartwell went up to Boston a month ago and spoke with some patriots. We've had enough of politicians talking and writing pamphlets. We need to organise for war.'

Aidan felt a stab of jealousy. It hurt to think that Cal had joined a secret society without telling him.

'Can I join?'

'You're too young.'

'But—'

'No.' Cal's voice was as stern as their father's. 'This is not like when we played at soldiers in the hayfield.' He tousled his brother's hair. 'I don't want you to get hurt.'

'I won't get hurt,' said Aidan. 'I can ride as well as you, and shoot even better.'

Cal resisted the automatic impulse to contradict him. 'And when you are sixteen, there will be fighting enough for all of us. Until then, this is man's work.'

Before Aidan could argue, Cal swung himself into the saddle and galloped out of the stable yard.

In the farmhouse parlour, Theo heard the drum of hooves. By the time he looked out of the window, Maverick and his rider were a cloud of dust on the farm track.

Theo's wife Abigail came in carrying a tray with a pot of tea. She set it on the table and poured two cups.

'I heard your argument from my bedroom,' she said. 'Did you have to be so hard on the boy?'

'What he is saying is treason.'

'If sons grew up believing everything their fathers told them, the world would never change. He must become his own man – as you did at his age.'

'That was different,' frowned Theo. 'I had no choice in the matter.'

'Neither did I, after I met you,' said Abigail archly.

Theo had arrived in America as an orphan. In a short time, he had become a hero in the frontier war against the French and their Indian allies. Against the odds he and his ragtag army had inflicted major damage on the French forces, winning the battle at Fort Royal, which turned the course of the war. He had fallen in love with Abigail and she became pregnant with Cal, to her family's fury. Fame and victory had provided him with a certain amount of money, which he had invested in a merchant business from the port of Boston. The business had thrived, for Theo had learned his trade in the bazaars of Calcutta and could out-haggle even the meanest Yankee. Later, he had bought this farm in a township some twenty miles from Boston.

Theo slumped in his favourite chair and sipped his tea. Even the drink was tainted with the sour taste of politics. Cal had refused to drink tea, ever since the British government put a tax on it.

'I fear for what will happen to him, if he does not stop this madness,' said Theo. 'It's more than politics. The government will hang traitors.'

Abigail glanced out of the window, where Aidan was picking his way across the stable yard.

'I am more worried for Aidan. Where Cal leads, he will follow. He idolises his older brother.'

'I idolised my older sister Constance, once,' said Theo. 'It brought me nothing but heartache.'

Cal returned for supper, as he had promised. He stared at his plate, made no conversation, and retired to bed early. Aidan followed. Shortly afterwards, Theo and Abigail extinguished the candles and went to their bedroom.

At a quarter to midnight, Cal rose from his bed. The horses snuffled and whinnied as he opened the stable door, but they calmed at the familiar sound of his voice. He saddled Maverick, and retrieved a heavy bundle hidden under a pile of hay. He tied it to the saddle and wrapped cloths around the big stallion's hooves so that they would make no noise on the cobbles. He led the horse by the bridle until they were clear of the farm before he took off the cloths and started to ride.

He was convinced nobody had seen him depart.

The night was dark. The moon hid behind ragged clouds, giving the merest light to guide him along the road. He was terrified that Maverick might catch his hoof in a hole, ending everything before it began. But the sure-footed horse did not let him down. Soon terror was replaced by elation: the midnight ride, the smell of the horse and the cold wind in his face. Maverick's hooves struck sparks from the stones in the road, flickering around his feet. It was apt, Cal thought. Tonight, he would ignite a revolution.

The others were waiting for him at the bridge. Dim figures circled their horses, cracking nervous jokes and checking their weapons. Some had dressed as Indians; others wore scarves wrapped around their faces and their hats pulled low. They had been busy. Most of the bridge timbers had been lifted and carried to the riverbank, leaving only a few planks spanning the river.

'You're late,' said one of the riders. His face was hidden, but Cal recognised the white blaze on the horse's nose. It belonged to Sam Hartwell.

'I had to wait till Pa was asleep,' Cal explained. 'Otherwise, I couldn't have brought this.'

He unwrapped the blanket tied to the back of his saddle. Moonlight gleamed on the long, lethal barrel of his father's rifle.

The other boys gasped. All of them could shoot, and had rifles hanging on the wall at home. Some of the bolder ones had brought them. But this was different. This was the weapon of a hero, the gun that had chased the French out of North America and won the battle of Fort Royal. Cal's father rarely spoke of his exploits to others, but Cal had recounted the stories.

They gathered round, touching its blackened brasswork and scarred wood.

'He'll thrash you if he knows you took it,' warned Sam, jealous of his friend.

'It'll be back by sunup and he'll never know,' said Cal. 'Unless we stand around talking all night.'

Without waiting, he kicked his horse and rode over the bridge. The skeletal timber seemed too narrow and frail to hold the weight of the boy and his horse, but Maverick picked his way across unerringly. Sam, not wanting to be outdone, spurred after him. The others fell in behind, until only one – George Hartwell, Sam's younger brother – was left on the far bank.

'You stay here,' Cal told George. 'You know what to do.'

George clutched his rifle and gave a trembling salute. The others tipped the remaining bridge timbers into the stream, until only a single plank remained. Cal circled around and kicked Maverick into a canter. Riding with his friends around him and his father's rifle slung over his shoulder, Cal felt nothing but pure savage joy. Confidence coursed through him; stealth was forgotten in the thrill of the moment. The horses' hooves drummed on the road. Some of the boys could not help letting out whoops of delight, intoxicated by youth and war. It was like every game of soldiers they had ever played, but now marvellously real.

No one could have missed their progress through the townships and farmsteads of Massachusetts colony. But the shutters on the houses remained closed, and anyone who heard them stayed in their beds. These were dangerous times to be abroad.

Soon the air thickened with the salty smell of the sea. They dismounted and tethered their horses to a rail fence, hidden from the road by a copse of trees. No one joked or hollered now. The deadly seriousness of what they were about to do was sinking in.

A squat tower stood on a hill ahead, silhouetted against the starry ocean sky beyond. A fire smouldered in a brazier, downwind and a safe distance away. One spark inside the tower would turn the hill into a crater. Three sentries huddled around the brazier, talking in low voices.

'I cannot believe they do not defend it better,' whispered Cal.

'That fool of a governor has underestimated us again,' said Sam. 'We will make him pay for his mistake.'

The tower was the British royal arsenal. In all their years of rule, the British had never allowed powder mills in their colonies. Every grain of gunpowder had to be imported from Britain. In Massachusetts, this was where it came to be stored.

There was a pause. The members of the Army of the Blood of Liberty stared uncertainly at each other. They had spent months discussing their plan, but now they were ready for action, no one was willing to make the first move.

'Enough,' said Cal. 'I did not come here to skulk in a ditch.'

He jumped back on his horse and, with a twitch of his reins, brazenly rode up the path towards the arsenal.

The sentries saw him coming. They ran forwards and levelled their muskets.

'Who goes there?'

'A friend,' gasped Cal, making his voice hoarse and ragged. He had hidden his rifle from sight. 'I came from Fairfield. A group of men are dismantling the bridge.'

The soldiers looked agitated.

'They mean to cut us off,' cried one. 'Without the bridge, the general cannot reinforce us from Boston.'

A lieutenant emerged from the guardhouse. He looked Cal up and down, reassured by his well-cut coat and polished boots.

'The devil you say!' he cried. 'Sergeant, muster the men. We will march out to Fairfield and teach those Yankee rebels a lesson in the King's power.'

Soon all the guards except two had formed a column outside the tower. Their white cross belts gleamed in the darkness. Cal led them back to the bridge, walking his horse so they could keep up. He spoke cordially with the lieutenant, amused at how easy it was to fool the man. The lieutenant was garrulous. He had asked the governor many times for more men, he complained; had begged him to move the powder store to the safety of Boston, never mind the risk to civilians. The governor insisted that moving the powder would be seen as an act of weakness.

Cal nodded. It was not hard to feign sympathy. He only had to repeat the things he had heard his father say.

At last they reached the bridge.

'Where are the rascals?' The lieutenant advanced towards the bridge, holding his lantern high. He wondered if he had been hasty in trusting Cal. 'If you have brought us on a fool's errand . . .'

His voice trailed off as he took in the view of the dismantled bridge. Only one narrow board remained, spanning the river like a tightrope. The water flowing freely underneath was clearly visible.

'We must have interrupted them at their work,' said the lieutenant. 'They will learn they cannot get away so easily.'

'They could be miles from here by now,' said his sergeant.

At that moment, fire flashed in the darkness. A shot rang out from the far bank, though the bullet went well wide. It was a deliberate shot off target, though the British were not to know that. George Hartwell had played his part to perfection.

'Get over the bridge!' shouted the lieutenant. 'We cannot let them destroy it before we cross.'

In single file, his men ran across the plank and fanned out on the other side, muskets aimed uncertainly on the darkness. Soon Cal was the only one left behind.

'Come over,' called the lieutenant. 'You must ride to Boston and inform the general we need reinforcements.'

Cal dismounted and walked to the river's edge. With a deft kick of his boot, he knocked the last plank off its support. Then he manhandled it with all his strength until it fell in the water with a splash. The rushing current swept it away.

The lieutenant stared at Cal. In the darkness, he thought it must have been an accident.

'You clumsy oaf!' He glanced over his shoulder, though no more shots had been fired. 'Now you are stranded on the wrong side.'

'On the contrary,' said Cal. 'It is you who are on the wrong side. I am exactly where I want to be.' He tipped his hat. 'You may give my regards to the general yourself – when you are on the boat to London, where you belong.'

And before the astonished soldiers could realise what had happened, he turned his horse and galloped back to the arsenal.

By the time he returned, the operation was in full swing. The Army of the Blood of Liberty had made short work of the remaining sentries. They lay trussed up in the guardhouse, tarred and feathered, while the stout door to the magazine stood wide open. By the light of many lanterns, men rolled out the casks and loaded them onto hay wagons, which had appeared as if from nowhere. They laughed and sang as they worked, drunk on their victory. The scene was more like a carnival than a military operation.

Cal found Sam Hartwell in the throng.

'They will see these lights all the way from Boston,' Cal worried.

'Let them,' Sam answered. There was brandy on his breath. 'Now that the bridge is down, General Gage himself can do nothing to stop us.'

'There are other bridges.'

'We will be gone long before the British can cross them.'

'Then we had best hurry.'

Cal joined the line of men passing the barrels down to the waiting wagons.

'There's enough powder here to blow up the Houses of Parliament!' shouted one of his friends.

'Or start a war,' said another.

'And finish it,' added a third.

Cal didn't answer. He was staring at one of the youths coming out of the tower. He was shorter than the others, struggling with the weight of the barrel he carried, which half-hid him. A scarf covered his nose and mouth. Yet for all that, there was something unmistakably recognisable about him.

Cal strode over and snatched the barrel from the youth's hands. Behind the scarf, his eyes widened. The boy turned to go; Cal reached out to grab him. His hand caught the scarf and pulled it away.

'Aidan?' Disbelief gave way to fury. He lifted his brother and pinned him against the wall. 'Ma and Pa will kill you if they knew you were here.'

'You're here,' said Aidan.

'That's different. I told you – this is not for you.' In his anger, he could hardly speak. 'How did you find me?'

'I stole a horse, followed you to the meeting place. After that, it was easy.'

'I won't let you put yourself in danger.'

'I won't let you hog all the glory for yourself.'

They stared at each other. If they had been back at the farm, they would have settled this with their fists. But it would be stupid to start a fight in the middle of a military operation.

And then he heard it.

'What's that?'

Over the clatter of barrels and general merriment, no one else had noticed. But Cal had keen ears, and a sharp sense for danger. He listened closely.

The noise came again. The urgent blast of a horn.

Cal let Aidan go and jumped on top of a hay wagon. From its height he could see clearly down the hill. A line of lights was strung out across the valley, moving towards them at a brisk speed. They were torches, carried by men on horseback with flowing capes and bright, sharp blades.

'Dragoons!' Cal shouted. 'The dragoons are coming.'

He had never expected them to arrive so fast. They must have swum their horses across the river – unless they had had advance warning of the raid.

He saw Aidan standing beside the cart, his young face looking up expectantly.

'Are we going to fight?'

In an instant, the merry mood around the tower turned to chaos. Some of the young men fled, others formed a line facing the charging dragoons. They seemed small compared to the long rifles they carried.

'We have to get the powder away,' said Cal. He glanced at Maverick, tethered to a rail in front of the guardhouse. 'Do you think you can ride him?'

Aidan's eyes widened with shock and delight. Cal had never let him touch his horse before, had boxed his ears when he even sneaked into his stall and tried to stroke him.

Aidan took Maverick's bridle gingerly. The horse twitched to feel the unfamiliar hand on the rein; Aidan shied away. But he would not let fear hold him back. Lifting his foot as high as it would go, he stepped into the stirrup and hoisted himself into the saddle. It seemed impossibly high.

'Now get away from here as fast as possible,' said Cal, leaping from the wagon.

Aidan's face fell as he realised why Cal had entrusted him with the horse.

'I want to fight.'

'This is no place for you.' Cal glanced at the ragged line preparing to face the dragoons. Their rifles were unsteady in their hands, elevated at all angles like straws from a haystack. 'In a few moments, this will be a bloodbath.'

He slapped Maverick hard on the hindquarters. The horse sprang forwards, almost throwing Aidan from the oversized saddle. Cal waited long enough to see him regain his balance and disappear into the night. Then he jumped up on the wagon again, snatched the whip from the driver's seat and cracked it over the horses' backs. He had to get the powder away.

The Army of the Blood of Liberty fired. In the forests of the back country, any one of them could have hit a squirrel from two hundred paces. In the dark, with the King's cavalry bearing down on them, their volley was uneven and let loose too soon. Their shots went wide or buried themselves in the earth.

The dragoons touched their spurs and galloped forwards, closing the gap while the young men struggled to reload. Smoke and noise and panic made their fingers fumble. The dragoons, the cream of the British army, did not hesitate. Riding almost knee to knee, they made a solid wall of steel and horseflesh bearing down on the defenders.

Cal turned his attention to his own horses. The musket shots had frightened them into full gallop, sending the heavy-laden wagon hurtling down the track. It jolted him nearly out of his seat. It took all his strength on the reins to stop the wagon careering into a ditch.

He heard screams behind him, a few shots and the sickening sound of hooves snapping bone. He risked another glance back.

The torches around the powder magazine revealed carnage. The Army of the Blood of Liberty was no longer an army, though there was plenty of blood being spilled. The dragoons rode over the defeated rebels, allowing their horses to trample them and kick in their skulls. Some of the young men fought with whatever came to hand; others tried to surrender. The dragoons butchered them all. They had been frustrated in Boston for months, listening to the ridicule and threats of the patriot citizens. Now they had their chance to teach the rebel colonists a lesson.

The dead were boys Cal had grown up with, friends he had known all his life. To see them crushed or dying on the end of British sabres left him numb. All those long evenings sitting around talking of bloodshed and liberty had not prepared him for this. He prayed Aidan was now far away.

All Cal wanted to do was to make sure his friends had not died in vain. If he could deliver the powder safely, it would change the fortunes of the rebel army at a stroke. Cal held on tight to the panicking horses as they galloped into the night. The wagon swayed and rocked. It was like riding a log in a rushing river. He could only cling on.

He passed a milestone and joined the coast road. Away to his left, the ocean lay calm and untroubled in the moonlight. The road wound along the shore, cresting hills and splashing through the little streams that flowed into the sea. The horses began to tire. Cal eased his grip on the reins.

The dark shapes of farm buildings lined the road. Cal didn't stop. Perhaps the inhabitants were patriots, willing to hide his wagon and its cargo, but he did not want to take the risk. By morning, the British would have patrols searching every property in the county, and it would go ill with the farmer if they found a wagonload of stolen black powder in his barn.

The wind off the sea drove the clouds away. The moon shone through, lighting up the land in a palette of grey and silver. Cal glanced back.

His heart stopped. There were horsemen, half a mile away and closing fast. The dragoons. The moonlight picked out the white belts and silver buckles on their uniforms, and the naked steel of the swords they carried.

He lashed his team with his whip, goading them back up to speed. The wagon bounded forwards. Its wheels spun so fast he thought the axles would snap.

But the tired horses could not keep up that pace for long. Yoked to the heavy-laden wagon, straining every muscle to keep it moving, they could not possibly outrun the cavalry, who were fresh and hungry for blood. A hill loomed ahead.

Cal's mind raced through his options. He could abandon the wagon and run for it, but with a clear moon he would struggle to outpace the dragoons. If he was caught, he would either be killed on the spot, or more likely taken to Boston to be paraded as a rebel before being publicly executed. As a traitor, they would hang him until he was nearly dead, then disembowel him and burn his entrails in front of his dying eyes, before tearing his body into four pieces.

He would not abandon the powder.

Two of the dragoons broke out of the pack and galloped ahead. They meant to chase him down before he reached the top of the hill, when the downward slope would give the wagon more momentum. Cal lashed his horses. Their coats steamed, and foam flecked their nostrils. They strained against the traces with all their strength, as if they understood how desperate his danger was.

The summit loomed, but the dragoons' outriders were getting closer. The two horsemen spread apart like the jaws of a trap, coming up either side of the wagon. There was nothing Cal could do. He still had his father's rifle slung across his back, but it needed all his strength to steer the wagon. He could not remove his hands from the reins.

In the corner of his eye, he saw one of the dragoons come up on his right. The other came abreast to his left, a flashing menace steering his mount closer and closer to the rumbling wheels. For a moment, the three of them rode in line.

A sabre slashed at Cal's head. He jerked out of the way just in time. The blade struck the seat beside him and was impaled, quivering in the wood. At full gallop, the dragoon tried to pull it free. As he did so, Cal yanked on the reins so that the wagon veered suddenly across the road.

The dragoon had come in too close. The wagon's metal-rimmed wheels slammed into his horse's foreleg and snapped the bone with a crack. Even above the thunder of hooves, the rattle of wheels and the jangle of harness, the beast's scream was plain and terrible as it collapsed in a tangle of limbs. The wagon's rear wheels nearly broke the horse's neck as they raced by.

Cal hauled on the reins again, dragging the wagon back to the centre of the road. It was like trying to steer a charging buffalo. It moved, but terribly slowly. A ditch ran along the side of the road. For a heart-stopping moment, his right front wheel hung above it, spinning over the void. He felt the cart begin to drop into it. If he hit the ditch at this speed, the cart would be smashed to pieces.

Then the wheel caught the edge of the road, and bounced back onto it with a bump that tossed Cal two feet in the air. The reins and the whip were thrown out of his hands.

The team of horses slowed. Cal could see the reins dragging along the ground between the traces. He had to get them back. He unshouldered his rifle and laid it aside. Hanging off the seat one-handed, he lowered himself into the small space between the wagon and the horses. The wheels rumbled beside him; the horses' hooves pounded inches from his face. The dust they threw up choked and blinded him. He grasped for the reins. The rushing ground scraped his fingertips raw, tearing his nails to bloody stumps. The pain was immense, but he forced himself to keep trying until his hands closed around the leather.

He hauled himself up onto the seat again. He spat dust out of his mouth and rubbed it from his eyes.

A sharp point pricked his ribs.

'Stop the wagon,' said a cut-glass English voice imperiously in his ear.

The second dragoon was standing on the running board, his sword held to Cal's breast. He must have ridden alongside the wagon and then leaped aboard while Cal was retrieving the reins. To jump from a galloping horse to a wildly veering wagon was no small feat, but Cal could not appreciate it. He cursed the man for his horsemanship, even as he heard another horse galloping behind the wagon. There must be more dragoons on his tail.

There was nothing he could do. At the least movement, the dragoon would run him through. The sneer on the man's face left him in no doubt.

Yet something stubborn inside Cal would not yield. He snapped the reins, urging the horses to up their pace. He wished he had time to grab his rifle, use the flint to make a spark that could ignite the cargo of powder. At least then his death would not be for nothing.

'You've had your warning . . .!'

The dragoon tensed his arm. Cal braced himself for the lunge. In the split second before it came, he wondered if being stabbed by the sword would hurt. His thoughts flashed to his friends massacred at the arsenal, and he took courage from their example. He would not die less courageously than they had.

The sword lunged. It was inches from his chest; it could not miss. Yet in those few vital inches, the blade went askew. It angled up, missing Cal's heart and cutting through the cloth of the shoulder of his coat.

There was someone else on the wagon. A pair of arms had wrapped around the dragoon's chest, tugging and beating him. It was not a fair fight. The dragoon was nearly six feet tall, while his attacker appeared to be more of a boy than a man. The Englishman grabbed the arm that held him and forced it back until it almost snapped. The boy cried out in pain.

Cal wrenched the sword's hilt from the dragoon's hands. Without thought or hesitation, he reversed the blade and plunged it into the dragoon's chest.

The man went limp. Before Cal could withdraw the sword, a rut in the road jolted the cart. The dragoon tipped over the side and somersaulted to the ground. The wagon bounced again as the wheels rode over his body, crushing whatever life was left in him. Cal gathered the reins tightly.

He stared at his saviour. It was Aidan.

'How did you get here?' he gasped. And then, not waiting for an answer, 'You saved my life.'

Over his shoulder, Cal saw Maverick loping along, easily keeping pace with the wagon.

'Maybe you are not as useless as I thought,' he said, trying to hide his emotions.

Aidan's eyes glowed with defiance.

Cal saw blood on Aidan's shirt. 'Are you hurt?'

Aidan grinned and showed him a hole in the fabric. 'You rammed that dragoon's sword so far through him you nearly skewered me as well. My first war wound. It is only a scratch.'

'There is time yet for another. There are more dragoons coming.'

Looking back, Cal could see them riding up the road behind. He handed the reins to Aidan.

'Drive on to Duxbury. There are patriots there who will take charge of the powder. I will slow our pursuers.'

His rifle still lay on the floor of the wagon where he had discarded it. Cal slung it over his shoulder, then whistled to his horse. Maverick cantered closer, until he was barely a foot from the moving wagon. Cal reached out, grabbed the pommel of the saddle and sprang. His leg went over, and he landed cleanly in the saddle. Maverick didn't break stride.

The wagon raced down the far side of the hill, swaying wildly as Aidan struggled to steer it. Cal prayed his little brother could regain control. He circled Maverick around. Some way back, he found the dead dragoon's horse, munching grass at the side of the road. The dragoon's carbine was still holstered beside the saddle, along with a finely made pistol. Cal took them both.

There were three dragoons galloping towards him. Cal dismounted, to steady himself, and aimed the rifle, which had the longest range. Kneeling, he trained it on the leading horseman. His arms ached from driving the horses, but they did not tremble as he sighted his enemy.

It was a long shot, against a moving target in the dark. The flash of powder blinded him, so he didn't see the bullet strike. As his vision cleared, he saw the horse still galloping towards him. But there was no rider. He lay in the road, writhing and screaming, as the other two dragoons rode past.

Calmly, Cal reloaded and fired again, at the next-nearest dragoon. But this time, his target swerved and the bullet went wide.

The remaining men were closing quickly. With no time to reload the rifle, Cal had two bullets ready, one in the carbine and one in the pistol. But both his weapons were short-range: he could not be sure of hitting the targets until they were nearly on him.

He swung himself back into Maverick's saddle. He levelled the carbine, forcing himself to hold steady until the dragoons were so close he could see the sweat foaming on their horses' flanks.

A hardened soldier would have aimed for the horse as the bigger target. Cal, still raw and unwilling to harm an innocent animal, shot at the rider. He missed. He threw the carbine aside and drew the pistol. The men were so close now he could not afford another wasted shot. The pistol exploded in the darkness, and one of the dragoons went down.

Only one remained. But he was on him. A sabre sliced at Cal, and he parried it desperately with his pistol. It stopped the blow, but the pistol was knocked spinning out of his hand.

The dragoon circled around to come at him again. Cal had no weapons, not even a knife. As the dragoon closed at speed, Cal's only defence was the horse under him. He tugged the reins and kicked Maverick's flanks. The horse bounded forwards, leaping over the ditch at the roadside into the adjacent field just as the dragoon's sabre whistled through the air where Cal's head had been.

With a 'huzzah' like a fox hunter, the dragoon gave chase. Cal had an advantage: he had been roaming this country since he could walk and knew it like his own garden. But the dragoon rode like the Devil himself. Even in the dark over unfamiliar ground, he cleared every fence and ditch. No matter how hard he rode, Cal could not shake him.

Galloping over the damp earth was draining Maverick's strength. His ears were back, his flanks white with sweat. Cal didn't dare look around, but he could hear the jangle of the dragoon's spurs edging closer and closer. He rode through a small stand of trees, face pressed against Maverick's mane so that he did not have his head whipped off by a low branch. As they emerged from the woods, he saw another fence ahead and managed to balance himself before Maverick launched them over it.

They had come back onto the road – on high ground, where the road hugged close to a cliff. Cal rode on, trying to coax every last ounce of strength from his tiring horse. It was like a nightmare, chased by a remorseless enemy who never seemed to lose pace. The dragoon was almost alongside him. Cal swayed and veered, dancing to keep out of reach of the flickering sword point, but he was running out of options.

Maverick slowed. The horse had given his all. Cal looked back. In the moonlight, the dragoon's helmet hid his eyes in shadow, but his mouth was open in a warlike snarl. He raised his sword as he spurred alongside Cal, ready for the stroke that would slit him from shoulder to belly.

With the last of his strength, Maverick leaped. Cal wasn't ready for it. The jump almost bounced him out of his saddle. Without thinking, he clenched his thighs against Maverick's flanks and wrapped his hands in the horse's mane. He didn't know why the horse had launched himself. All he saw was a dark blur sweeping beneath him, before the thud of the horse's landing nearly unseated him again.

A crack in the ground yawned behind, a narrow gully where the cliff had crumbled away. Maverick had seen it and reacted in time. The dragoon's horse galloped into the hole, smashing into the opposite bank so hard it broke its neck. The dragoon was thrown from his saddle. He flew over the cliff edge, bouncing down the steep slope until he landed in a tangle of limbs on the rocks below.

Cal drew Maverick to a halt, horse and rider breathing so deeply their hearts might burst. Cal hardly had the strength to lift his head, but as the pounding in his ears subsided he heard a familiar rumble a distance away. He looked up.

He was in a dip between two hills. The road came down the slope behind him, bent inland to avoid the gully where the dragoon had fallen, then straightened towards the summit of the next hill. Almost at the top, was the wagon. Cal saw the powder kegs piled in the back, and the small figure of Aidan perched on the driver's seat. Fixed on his task, Aidan hadn't seen the battle behind him.

The wagon was safe. Cal felt a surge of fraternal pride: he wanted to hug his brother. They had done it together. Sam Hartwell and all the friends they'd lost had not died for nothing.

But something was wrong. As Aidan reached the top of the hill, Cal could see his silhouette come into sharper focus. Not against the stars, but against a dull orange haze glowing behind the hill.

The wagon seemed to pause at the summit, then disappeared over the other side.

Cal felt a terrible sense of dread. Forgetting his exhaustion, he kicked Maverick forwards. The horse responded sluggishly. He was half lame, too exhausted to muster more than a trot. The orange light grew brighter as they climbed the hill, but however much Cal kicked, begged and cajoled the beast, he was too slow.

They crested the hill and Cal's heart stopped. The British were there. How they had managed it – if word had raced ahead, if someone had betrayed them, if it was sheer bad luck – he didn't know. But there they were. Waiting for him.

They had felled trees across the road at the bottom of the hill. Braziers burned at either end, lighting up a dozen soldiers with fixed bayonets behind the barricade. There was no way through.

Further down the slope, Cal could see Aidan leaning back on the reins, trying desperately to slow the horses. But the wagon kept rolling. It gathered pace as its momentum took it down the hill.

Suddenly Aidan fell back. The horses pulling the wagon broke free and galloped away. In horror, Cal realised the dragoon's sabres must have nicked the harness: now it had snapped. The wagon continued on, out of control. It was going to smash into the barricade.

'Jump, Aidan!' Cal screamed at the top of his lungs.

He thought Aidan would do it. His little brother stood up on the driver's box, looking around in disbelief. He seemed poised to leap. But whether he couldn't bring himself to make the move, or if he stayed loyal to the last to his brother's instructions not to leave the wagon, he didn't try to abandon the vehicle.

Cal kicked Maverick's flanks and charged forwards, thinking he might yet snatch Aidan off the cart. Panicked by the sight of the runaway wagon rushing down on them, some of the soldiers started to flee. Others watched open-mouthed, but one or two with cooler heads opened fire. Muskets flashed.

The wagon hit the barricade with the speed of a charging bull. The front wheels shattered; the frame snapped. The soldiers were skittled like ninepins. The braziers were knocked over, spilling their hot coals. Kegs of gunpowder were hurled in the air and smashed open. Cal saw Aidan thrown high, tossed over the barricade and landing on the far side like a rag doll.

One of the powder kegs rolled away across the road. Its staves had cracked, making it oscillate like an egg, and leaving a trail of black powder spilling through the gaps. It trundled lazily across the road in the direction of one of the toppled braziers, towards the embers glowing in the dust.

The barrel nudged up against them and stopped.

A flash shot across the road like lightning as the powder trail ignited. Then the landscape vanished in a ball of fire, so vast and bright it was as if the noon sun had appeared in the middle of the night. Cal shielded his eyes. A split second later the force of the blast punched him hard and he was nearly thrown from the saddle. The noise punctured his ears like a thunderclap, followed by silence as he went deaf.

Peering through his fingers, he saw the scene like some soundless vision of Hell. Smoke poured into the night. The frame of the wagon burned like the skeleton of an enormous dying animal. More fires flared as other barrels caught alight and exploded, making a dull popping sound in his shocked ears. Fragments of wood and men lay strewn over the ground.

Aidan was somewhere in the inferno. Ignoring the blood running from his nose, the ache in his ears and the smoke in his eyes, Cal urged Maverick forwards. The horse reared onto his hind legs, shying away from the fire. Even Cal could not persuade him on. He dismounted and ran through the burning debris, remembering just in time to unbuckle his cartridge box so it did not explode in the heat. The fire scalded his face and burned his skin, but Cal was insensible to pain. He scrambled over the remains of the barricade and jumped down on the far side.

Aidan lay where he had fallen, a shadow spread-eagled on the ground. Cal ran to him. The sleeve of Cal's shirt was on fire, but he ignored it. He kneeled beside Aidan and tried to lift him.

The moment Aidan's head left the ground, it flopped back like a broken hinge. The force of the landing had snapped his neck. He had died instantly.

Tears ran down Cal's face, cool against the blisters bubbling up on his seared skin. His brother was dead. The powder was destroyed. All was lost.

Something stirred on the ground a distance away. A British soldier lay under one of the logs that had been thrown back by the force of the blast. He was alive.

Cal walked over and looked down. The log had broken the soldier's leg and pinned him to the ground, but it had also shielded him from the violence of the explosion. The eyes staring up at Cal were raging.

'Get this bloody weight off me,' the soldier said through gritted teeth.

Cal hesitated, paralysed by a storm of emotions. The soldier's fury seemed to exhaust itself.

'Please,' the soldier begged.

He was helpless. Cal crouched down beside him. He noted the relief in the man's face as he reached for the log. It was heavy, but Cal was used to clearing brush and chopping firewood on the farm. He could save him.

But no one had saved Aidan.

A great emptiness opened inside Cal, as if his heart was collapsing into itself. How would he tell his father? His mother? He imagined walking into the kitchen in the farmhouse, his mother's smile crumbling to despair. The fury rising in his father's eyes.

It was not my fault Aidan followed me, he told himself, trying to make himself believe it. *It was not my fault*. However many times he repeated it, he knew his father would never accept it.

A long, wickedly spiked bayonet was tucked in a loop on the soldier's belt. Cal pulled it out. Guilt rose inside him to an almost unbearable pitch. He wished he had ridden Maverick right into the fireball when the powder kegs went up, to obliterate himself and his shame. The sharp point of the bayonet glimmered in the firelight. He wanted to drive it into his heart.

It was not my fault.

Guilt hardened to anger. He hurt so badly, but his father would offer no comfort. He would blame him for everything. It was so unfair.

Hot liquid dribbled down his face. He wiped it away, thinking it must be tears and ashamed of it. But when he looked at his hand, he saw it was wet with blood.

Had he been hurt? He looked down, focusing on his surroundings again. The British soldier lay beneath him, with the bayonet piercing his throat. The blood on Cal's face must have fountained out of an artery, though it had already subsided to a dribble. The soldier's neck was a mess of open wounds where he had been repeatedly stabbed, so hard that in the end the bayonet had gone right through his neck and stuck upright in the earth beneath.

I must have done that, thought Cal, though he had no memory of it. He wiped the blood from his eyes and stared at the bloody pulp that had once been a soldier.

Cal began to shake so hard he thought his neck might snap. Bile rose in his throat. It was the first time he had killed a man in cold blood.

He was unarmed, a voice in his head protested. *You murdered him*. But another voice answered: *you did this for Aidan* – and that voice was warm and comforting. His father could say what he liked; it was not Cal's fault Aidan was dead. He had died for the same reason the soldier had – for the revolution. For freedom. Theo would never understand that.

Cal glimpsed his face in the soldier's shiny buckle, and almost shied away in horror. He looked like a terrible, inhuman thing:

burned, bloodied and blistered, his mouth open in a snarl. He hardly recognised himself.

I will not let you die in vain, he promised Aidan. *I will not let us lose this war.*

Whatever he had to do, however many Englishmen he had to kill, he would do it. He would make his father understand.

It was not my fault.

Robert Courtney had never imagined there could be so many ships in the world. But then, he was beginning to realise there was so much about the world he'd failed to imagine. All the way from Gravesend, the Thames was choked with shipping, moored so close together you could almost have crossed the river on their tangled yards. Heavy Indiamen bringing tea from China, sugar from Jamaica and calicoes from India. Ships bringing furs from Canada, spices from the East Indies, ivory from Africa and whale oil from Greenland. At Woolwich, lighters unloaded saltpetre from Bengal. It would be milled with sulphur and charcoal, then loaded onto other ships as black powder to fight the wars that kept all this confusion of commerce in motion across the globe.

And then there was London.

Rob saw it first as a smear of dark smoke hanging over the horizon.

'Is that a brush fire?' he asked Cornish.

The captain chuckled. 'That is the smoke of a hundred thousand homes.'

Rob thought he was joking. Then he saw London and realised Cornish had understated it. The city was as big as a forest: chaotic, dark and filled with noise. It stretched as far as he could see, with buildings that seemed as high as the cape at Nativity Bay.

'How can so many people live in one place?' he wondered. 'How do they eat? Where do they hunt?'

A brightly dressed group of women waved from the shore. They lifted their dresses to show their petticoats and blew kisses. Rob waved shyly back, though he could not understand what they were saying.

'You will find life here very different from what you are used to,' Cornish said with a smile. But there was concern in his eyes. He had not thought until now how overwhelming the city might be to a boy who had grown up as Rob had.

The *Dunstanburgh Castle* moored at Monsoon Dock and began offloading her cargo into the lighters. The crew queued to receive their pay. Their rough sailors' clothes had been put away, and they wore extraordinary garments: gaudy striped trousers, long-toed shoes, shirts decorated with tassels, fringes, brass and silver buttons and every kind of ornament.

'Is that the fashion in London?' Rob wondered.

All he had to wear was one clean shirt and a pair of breeches he had kept safe at the bottom of his sea chest.

One of his messmates beckoned him over. 'Come ashore with us, Rob. We will show you all the finest sights of London town.'

He said it kindly – Rob was popular with the crew – but the roars of laughter from his companions left Cornish in little doubt what they had in mind.

'The sight of a fine whore's arse, you mean,' said one of the men.

'Rob is coming with me,' Cornish announced, giving the boy no say in the matter. 'We will dine together tonight.' He saw the disappointment on the boy's face. 'There will be time enough tomorrow to see the town.'

The moment they stepped ashore, the noise and the smell increased tenfold. The only thing Rob could compare it to was standing in the middle of a herd of stampeding elephants, thundering and braying.

'Wait here,' Cornish told him. 'I need five minutes with the customs inspector. I have a bottle of brandy to deliver.'

Rob could barely stand still. The energy of the city elated him. He wanted to run, to see every street and every building and every secret the city had to give up. He stood on the quay, taking in the sights with eyes as wide as a newborn calf. If he ever had doubts about his decision to leave Nativity Bay, he had none now.

'Thief!' cried a voice, its urgency cutting through the hubbub. 'Stop that thief!'

Rob's attention snapped back to the wharf in front of him. A tall, gaunt man in ragged shirt and trousers was running at surprising speed, clutching a leather bag that looked as if it was worth more than all his clothes put together. A young man in a plum-coloured coat and striped yellow breeches was chasing after him, though the press of the crowd held him back.

Rob read the situation in an instant. He stepped forwards smartly so that the ragged man charged into him. The man was almost knocked off his feet by the force of the impact, but Rob stood firm. He put his hands on the leather bag.

'I do not think that belongs to you,' he said.

The man lifted his head, surprise hardening to fury in his eyes. He let go of the bag.

'Don't belong to you neither.'

The bustle on the wharf ceased. A circle had formed around Rob, watching the confrontation unfold. Suddenly the onlookers drew back with gasps. A knife had appeared in the thief's hand.

Rob was unarmed. Yet despite the blood pumping hard in his veins, he felt unnaturally calm. He looked the man in the face.

'If you go now, it will be easier on you.'

With a cry of anger, the man lunged at him with the knife. Rob had never fought an armed man before, but he had a Courtney's instincts. As the man started to move, Rob turned his body sideways, swaying out of the way. The knife stabbed the space where his stomach had been a split second earlier. Rob did not bother with the knife. He was inside the man's guard. He brought a knee up into the man's groin, and as he doubled over Rob swung a heavy punch into his face.

The man dropped the knife and fell to his knees. Rob put his foot on the blade so his opponent could not reach for it. He waited for the man to come at him again.

But the thief had had enough. Scrambling to his feet, he pushed through the watching crowd and made his escape.

'That was neatly done,' a voice complimented Rob.

The man in the plum-coloured coat had arrived. Close to, Rob could see he was not much older than Rob himself. He had a handsome face, with sharp cheekbones and tousled hair tied back with a velvet bow. His lazy, almond-shaped eyes darted about with almost feline precision.

'Hugo Lyall,' he introduced himself.

'Robert Courtney.'

Rob was still clutching Hugo's leather bag in his hand. Hugo reached out and took it.

'I owe you a debt.'

'It was nothing.'

Now that the fight was over, the heat had drained from Rob's veins. He felt slightly dizzy.

Hugo noticed it. 'You are trembling.'

'It is just the excitement. I have never fought a man before.'

'Never?' Hugo's eyes widened in disbelief. 'You gave a good account of yourself for an amateur. I have seen prizefighters who would have been proud of the blow you gave him.'

Rob grinned at the compliment. 'I once had to fight off a shark. It is not so different.'

Hugo laughed. 'Now I am certain you are pulling my leg.'

Rob pulled open the collar of his shirt and showed him the shark's tooth on the cord around it.

'I kept a souvenir.'

Hugo had stopped laughing. He stared at Rob with intense curiosity.

'Where do you come from?'

'Africa.'

'Ah. Blackbirding on the Guinea coast?'

Rob smiled, not sure what he meant. 'I grew up there.'

'Are you Dutch?'

Rob's accent was hard to place.

'British.'

Hugo squinted. 'But no Englishman grows up in Africa.'

Rob wasn't sure what to say. 'I did.'

There was a pause. Rob had the feeling they were talking at cross purposes, somehow, but he did not know what to say. Hugo broke the impasse.

'I am forgetting my manners. You saved me a considerable sum of money, at great personal risk. Let me at least buy you something to drink.'

Rob hesitated. He glanced over his shoulder towards the customs house.

'I should wait for Captain Cornish.'

'Nonsense.' Hugo had a confident way of speaking which made every objection seem not just trivial, but mean-spirited. 'He will find you.' He grabbed Rob's hand and tugged him forwards. 'And I have some friends who would like to meet you.'

Rob couldn't resist. And he could certainly use a drink.

'I would like that.'

Hugo guided him to a tavern a little way from the dock. The air was thick with pipe smoke and laughter, every corner crammed with men sipping drinks, gambling and arguing. Half a dozen young men, Rob's age or a little older, sat squeezed together on benches. They must have been there for some time because they had empty glasses and several empty wine bottles. They all had a common look about them – not so much as a family, but like a certain breed of dog. Tousled hair tied back in bows, cotton shirts with lace cuffs, upturned chins and half-closed eyes which seemed to watch the world from a superior angle.

'This is Rob,' said Hugo. 'He saved me from being robbed.' He laughed at his inadvertent pun.

'By a tart you tried to bilk?' jeered his friends. Hugo ignored them.

'Rob comes from Africa.'

'Did you ride elephants?' asked one.

'Or lions?' said another.

'I've shot elephants,' said Rob.

'And fought sharks,' added Hugo proudly, as if he was in some way responsible for it.

They studied him with greater interest.

'Good Lord,' said one. 'I do believe he means it.'

'Are you a gentleman?' enquired one of Hugo's friends.

'Don't be ridiculous,' said another. 'They do not have gentlemen in Africa.'

'I say he is nothing but a common sailor. Look at the tattoo.'

Rob tugged his sleeve down to cover his tattoo. He was starting to feel like an exotic beast displayed in a cage. And he was beginning to worry about how Cornish would find him.

'I must go,' Rob said.

There was much braying and protesting.

'Stay for a drink,' they said. 'Tell us stories of Africa.'

Rob edged away. Hugo stood and accompanied him the way they had come.

'I apologise if my friends seem uncouth,' he murmured.

'I'm sure it means nothing.'

'It means they're bloody drunk.' He looked Rob in the eye. He had clear, open eyes that brimmed with good humour and fun; Rob found himself instantly warming to him. 'You really come from Africa,' he said again, half disbelieving.

'I do.'

'I have always dreamed of exploring the world. Where are you living now?'

'At present I am staying aboard ship.'

Hugo took an enamelled case from his coat, snapped it open and pulled out a small card embossed with his name and address.

'I stay at number 22 Wimpole Street. Call on me, if you can. I would like to hear more tales of your adventures in Africa, without so many interruptions.'

He handed Rob the card. Then, with a raffish grin, he disappeared back to his friends.

Rob found Cornish on the quay, searching anxiously through the crowd.

'I told you to stay where you were,' the captain scolded him. His concern at losing Rob now poured out as anger. 'You must be careful in London.'

Rob thought of his fight with the thief. With the safety of hindsight, it seemed like a thrilling encounter, the sort of thing his ancestors would have done. He decided Cornish would not appreciate the story.

'I made a friend,' was all he said.

'Who?'

'Hugo Lyall.' Rob showed him the card, then tucked it in his waistband. 'He seemed very nice.'

'Be careful,' Cornish warned. 'Not everyone in this city is what they seem.'

But Rob didn't listen.

Cornish worried for Rob. But he also worried about unloading his cargo quickly enough to beat the other merchants, getting the best price for his goods, paying the customs agents the bribes they would inevitably expect, repairing his ship after the long voyage, meeting his creditors and seeing his wife. Next morning, when Rob asked permission to go ashore, Cornish barely looked up from the thick ledger his head was buried in.

'Make sure you are back by sundown,' was all he said.

Rob hardly knew where to begin exploring London. After half an hour, his eyes hurt from staring and his head throbbed trying to take in so much. His senses were assaulted by noise, smell, movement, bustle and the most extraordinary array of humankind, as if all the most exotic beasts of the wilderness had come together at once, demanding attention. It was never-ending, a mass of humanity zigzagging and interacting as if it was performing an ancient ritual dance, the purpose of which Rob had no clue.

He could hardly move without a woman or a boy offering to sell him a pie or a pastry. He bought three, using some of the coins Cornish had given him for his wages. He had never spent money before. At home, if you wanted something you had to make it yourself. It was intoxicating to be able to buy things so easily, and there was so much choice. All the riches he had ever imagined the world to possess seemed to be in this one place – and people wanted him to claim a part of it, were thrusting their wares at him with a strange desperation. He was beginning to feel the attraction of plenty, of excess.

In Africa, Rob had been used to working under a hot sun, but here the crowds and the pressing buildings made the heat sweaty and draining. He bought a pint of ale to refresh himself, but that only gave him a headache. He became dizzy. He was certain everyone was staring at him, laughing at him as an ignorant newcomer.

He wandered aimlessly, until he was disorientated. He had never been lost in his life before. However far he wandered from Fort Auspice, he could always find a game trail or a watercourse to guide him home. Here, the high buildings hid the sun and boxed him in. Whichever way he wanted to go, it always seemed to be a dead end. He thought if he could only reach the river, he could follow it back to the docks. But he could not find it. How could such a vast body of water simply disappear?

He had almost begun to despair when he noticed a sign: Wimpole Street. He took Hugo Lyall's card, sweaty and smudged, from his pocket and read the address: 22 Wimpole Street. Much of the street was still vacant, or under construction, but there were a number of fine imposing mansions already complete. Number 22 seemed to be the finest of them all – a gleaming white stucco façade, six storeys tall, with pillars framing a large black door.

A liveried servant answered Rob's knock. To Rob's surprise, the man's skin was as black as that of the natives in Nativity Bay.

'*Sawubona*,' Rob said automatically, greeting him in the language he'd used with the servants at home.

The man scowled as if Rob had offered the most grievous insult. He looked down his nose at Rob.

'Yes?'

'Does Hugo Lyall live here?'

The servant looked Rob up and down. He took in the tar under his fingernails, the callouses on his hands and sunburn on his neck.

'Mr Lyall is not at home to visitors.'

Rob fished out the card. 'He told me to call on him.'

'He is not at home,' the servant repeated, louder and slower, as if speaking to a stupid child. And then, without waiting for a reply, he shut the door in Rob's face.

Rob stared at the closed door, confused and humiliated. Then, because he couldn't stand on the doorstep all day, he turned to go.

'Robert Courtney.' A familiar voice hailed him.

It was Hugo, dressed in a sea-green coat with a purple lining, stepping down from a carriage that must have cost more than the *Dunstanburgh Castle*'s entire cargo. His face broadened into a delighted, surprised smile when he saw Rob.

'Not run back to Africa yet?'

'I was lost,' Rob confessed. 'I was trying to find my way back to Monsoon Dock.'

'Then you are lost indeed.'

'If you could point me the right way . . .'

'Absolutely not,' said Hugo firmly. 'You look half dead. Come in and have a drink first.'

Rob demurred; Hugo insisted. 'I never had the chance to buy you the drink I promised yesterday.'

Rob was certainly thirsty. And after the hard anonymity of London, it was a relief to find someone who seemed genuinely glad to see him. He followed his friend past the scowling doorman and through a marble-floored hallway, up a flight of stairs to an opulent sitting room.

They lounged on silk sofas, while more black servants brought wine in silver coolers. Hugo raised his glass.

'Your good health.'

The chilled wine slipped easily down Rob's throat, as refreshing as spring water.

He gestured to the magnificent room. Everything about it seemed fit for a palace: gilt-framed mirrors and paintings, thick flock wallpaper on the walls, a harpsichord.

'Do you live here alone?'

'For the moment,' said Hugo. 'My father is away visiting his estates in the West Indies. He will not be back for some months.'

'And your mother?'

'She died when I was young.'

'So did mine.'

Their eyes met; a spark of kinship passed between them.

'I am sorry to hear it,' said Rob. 'I suppose it cannot have been easy.'

Hugo gave a braying sort of laugh. 'Indeed not. My father is a hard man.'

'So is mine.'

'He does not understand that I am different from him.'

'Nor mine.'

The hush in the room seemed to close tighter around them as they held each other's gazes. For the first time in his life, Rob felt there was someone who understood him. All his life he had longed for an older brother, someone to show him how to face the world in the way his father never could. Perhaps this connection was how it would feel.

'Clearly we have many things in common,' Hugo said. Then he broke into a grin again. 'Listen to us, feeling sorry for ourselves like a pair of girls. You have all of London to see, and I must hear everything you can tell me about Africa. Have you ever seen a camelopard?'

'I do not think so.'

Hugo looked disappointed. 'I hear they are as tall as a house, and brindled like a leopard.'

Rob realised what he meant. 'We call it a giraffe,' he told Hugo. 'Yes, I have seen many hundreds. And lions, too.'

'I saw one once, at a fair. It was a shabby, bedraggled creature. I felt so sorry for it, chained in captivity so far from its home. Yet even then, I could see the nobility in it.'

'They are beautiful animals,' Rob agreed.

'All I ever wanted was to become a pirate or an explorer.' A sad look crossed Hugo's face. 'My father forbade me, of course.'

'My father forbade me to come to London,' said Rob.

'But you came anyway?' Hugo looked astonished. 'You defied your father?'

Rob shrugged. 'Here I am.'

'You ran away to sea.' Hugo clapped his hands. 'You are a marvel, Rob. You must tell me the whole story.'

'It is not so extraordinary,' Rob said shyly. 'London is far more exotic.'

Still, he could not deny he was pleased with the attention. A servant refilled his drink, and Rob told his story. At first he was embarrassed at Hugo's attention, but the more he drank the more he spoke. He had never been so much the centre of attention, and he found he liked it. Hugo's questions, his obvious awe of Rob's life, made him want to tell his new friend everything.

He lost all sense of time. At Fort Auspice, the locals had made small beer from fermented maize, while there had always been bottles of wine and brandy picked up from the ships that called in Nativity Bay. But it had been served sparingly, on special occasions like Christmas and birthdays. Hugo drank it like water. And each time Rob protested he must go, Hugo asked another question that had Rob launching into another long answer. Soon his head was spinning with the alcohol, lost in a warm haze of laughter and chatter.

The day stretched into evening. Rob realised he was hungry, and mentioned it: in no time, he and Hugo found themselves at a table in a chop house, devouring hunks of meat and draining pints of wine. After that, Hugo decided they needed entertainment, so they staggered down to the Marylebone pleasure gardens, singing raucously.

Rob had brought a purse with a little of his seaman's pay and some of Louisa's money, but he had spent it all on clothes. Hugo had to pay the sixpence entrance fee.

'Where do you get your money?' Rob asked. Alcohol had made him uninhibited.

'My father.'

Rob tried to imagine how a man could earn enough to keep such a magnificent home.

'Is he a merchant?'

Hugo looked appalled. 'God, no. If he heard you ask that he would box your ears. He owns estates in the West Indies.'

Rob was having trouble focusing on what he said. 'Estates?'

'Sugar.' Hugo frowned. 'Really, if you wish to spend all evening talking of business, then you can spend it with my father's agent.'

Rob let the matter drop and gave himself over to the sights of the pleasure gardens. As much as London had overwhelmed him already with its size and splendour, this was even more extraordinary. They watched a boxing match between two women who tried to pummel the life out of each other, as if each had stolen the other's lover. The male crowd cheered and booed with such intensity it was as if their own wives were scrapping desperately to assuage a bitter jealousy. Rob noticed the women cling to one another in a clinch and one of them smiled knowingly, but he couldn't help staring intently at the bare flesh of their stomachs and thighs. They moved on to a bear-baiting, which made him feel sick to witness dogs so frenzied and the bear defenceless. He had an uncommon sympathy with wild animals, and he wanted to halt the performance, but his shouts of protest were lost in the raucous baying of the drunken crowd. A fire-eater restored his spirits as the performer spewed flame like a fantastical beast, a dragon from the dark depths of his fevered imagination. He felt that he might have died and been transported to a place where nothing but sensation resided. Everything was new and thrilling, a world dedicated to every pleasure the sun or moon could provide.

At last the gardens closed, and they staggered back to the house on Wimpole Street, by way of another two or three taverns. They collapsed on the silk chaises in the drawing room, and Hugo called for more wine, which came at once. Did the servants never sleep?

A grandfather clock in the hall struck two.

'Two bells,' Rob murmured drowsily.

Hugo laughed. 'Silly. It is two o'clock in the morning.'

Rob shook himself awake. 'But I was due back with Captain Cornish hours ago.'

'Tell him you got lost,' Hugo encouraged him. 'Stay a while longer. We may find some female company before long.'

Rob put out his hand to steady himself. 'I must go.'

He stumbled towards the door, out onto the landing. The huge staircase seemed to spin around him. He took one step, and almost pitched head first down the stairs.

Hugo grabbed his arm. 'You will break your neck on the stairs in the state you are in. Stay here.'

Rob knew he ought to go back to the ship. Cornish did not know where he was; he might be worried. But the house was warm, and Hugo was kind, and the wine in his blood made him suddenly terribly sleepy.

'Thank you,' he said. 'If you are sure it is not trouble.'

He sank into the feather bed, thinking how lucky he was to have found a friend like Hugo.

He did not feel so lucky the next morning. His mouth tasted like the inside of the bilge, his stomach tossed like a ship in a storm, and his head ached as if a cannon had gone off inside it.

He lay in the bed, rising only to stumble to the side and vomit into the chamber pot. It was nearly noon when Hugo put his head around the door.

'I thought sailors were supposed to have strong heads.' He seemed no worse the wear from the night before. 'A spot of breakfast will cure you.'

Rob meant to say that he should go back to the ship. But after emptying his stomach, he found he was ravenously hungry. Soon he was eating a plateful of eggs, while trying to answer Hugo's ceaseless stream of questions about Africa, and of his family's adventures. Hugo was as wide-eyed as a boy who had just had a genuine pirate walk into his drawing room.

'And what should we do today?' Hugo asked, when his plate was empty. 'The theatre? White's? There is so much you need to see.'

Rob badly wanted to spend the day with Hugo, and see more of the fathomless marvels London had to offer. But he knew he was already past due back at the ship.

'Captain Cornish will worry where I have got to.'

'The voyage is over,' Hugo pointed out. 'Are the crew not entitled to shore leave.'

'I suppose I am,' said Rob. 'But I do not have anywhere to stay ashore.'

'Of course you do,' said Hugo. 'You are staying here.'

Rob felt a lift in his heart. The prospect of staying with his new friend, with his sophistication and easy manners, felt like a dream he could hardly dare to realise.

'Are you quite sure?'

'For as long as you like.'

'But your father . . .?'

'He is not here to ask, and this house is far too big for one person.' Hugo saw Rob still had qualms. 'If it makes you feel better, I will write and tell him.' He winked. 'He will not get the letter for six weeks, and even if he objects it will take as long again to get a reply.'

'You are very generous,' Rob said. 'I fear I do not have much to offer in return.'

'Nonsense,' said Hugo forcefully. 'London was so dull before you came.'

The notion astonished Rob. 'I cannot imagine London ever being dull.'

'I cannot imagine why you would trade a life of wild adventure for this cesspit, but there you have it. With you, I feel I have stepped into the pages of a Daniel Defoe novel.' He rang the bell for a servant. 'It is decided. But if you are to cut a dash as a man about town, you cannot wear those frightful seaman's clothes. I have some old suits you could wear. They are no longer quite so fashionable as they were, but I can have my tailor adjust them for you.'

'That is very kind,' said Rob, 'but I have hardly worn in the clothes I have.'

He had grown up wearing canvas trousers and a cotton shirt; whenever one was worn so badly through that it could not longer be patched, his grandmother would run up a replacement that was to all intents identical. On Christmas Day, or if there was a baptism or a funeral, he had struggled into an old suit of his grandfather's. The notion of fashion was entirely alien to him.

Hugo took it a deal more seriously. Before Rob knew it, he was standing on a box in the middle of the drawing room, while an elderly man with a protruding chin and a red cap fussed about him with measuring tapes and pins.

'I should not be spending my money on clothes I do not need,' Rob fretted.

'You absolutely do need them,' Hugo insisted. 'If you are to stay in London any time at all, you cannot look like a tar just off the ship.'

That is what I am, Rob thought. But Hugo looked so pleased at seeing Rob in his fine new clothes, it felt churlish to say so.

Rob fetched his possessions from the ship. Saying goodbye to Cornish was not as awkward as he had feared.

'The ship will be in harbour for weeks while we refit for the next voyage,' said Cornish. 'I promised to bring you to London. Now you must make your own way.'

He spoke philosophically, but he could not hide the concern in his eyes. Rob had grown in every way since they left Nativity Bay, but he was still so young.

'You are able to support yourself?' Cornish asked.

'I have the money from my grandmother.'

'You will need more than that.'

Cornish led him down to his cabin and opened a chest. Inside, laid on sackcloth, were half a dozen long bull elephant tusks.

'These are for you,' he said gruffly.

Rob flushed. 'It is too much,' he protested.

'Consider it repayment of all the kindnesses your family has shown me these many years.'

Rob did not care about old family debts.

'I can make my own way.'

'No doubt you can. But it's a sight easier to start with something than with nothing.' Cornish saw the stubborn look in Rob's eyes, and sighed. 'If you will not take this as a gift, take it as an investment. If you have half an ounce of Courtney blood in you, you will turn it into a handsome profit. You can pay me back when you have made your fortune.'

Rob took one of the tusks. It took all his strength to hold it, and there were five more just as big in the chest. The weight reassured him. As determined as he was to live on his own wits, he could not deny that London was an overpowering and expensive place. Better to start with a little capital. Maybe then he would not feel quite so unequal with Hugo.

'Let them be a reminder of where you came from,' Cornish added. 'I know you have come to see the world, and maybe you will see more than you bargained for before it is over. But Nativity Bay is your home. We sail for the Malabar Coast in three months' time, and we will call again at Nativity Bay. There is a berth for you aboard this ship if you want it.'

'Thank you,' said Rob.

He was grateful to the captain. But he was also eighteen, on his own, with a full purse and the greatest city in the world at his feet. It was not a time for lingering doubts. By the time he reached Hugo's house and started to unpack, he had forgotten Cornish and was already looking forward to the night's adventures.

Hugo could hardly believe the chest of ivory. He ran his fingers along the length of one of the tusks, marvelling at its size.

'Imagine facing down the beast that carried this. You must be impossibly brave.'

Rob did not know what to say.

'The only ivory I have ever touched before is on a billiard ball. And what is this?'

He picked up the long canvas bundle that lay on the bed.

'Don't . . .' Rob began. but Hugo had already unwrapped it. The sapphire in the pommel of the Neptune sword shone as he held it up to the light.

'Sweet Jesus,' Hugo breathed. 'This must be worth a hundred thousand at least.'

Rob had never thought of it like that.

'It was my grandfather's. And his father's before him.'

Hugo unsheathed the blade and took a few theatrical swings. 'I knew you were a pirate.'

'It belonged to Sir Francis Drake.'

Rob wished Hugo would put it down, but he also wanted his friend to know how important the sword was. Hugo's wealth and breeding were so impeccable, it felt good to show that the Courtneys had their own noble pedigree.

'You really have lived the most extraordinary existence,' Hugo said, with so much admiration in his voice that Rob swelled with pride. 'Make sure you keep this safe.'

As soon as Hugo had left, Rob prised up a floorboard in the corner of the room and hid the sword under it, together with the bag of coins Louisa had given him. He was living under Hugo's roof; he hated himself for distrusting his friend. But any thought of losing the sword, however far-fetched, was unbearable.

The city was tumultuous: a jungle of brick, stone and soot, teeming with life. But it was not as difficult to navigate as Rob had first thought. Over the next weeks, he learned its rhythms and its geography, just as he had the bush at home. He could follow wagon traffic to a major crossroads, as he had once followed game trails to watering holes. Instead of streams, he followed the flow of humanity, watching how trickles grew into the great crowds that thronged the main streets. Instead of tall trees and prominent rocks, he learned to orientate his position by church spires and tavern signs. They had all looked the same to his overloaded eyes when he arrived, but he learned the differences. St Martin in the Fields was shaped like a termite mound; the tiered spire of St Brides, like a cake stand; and there was the stolid square tower of St George's that told him he was nearly back at Wimpole Street.

He also became familiar with many of the different taverns.

Like the jungle, the city had its dangers. Rob learned to be alert for the telltale signs: the rumble of wheels that told of a chaise ready to burst around a street corner; the creak of a window over his head, warning that someone was about to tip out the contents of a chamber pot; the shadow moving in a doorway down an empty alley, when he was coming home late at night.

Employing vigilance and instinct, he was soon able to find a destination, relatively safely, anywhere in London.

He spent many of his days with Hugo and his friends. But there were also times when they went their different ways. During those periods, Rob would go east into the City. He had struck up some friendships with the traders who thronged the court of the Royal Exchange. Tentatively at first, but ever more confidently, he began to trade on his own account. He started with the ivory tusks Cornish had given him. With the profits from that sale, he bought a consignment of tea from a ship that had come in late and was selling cheap, her captain desperate to be rid of the cargo. Rob held on to it for a few weeks, and then sold it on when prices rose again. He had a knack, he discovered, for sensing when a price was low, and when it was likely to rise.

He did not mention it to Hugo. He had learned early on that Hugo had fixed ideas of the world that no amount of argument could change. A man was a gentleman, or he was nothing. A gentleman did not engage in trade. Money was contemptible, except as a means to pleasure. Speaking of it was unforgivably dull. If Rob ever queried the price of an item, Hugo would tease him mercilessly as a penny-pinching old grandmother.

Rob did not entirely understand how a man as profligate as Hugo could give no thought to money, or how one obtained money without engaging in some kind of commerce. But the few times he pressed the question, Hugo grew moody, and Rob did not want to quarrel. So he kept his dealings on the exchange to himself.

Rob tried to invest his money wisely and make it grow. But as quickly as he earned it, it seemed to flow out of his purse again. There were so many ways to spend money in London, and Hugo embraced them all. He took Rob to the finest tailors, cobblers and milliners in St James's to buy new clothes, extravagantly bright fabrics of the kind that Hugo and his friends favoured. There were pleasure gardens, feasts, taverns, races, cock fights, gin shops, theatres: an infinite cornucopia of indulgence.

One day, they found themselves at Epsom Downs, in Surrey. Even in the heart of London Rob had rarely seen so much noise and colour. Gentlemen and their ladies watched from carriages drawn up alongside the track, while vertiginous temporary grandstands tottered above them. There were so many spectators crammed in, Rob feared they would crash over.

They sat in Hugo's phaeton near the starting line, watching the milling crowds and the jockeys preparing their mounts. The smells of hot pies, leather and horse dung filled the air. Hugo kept up a constant commentary on the people he saw:

their titles, incomes, families and scandals. Rob was more interested in the horses. One in particular caught his eye: a tall bay
with a black tail and fetlocks, who stamped his feet and tried to
bite any groom who came near.

'Whose horse is that?' he asked Hugo.

If Hugo knew, his answer was drowned out by a loud rattling
of traces and wheels as a large barouche rolled up beside them.
It had red wheels with black trim, burgundy woodwork trimmed
with gold, and a quartet of matched black geldings harnessed to
it. The leather top was pulled down, so Rob could see two pairs
of finely dressed men and women seated inside.

One of them – a young man with sandy hair and a pointed
nose, his arm fondling a blonde-haired young woman – greeted
Hugo.

'Fine sport today, eh?'

'Lord Tewkesbury,' Hugo whispered in Rob's ear. 'A notorious gambler. He once bet a thousand pounds on which flea
would be first to leap off a tart's backside.'

'Are you running a horse in the race?' he asked, more loudly.

'Indeed I am.' Tewkesbury pointed his cane at the tall bay
Rob had admired earlier. 'Sir Bors is mine.' He leaned forwards.
'Would you care to make a wager?'

Rob had never known Hugo refuse a bet, but against Sir Bors
even he demurred.

'That would be a damned waste of money. Sir Bors is the
finest animal in the field. I doubt you could get twenty to one
against him.'

Tewkesbury looked disappointed. 'I thought you were a man
of mettle, Lyall. But no doubt I will find someone with more
stomach.'

Rob could feel his friend squirming on the seat beside him.

'I will take the wager,' he called.

Tewkesbury lifted up a pair of gold pince-nez and squinted
at him.

'Who is this?'

'Robert Courtney.'

'Of the Devon Courtenays?'

'The Courtneys of Africa.'

Tewkesbury frowned. He felt sure he was being mocked, but Rob's expression was so direct it was hard to believe he was joking.

'I suppose it does not matter where you come from, if your credit is good. Whom do you think has the pace to beat my horse?'

Rob pointed to a wiry piebald colt he had noticed standing placidly in the background, while his grooms braided his mane into bunches.

'What odds will you give me on him?'

Tewkesbury gave a sharp, barking laugh. 'On Alcmaeon? Four to one. A hundred guineas on Sir Bors against your nag.'

The colour drained from Rob's face. As much as he had profited from his trades on the Exchange, most of his capital was currently invested in goods he could not sell quickly, except at a loss. He was about to say he did not have the money, when Hugo said suddenly, 'I will stand surety for Rob's wager.'

'Capital.' Tewkesbury reached out of his barouche and stretched out to shake Rob's hand. 'It is agreed.'

The carriage rattled on, forcing its way through the crowds. Hugo slumped into his seat and beckoned one of the ale-sellers to bring him a drink. The look he gave Rob was caught halfway between admiration and anxiety.

'What in God's name have you just done?'

'Why did you support me?' Now that Tewkesbury had gone, Rob was trembling.

'I trusted you knew what you were up to.' Hugo drained his tankard and stared hopefully at Rob over the rim. 'You do know what you're up to, don't you?'

'I have never gambled on horses before,' Rob said, honestly.

'Dear God.' Hugo gripped the side of the phaeton. 'What have you done?'

'Used my common sense.' Rob pointed to Tewkesbury's horse. His jockey, in red striped livery and cap, was leading him gingerly to the starting post. 'He looks very fine, but see how his ears twitch every time his hind left leg touches the ground. There is something not right there.'

Hugo whistled. 'Now I wish I had taken the wager. And the horse you chose? Alcmaeon?'

'I cannot say.' Rob wished he could explain that growing up on a farm in such close proximity to animals both tame and wild had given him a sort of intuition to their needs. 'There is a calmness about him that I liked. An intent.'

'You risked a hundred guineas on your feeling?'

'Actually, it was your hundred guineas I risked.'

Hugo buried his head in his hands. 'Then God have mercy on us both.'

The horses were marshalled into position. The race stewards mounted a wooden tower that had been erected by the starting post. It took some time to be ready, as the bay colt kept tossing its head and bucking about, disturbing the other horses in the line. The piebald, meanwhile, stood placidly, feet planted square and ears pricked up.

'Look at Tewkesbury,' said Hugo in disgust. His barouche was drawn up near the start, surrounded by a crowd of braying sycophants. 'Let us hope we wipe the smirk off his face.'

Sir Bors had had enough. Ignoring the best efforts of his jockey, he suddenly started forwards. The stewards, faced with the unappealing prospect of calling him back, chose the path of less resistance and promptly blew the horn to start the race.

'That is unfair!' Rob cried.

Boos rose from the crowd, though not from those around Tewkesbury. Sir Bors was a length ahead of the field before any of the others had started. His powerful legs bounded forwards; his hooves dug deep divots out of the turf. The others could barely keep pace. They raced past Hugo's phaeton in a blur of colour and noise. Then they were gone.

'Yours is last,' said Hugo dolefully.

The piebald colt was keeping a steady pace near the back of the field, galloping along with no great intent.

Rob stood up on the seat, shading his eyes to follow the distant horses as they made their way around the course.

'Alcmaeon is moving up.'

It was true. Without seeming to exert himself, the piebald horse had passed two riders already. But it was scant consolation. Sir Bors had powered further ahead, and now had four lengths on the rest of the field.

'Tewkesbury will be unbearable,' lamented Hugo. Absently, he took a letter from inside his coat, stared at it, then returned it to his pocket. 'And if my father hears how I have been using my allowance, he will be furious.'

'Alcmaeon is still in it.'

The horses had reached the far corner, too far off to see clearly. But Rob's keen eyes could see a blur of grey moving through the field.

'He is only competing to be second.'

Even from that distance, every man and woman on the course could see Sir Bors still retained his imperious lead.

The noise of the spectators swelled as the horses rounded the final corner, into the long straight that led up to the winning post. Sir Bors stood out from the field, who were bunched together behind him.

'Alcmaeon is gaining on him,' said Rob, pulsing with excitement. He stood on his tiptoes, watching the two horses gallop down the straight. Alcmaeon had pulled clear of the chasing pack and was drawing closer to the big bay. Both jockeys hunched low in the saddle, whipping every last bit of pace they could out of their mounts as they bore down towards the finish line.

'There is not enough time for him to close the distance,' said Hugo.

With his long legs and powerful frame, all Sir Bors needed was to keep up his pace for another furlong. But . . .

'Look!' cried Rob.

Sir Bors's head was going down. Sweat foamed on his breast. Each thunderous step seemed slightly shorter than the last. His eyes bulged, his nostrils flared, but he could not eke out those final yards.

'*Come on!*' bellowed Rob, thrilling with the chase. The two horses were neck and neck now, the finishing line only a few yards distant. Thrashing with his whip, Tewkesbury's jockey managed to coax one last burst of strength from the horse. He edged ahead. The ground shook with the thunder of hooves.

It was too much to ask. Sir Bors was spent. Alcmaeon surged past him and crossed the line a nose in front. The grandstands and the carriages erupted in frenzied cheering. Only the party around Tewkesbury's gilded barouche did not join in.

Rob sought out his rival and tipped his hat, enjoying the chill glare he got in return. Victory flowed hot in his veins. Hugo flung his arms around him and almost knocked him off his feet.

'You did it.' His eyes shone. 'I knew you were a marvel. Think how much you will enjoy spending your winnings.'

'Our winnings,' said Rob. 'You backed me. We should share the profits equally.'

'And spend them as quickly as possible.' Word of the wager had already spread, and crowds were starting to gather around the phaeton to toast their health. 'I do not know which I like better – being four hundred guineas richer, or seeing you prick that bastard's pride.'

'Four hundred guineas,' Rob repeated, hardly believing it. It was as much as he had ever made trading at the Exchange – and less work, too. For a moment it was tempting to believe he could do it again, that the horses would always come in and he could make an easy living by gambling.

Then he remembered how close Sir Bors had come to winning the race. This was a lucky moment, nothing more. He should celebrate it, savour it, and not expect it to happen again. Fortunes would be made by hard work, not chance.

A new thought rose in his mind. Before he could second-guess himself, he said, 'We should go to sea together.'

'What?'

Rob had spoken on impulse, yet the moment he said it, he felt the rightness of the idea strong inside him.

'The *Dunstanburgh Castle* sails for the Malabar Coast in a fortnight. Her captain has already offered me a berth, and I am sure there would be space for you, too.'

Hugo frowned. 'I do not think I would make much of a sailor.'

'We would not be going simply as seamen. We will use the money we have won to buy a cargo and trade it in India, on our own account. Cornish will give us space in his hold. We will see the world, and make ourselves princes.'

Rob could see the idea taking root in Hugo's mind. In the midst of the crowd of drunken spectators, the air thick with beer and mud and dung, he was seeing the dusky coasts of the Orient: saffron, gold and ivory.

'Is it not what you dreamed of?' Rob said. 'Break away from your father. Make your own way in the world – stand on your own feet. Think how proud your father will be when he sees what you have made of yourself.'

'Proud?' said Hugo softly.

Something still seemed to be gnawing inside him – doubt; fear? Rob could not tell. Then his face softened. The tension inside him seemed to release. He looked up, his gaze meeting Rob's with delight in his eyes.

'We will conquer the world together.'

Rob felt the same thrill he had when his horse crossed the line, the sense of possibilities crystallising into fact. In his mind, he was already halfway across the ocean.

'We should return to London at once. Tomorrow, we can start choosing our cargo.'

'It will be marvellous. Though not tomorrow.' Hugo's face darkened. He took out the paper Rob had seen him holding earlier. 'I have had a letter from a friend of my father's. Some tedious drone, he is something in the government. He has asked to see me tomorrow morning.'

'Do you know why?'

'No doubt my father has asked him to lecture me on my short-comings.' He sighed. 'I shall have to listen to him, I suppose, commending me to the merits of sobriety and continence. And afterwards you and I will plan our adventure.'

It was a trivial thing, yet still Rob felt a stir of unease, as if Hugo's father had magically heard their plan and reached across the ocean to stop it. Hugo saw his concern and laughed.

'Do not worry. I will take my medicine, and the next thing my father knows I will be writing to him from Calcutta. Now let us have another drink to celebrate.'

Next morning, Hugo approached the door to a great house on Portman Square. He had been there quite often as a child, trailing after his father, but that did not quell the shaking in his knees as he stood on the doorstep.

He presented his card to a liveried servant. 'Baron Dartmouth asked me to call.'

Stepping into the house was like entering another continent. Persian carpets covered the floors, and the walls were hung with silks. There were elephant tusks, fine porcelains from China, and statues of strange gods with animal heads. The sight of so many exotic treasures should have thrilled Hugo – it was, if he thought about it, how he imagined Rob's home must look. But he barely noticed them.

Baron Dartmouth received Hugo in his study, sitting behind a carved teak desk. A tiger skin was stretched out on the wall behind him, between portraits of his illustrious ancestors. A hookah pipe filled the room with the aroma of sweet tobacco. Dartmouth wore a wig, which most of London had long since abandoned as outmoded. Hugo had heard rumours he wore it because every hair on his head had been burned off in battle. Other rumours were more outlandish still: that he had fought as a mercenary in India; that he could kill a man with a steel whip. Most terrible of all was his right hand, a prosthetic made of gold that gleamed at the end of his coat sleeve. Men said that he had lost the hand by ramming it in a tiger's mouth and choking it to death. Nobody ever dared ask if the rumours were fact, because everyone understood the underlying truth. Baron Dartmouth was capable of anything.

Dartmouth took a long draw on his pipe. Smoke bubbled up through the water.

'Tell me about Robert Courtney,' he said, without preamble.

Hugo was astonished. Dartmouth was one of the richest, most powerful men in England. As President of the Board of Trade and Plantations, the entire commerce between Britain and her colonies passed under his eye. He could make or break traders, firms, even whole ministries with a single word. The thought that he should trouble himself with the exploits of two young men amusing themselves in London was beyond Hugo's comprehension.

'How do you know about Rob?' was all he could manage to say.

Dartmouth fixed Hugo with a pair of glittering black eyes.

'I received a letter from your father.'

That explained some of it. As one of the most prominent West Indian sugar planters, Hugo's father had long relied on Dartmouth. Hugo could remember the two men talking business, conspiring together, on those childhood visits. The connection had been profitable for both men. When the sugar interest was under attack in Parliament, by free traders or sanctimonious abolitionists, Dartmouth saw to it that their protestations were ignored or crushed. In return, Lyall and his fellow planters made sure that a healthy part of their vast profits found its way into Dartmouth's own coffers.

But it still did not explain Dartmouth's interest in Robert Courtney.

'Rob Courtney is new to London. He has been staying with me.'

'So your father tells me. What do you know of him?'

Hugo tried desperately to think. 'His family comes from Africa. He grew up there. He arrived in London some three months ago. We met by chance. He is my friend.'

Dartmouth's mouth twisted in a sneer, as if Hugo had admitted some particularly shameful and depraved habit.

'Does he have other friends in London? Allies who would help him?'

'None that I know of.'

'Has he ever mentioned me?'

Hugo shook his head. Dartmouth and Rob were so different, he could not conceive of them occupying the same sphere of existence, let alone that they would overlap.

'I am certain he is as ignorant of your person as he is of the back side of the moon.' And then, suddenly terrified he had insulted Dartmouth: 'He is quite innocent. Rather naive.'

Dartmouth sat back in his chair, thinking hard. There was something monstrous in the way the folds of his brow furrowed, the way his hooded eyes turned inwards. Even the act of thinking was pregnant with menace.

Hugo waited, his mind a tangle of confusion. So far as he was concerned, the man in front of him had only ever been Baron Dartmouth, the title as fixed and eternal as the king of England. But now a vague memory stirred itself inside him: a dinner party years ago with his father's friends, the cabal of planters discussing their benefactor. One of them, an old West Indies hand who had held his estates since the reign of Queen Anne, had been forthright in his drunkenness.

'Baron Dartmouth is no better than a jumped-up nabob. I knew him when he was plain Christopher Courtney.'

Curiosity got the better of Hugo. 'Am I right that your lordship's family name was Courtney, before you were ennobled?'

'What of it?' Dartmouth's voice was soft as a rapier sliding into flesh. It made Hugo regret ever speaking – but now he had started, he had to answer Dartmouth's question.

'I wondered . . . if he might be your family.'

The words provoked the most extraordinary reaction. Almost before Hugo had finished speaking, Dartmouth was on his feet. If there had not been a desk between them, Hugo feared the baron would have grabbed him by his lapels and thrown him against the wall.

'I have no family!' Dartmouth roared, spitting venom from his lips. 'My uncle Tom fled to Africa as a murderer. He died childless and unmourned. My father Guy was the only surviving heir of that line of Courtneys. Do you understand?'

Dartmouth leaned on the table, breathing hard. He had been born Christopher Courtney, though that was a name he seldom used now. It had taken him twenty years of painstaking argument, lobbying and bribery to have his relatives declared dead without issue, so that he could secure the title of Baron Dartmouth that had belonged to his grandfather.

Hugo didn't care. All he wanted was to escape as quickly as possible.

'It must be a coincidence,' he muttered, fumbling towards the door. 'I apologise for troubling your lordship.'

'Wait!' Dartmouth roared. 'I have not finished with you.'

Hugo froze.

'Tell me everything you know about Robert Courtney. The least detail, however trivial.' Dartmouth leaned forward. 'If you hold anything back, anything at all, and I learn of it, you can be sure you will regret it.'

Hugo struggled to think, desperate for any crumb of information that might satisfy Dartmouth and let him escape.

'He has a sword – a truly magnificent weapon. A family heirloom, I think. It . . .'

Hugo trailed off. Trying to avoid Dartmouth's eye, his gaze had landed on a full-length painting behind the desk. It showed a strong, proud man dressed in the fashion of the previous century. The picture must have been painted almost a hundred years ago; the paint was faded, the varnish cracked and yellowed. Yet one spot shone almost luminous from the dull canvas. A great blue sapphire, set in the pommel of the sword that the man's hand rested on.

Dartmouth was still as he followed Hugo's gaze.

'What sword?' he asked, in a voice that suggested he was capable of murder.

Hugo wiped his brow. 'It is only a superficial resemblance.'

'*What sword?*' Dartmouth slammed his fist on the desk and the hookah pipe toppled over. The smouldering coal landed on a piece of paper and set it alight. Dartmouth ground out the fire with his golden hand. 'Is it true? After all these years, has a Courtney arrived in London with the Neptune sword?'

Hugo could not tell if Dartmouth expected an answer, or if he was speaking to himself. He flinched as the black eyes fixed on him again.

'I must know everything. Where he lives, how he came here, who else is with him and *what he wants*.'

'Yes, my Lord,' Hugo croaked. He did not want to betray his friend, but at that moment he would have said anything Dartmouth wanted to hear, if he could only get out of there.

Dartmouth had not finished with him yet. 'There is more in the letter from your father.' He tossed the paper across the desk. 'Read it.'

Hugo took the paper and held it up to the light. His face, already pale, seemed to grow white; his hand shook as if with a palsy.

'He says he will cut me off,' he whispered. 'All my allowance. What will I do?'

Dartmouth smiled evilly. 'Go on.'

'He means to buy me a commission as a lieutenant in the army and have me posted to the garrison in the East Indies.' Hugo dropped the paper. 'Those are fever islands. No man stationed there lives six months.'

'Your father has heard enough of your debauches, the way you squander the fortune he worked so hard to build. It is time you became a man.'

Hugo hugged his arms to himself, as if curling into a ball. 'No.'

'But . . .' Dartmouth let the word hang in the air, dangling like a hook. 'Your father and I have a long association. I flatter myself he respects my counsel. If I were to put in a good word for you, perhaps I could soften his opinion of you. Maybe I could even change his mind from this course of action.'

Hugo bowed his head. 'What do you want from me?'

Dartmouth did not speak for a moment. All the time he had been speaking to Hugo, a deeper part of his mind had been turning rapidly. When he had received the letter from Hugo's father alerting him that a boy named Courtney had arrived from Africa, he had almost dismissed it as happenstance. But he had not risen to the heights of power by being careless – and some inner instinct had warned him he should look into it. Now there was no doubt.

His left hand fingered his right wrist, where the golden hand was buckled on to the stump of his arm. The arm still ached, but that was nothing compared to the pain in his heart when he thought of the Neptune sword. It was the greatest heirloom the Courtney family possessed. Almost seventy years earlier, he had held it – and Tom Courtney had cut it out of his hand. In the years since, Dartmouth had made himself the richest man in India, perhaps the richest in the British Empire. He had amassed more gold, land and titles than any Courtney before him. Only one trophy had eluded him. And now the tides of fate had brought it to his doorstep, in the hands of an ignorant boy. Tom Courtney's grandson – it could be no one else – had come to London.

He leaned forwards across the desk, taking a small pleasure from the way Hugo shrivelled into his seat. He had waited years for this moment. And now this snivelling creature would be the instrument of his vengeance.

'This is what you will do . . .'

'You look very pale,' Rob said. 'Was the meeting with your father's friend so dreadful?'

He and Hugo were sitting together, taking a late breakfast. Rob tucked enthusiastically into his plate of devilled kidneys, but Hugo barely touched his food. His face was grey, his eyes dark-rimmed. He looked as if he was on the verge of tears.

Hugo pressed his fork into one of the kidneys. Blood oozed from its smooth flesh. Something seemed to be knotted up inside him.

'What is wrong?' Rob asked.

'Dartmouth gave me a letter from my father.' The words rushed out of Hugo's mouth. 'He means to cut me off without a penny.'

'Is this because of me?'

'It is nothing to do with you. He has always despised the way I live. His friends write to him and whisper poison in his ear. Now his patience has snapped. He will buy me a commission in the army and send me to the fever islands.'

Rob had never heard him so heartbroken. All the time he had known Hugo, his friend had been bursting with energy and good humour. To see him like this now was like seeing a hunting dog with its legs broken.

'It does not matter what your father thinks,' he said, consoling Hugo. 'Remember what we agreed yesterday? You will be free of your father's purse-strings. We will be trading on our own account.'

'But that is what I mean,' said Hugo. 'Without my allowance, I have nothing with which to buy our cargo for India.'

Rob considered the question. He had the money from the wager, but that would not go far enough. He certainly did not have enough to pay Hugo's share as well.

Some of Hugo's despair began to colour his own thoughts.

'Is there nothing we can do?'

'You should go ahead without me,' said Hugo. 'I will take my fate.'

'No.' Rob could not fail his friend. 'You have been so generous to me. I will pay for both of us.'

'I cannot let you do that.'

'You staked me the money to bet on Alcmaeon,' Rob reminded him. 'It is the same thing. Consider it an investment in our future fortune.'

Hope began to dawn on Hugo's face. 'Do you have enough? For both of us, I mean.'

'Another month or two and I will certainly earn it.'

Hugo bit his lip. 'That is too long. My father will be home in a fortnight, and then I will be powerless.'

Rob's optimism faded. He stared at Hugo, trying to convey to him how much he wanted to help, though his mind could think of nothing.

As their eyes met, an idea seemed to occur to Hugo. He put down his fork; his eyes sparkled.

'Perhaps there is a way.'

'Tell me.'

'I will show you.'

He made Rob dress in his finest clothes, and insisted he bring the Neptune sword. Rob was reluctant.

'Are we going to steal the money?' he asked.

Hugo laughed. 'I knew you had a pirate's instincts,' he said. 'But this will be a more sedate transaction.'

'You know I will not sell the sword.'

'I would never ask you to do that,' Hugo reassured him. 'But you must trust me. It is a curious fact of money, that it is very hard to come by unless you have it already. And then it is ridiculously easy.'

They took the carriage to a trading house on Cornhill. A man named Spinkley with a gold tooth welcomed them into his office.

'Spinkley is my father's agent,' Hugo explained. 'He handles all his financial arrangements. And mine, too.'

'Is your father in the sugar interest, too?' Spinkley enquired of Robert unctuously.

'Robert's family have interests in Africa,' said Hugo, before Rob could speak. 'Extensive trading business.'

Spinkley peered over the tops of his glasses. He smiled.

'I confess, I am not aware of the family.' He mused for a moment. 'Courtney. You are not by chance related to Baron Dartmouth?'

'I don't believe so, sir,' said Rob uncertainly. He was uncomfortable with the conversation. He felt as if he was playing a part in a charade, without any idea what he was supposed to do.

But Hugo had a way of making doubts disappear.

'My family and the Courtneys are the greatest of friends. My father would vouch for Rob in an instant.'

'If he were here,' said Spinkley, 'and not five thousand miles away in the West Indies.'

'He will return,' said Hugo, airily. 'And when he does, you would not want him to find out you did not make my friend welcome. It might cause him to question whether you valued his own custom.'

'I never meant to imply . . .' Spinkley blinked rapidly. 'I can have my clerk to draw up a contract this instant.' A sly tone came into his voice. 'Of course . . . you have collateral?'

Rob barely understood what he was talking about. Hugo nudged him in the ribs.

'The sword,' he whispered.

Unwillingly, Rob took out the Neptune sword and laid it on the desk. Spinkley's eyes bulged so far Rob thought they might drop in his teacup.

'This . . . ah . . . puts a very different complexion on matters,' he said. 'This will be perfectly satisfactory.'

They waited while the clerk produced the contract. It seemed a long document. Rob began to read it, though with its talk of *encumbrances* and *replevin* and *compound interest* it might as well have been written in French.

'You are too assiduous,' Hugo teased him. 'Do you mean to read every word? Just sign the damn thing and take the money, before Mr Spinkley gives it all away to a deserving orphan.'

Rob signed. They left the bank with a fresh purse of coins, and a letter of credit for more. Most importantly, Rob still had the sword clutched tight in his hand.

'You are certain he cannot take it,' he asked Hugo, for the third time.

'Only if you do not pay him back. But that is not something to worry about.'

Rob did not entirely share Hugo's confidence. Any risk to the sword, however trivial, alarmed him. But at that moment, they stepped out of the building and were suddenly confronted by a small crowd who had gathered there holding sheaves of handbills. A man with hollow cheeks and a pointed chin saw Rob coming down the steps and thrust a leaflet into his hands.

'Do you tolerate slavery, sir? Then you tolerate inhumanity itself.'

Rob was so surprised he took the leaflet. He looked up. The man's burning blue eyes seemed to bore through his soul. Rob felt naked.

Hugo took the man by the lapels and almost threw him down the street.

'Away with you and your vile slanders!' he roared. 'Let honest men go about their business, or I will tan your face so black you could pass for a Negro.'

The hollow-cheeked man dusted himself off. He gave Rob and Hugo a look of disgust. Then he turned away to accost another customer going into the building.

Rob had to hold Hugo back to stop him striking the man again. He had never seen his friend so angry. He steered him to a coffee house and ordered coffee with brandy. It was only then that he realised he was still clutching the pamphlet in his fist. He flattened it out.

The cover showed a black man kneeling, wrapped in chains and staring up at the heavens. The legend above said, 'Am I not a man and brother?' Inside was a picture of a naked black woman hung from a gibbet by her ribs. Her tongue lolled out; her arms and breasts had been cut off.

'Who can deny the nature of that disgraceful branch of commerce, the purchasing of our fellow-creatures from the coast of Africa to supply our West Indian sugar islands . . .?'

Before Rob could read any more, Hugo snatched it from his hands. He held it over the candle on their table and let it burn to ash.

'What was that?' said Rob, astonished. 'Who were those people?'

'Abolitionists,' said Hugo venomously. 'Anti-slavery campaigners.'

'But what has that to do with us?' Rob could not shake the image of the mutilated woman from his mind.

'Because we use slaves on the plantations.'

Robert stared at him in horror. 'Slaves?'

'Of course. Cutting cane is beastly work. How else would we get it done?'

'But . . .' Robert could not think what to say that would not mortally offend his friend. He remembered what his grandmother Louisa had said. *No human being should ever have to suffer that.*

'Is it not monstrously cruel?'

'Not at all,' said Hugo. 'You sound like one of those abolitionist lunatics. We treat the slaves like our own children. And the blacks are quite helpless, you know. If we did not feed and clothe them, and direct their labour, they would starve to death.'

The Africans Robert had known at Nativity Bay were not like that. They were resourceful, brave, and had taught the Courtneys everything they needed to know to survive in the unforgiving landscape.

Hugo saw his doubts. 'Have you ever been to the West Indies?'

'No.'

'I have. I promise you, for the Negroes it is the best life they could hope for.'

Hugo sounded so certain. Perhaps the blacks in Jamaica came from some different tribe from the sturdy warriors around Fort Auspice.

'I did not mean to offend you,' Rob said humbly.

'In any event, that is my father's business. Soon I will have no part of it.'

The next fortnight passed in a blur of activity. Rob spent his days in the city, haggling and purchasing and racking his brains for every scrap of information he had heard about conditions in India from the sea captains who had passed through Nativity Bay. It seemed that steel blades and muskets were much sought after in Bombay, and also tobacco and spirits.

'It sounds a blood-curdling place,' said Hugo, when Rob told him. 'Do they do nothing but fight and indulge their vices?'

Weapons were hard to come by in London, but there was no shortage of tobacco and brandy to be had. Rob contracted for as much as he could afford, and found a warehouse not far from Monsoon Dock where he could store it until Cornish was ready to load. It was an old, timber-framed building, far less sturdy than the newer brick-built warehouses around it. But it was cheap, and the foreman seemed honest.

'As long as it does not fall down in the next fortnight, it will serve our purposes,' Rob decided.

He looked forward to the voyage. London might promise pleasures beyond counting, but after three months – impossible as it seemed – he had grown bored of it. He longed to be back at sea, feeling the ship like a living thing that needed to be loved and handled and tamed. To him, somehow, that cramped wooden world barely a hundred feet long held more freedom than all the fleshpots of London put together.

Hugo seemed even more keen to be away. He looked constantly at the clocks, as if he could browbeat time itself into moving faster. Three times a day he would rehearse with Rob the sailing times: the loading schedule, the phases of the tides, the route downriver.

'Anyone would think you were being chased away by a horde of pirates,' Rob teased him.

'My father may return any day,' Hugo fretted.

'What if he does? He cannot stop you going.' Rob laid his hand on Hugo's arm. 'I know how hard it is to go against your own father. But you do not need his money, and you certainly do not need his permission. You are your own man now.'

Hugo smiled. The words seemed to console him. 'What would I do without you?'

At last they exhausted the credit Spinkley had given them. The warehouse stood piled high with casks of brandy and bales of tobacco, so much that Hugo wondered if it would all fit in the Indiaman's hold.

'We will find out tomorrow when we load,' said Rob.

Hugo stared up at the stacked barrels. 'How much have we spent?'

'Ten thousand pounds.'

'And how much do we stand to profit?'

Rob shrugged. 'I would hope we would clear at least as much again.'

He knew from Cornish that when it came to haggling, the merchants in Bombay would make the factors and traders in London look like innocent lambs, but he was confident in his ability.

'We should celebrate our good fortune,' Hugo declared. 'Our last night of freedom.'

'There is a kind of freedom aboard a ship,' Rob pointed out.

'Maybe so,' Hugo allowed. 'But salt beef does not sate all appetites.'

The sort of appetites he meant soon became clear. They drank, they ate, and eventually found their way to a tall house on Tenterden Street. The windows were discreetly curtained, but inside every inch of the walls was covered with gilded mirrors, and paintings of naked women being ravished by antique gods. Some of the paintings seemed to have come alive, for in every corridor and drawing room paraded young women in advanced states of undress. Their creamy breasts peeked over the tops of their dresses, which split at the waist to reveal inviting shadows between their thighs. The mirrors on the walls reflected them back endlessly from every angle.

Rob chose one named Mary, a Dorset girl with pink cheeks and a kindly smile. When she put her hand on his manhood, he almost climaxed immediately. But she was a sensitive girl, well trained, and she knew if she gave him his money's worth he would come back for more. She coaxed and teased him for nearly an hour before she released him. He thought he had died and gone to Heaven.

'Was that your first time?' asked Hugo, afterwards. They lounged on sofas, both naked.

'No,' said Rob indignantly.

He was not entirely inexperienced. At Nativity Bay, one of the servant girls used to take him, giggling, behind the storehouse and let him touch her breasts while she rubbed against him. On the *Dunstanburgh Castle*, he had picked up a colourful and wildly extravagant impression of sex from the sailors' conversations. But never anything like this.

'I don't believe you,' said Hugo. 'Not with that enormous smile on your face.' He lounged back on a chaise, holding a glass of sparkling champagne. 'To our voyage,' he toasted.

'To our voyage.'

'May we come back as rich as Satan.'

Rob laughed. His mind was still in a delicious haze of Mary's musk and champagne.

'Does it excite you?' Hugo asked. 'To be following in the footsteps of your ancestors? Your grandfather sailed from London nearly a hundred years ago to make his fortune, and now you will do the same.'

Rob had told him the story many times, but Hugo could never remember the details properly. Luckily, he never tired of hearing it again.

'Tom Courtney was my *great*-grandfather,' Rob corrected him.

'And that magnificent sword you own – that was his?'

'It was presented to *his* grandfather by Sir Francis Drake himself. It has been in our family for seven generations.'

'What an extraordinary family.' Hugo upended the last of the bottle into Rob's glass. 'I look forward to meeting them.'

'I hope they do not disappoint you.' A strange wave of melancholy swept over Rob as he remembered his parting with his father. 'Tom Courtney died years ago. My grandfather was the last link to that age, and he died before I left. You will find the Courtneys of today rather diminished.'

'Then you and I will write a new chapter of that history,' said Hugo, 'and in a hundred years, your great-grandchildren will tell tales of the great deeds of Robert Courtney, and despair of the pygmies who live in that time.'

'Maybe,' said Rob doubtfully.

It was what he dreamed of most of all, though it was hard to imagine anything he could do that would match the exploits of his famous ancestors. Sometimes the weight of it could be almost unbearable.

'At any rate, you can judge for yourself when we reach Nativity Bay.'

Rob tried to imagine Hugo at Fort Auspice, with his urban polish and drawling wit. He could not think how his father would react.

Hugo beckoned to one of the girls for another bottle of champagne. When she bent over to pour it, her chemise rode up to reveal the cleft of her naked buttocks in a most enticing way. She dipped a finger in the champagne and sucked it suggestively.

'Will there be anything else?'

Hugo saw the look on Rob's face.

'I believe my friend is ready for more.'

'We should see to the cargo,' Rob protested weakly.

'We should see to your other needs first.'

Hugo waved to the girl. She kneeled beside Rob so that her golden hair draped over his naked thighs. She took his manhood in her mouth and started flicking it lightly with her tongue.

'Remind me exactly where Nativity Bay is to be found?' said Hugo. 'You know I have no head for geography.'

'On the east coast of southern Africa,' Rob said. The girl's tongue was sending shots of delight through him, and it was hard to concentrate.

'It sounds impossibly exotic. Is there civilisation nearby?'

'Cape Town,' said Rob with a little gasp. 'But that is a thousand miles away.'

'Are you sure we will be able to find it?'

'It sits in the lee of a cape, with a summit shaped like a whale's back,' Rob assured him. 'I would know it by sight in an instant.'

'Then let us look forward to seeing it together.'

'Mmmmm,' nodded Rob, as the girl's eager mouth closed around him.

Next morning, for the first time since Rob had known him, Hugo was awake before Rob. Rob found him in his dressing room, standing over a chest that was overflowing with clothes. More garments lay strewn around the room.

'You will not want this finery at sea,' Rob teased him, holding up a pair of striped silk breeches. 'In any case, we are not sailing for another three days. Today we are only loading the cargo.'

'I cannot wait to be away,' said Hugo fervently. 'Every day we delay I fear some disaster.'

'Save your fears for when we are at sea. That is where the true dangers lie.'

It was a clear, bright morning. Rob's body still glowed with the memory of his encounter with Mary, coupled with the excitement of their new adventure. He felt as if he was swimming with a strong tide at his back, rushing along, and there was nothing he could not do. Perhaps Hugo had been right. Perhaps one day his exploits would stand comparison with the great Courtney heroes of old.

The feeling persisted as Hugo's coach rattled through the morning streets of London. Watching the passers-by, seeing the shops and the great mansions and monuments, it was hard to believe how much they had overwhelmed Rob when he arrived. Now they were familiar – commonplace, even.

But as they approached the docks, bouncing over the narrow cobbled streets, an uneasy note intruded on his happiness. First there was the smell, a bitter odour tickling his nostrils in the open carriage. The crowds in the street grew tighter; the coachman had to slow down. Everyone seemed to be hurrying in the same direction.

The smell of smoke grew stronger. A haze covered the blue sky, growing steadily thicker.

'What is happening?' Rob called.

Fear rose inside him. The coach had stopped, unable to get through. He leaped down and began pushing his way forwards through the throng. The crowd were talking around him, though he heard only snatches, like the chattering of a great flock of birds. But one word cut through it all. *Fire.*

He came around a corner and stared. He should have been looking at the warehouse where they had stored their goods – but it was not there. The buildings either side of it still stood, their red brick walls scorched black. In between, there was nothing. Through the pall of smoke still rising from the heap of charred timbers, he could see only the river and open sky beyond.

His legs went weak. If not for the crowd pressed so close around him, he might have fallen. Everything he had owned, the cargo he had pinned his future on – gone.

There was a rumble and a crash, as another part of the building collapsed on itself. It was hard to believe there was anything left to fall, but clearly the fire still smouldered: a fountain of sparks leaped up from the shifting timbers. The crowd shrank back, but Rob moved against them, like a moth drawn to the flames. He stood in front of the crowd, alone, staring at the wreckage of his ambitions. All the money he had borrowed, all the hopes he had bought with it, turned to ash.

Hugo emerged from the throng and stood beside him. Rob felt another tremor of despair. He had led his friend into this scheme. How could he look him in the eye now?

'This is terrible,' Hugo breathed. 'You have lost everything.'

His words jarred Rob. 'You mean *we* have lost everything.'

Before Hugo could respond, another man pushed his way out of the crowd. Even in the dull light, Rob caught the flash of a golden tooth in a thickset mouth. It was Spinkley, Hugo's father's agent. How had he come so quickly?

The agent stuck his hands in his pocket and surveyed the scene.

'Terrible, terrible, such a loss.'

A nasty suspicion began to grow in Rob's mind.

'How did you know to find me here?'

'Bad news travels quickly. And I must protect my investment.' Spinkley gestured at the smoking ruin. 'There is a rumour that all your trade goods were held in that warehouse.'

Smoke had got into Rob's lungs. He felt his throat constrict. 'That is true.'

'Then I cannot have any confidence in your ability to repay. I regret I am calling in the loan.'

Rob's stomach flipped. 'So soon?'

'It is in the contract you signed.' He held up the document with Rob's signature scrawled on it. It might as well have been a death warrant.

'I do not have the money to pay you.' Rob could hardly force the words out.

'Then I claim your collateral.'

'The sword?' The ground seemed to sink beneath Rob's feet. He felt he was falling into a pit, slithering down a crumbling face that turned to dust whenever he tried to grab it. 'You want the sword to repay the loan?'

'That is the nature of collateral.' Spinkley spoke perfectly dispassionately, as if this were merely a dry business of numbers, as if he had not noticed that Rob's life lay in ruins. 'Although to be precise, the sword was only collateral for the principal loan. There is also the interest to consider.'

'Interest?'

'A further two hundred pounds.'

He showed Rob another piece of paper, copied from a ledger. Numbers written in red ink, spiralling quickly upwards.

Rob had a quick mind for figures. He understood the voracious logic of the arithmetic, how a simple percentage could feed off itself until it far surpassed the original amount. That, after all, was how he had intended to make his fortune, one trade building on the profits of the next. But now the process was reversed, he saw how it became an inescapable trap.

'How am I to repay this?' he asked in a small voice. 'The sword is all I have. If it is not enough . . .'

'That is not my concern.' Spinkley folded the papers in two. His fingers rasped along the crease with a noise like slitting a man's throat. 'By the terms of the contract, you must pay back the principal and the interest when I demand it. If the sword does not satisfy the debt, you will go to the debtors' prison until you have paid it in full.'

Rob felt the jaws of the trap closing around his neck. He could hardly breathe. He had heard about debtors' prisons, like the notorious Marshalsea in Southwark which was run as a private enterprise for profit, trading in human misery. Hugo's friends sometimes joked about it but there was always fear in their eyes. It was the spectre that haunted their debt-ridden dreams. Under the terrible logic of the prisons, the prisoner had to pay for his accommodation, so that the longer he stayed the more indebted he became. Those who could not pay were tortured with hot irons, thumbscrews and crushing iron skullcaps. If a man died in the night – which happened often in the overcrowded, windowless cells – he would be unrecognisable by dawn. The rats would have chewed off his face.

'How long do I have?' asked Rob.

Spinkley made a show of thinking about it.

'By the terms written here, you have until noon today.'

Rob stumbled away in a daze. The unfeeling crowds jostled him, oblivious to his despair. In Africa he had faced lions, elephants, even the shark. Debt was nothing but paper, ink and broken promises. Yet somehow he felt more powerless, trapped by an invisible beast he could not fight or even understand.

In his confusion, he didn't see Hugo following him until his friend grabbed his arm.

'What will you do?' Hugo asked.

'What can I?' Rob was furious with himself for letting himself be snared by the moneylender. 'Could you lend it to me?'

'You know I am at the end of my credit with Spinkley as it is. All I could do is borrow the money from him, and he would refuse at once if he guessed the reason. He might even call in my own debts.'

'But half of that cargo was yours.'

Hugo stiffened, and seemed to shrink away a little. 'You put up the collateral and took the money. The loan is in your name. Do not try to drag me into this business.'

'*Drag you into it?*' Rob could not believe what he heard. 'But we are in this together. This has always been our joint adventure.'

Hugo shrugged. A coldness had taken over his face, and if Rob had had time to consider it, he might have thought it reminded him of a boy watching a kitten drown in a pond.

'I am sorry, Rob. You are on your own.' As if to underscore the finality of his words, a cacophony of church bells began to chime ten o'clock in the distance. 'Spinkley's bailiffs will be at my house in two hours to claim whatever they can.'

Only one thing mattered now.

'The sword,' Rob said. 'I cannot let him get the sword.'

'But that is your only collateral. Your only hope of avoiding the debtors' prison.'

Rob didn't hear him. He had started to run.

Hugo's carriage was still waiting, but Rob was like a hunted animal, trusting to nothing but himself. He ran – through the streets, the teeming city he thought he had tamed, the familiar landmarks that now seemed cold and impervious to his plight – until he reached the front door of the house on Wimpole Street. His head ached and his stomach churned, though whether that was from the shock of his loss or the effort of running he didn't know.

He pounded on the door until Hugo's footman opened it. Rob almost knocked him over in his haste to push past. He took the stairs three at a time to his room and pried up the floorboard where he had hidden the Neptune sword.

Sunlight shone through the curtains, so that the sapphire in the pommel glowed like the depths of the sea. Before, Rob had only noticed its beauty. Now he saw it with the greedy eyes of a desperate man. He wondered how much the gem would fetch if he pried it out and sold it to the jewellers in Hatton Garden. How much the gold might be worth melted down.

The thought made him ashamed. Was this what he had come to? Better to die than dishonour his family legacy this way. The Courtneys had wielded that sword in battle against Spanish galleons, Dutch privateers, Indian pirates and the villains of three continents over nearly two hundred years. One day, Rob would see it in the hands of his own son.

He would take his punishment if he had to. But if he could avoid it, so much the better. He thought of what his grandfather Jim would have done in his position. Jim would not have surrendered meekly to greedy men like Spinkley, simply because they claimed authority. He would not have let them trap him in their snares of paper.

Jim would have done what he did the day he rescued Louisa from the sinking convict ship. He would have escaped.

Rob threw a few clothes into his bag and wrapped the sword in a coat. He probably should say goodbye to Hugo, but he had evidently not returned yet. Rob guessed he wanted to be well clear of Spinkley's men when they came.

A hammering sounded from the front door. Looking out of his window, Rob saw a gang of stout-looking men armed with cudgels gathered around the steps. Spinkley had lost no time sending his bailiffs. It was not even twelve o'clock.

Rob heard the footman open the door smartly. A shouted conversation followed, and then feet pounding up the stairs. Rob did not wait. He slipped out of his room onto the landing, took off his shoes so that he would not make a sound and ran down a corridor in his stockinged feet. He threw open the sash window that opened onto the rear garden and dropped his bag out.

It was too high for Rob to jump. And the bailiffs were almost there. Rob darted through a side door just as they reached the top of the stairs. From inside a cupboard, Rob heard them run into his room, then emerge again onto the landing. One man ran past where he was hiding, making the door tremble on its hinges.

Rob heard him pause by the window.

'Look here,' cried a gruff voice. 'There's a bag in the garden. He must have gone out the window.'

The footsteps receded. Rob counted to twenty, then let himself out. He did not dare descend the stairs. Instead, he climbed to the servants' quarters at the top of the house. The ceiling sloped low over his head, but there was a window in the gable that led onto the roof. Rob climbed through.

The city was small and muted below, but the height didn't worry him. It was like being up in the rigging of a sailing ship. The fresh air and the thrill of escape cleared the fog from his mind. It gave him a sharp purpose.

In his stockings, with the sword tied over his back in a makeshift sling using the sleeves of the coat, he ran unerringly along the ridge of the roof. At the end of the row of houses, he let himself down a drainpipe – as easy as sliding down the backstay – and climbed over a wall into the street.

There was no question of where to go. Apart from Hugo, he only had one friend in London.

Exhausted as he was by having run halfway across London, it took more than two hours to walk back to the docks. The crowds thickened as the day drew on, slowing his progress, but he didn't mind. They offered protection, the chance to be anonymous. It reminded him of the wildebeests he had seen in Africa, herding together in their thousands to safeguard themselves from the lion's teeth, or the hunter's gun. Before, he had only ever seen them down a gunsight. Now, he saw how the world looked through their eyes.

He told himself he should not be so afraid. The bailiffs could not possibly know where he would go in this vast city. The further he went from Hugo's house, the safer he was, the more he began to relax. At last, he saw the masts of the ships at anchor rising over the rooftops and hurried ahead. Even among the hundreds of vessels clogging the river, he could make out the *Dunstanburgh Castle* in an instant, swinging easily at anchor as the tide turned. He was safe.

He was about to go down the steps to catch a boat when a voice stopped him short.

'Robert?'

Rob turned to see Hugo hurrying up the street behind him.

Rob embraced his friend. 'Thank God you are here. I did not want to leave without saying goodbye, but Spinkley's men left me little choice.' He paused. 'How did you find me?'

Hugo smiled. 'I knew you had nowhere else to go.' He noticed the bundle Rob was carrying. 'Is that the sword?'

'I could not let Spinkley get his hands on it.' A wave of exhaustion hit Rob. Suddenly, he felt on the brink of tears. 'I know it is a cowardly thing to do. But this sword is all I have here of my family.'

Hugo touched his arm gently. 'It is quite understandable. I know how precious the sword is to you.'

Rob became aware that the crowd around him had gone still. He glanced about him. Four large men with bruised faces and clubs in their hands had appeared, forming a ring around him that pushed everyone else on the bustling dock away.

Rob tried to move. Hugo's hand tightened around his arm, holding him still. The men with the clubs pressed closer.

'What . . .?'

A figure appeared over Hugo's shoulder, a horribly familiar mass of chins and flesh, and the sparkle of a gold tooth.

'I am obliged to you, Mr Lyall,' said Spinkley. 'You have helped apprehend a great villain.'

Rob stared at Spinkley, and then at Hugo.

'What is this?'

'What it looks like.'

'You . . .' There were not words to express the betrayal he felt. 'I trusted you.'

'I had no choice. I owe Spinkley far more money than you. If my father cut me off, I would have a choice between the debtors' prison and the garrison of some fever-ridden island.'

'You led me to borrow all that money. You knew the warehouse would burn down.' Rob struggled to comprehend it. 'I thought we were friends.'

He thought he saw a flicker of guilt in Hugo's eyes, though it passed so quickly he could not be sure.

'I had no choice,' Hugo said again, desperate for Rob to believe him. 'There are powerful men who want you destroyed.'

One of Spinkley's men stepped forwards and grabbed the bundled sword. Rob refused to release it. The two men struggled. Then a blow from a club struck Rob's upper arm and it went numb. The sword was pulled from his grasp.

The bailiff handed it to Spinkley. He unwrapped it, holding it up to admire the workmanship.

'Really, it is quite exquisite.'

The sight of the sword in those fat, greedy hands was like a blade through Rob's heart. He lunged at Spinkley, but the bailiffs held him back.

'Do not blame yourself, young Courtney,' Spinkley told him. 'Almost from the moment you arrived in London, your destruction was inevitable.'

Rob struggled against the hands that held him. He craned his head to get a glimpse of the *Dunstanburgh Castle*, hoping that Cornish might spy him and send help. But no one stirred on her decks.

'You have the sword!' he cried. 'Does that not satisfy the debt? Why don't you let me go?'

'With the interest you accumulated, this is not enough to pay what you owe.' Spinkley fondled the weapon, staring at the jewelled pommel as if he wanted to lick it. 'Take him to the Marshalsea prison.'

All the terrible stories Rob had heard of the debtors' prison hit him like a hammer blow. Without friends or family to pay for his upkeep in the more comfortable gentlemen's wing, he would be sent to the common side, where men were crammed in foetid cells without even space to lie down. He would never escape.

He stared at Hugo, looking for some trace of pity.

'Please . . .' he begged. 'Do not let them do this. For our friendship.'

Hugo could not meet his eye. 'I am sorry, Rob. I did not want it to end this way.'

He turned with a swish of his coat and disappeared up the busy street. Two of the bailiffs grabbed Rob, while the other two began to open a path through the crowd.

Rob let his knees buckle so that all his weight dropped onto the men holding him. Before they could tighten their grip, he stamped down as hard as he could on one of the bailiffs' feet.

The man let go. Rob twisted around and sank his teeth into the other bailiff's hand. There was a howl of pain; Rob was free. He sprang away towards the wharf. The Thames was rank with sewage and strong currents, but Rob was a good swimmer. If he could reach the *Dunstanburgh Castle*, he might be saved.

A hand reached out for him. It missed his shoulder, but caught the billowing fabric of his shirtsleeve, tugging him back. Rob threw himself forwards. The sleeve tore away and was left behind as he lunged towards the edge of the wharf. Five more paces . . .

He never saw what tripped him – one of the bailiff's clubs, or a mooring ring, or a bystander who thought he was doing his civic duty. All he felt was a rap against his shin, and then the pavement came flying up to meet him. He struck his chin and sprawled on the ground.

He was so close to the river his arms stretched over the edge of the wharf. He could see the brown water flowing almost under his nose. He was so close. Shaking off the pain in his skull, he pushed himself up for the final lunge.

A heavy weight crushed him to the ground. One of the bailiffs had leaped on top of him. Rob tried to throw him off, but the man was too heavy. The bailiff held his cudgel against Rob's neck and pushed until he almost broke Rob's windpipe. The others gathered around, aiming vengeful kicks at Rob's head and ribs. He no longer had any thought of escape. All he wanted was to protect himself.

Through a haze of pain, Rob heard Spinkley's agitated voice shouting, 'For God's sake do not kill him! Baron Dartmouth wants his prize alive!'

The beating stopped. Rough arms hauled him to his feet. One of the bailiffs wrapped Rob's torn shirtsleeve around the bleeding bite on his hand. He gave Rob a look that promised more pain as soon as Spinkley's back was turned.

'Get him out of my sight,' said Spinkley. His face was flushed from the effort of chasing after Rob; his coat was askew. 'Put him in the Marshalsea and tell the jailer to go hard on him. We will break his rebellious spirit once and for all.'

'Halt!' cried a voice.

Despite his pain, Rob looked up. A tall man in a blue navy uniform had appeared, a lieutenant's stripe on his sleeve. A group of sailors in short jackets and trousers accompanied him. He pointed to the tattoo on Rob's bare arm, exposed where the shirtsleeve had been ripped away.

'This man is a sailor.'

'He is a prisoner,' said Spinkley testily.

The lieutenant looked down his nose at Spinkley. He was not an old man, but his hair was powder-white, cut short so that it stood straight up from his scalp. His face was taut, so that the skull bones underneath jutted with unsettling prominence. His eyes were a piercing blue.

'By order of the King, I am empowered to press any seaman I find into His Majesty's navy, to fight in the war with America. I am seizing this man.'

Spinkley drew himself up to his full height.

'As you will know, it is expressly prohibited for the navy to take any man who is imprisoned for debt. As Mr Courtney is.'

'I see no prison.'

'We were on our way there this instant.'

'Has he been charged before a magistrate?'

'No!' blurted out Rob. 'I am a sailor. I shipped on the *Dunstanburgh Castle* under Captain—' He broke off as one of the bailiffs slapped him across the mouth. But there was doubt in their faces. The lieutenant had a dozen armed sailors with him, a sword at his side and a pistol in his belt.

'This is outrageous,' spluttered Spinkley. 'What is your name?'

'Lieutenant Henry Coyningham, of His Majesty's Ship *Perseus*.'

'Do you know on whose orders I arrested this man?' said Spinkley.

Coyningham waited expectantly.

'Baron Dartmouth, the President of the Board of Trade and Plantations. If you defy him, I promise you will end your career commanding a fishing boat in the fever islands.'

Coyningham gave a shrug. 'If your patron wishes to complain, he may take it up with the Admiralty. They will not censor me for doing my duty.'

Two of his men grabbed Rob roughly and led him to a knot of sad-looking men waiting with the other sailors. The bailiffs tapped their clubs in their palms, but they were overmatched and they knew it. There was nothing they could do.

Rob fell in with the pressed men, shuffling into the middle of the group for protection. The man beside him looked up.

'You must have offended someone right royally. What did you do?'

Dazed, Rob could only shake his head. 'I wish I knew.'

The man stood a head shorter than Rob, but he had meaty hands, strong arms and a stocky frame. A black eye and a crooked nose said he had used his fists in anger, and recently, but his face was kind. When he grinned, it was the first sincere smile Rob had seen since what felt like eternity.

He stuck out his hand. 'Angus MacNeil,' he said in a soft Scottish accent.

Robert shook his hand. 'Robert Courtney.'

Up front, Spinkley had departed with a final round of curses and threats and dark looks at Rob. The lieutenant turned his back on him and shouted orders to his sailors.

'Move on. We need a dozen more men if we are to earn our keep – and we must have them in the pressroom by nightfall.'

By next morning, Rob wondered if he had been saved after all. There seemed little to choose between the navy and what he had heard about the Marshalsea prison. From the wharf, he was taken to a room above a pub that the lieutenant had hired for the purpose. When it was full, the recruits were transferred to a tender and taken downriver to a mastless hulk anchored away from shore. Rob and the others were prodded down a ladder into an airless room on the orlop deck. A grating was put over them, with four marines standing guard.

'They treat us no better than prisoners,' complained one of the recruits – a youth named Thomas who looked to be on the verge of tears. 'I volunteered for this. They should not treat me like a felon.'

'I was in prison till yesterday, when the lieutenant called,' said Angus. He had a blunt manner of speaking that reminded Rob of his grandfather. 'I promise you, this is better.'

'Why were you in prison?' Rob asked.

'Mayhem.'

'What does that mean?'

'Mayhem is a criminal offence consisting of the deliberate maiming of a person which leaves said person unable to defend himself in combat.' He sounded as if he was reciting a charge sheet. 'In English, it means I cut a man's arm off.'

Rob wasn't sure what to say; but nor did he want Angus to take offence at his silence.

'Did he deserve it?' Rob asked.

Angus shrugged. 'I thought so. I asked him to stop what he was doing, and he refused.'

'What was he doing?'

'Fucking my wife.'

Rob considered that. 'I'd say it was lucky for him you only cut off his arm.'

Angus laughed. 'Aye.'

T en miles upriver, Hugo Lyall had the luxury of more agreeable surroundings. But the plush carpet underfoot; the fat sofas trimmed with gold brocade; the glass of the finest port in his hand: none of it gave him an ounce of comfort. Not with Baron Dartmouth's acid stare eating through him.

'He escaped?'

'The purest chance,' Hugo pleaded. 'Nothing could have prevented it.'

'You were there. *You* should have prevented it.' Dartmouth tapped his artificial hand on the table. 'You know what I do to those who fail me.'

Hugo swallowed. 'He cannot have gone far.'

'The press gang will have taken him to the hulks at Deptford,' added Spinkley. He had been summoned with Hugo, sweating profusely in his thick coat. 'It will be some days still before he is assigned to a ship.'

Dartmouth said nothing. He raised his gold hand and drew it across his throat.

Hugo's mouth dropped open as he realised what Dartmouth wanted of him.

'You can hardly expect me to break into a man-of-war and murder someone.'

Dartmouth studied him. Whatever happened, he must not be implicated. But if he left Hugo to his own devices, there was no telling what mischief the young fool would cause.

'There is a man I know,' said Dartmouth at last. 'He can take care of such matters discreetly. I will send him to call on you. You will make the necessary arrangements with him.'

Hugo nodded. A week ago, he would not have imagined himself capable of even striking a man. He had known that he was driving Rob to ruin, that the warehouse would burn and leave him penniless, but he had still clung to the excuse that

Rob would not be hurt. Now, even murder seemed better than having to face that terrible stare.

Dartmouth still had not finished with him.

'The other matter we spoke of. You did as I instructed?'

'Yes,' said Hugo eagerly, thankful that the conversation had moved away from murder. 'I asked Rob how to find Nativity Bay.' He repeated what Rob had told him, about the bay and whale-backed promontory a thousand miles from Cape Town. 'He says he could not miss it.'

Dartmouth grunted. 'And the sword?'

Spinkley pulled out the bundle, still wrapped in the coat.

'I had thought,' he said, 'that your lordship might permit me to keep it.'

Dartmouth raised his hooded eyes. '*You?*'

'In consideration of my aid in this matter. Robert Courtney owed me a great deal of money, and, ah . . .'

'If you wish to leave this room alive, you will give me the sword this instant.'

Spinkley laid the bundle on the desk. The coat fell open, bathing Dartmouth's face in reflected golden light. Dartmouth leaned over it, slavering like a dog presented with a bone. His reflection gazed back at him a hundred times in the many facets of the sapphire.

'I am sure your lordship would want to compensate me for the losses I have incurred,' Spinkley said.

Dartmouth raised his head. He pulled the sword from its scabbard and sliced it through the air, so close to Spinkley's face it almost took the skin off his nose.

'Go!' he bellowed.

Spinkley did so, followed by Hugo, who would not have run faster if all the devils of Hell had been chasing him.

After they had gone, Dartmouth stared at the sword for a long time. Eventually, he took up his pen and wrote a letter to his son, Gerard Courtney, in Calcutta. His writing was crabbed and awkward, a tangle of angry scores and splashes of ink. After he lost his hand, he had had to teach himself to do everything left-handed. He wrote furiously, the thirst for revenge dripping from his pen.

Tom Courtney's heirs live in Africa at a place called Nativity Bay. You will find it some thousand miles north-east of Cape Town, behind a cape that takes the shape of a whale. If you honour your duty as a Courtney and as my son, you will engage a ship forthwith and scour that coast. I need not tell you what to do when you find them.

When last I wrote, I told you that Tom's great-grandson Robert had arrived in London. But do not worry on that account. By the time you read this, he will be dead.

Rob woke from a nightmare. He'd been dreaming he was back in Nativity Bay, swimming in the azure waters. A shark had approached, and however fast Rob swam he could not escape. The jaws closed around him, squeezing tighter and tighter until Rob felt his bones snap.

He woke with a spasm. The jerk shook Angus, lying beside him; he rolled over in his sleep and knocked the man next to him. The recruits were jammed so tight in the press room, the least movement would disturb all of them.

He lay awake, listening to the darkness around him. It must be nearly dawn: a grey half-light seeped through the gunport that had been cracked open for air. Rob had thought the hammocks on the *Dunstanburgh Castle* were packed close, but that was luxury compared to the press room. If this was how the navy treated its recruits, what would life be like when he finally boarded their ships?

It was better than the alternative.

But it was little consolation. Ever since he was small, he had hated to run away from danger. More than once, in the African bush, his stubbornness had earned him scars and broken bones. Now he was fleeing from his debts, evading his enemies and leaving behind the only precious thing he owned: the Neptune sword.

If he jumped ship, he would be a deserter as well as a debtor. Instead of jail, he would be looking at the hangman's noose. And to the list of his enemies would be added the might of the Royal Navy.

His enemies. He had come to London – he thought – without an enemy in the world. How had he made such powerful foes? Certainly he owed Spinkley money, and perhaps Spinkley had turned Hugo against him. But he had seen something in both their faces that was more than greed. Fear. They were afraid of someone.

Spinkley had said he was working for Baron Dartmouth, but who was that? Rob had never heard of him, had no inkling why such a powerful man should even have heard of Rob, let alone want him dead. He must have misheard.

He was wondering about it when he heard a sound on the other side of the room. It was someone standing, then a thump and a curse. Unused to the ship's low decks, the man must have hit his head.

That surprised Rob. All the men who had been pressed were experienced seamen. Like Rob, they ducked instinctively the moment they descended the ladder.

It must be the new arrival, Rob decided. A stringy man named Lendal, with a pockmarked face, who had arrived before dusk. All evening, he had sat listening to the chatter in the hold, saying nothing. He wore his hat low, even in the close confines of the hold. Beneath the brim, Rob had had the uncomfortable feeling that the man's eyes were watching him.

Now Lendal was coming across the room, carefully picking his way between the sleeping men. There was hardly space to move: several complained angrily in their sleep as his foot caught them.

He was coming towards Rob.

A beam of dawn light reflected off the river and through the gunport. It gleamed on a thin sliver of sharp steel in Lendal's hand.

He had a knife.

Rob was unarmed. He had nothing but the clothes he had been wearing when the press gang took him. He forced himself to remain still, keeping his eyelids almost shut lest any glimmer in his eyes show he was awake. Under his blanket, he tensed his muscles to spring. He could see Lendal edging closer, a shadow in the darkness. Rob made himself wait. Surprise was his only weapon. He had to make it count.

Lendal stepped over Angus. He squatted beside Rob. Rob wondered what Lendal planned to do. He could only afford one stroke. If he made any mistake, Rob's screams would wake the others and Lendal would be caught in the act of murder. But it would be difficult to kill Rob both quickly and discreetly. Locked in the hold with marines on guard above, he could not escape before the body was found.

Lendal must have reached the same conclusion. He changed his mind. He slipped the knife into his boot, and unwound a cloth from around his neck. He wrapped the ends in his fists, pulled it tight and leaned towards Rob's neck.

He means to strangle me, Rob thought.

He waited, until he could almost feel the fibres of the cloth tickling his throat.

With a snap of his arms, he seized Lendal's wrists and twisted him away. Caught off balance, Lendal tumbled over hard onto Angus, who grunted. He tried to sit up, tangling his limbs with Lendal's. In the confusion, Rob felt for Lendal's foot and pulled the knife out of his boot.

The struggle ended suddenly as Rob put the blade to Lendal's throat.

'Who are you?' he hissed. 'What are you doing?'

Lendal tried to shake the knife off.

'I was looking for the head,' he said, sounding aggrieved. 'Can't a man go for a piss in peace?'

'You tried to kill me.'

'I tripped.'

'Why? Who sent you?'

Lendal spat in his face. Rob pushed the knife against his throat. Lendal's eyes widened, white in the gloom, as he saw he could not lie his way out.

'*Who?*'

'No one.'

Silence. Rob pushed the knife so hard against the skin that blood beaded on the blade. It was as close as he had ever come to killing a man, and he wondered if he would have the courage to push the knife the last fraction of an inch if he had to.

There was a sharp movement behind him, a thump and a squeal. Angus leaned in close, dangling something over Lendal's head. It seemed to be alive, wriggling and squirming as it hung from his hand.

'I caught a rat,' he said casually. 'You know what it'll do to that pretty face of yours if I let it? It'll eat you up, one nibble at a time. Little teeth, take a while to gnaw through into your brain. But it'll get there, I promise you.'

Lendal started to shake. Angus lowered the rat, so that its scrabbling paws scratched Lendal's cheek below the eye.

'Take him off me!' screamed Lendal.

The noise had woken the other men in the room, but Rob ignored them.

'Who sent you?' he asked again.

With the rat squealing and writhing over Lendal's face, Rob had drawn back. Only a little – but it took the knife away from Lendal's throat. Lendal saw his opportunity. He lunged for Rob.

In the dark, Rob scarcely knew what happened. As Lendal grabbed for the knife, the rat fell and scurried off. Angus was knocked aside. Lendal's hand closed on Rob's, trying to pry the knife from his fingers.

Rob tightened his grip, wrestling Lendal for the weapon. It jerked back and forth between them. Rob was the bigger man, but Lendal had a desperate strength. What fear or hate must drive him, to still think of attacking Rob in front of so many witnesses?

Afterwards, when Rob remembered the fight, he realised it must have taken mere seconds. At the time, it seemed like an eternity of struggle, darkness, and the sharp tang of iron as he and Lendal wrestled the weapon between them. Rob felt the hilt begin to slip in his sweaty palms. Lendal was pulling it away from him, and Rob did not have a good enough grip to resist.

He did not fight it. Instead, he put all his weight behind it, driving the blade back towards Lendal much faster than his enemy expected. At the same time, he twisted the handle, so that the blade was angled straight at Lendal's neck.

The blade was so sharp he felt only the slightest resistance as it sliced open Lendal's throat. Hot blood spilled over his hands. Lendal went limp. There was a loud thump as his skull hit the deck. Then he lay still.

Rob dropped the knife. It was the first time he had killed a man, and his mind was in turmoil, but even as the blood dripped from his hands his mind repeated one question.

Why? Why did he try to kill me? Why, even after I caught him, did he still try to attack me? He must have known he could not escape.

Rob could ponder that later. He was locked in a stinking hold, with thirty other men and a corpse he was responsible for.

'How do we get rid of him?' Rob asked, breathing hard.

'Out the head,' said Angus.

He tore aside the curtain that screened the privy. Standing on one leg, he stamped his foot through the wooden boxing that surrounded the hole, pounding again and again against the iron grating beneath.

With a splintering of wood and a splash, the grating came free and dropped into the river. Rob and Angus lifted Lendal's body between them and jammed him through the gap. They wiped the blood off their hands onto his shirt.

Rob twisted Lendal to squeeze him through, ignoring the men behind him who had woken up to this extraordinary scene. For a thin man, Lendal was surprisingly heavy.

'It's lucky he's a wee thing,' grunted Angus. 'He fits through a space made for a little shit.'

The corpse's shoulders popped through the hole. The rest of him fell rapidly and splashed into the river below. Angus peered after it.

'Tide's on the ebb,' he declared. 'He'll be halfway to Sheerness before anyone finds him.'

Rob leaned over the toilet and vomited into the river. When he turned around, he saw two dozen pairs of eyes watching him. The men were awake and had seen what he had done. If Rob had anything left in his stomach, he would have voided his guts again.

'I think we're all agreed what happened,' said Angus calmly. 'Mr Lendal decided he didn't fancy the sailor's life after all and broke through the head before we could stop him. Ain't that right?'

No one answered. One of the seamen – an old collier from Newcastle – spat out a wad of tobacco.

'Didn't like the bugger nohow.'

Light flooded the room as the hatch was thrown open. Lieutenant Coyningham's petulant face peered through the opening.

'Enough loitering. You are to come with me aboard HMS *Perseus*.'

He squinted into the darkness, seeing the broken wood around the toilet. It was lucky in the dark he could not see the blood on the floor.

'What happened here?'

'It was Mr Lendal, sir, the new volunteer,' said Angus. 'He escaped through the shi—'

'I can see where he went,' said Coyningham. 'How long ago?'

There was a general shrugging of shoulders.

'He went in the night,' said Angus.

'I will alert the shore parties. He will be lucky to survive the currents.'

The collier shook his head sadly. 'I'm afeard he weren't a strong swimmer.'

'Then the Devil take him.' Coyningham beckoned them up. 'Now on deck with you. The last man up will feel the taste of the lash.'

As they climbed the ladder, one of the younger recruits asked, 'Where are we going?'

Coyningham looked as if he might strike the youth for speaking out of turn. Then he relented. He bared his teeth in an ugly grin.

'You are going to teach those damn Yankee colonists a lesson in obedience to the King.'

I t was difficult wearing a ship on your head. But that was the latest fashion, and the Comtesse de Bercheny was never less than fashionable. Her hairdressers had been working since dawn, piling her long golden hair into a great *pouf*. They had stretched it over wire frames, tortured it with hot irons and pins, and hardened it in position with so much paste you could crack an egg on it. Atop that, they set a papier mâché model of a ship in full sail, with the white fleur-de-lis banner of King Louis XVI streaming from its masthead.

The *comtesse* waved to the gathered crowds as she descended from her gilded carriage. She had been born Constance Courtney, but she had left that name behind so long ago she hardly remembered it. She had married a French captain, whose wedding gift to her had been an early death. Barely pausing to mourn, she had worked her way up the ranks of the French aristocracy with ruthless ambition: from the captain to a colonel, from the colonel to a general, and finally to her present husband, the Comte de Bercheny. It had not always been smooth – she had faced death more than once. But she was a resourceful woman, and somehow she had survived while her former lovers were all discarded or deceased. She sat at the height of French society – an intimate friend of the new queen Marie Antoinette, the first name on the guest list for every ball – and stood at the centre of attention now, as she stepped onto the quay at the harbour of Brest.

A young man in a commander's uniform saluted her. His uniform shone bright and new, from the gleaming buckles on his shoes to the glittering gold lace that trimmed his hat. He had fine fair hair, and a haughty face which had been educated to expunge every emotion. Yet even he could not hide his excitement.

'Étienne.' She kissed him on the cheek. 'You look very handsome.'

He took Constance's arm and steered her towards a row of officers lined up to receive her.

'I am glad you are here, *Maman*,' he murmured in her ear. 'I know how you have worked for this moment.'

She handed him a sealed packet from her bag.

'The King himself signed your commission two days ago.'

She nodded graciously to the first lieutenant as he bowed to her, noting how his eyes lingered on the swell of her breasts where they squeezed out of her bodice. She favoured him with a smile. She knew the effect she had on men. She enjoyed toying with them, though it was a long time since she would have bothered with a mere lieutenant.

'And which is your ship?' she asked her son, looking at the crowded fleet in the harbour.

Étienne handed her a brass telescope, a delicate instrument that had been a gift from his father in Paris. Holding her bare shoulders, he steered her until she was pointing in the right direction. Among the scarred old two- and three-decker ships of the line at anchor, one ship almost gleamed on the water. The red paint on her gunports was still wet, the tar shiny on her rigging. The sails brailed on her yards were virgin white, not yet stretched by storms and rain. At the front, the figurehead of a gold-beaked hawk leaned ravenously over the water, its wings streaming back around the bow as if she were dropping on her prey.

'The ship seems so small,' said Constance. 'Will she really carry you all the way across the ocean?'

'The *Rapace* is the finest ship afloat,' boasted Étienne, with the fervour of a child with a new toy. 'Forty guns, and with the wind off her quarter she will veritably fly. She can outrun anything larger and destroy anything smaller.'

Constance embraced him. Étienne was her first son and her favourite: strong, handsome and fierce. He was almost as ruthless as she was. She did not spoil him – she needed him to be hard, and he was too proud to accept charity in any case – but she worked tirelessly at court to promote his interests. More than one admiral had received a private audience in her boudoir. How else would a young cadet, barely twenty, be given command of the newest ship in the navy?

'I hope you burn the English navy to ashes,' she said, with sudden vehemence.

Étienne gave her a warning look. 'You forget, we are not at war with England,' he reminded her loudly, for the benefit of the assembled crowd.

'Of course,' said Constance. 'How silly of me. Old instincts die hard.'

The crowd laughed appreciatively. They understood that peace between England and France was a diplomatic fiction. It was nothing but a breathing space between wars. The last time France and England fought, France had lost an empire in North America. France was ready for revenge, and the only question was when the government would feel bold enough to take it. War was fermenting between Britain and the American colonies. King Louis would wait for the colonists to weaken their masters – and then he would strike.

What no one on the quay knew, except Constance and Étienne, was that the first manoeuvres of the war were already in motion. The document Constance had brought from Versailles was not a regular commission. It authorised Étienne to act as a privateer in the rebel navy of the American colonies. The ship was French, and the crew were French, but they would fight under an American flag in the name of the new American republic. Another fiction, another lie.

But Constance knew, better than most, that lies and fictions could kill far more suddenly than the truth.

'Come back in glory,' she murmured in Étienne's ear.

A few successful battles, bloodying British noses and capturing their ships, would make him a sensation in Paris. Her sycophants in the press would write him up as a hero, while her allies would ensure that his name was spoken at every *salon* and *soirée* in the city. Then an advantageous marriage into the topmost echelons of aristocracy, and her ascendancy would be complete.

But there was more to it than ambition. Twenty years earlier, a British army had left Constance to die in an Indian dungeon. It had been the worst ordeal of her life; she had crawled out of it barely alive. She would have ended her life in an Indian brothel if a French officer had not rescued her. She never forgot a debt. Every shot her son fired against British ships would strike another blow for her revenge.

Étienne stiffened and saluted. Out on the *Rapace*, a gust of wind snapped the white flag from the masthead.

'I will make you proud, *Maman*. The British ships will be easy prey. I will send you the head of the first captain I capture, wrapped in his own flag.'

Constance moistened her lips with her tongue. 'My dutiful son.'

Rob had thought shipping on the *Perseus* would be much like the merchantman he had sailed on with Cornish. In some ways, indeed, it was. The sails, the lines and the rigging were the same. The layout of the decks, the structure of the hull were similar enough. The wind, the waves, the points of the compass were familiar.

Everything else was different.

The *Dunstanburgh Castle* had worked her way from India to London with a crew of fifty. The *Perseus* was little larger but carried over two hundred. The difference was the guns. Captain Cornish had carried a few to scare off pirates, but each one took up tonnage that could more profitably be used for cargo. On the *Perseus*, the guns were her reason for existence. They sat like crouched beasts along her main deck, long twelve-pounders that could throw a ball over a mile. In battle, it needed six men to service each gun, and more to keep handling the ship.

The ship was a hundred and twenty feet long. Yet for all the crew worked and slept at close quarters, there were invisible barriers that a man crossed at his peril. The officers were distant, the captain almost as remote as God. Unlike Cornish, who had roamed the deck chatting to the men, Captain Tew was a stiff figure on the quarterdeck.

Another difference was the discipline. Rob learned about this on his first morning aboard, when the boatswain's mates came down to the lower deck using their starter ropes liberally to get men out of their hammocks. Aboard a merchantman, the crew were freely employed and could leave a captain who mistreated them at the next port. In the Royal Navy, most of the men were there against their will. The officers and petty officers treated the sailors as somewhere between criminals and animals. Orders were shouted, mistakes punished, and at the least delay the rope ends came out again. Rob was astonished that the crew didn't mutiny. Yet they seemed to accept the conditions without question.

'Cap'n Tew's a firm man, but he's fair,' said one of Rob's messmates at dinner that evening, a grizzled old gun captain named Hargrave. 'He knows in battle it's discipline as keeps a crew alive.'

'Not like the Bloodhound,' chimed in another. The Bloodhound was their nickname for Coyningham, the first lieutenant. 'He's a bad 'un. If the cap'n didn't keep 'im honest, he'd flog us until the scuppers choked with our blood.'

'He saved me from prison,' said Rob loyally.

The gun captain stared at him, one eye closed. 'He took you to make his quota. He didn't give a piss if you was off to prison or the House of Lords.'

Next morning, the new recruits assembled on deck to be assigned their new stations. Coyningham prowled the line, glaring at the men.

'Where did you serve before?' he asked Angus.

'Gunner on the *Repulse*, sir,' Angus answered. 'Three years.'

Coyningham nodded. Then, without warning, he stamped his boot down hard on Angus's bare foot.

Angus gasped with pain. His body went rigid. He gritted his teeth and balled his fists so tightly the knuckles went white. Coyningham laughed.

'You will have to move a damn sight faster than that. If that had been the trucks of a gun carriage, you would have lost your foot.'

Anger boiled in Angus's face. For a moment, Rob feared his friend would strike the lieutenant. Coyningham almost seemed to be encouraging him. He wanted an excuse to punish Angus. Not to make an example of him, but to hurt him.

'Angus's feet are so big, he'd probably stop the cannon better than a chock of wood,' said Rob.

It broke the tension. The men around him laughed. Angus took a deep breath and collected himself. But Coyningham wheeled around to Rob.

'Your name?'

'Rob Courtney, sir.'

Coyningham's piercing blue eyes met Rob's. The salt air seemed to irritate them, for the eye sockets around them were bloodshot and red. A tear brimmed on his eyelid. Yet you would not mistake it for softness.

'Do you think discipline aboard this ship is a laughing matter?'

'No, sir.'

Rob was not easily cowed, but it took all his strength to stand up against the hostile energy blazing off Coyningham. He looked ready to strike Rob.

But he did not. Rob was tall and well built, but more than that, there was an inner strength inside him that any man could see. It had not flinched from Coyningham's anger, and that unsettled the lieutenant. Like any bully, he did not like a man standing up to him.

Instead, he looked for easier pickings.

The next in line was a London boy named Thomas, little more than thirteen years old. Rob had heard him crying in his hammock in the night.

'Have you been to sea before?' Coyningham asked.

The boy shook his head, but said nothing. His silence enraged the lieutenant.

'Answer me when I ask you a question, God damn you.'

'No,' sniffed the boy.

Coyningham gave him a slap across the cheek. 'If you ever speak to me, you address me as "sir". You understand?'

'Yes,' said the boy. 'I mean . . . yes, sir.'

Too late. Another slap caught his mouth and made his lip bleed. Coyningham stepped back, his face flushed.

'Take off your trousers,' he told the boy.

A murmur of disquiet went down the line. Coyningham stopped it with a look. The boy was too frightened to disobey. He undid the rope belt and let his canvas trousers drop. He was barely old enough to have grown hair on his balls.

Coyningham studied him. One hand drifted to the crotch of his breeches.

'I want to see your arse move. Up to the crosstrees.'

The boy's eyes widened in terror. 'Sir?'

'You heard me,' Coyningham repeated. He pulled out a watch. 'If you are not at the main top in one minute, I will make that arse so sore you cannot sit down for a week.'

The boy looked up. The crosstrees were two thin planks fastened to the top of the mast, so far up they were barely visible from the deck.

'I can't go up there, sir,' Thomas pleaded. 'I can't climb a ladder. I get dizzy, I fall.'

Coyningham snatched a starter rope from the master's mate and lashed him across the buttocks.

'Get up there now,' he screamed in a sudden fury, 'or I will throw you in the sea!'

Another bite of the rope overcame the boy's terror. He grabbed the shrouds, flailing like a kitten in a tree, and started to climb the ratlines.

The men on deck had stopped what they were doing to watch. It was a blustery day, with a skittish breeze that made the ship twitch and roll. Every step that Thomas took seemed to make his limbs heavier. The higher he went, the slower he climbed.

Eventually, he reached the main top, fifty feet above deck. He squeezed through the lubber's hole onto the platform and slumped against the mast. Some of the men cheered, but Coyningham raised his hand to silence them.

'You are not yet halfway!' he shouted through a speaking trumpet. 'On with you.'

Thomas hugged the mast and would not move. Coyningham looked to the marine sentry standing by the main hatch.

'Is that musket loaded?'

The marine nodded. Coyningham took the gun, put it to his shoulder and fired it in the air. He was careful to aim well clear of the rigging, but Thomas was not to know that. He started moving again as quickly as if the ball had grazed his buttock.

He had not gone more than a few yards when he stopped. He clung to the shrouds, pitching like a pendulum as the ship rolled.

Coyningham's face was crimson with fury. 'On!' he shouted through the trumpet. 'On, or I will flog you to ribbons!'

Thomas didn't move. Coyningham handed the musket back to the marine.

'Reload.'

On the topmast, Rob saw Thomas glance at the sea below. The boy was too far up to see his face, but Rob could sense his desperation. He had seen it in Africa, in crippled beasts that could no longer drag themselves to the watering holes. A madness beyond reason, the moment when life became too painful to live.

He means to jump, Rob thought. *If Coyningham does not shoot him first.*

Before anyone could stop him, Rob ran to the shrouds, spun himself out on the channels and raced up the rigging, deft as an acrobat. Coyningham's shouts followed him up, so furious Rob wondered if he might after all fire the musket into the rigging. If so, Rob would be in the line of the bullet. He kept climbing, over the side of the main top, scorning the lubber's hole, and on up the topmast rigging. Thomas was just above him, peering down at the sea with a wild look in his eyes.

The rigging was too narrow for Rob to climb up beside Thomas. He swung himself around on to the underside of the shrouds. If he let go, or lost his grip for a second, he would plummet to the deck.

He came face to face with Thomas, the two of them swaying on the shrouds with nothing but the ropes between them.

'It's all right,' Rob told Thomas. Letting go with one hand, he reached around and put an arm on the boy's shoulders. 'I will help you.'

'I cannot go down!' cried Thomas. His face was a mask of tears, his body shaking like a feather. 'I cannot.'

'Of course not.' Their faces were so close together Rob could speak gently, even with the wind whipping around them. 'We still need to get you to the crosstrees.'

Thomas's eyes went white with terror. Rob grabbed his wrist and held it firmly against the rigging.

'Do not do something you will regret,' he said, in a calm voice. 'If you give up now, Coyningham will have his victory and every man on this ship will suffer for it.'

'But what can I do?' The panic was returning. In a moment, Rob would lose him. And Rob could not stay where he was much longer. His right arm was beginning to ache from holding his body against gravity. The wind tugged at his body.

He lifted the boy's hand off the rigging and onto the next rung up. He held it there and looked him in the eye.

'Keep your gaze on the horizon. I will help you to the crosstrees. You will show Coyningham he cannot break you.' Rob nodded towards the deck below. 'There are two hundred men who want to see you succeed. Let us give them something to cheer.'

The wind whistled through the shrouds. The ropes creaked, canvas snapped and the waves broke around the hull. There was shouting on deck, but neither of them could make out the words. Rob held Thomas's gaze so the boy had nowhere else to look, then slowly lifted his gaze to the horizon.

Thomas's eyes followed. One hand tentatively let go of the rigging and hovered in mid-air, trembling.

He reached up and grabbed the next ratline. Then the next, and the next. Rob heard cheers from the deck. He followed Thomas up, whispering to him, the way he would to a frightened animal.

They reached the crosstrees. Thomas hooked one leg over and hauled himself onto the narrow spar. He and Rob sat face to face, looking out over the implacable ocean.

'I thought I would die,' said Thomas.

'I would not have let that happen,' said Rob, though his stomach churned to think how close he had come. 'We will look after you.'

The climb down was quicker. Rob could feel the fear ebbing away from Thomas as the deck came closer and he learned to trust the ropes. A cheer went up from the men as he took the last rung and dropped onto the solid planking. Rob swung down on one of stays and landed beside him in the crowd of sailors.

Angus handed Thomas his trousers. The boy tugged them on, stealing an anxious look at Coyningham.

But the lieutenant had lost interest in him. He bore down on Rob as if he meant to floor him with a punch.

'How dare you undermine my authority?' he bellowed. 'Master at Arms! Seize this miscreant and clap him in irons.' He leaned in close to Rob's ear. 'When I have you chained down in the brig, you will see what I can do to you.'

Then suddenly he straightened. The master at arms stopped midway across the deck and turned to face aft.

Captain Tew had emerged from his cabin. He strode across the deck to where Rob and Coyningham stood. He had a stern face, with steel-grey eyes that seemed to miss nothing. He wore his hair powdered, an old-fashioned style, but on him it added to his authority.

'I heard a shot,' he said. 'I do not care to have weapons discharged on my ship without my command.'

The bravado had drained from the lieutenant.

'I was ... ah ... testing the men's suitability for working aloft. Giving them a taste of battle.'

Tew nodded. He turned to Rob.

'I saw you in the rigging. That was nimble work. What is your name?'

'Robert Courtney.'

'I need topmen like you who can work this ship within an inch of her life.'

Rob touched his forehead. 'Yes, sir.'

Tew raised his voice so that all could hear.

'But I cannot have men on board who cannot control their fear.' He turned to Coyningham. 'Courtney and the boy will serve as topmen in the larboard watch, under Second Lieutenant Verrier's command. I expect to see the boy dancing on those yards like a monkey before we sight America.'

Thomas went pale, but Rob whispered in his ear, 'I will teach you.'

Coyningham tried to suppress his fury. 'And what of the punishment?'

Tew cocked an eyebrow. 'The man was helping his shipmate. I saw no disobedience. You may dismiss the hands.'

Coyningham swallowed his pride. The men were smirking at his discomfort. Rob thought the lieutenant might explode with the effort.

'Dismissed,' he barked.

He strode to the gunroom, while the men moved towards the galley.

Rob wanted to thank Tew, but the captain had gone to the quarterdeck. He was aloof, untouchable once again.

'Be careful,' said Angus. 'You have made an enemy of the Bloodhound, and Captain Tew will not always be able to rescue you.'

Rob knew what he said was true. But on a ship a hundred and twenty feet long, what could he do?

'It is a long way to America.'

After that baptism of fire, the atmosphere changed aboard the *Perseus*.

Rob loved his work. Whatever the hour or weather, he never grew tired of climbing into the lofty tops of the ship, far removed from the cares below. He was reliable and the other topmen trusted him. He was positive, always ready with a joke or an encouraging word, and they liked and respected him. They saw how he tutored the boy Thomas, coaxing him up the rigging every day, and they admired him for it. Day by day, Thomas grew more confident.

Up on the yards, fixing lines or wrestling with the unruly canvas, there was an easy camaraderie unlike anything Rob had known. The topmen were his family.

He loved the ship, too. The *Dunstanburgh Castle* had been a fine vessel, but she lumbered like an ox compared to the *Perseus*. All frigates were fast, and this one was the fastest in the British fleet. The secret, Rob learned, lay under her hull. She was the first ship to be given copper sheathing on her bottom. The metal prevented weeds and barnacles clinging to her structure and dragging on her progress. Sometimes, when the ship heeled over in a strong wind, Rob would look over the side and see the edges of the copper skin still shiny from the shipyard. More often he was up at the masthead trimming the sails, for Tew was always trying to coax a few more knots out of his ship. Standing on a yard with the wind whipping around him, the ship plunging through the waves, Rob felt like a bird of prey swooping through the air.

On deck, life was harder. Lieutenant Coyningham had not forgiven Rob for humiliating him in front of the men and the captain. Rob learned to dread the heavy tread of his riding boots marching across the deck. Being in the second lieutenant's watch brought him some respite, but when Coyningham was on deck Rob always had to be on his guard. There would be some new humiliation – an order to scrub the heads, or find some rope buried in the bottom of the hold among the rats. And if Rob was not quick enough, the boatswain's mate had a ready arm and a mean temper, which Coyningham gave free rein.

'Why is he so cruel?' Rob wondered, sitting with his messmates one evening. 'He seems to have a kettleful of rage boiling inside him.'

'He can't bear it that he didn't get command of the *Perseus*,' answered Hargrave, the old gun captain. He had served five years aboard the ship, under her previous captain. 'Last year, we was sailing home from Antigua when old Captain Tennant caught fever and died. Coyningham took command. He thought when we got back to London he'd be promoted captain – but he wanted to be sure. So when we ran into a Yankee privateer that had been sailing those waters, he sniffed a chance for glory.'

Hargrave stared out of the gunport, as if he could see the enemy ship still sailing off their quarter.

'We were near a pair of islands, with a reef running between them. The Yankee was a small thing, knew we'd win a fight, so she showed us her stern and put on all sail. Slipped across the reef and ran.

'Coyningham ordered us to give chase. But the sailing master refused to do it. Said the water was too low and we'd tear our guts out on the reef. Coyningham swore and screamed, but the master wouldn't bend. And the men was with him.'

Rob could imagine the scene. The humid air, the desperate urgency, and the line of white water frothing over the reef.

'What happened?'

'Coyningham hanged the master for mutiny.' Hargrave spat a wad of tobacco out through the gunport. 'Would have hanged the whole crew, too, if he didn't need us to get the ship home. Probably wished he had done, too, when we came back. Admiralty heard what had happened, blamed Coyningham for losing control of the vessel, and gave command to Captain

Tew instead. So far as Coyningham sees it, it's all the men's fault that he lost his command.'

'No wonder he is so harsh with the men,' said Rob. Hargrave shook his head.

'He always had a mean streak. Only now he don't try to control it.' He stared across the table at Rob. 'Be careful. He looks at you and he sees a man that'll stand up to him. One way or another, he'll try and break you.'

They had not been at sea a week when Rob witnessed his first flogging. One of the new recruits, a landsman, had sworn at Coyningham's provocation and been charged with insubordination. Coyningham ordered a dozen lashes.

The drummer boys beat the men to quarters. The marines lined up on the quarterdeck rail, bayonets fixed, while the victim was stripped of his shirt and lashed to a grating that had been leaned against the waist of the ship. The rest of the crew assembled on the main deck. The boatswain's mate took the cat-of-nine-tails from its baize bag and swung it a few times to loosen his shoulder. The ropes fanned out in the air, nine thin strands each studded with tight knots. It did not look dangerous, but a dozen strokes would cut a man's flesh to ribbons.

Tew read the Articles of War. His lips were pursed in distaste – Rob could see he did not favour the punishment. But he was the captain, and he was obliged to support his officers. He could not allow any breach of discipline.

The boatswain's mate stepped forwards, cocked his arm and unleashed the whip with all his strength. The prisoner moaned and bit down on the leather patch between his teeth. Nine livid red weals blazed across his back, spotted with blood.

A solitary drum beat a single stroke. Coyningham wiped spit from his lips on the sleeve of his coat.

'One,' he said.

After three lashes, the man's back was raw. After six, it was a bloody pulp. By nine, the cat was so soaked in gore that every twitch sent sprays of blood across the deck. Some landed on men's faces.

The drum beat for the last time.

'Twelve,' said Coyningham. His face was flushed, and there was an unsightly bulge in his trousers which he was discreetly trying to cover with his hand. 'Cut the prisoner down.'

The boatswain's mate took a bucket of seawater and threw it over the sailor's back. The sailor screamed as the salt stung his bleeding flesh, though it was the kindest thing they could do. With luck, it would clean the wounds and stop rot setting in.

The men were dismissed. The sailor's friends took him away. Rob was about to follow – he had saved his rum ration to give to the man to dull the pain – when he heard Coyningham's voice behind him.

'You are not dismissed, Courtney.' Coyningham pointed to the blood that spattered the deck. 'On your knees and clean it up. If I find one spot when you are finished, you will lick it off.'

Rob knuckled his forehead. 'Aye, sir.'

Coyningham leaned in close. 'Get used to it, Courtney. Soon enough, I will have a taste of your blood.'

One day, Tew summoned Rob to the stern cabin. It was the most luxurious space on the ship, though even here you could not forget the ship's purpose. Two hulking twelve-pounders sat fast on their tackles. In battle, the furniture would be stripped away and carried into the hold.

Tew sat at a desk studying a chart. He barely looked up as Rob entered.

'You see the book?' he barked. A slim volume sat on the desk. 'Read it.'

Rob opened the cover. There was an inscription on the flyleaf in a childish hand: 'To Daddy, Come back safely, love Edward.' Rob turned hurriedly on to the first page.

'"I was born in the year 1632",' Rob read, '"in the city of York, of a good family, though not of that country, my father being a foreigner of Bremen, who settled first at Hull. He got a good estate by merchandise, and leaving off his trade, lived afterwards at York, whence he had married my mother, whose relations were named Robinson . . ."'

He trailed off. 'Shall I go on?'

'That is sufficient.' Tew pointed to the chart. 'Can you show me our latest position?'

Rob took a pair of dividers and plotted where he thought they were. He made a small pencil mark to show the place.

'You are confident,' Tew observed. His watch showed it was not quite noon. 'The master has not yet taken his sighting today.'

'I overheard him when he took it yesterday,' Rob explained. 'Knowing our course and speed, I would guess we are about here.'

Through the open skylight, he heard the ship's bell strike eight bells. Midday. There were shouts, and feet stamping across the deck above as the master gathered the midshipmen to shoot the sun with their sextants.

'We will find out soon enough if you are right.'

Tew sat back in his chair, studying Rob with his grey eyes. Unsure what was expected of him, Rob stood in silence.

'You have the makings of a fine sailor,' said Tew. 'The men respect you. Even the old hands take their lead from you.'

Rob blushed. 'I only try to do my best, sir.'

'Where did you learn to read?'

'My grandmother.'

'And navigation?'

'Captain Cornish taught me on my last ship.'

'Indeed.'

Outside the door, the marine sentry stamped his feet to announce a visitor. A freckled midshipman peered nervously in.

'The master sends his respects, sir, and wishes to inform you of our latest position.' He read a series of co-ordinates off a scrap of paper, then scurried away as Tew dismissed him.

Tew took the dividers and plotted the position on the chart. He marked it with a small cross. It was a hair's breadth away from the position Rob had reckoned.

'You were able to make that calculation in your head?' Tew's gruff manner could not hide the admiration in his voice.

'Yes, sir.'

Tew put down the dividers. 'How long did you serve aboard your last ship? It was three years, was it not?'

'Nine months, sir,' Rob corrected him.

Tew fixed him with a frown. 'You may have a fine head for figures, but on this question your memory is faulty. It was three years. I am quite certain of it.'

Rob sensed this was not the time to argue.

'I am promoting you to master's mate,' Tew said. 'In order to do this, I must certify to the Admiralty that you have served at least three years at sea.' He stared at Rob. 'That is why I fear you have mis-recollected your time aboard the *Dunstanburgh Castle*. It was three years, was it not?'

'I believe it must have been, sir.'

'Then there is no obstacle.' Tew stood and shook Rob's hand. 'Congratulations, Mr Courtney. You will assist Mr Verrier, the second lieutenant. I expect great things from you.'

Rob could no longer keep the grin from spreading across his face.

'Thank you, sir.'

He stumbled out of the cabin in a daze. To his surprise, a group of his messmates were clustered around waiting for him. They thumped him on the back and cheered when they heard his news, while Angus pressed a cup of rum into his hand.

'Well done,' said Angus.

A shadow fell over them from the quarterdeck, sharp in the tropical sunshine. Even without looking up, Rob recognised the stiff neck and beaked nose. His friends went quiet.

'Back to work!' shouted Coyningham. 'Back to work, or you will feel the touch of the lash.'

'He cannot flog you now,' said Angus, 'but do not think you are safe. He will find some other way to bring you down.'

Rob did not forget Angus's warning. He kept his guard up, never trusting that his new rank or the captain's favour would protect him. He had seen the look in Coyningham's eyes.

But soon enough, Rob had new worries to concern him. A steady breeze gave them swift passage. Each day, the marks on the chart drew nearer the coast of America. Every man aboard felt the anticipation – and the danger. Captain Tew exercised the guns twice a day, using live powder and shot so the gun crews could practise their aim on pieces of driftwood. The tension in the ship was palpable.

One of the drawbacks of Rob's promotion was that he spent more time on deck, away from the tops where he loved to be. But he still managed to contrive reasons to climb the rigging. One afternoon, he had gone aloft on the pretext of checking the buntlines. All was shipshape – the men knew Rob would inspect them in person and kept them in good order – but he dallied for a few moments, enjoying the respite from the bustle on deck. He stared into the distance, remembering something Louisa had said.

'You gaze at that blue horizon and long to discover what is beyond it.'

He had sailed over the horizon, and halfway round the world from Africa. What had he discovered? Coyningham's sadism, Spinkley's greed, Lyall's debauchery. Rob had been swindled, beaten, imprisoned and almost murdered. Perhaps his father had been right. Perhaps he should have stayed safe in the walled paradise of Nativity Bay.

But then he would never have seen the marvels of London, met Angus, or known the camaraderie of the gun-deck. Angus was a true friend, loyal and always ready with a razor-sharp quip. He understood the value of teamwork, and underneath that world-weary exterior beat a kindly heart. When Rob looked back at the youth he had been a year ago, he cringed at his naivety. If he had not left Fort Auspice, he would have remained a child all his life.

'In any event,' Rob told himself, 'you cannot return until you have reclaimed the sword.'

It hurt every time he thought of it. Part of the reason he drove himself so hard aboard the ship was the guilt that he carried. It ached like an open wound. Up on the yards, or lying in his hammock at night, it was always in his thoughts. There was the pain of his betrayal by Hugo, the burning injustice of the way he had been tricked by Spinkley. But most of all there was one, simple question: *why?*

He ran through his memories so often he could see them in his sleep. He pored over them, sifting them for any hint or meaning. Very quickly, he saw that one name linked everything that had happened in London.

Spinkley at their first meeting: *You are not by chance related to Baron Dartmouth*, and then on the docks, *Do you know on whose orders I arrested this man?* Was it Dartmouth who had also sent Lendal to murder him in the hulk's hold? *Why?* How would such a great man even come to know of Rob's existence, let alone decide to ruin him?

Rob asked his friends in the crew if they had heard of the man. Most knew no more of the peerage of Great Britain than they did of the dark side of the moon. But one, a clerk named Williams who had joined the navy in a fit of despair after his wife cuckolded him, was better educated than most.

'Baron Dartmouth is First Lord of Trade and Foreign Plantations.'

'Do you know anything more?'

Williams had shrugged. 'I read about him in the newspaper. It's not like he had me to tea.'

It had left Rob none the wiser. 'Why would a Lord of Trade want to kill me?' he wondered.

'He's responsible for the American colonies,' said Williams. 'Where we're going.'

'But I never meant to go to America. I am only here because Dartmouth chased me into the arms of the navy.'

Rob was more confused than ever. Was it possible he was related to a peer of the realm? He knew there had been many branches of the Courtney family tree over the centuries. But even if he was, what could have drawn Dartmouth's attention – or his implacable hatred?

However much he thought about it, he could not fathom the answers.

'Perhaps I will find out in America,' he thought now, his legs dangling from the crosstrees.

Something appeared in the distance, breaking into his thoughts. Rob's gaze snapped to the horizon.

For weeks, there had been only grey waves as far as the eye could see. Now, suddenly, a low smear broke the monotony, the leading edge of a vast continent.

Rob took a deep breath and shouted down to the deck.

'Land ho!'

He stared at the distant land, wishing he had brought a spyglass so he could observe it in more detail.

America.

Cal Courtney joined the Continental Army camped outside Boston. He was a hero. The attack on the powder magazine had been a failure, but it was an *heroic* failure. He was toasted, saluted, and commissioned as a lieutenant. Men clapped his shoulder and shook his hand and murmured, 'God rest your brother.' Cal tried not to let them see him wince.

The army was a rabble. No uniforms, no tents, and little regard to rank. The men were volunteers, not professional soldiers. Coopers and clerks, blacksmiths and booksellers, farmhands, tanners, wheelwrights and vagrants. When they formed up for inspection, they looked barely more professional than the hotheads of the Army of the Blood of Liberty. But Cal loved it. After so many years in secret, trying to hold his tongue in front of his father and hiding his pamphlets under the bed, it was a release to be able to talk openly. With his comrades, he sat around the campfires until dawn talking of Thomas Paine, Congress, the rights of man and the cause. They drank toasts to George Washington, and death to the tyrant King George. At last he could express himself. This, he felt, was the meaning of liberty.

Though it had come at a price.

He had not only lost his brother in the raid on the powder magazine. When he slunk home from the raid, bloodied and burned, he had hardly been able to face his parents. His mother had read the news about Aidan in his face, even before he could stammer it out. He would never forget her scream – nor the tears that brimmed in his father's eyes.

It was the first time Cal had ever seen Theo cry. For a moment, the two men had stared at each other, united in grief, and Cal had felt closer to his father than he had in years. He wanted to embrace him, as he had done when a child.

Then his gaze had turned to fury.

'You killed your brother!' he shouted. 'You killed your brother. And for what?'

'He died a hero,' Cal insisted – bellowing, though he did not realise it. 'For a cause.'

'He died because you would not do as you were told. You speak of a cause, but you are a traitor to your family, and that is the greatest cause of all.'

Theo looked as if he might try to box Cal's ears. But something had snapped inside him, and when he tried to raise his fist it fell back, like a fire starved of kindling. He had nothing left in him.

Cal went to his room, packed his few belongings, and left. No one tried to stop him. His mother was sobbing in her bedroom, while his father simply stayed in the parlour.

Just as he was passing through the gate, he heard a door open behind.

'Cal?'

His heart lifted, he looked back. His father stood in the farmhouse doorway, his face lined and wet with tears. He seemed to have aged twenty years in fifteen minutes.

'Father?'

He longed for a smile, for a trace of warmth that might lift the burden of guilt he felt. But his father's face set hard.

'Go. You are no longer my son.'

Cal ran and did not look back. Later, there were times when he would wake in the night, a silent scream echoing through his body. He would weep bitter tears at life's cruelty, his own stubborn nature, the collision of fate that had ripped his father from his soul. At other times, when the mails came, Cal found himself hoping there would be a letter from his parents. Then he would scold himself, and harden his heart again.

You do not understand, he raged, speaking in his mind what he could not say to his father. *It was not my fault. There was no other way. If you and men like you had stood up to the King of England, maybe we would not have to fight now. It was not my fault.*

It would have been easier if he had someone to fight. Every time he thought of Aidan, he thought of that desperate clifftop battle. He wished so hard the outcome had been different, he thought his heart would split open. The prospect of action was like the promise of salvation, as if by fighting he could change the battle he had already lost.

His enemies were not far off. If Cal climbed the hills, he could see them clearly across the water, bottled up in Boston: parading on the common, guarding the long wharf, or marching through the streets. Often they came within rifle range. But General Washington had forbidden his troops to fire unless given the order. They had to conserve their gunpowder. Cal had heard a rumour that if every man in the army was called into action, they would not have ten shots apiece.

He wished he had saved the powder from the arsenal. He wished Aidan had not died.

Cal waited, as summer turned to autumn and the dreaded camp fever began to take hold. The thrill of liberty wore thin. They dug latrines, chopped firewood, marched up and down the drill ground until their feet were raw. They cleaned muskets that had never been fired.

Even with a full supply of powder the army could not hurt Boston. The city was surrounded by water on every side except for a narrow neck that joined it to the mainland. The British had dug in to withstand an almighty siege, while their men-of-war in the harbour covered any approach by water. The Americans had few cannons, and none of the big siege guns that would be needed to take the city.

One day, Cal was pissing in a latrine when he overheard two officers talking. They were lamenting the lack of guns.

'Everything is a matter of position,' said one, a red-faced colonel. 'I was with Ethan Allen and his boys when they took Fort Royal last spring. We captured two dozen cannons the British had left behind, twenty-four pounders and mortars. If we had those here, we'd have Boston at our feet.'

'But they're on the wrong side of the mountains,' said his companion, also a colonel. 'And there's no way to get them across.'

'You're wrong,' Cal interrupted.

The two colonels looked up, disconcerted to be interrupted by a lowly lieutenant.

'You should mind your manners, sir,' said one, 'or I will mind them for you.'

'Where are you from?' asked the other.

'Massachusetts,' said Cal.

'And how do you reckon to tell two Green Mountain men how the land lies in Vermont.'

'My father is Theo Courtney,' said Cal. The two colonels exchanged glances. They knew the name. 'He helped take Fort Royal from the French in the last war. He often told me the stories. He said there was a secret path across the mountains the French used.'

The colonels considered that.

'Where is it?' asked one.

'I don't know,' Cal admitted. Then, raising his voice as the colonel began to jeer at him, he said, 'But I can find it.'

'You are wasting our time,' said the colonel. 'How could a Massachusetts man find paths over mountains that we do not know about?'

'There's a man who can show them to me. An Abenaki Indian, a friend of my father's from the old days.'

'The Abenaki fight with the British.'

'Indeed.' Cal grinned. 'But I have a plan.'

Ten minutes later, he was in a comfortable study in a nearby farmhouse, explaining his proposal to an increasingly intrigued general. Two days later, with the first winds of winter swirling around Cambridge, he rode out from the camp with fifty men and a captain's commission in his saddlebag. None of the men wore uniform, and they rode horses that had not been branded with the Continental Army's mark.

Not so long ago, the Abenaki village had been the frontier between the British and French empires, as the two great powers battled for control of North America. The French had lost, but the peace had been brief. The palings that made a stockade around the log huts of the village were freshly cut, their points still sharp.

The Abenaki scouts had met Cal ten miles away, as soon as he crossed into their lands. He had expected it. This was a time of war. Cal had left most of his men camped a day's march away, bringing only one lieutenant and one sergeant to avoid being seen as a threat. Even so, the Abenaki kept a close eye as they escorted him to their settlement.

The headman of the tribe, the sachem, came into the clearing in front of the longhouse. He was not the biggest man, nor particularly old, but he had wise eyes and a presence that brought stillness into the bustle of the village. The men around him gripped their tomahawks and guns. Strangers were not welcome in these troubled times.

Cal swallowed. 'The son of Siumo the Hawk sends his greetings,' he announced.

The sachem squinted, as if trying to remember past events. Then he tipped back his head and laughed.

'Caleb Courtney!' he cried. 'Can it be?'

Cal gave a shamefaced grin. The sachem strode forwards and wrapped him in a warm embrace. He smelled of bear fat and woodsmoke.

'The last time we met, you were a little cub,' he said. 'Now look at you. A grown man.' He touched the rifle slung across Cal's back. 'And a warrior. It is good to see you.'

'It is good to see you, too, Moses.' Cal knew the Abenaki chieftain had other names, other titles, but Cal had always known him by the name the Abenaki had been given by French missionaries.

Moses brought Cal and his men into the longhouse and seated them by the fire.

'How is your father?'

When he was Cal's age, Theo Courtney had been captured by the Abenaki and adopted into their tribe. He had lived for a year as an Indian, learning their ways and their knowledge of the forest. They had named him *Siumo*, the hawk. Moses had been his companion and his best friend. When Theo returned to the British army, Moses had gone with him and enlisted. After the war, he had accompanied Theo and Abigail – with the infant Cal – to Massachusetts. Cal had memories of sitting on Moses' knee by the fire on winter nights, while Moses and Theo swapped tales of their exploits. Later, Moses had grown bored of life in the colony. He had returned to his village and become sachem of the tribe.

'My father is well,' Cal lied. 'Though he will be happier when the rebels have been thrashed, and the good rule of King George is assured in the colonies.'

He struggled to remain passive as he said it, watching Moses for any sign he might have guessed the truth. He hated having to lie to a man he had known all his life: it felt a shameful thing to do. But it was the only way.

Moses was my father's friend, he reminded himself. The thought tapped into a bitterness in his heart that drowned any guilt.

'And you?' Moses looked at the men with Cal. 'Are these men British soldiers?'

'We are scouts,' said Cal. 'You know the rebels took Fort Royal last spring?'

Moses sucked a deep draught on his pipe and nodded. 'That was a bad loss. It has made the forest a dangerous place for us. The tribe goes hungry when we can no longer be safe where the ancestors hunted.'

'The British are planning a new campaign in the spring.' Cal had had plenty of time on the march from Boston to perfect this story. 'I know you and my father found a path over the mountains. If you show me the path, we can use it to bring our guns here this summer and retake the fort.'

Moses was deep in thought. He was not yet forty, but the cares of his life had scored creases into his face like a much older man.

'It is dangerous,' he warned. 'The rebels have many patrols on the way to the mountains. If they know I am helping you, they may attack our village.'

'If you don't,' said Cal solemnly, 'your people will starve.'

Moses nodded and stared into the fire. A sachem's job was to keep his tribe safe, living from season to season as their ancestors had for generations. He was too young to remember a time before the white men came, with their guns and alcohol and wars started by kings he had never heard of. But he was old enough to have heard stories of the old days from his grandparents, of a time when the world was safe and known. Moses' life had been spent twisting like a leaf in a hurricane, making alliances with men he could not trust, knowing the outcome might be decided in palaces thousands of miles away across the great ocean. Every choice was like shooting a rifle in the dark, knowing you might hit the wolf – or your own child.

But Theo Courtney had saved his life more than once, and never betrayed him. Moses trusted his son.

'I will show you the path.'

The temperature dropped as they climbed into the mountains. The trees were bare and leafless. Cal was astonished to see how lightly the Abenaki moved through the forest. Growing up in Massachusetts, he had prided himself on his woodcraft. But compared to Moses, he was a bull ox blundering through the woods after a hummingbird.

'When he was young, your father could move like a snake,' Moses reminisced. 'Now I am certain he must be old and fat.'

'He is a different man,' Cal agreed, tightly.

Moses chuckled. 'And your brother Aidan?'

'He is dead.'

Moses' laughter died on his lips. 'How?'

'He joined a secret band of patriots.' The truth made the best lie. 'He died trying to steal powder from the British arsenal.'

'It must have broken your father's heart,' said Moses gravely.

Cal stared into the distance. In his mind, he was back at the farmyard gate, looking back at his father standing on the doorstep. *You are no longer my son.*

'It was hard for all of us.'

He lapsed into silence. Moses, seeing his sorrow, did not press him. They walked on together, climbing steadily, until they came up against a sheer rock face. The mountain loomed over them, the pines swaying softly in the winter breeze.

'This is the path,' said Moses.

'Where?' said Cal.

Moses led him up to the cliff face. Cal could see there was a narrow gully behind it, leading up the mountainside. The cliff curtained it off almost completely.

'This is the way your father and I went,' said Moses. 'From here, you go to the top of the mountain and then along the ridge to the fort.'

Cal looked up. The gully was steep and rocky, so narrow you could barely imagine fitting a gun through it. It would take ropes, levers, and almost impossible determination to haul them over the mountain this way.

But he was eighteen, and he had been polishing his boots in Washington's army for months. Nothing was impossible.

'Can you take me to the top?' he asked Moses.

It was a hard climb. Near the ridgeline, they came to a place where the gully forked. A distant look came into Moses' face.

'This is where we fought the French,' he said. 'Your father led sixteen men against a thousand and defeated them.'

Cal knew the story. He did not want to hear it again.

'How about you?' he asked. 'Were you never tempted to join the patriots?'

Moses wrinkled his brow. 'How is a man a patriot if he fights against his rightful king?'

'I meant the rebels,' Cal corrected himself.

'I swore loyalty to King George eighteen winters ago. I will not break my oath.'

'But the Abenaki fought against the British before they fought with them. Why not again?'

'The British are our best hope,' said Moses. 'They honour their treaties with us. They leave us free to live and hunt in our own lands. But the colonists defy them. They come over the mountains and the rivers, they claim land and build farms and call it their own. And when we fight our claim, they kill us. Tell me, why is a white man who fights for his land a patriot, but an Abenaki who does the same a criminal?'

Cal had no answer.

The gully opened out as they gained the ridge at last. They followed it west for several hours, in a cold drizzling rain, until they came to an open knoll at the end of the mountain spur, overlooking the lake. From the cliff edge, Cal could see Fort Royal below.

It was not the fort that Theo Courtney had taken some seventeen years earlier. That had been blown to pieces when the French general fired the gunpowder magazine, rather than surrender to the British. The rubble had been used in the foundations of the new structure, a five-pointed star with stone bastions and timber revetments on a promontory commanding the lake. Looking down into it, Cal could see the striped flag of the colonies hanging defiant from its flagpole.

And there were the guns. Their mouths were plugged against the rain, their touch holes covered with canvas. But even muzzled, Cal could feel their power. They squatted low on the ramparts, like great cats poised to spring.

'Wait until we get those to Boston,' Cal said under his breath. 'We will blast the British to pieces.'

'What do you mean?' said Moses.

Cal froze. He had thought he was alone, but the Abenaki had stolen up behind him without a sound.

'Nothing,' said Cal shortly.

'Why do you speak of turning the guns on your own people?' Cal tried to ignore him, but Moses continued, 'Why do you sneer every time you say "the British", and call the rebels "patriots"? Why are you here?'

Moses advanced. Cal took a step back – and stopped suddenly as he felt the cliff edge under his foot. He was caught between Moses and a thousand-foot drop. There was no escape. He had a pistol in his belt, but the powder would be wet from the rain.

'Let me explain,' said Cal.

Moses lifted his head. 'I am listening.'

Cal opened his mouth – but no words came out. A thousand excuses ran through his head, but none of them seemed plausible. All he could feel was the great void behind him, sucking him back, and Moses' eyes fixed on him.

Cal was young, his emotions never far from the surface. The Abenaki chief had spent a lifetime getting the measure of men. He read the truth in Cal's face.

'These guns are for the rebels,' he said.

Cal said nothing. He felt a great pressure squeezing his chest, as if he was being crushed between two stones. Part of him wanted to run, and that made him flush with shame. If he failed in this mission, he would have failed the revolution. Aidan would have died for nothing.

Moses put out his hand. 'Whatever foolish thing you have done, it is not too late. You are still your father's son.

With a roar, Cal threw himself forwards, tackling Moses below his shoulders and driving him back. The Abenaki had not expected it. They staggered backwards together, then collapsed in a heap.

Cal was bigger, but the Abenaki had a wiry strength. He rolled Cal over, twisting and writhing like a snake. Cal fumbled for the knife in his belt, but with Moses gripping his arms he could not get hold of it.

There was a tomahawk in Moses' belt. Cal felt it slapping against his leg as they wrestled. He tried to reach it, but Moses pushed him on his side, trapping Cal's arm under his own body weight. With a howling war cry, Moses grabbed the tomahawk. He sat on Cal, pinning Cal's free arm with his thigh, and raised the tomahawk.

'If you were not your father's son, I would split your skull.'

'I am not my father's son!' Cal cried.

Moses paused. The warrior-mist cleared from his eyes. He looked down at Cal and saw the spitting image of the young Theo Courtney he had befriended many years ago. The past seemed like a foreign country and the present was so difficult to navigate. It confused him with its changing alliances, vicious conflicts and how easily friend could become foe. He did not want to destroy what was important to him. He could not kill the boy.

He lowered the tomahawk. 'Let us be friends,' he said. 'Go home, and forget this quarrel.'

It was a good offer – but for one thing.

'I cannot go without the guns.'

'Then how—?'

Too late, Moses saw the knife in Cal's hand. Cal had managed to pull it from his belt. He jerked his hand free, and held the knife at Moses' chest.

The Abenaki's eyes went wide. 'What have you become?' he whispered.

'I do not want to kill you.' Cal's hand was trembling, which made him ashamed. 'You have shown me the path I needed. If you give me your word you will not reveal what we are doing, I will let you go.'

Moses' gaze was unyielding. 'That would betray your father.'

'And what about his son?'

Rage rose in Cal's heart. Could he really kill the man who had held him on his knee as a baby? If he did not, he could never return to the Continental Army.

Moses could see his indecision.

'For the love of your father—'

He broke off as Cal's left fist smashed in to the side of his face. He swayed sideways; Cal lunged up. He only wanted to get his enemy off him, to pin him down so he could force him to submit. But Moses had a warrior's reflexes, and the tomahawk in his hand. Instinctively, he started to bring it down towards Cal's head.

He had forgotten Cal's knife. Cal still held it; as Moses bent towards him, he instinctively lifted his hand to protect himself. Before either man knew what was happening, the blade plunged into Moses' heart.

The tomahawk dropped to the ground, its handle striking Cal a glancing blow across his head. The Abenaki chieftain shuddered, then went still. Blood pumped out of the wound in his chest, covering Cal's hands and running down his arms to soak his shirt. He let go of the knife, threw the body aside in horror, and scrambled away.

He paused, panting, at the cliff edge. Part of him wanted to hurl himself over it, to obliterate what he had done. He could not look back. Even thinking of the trusting Abenaki made something grind in his heart, as if he had killed his own father.

His father. Theo's last words echoed in Cal's mind: *You are no longer my son.* Flames of anger began to lick up inside him, cleansing the guilt. Moses' death had been an accident; he was not to blame. Or perhaps it was inevitable. The Abenaki had allied themselves with the British, so killing them had been his duty, no less – another prick in the belly of King George's military might. This was war, and Moses had been the enemy.

Cal looked out over cliffs. Far below, he could see the star-points of the fort, and the black guns sitting on her ramparts. The sight calmed him.

He had done what he had to do.

Off the coast of Long Island, the *Perseus* rendezvoused with a cutter from New York. The boat brought news of the war's progress. The rebellion had become more widespread; the Continental Army was besieging Boston. The colonists had no navy, but blockade runners and privateers were rife along the Atlantic seaboard.

'They cannot engage us in battle,' said the cutter's commander, sitting in Tew's cabin. 'But they are damned hard to defeat, and they sting us where they can. General Howe's troops in Boston are cut off by the siege. They receive their supplies by sea. If the American privateers take too many of our transport ships, Howe's men will be starved into surrender.'

The *Perseus* was ordered to patrol the coast of Connecticut, Rhode Island and Massachusetts, intercepting any ships who crossed her path.

'Though what their Lordships in the Admiralty expect me to achieve by that, I cannot fathom,' said Tew. 'It is almost five hundred miles of coastline, and you can be sure that the Yankees will know every bay and inlet. They are past masters at smuggling contraband ashore. That is why they are so averse to paying the King's taxes.'

Rob thought about the challenge. At Portsmouth, the fleet of the Royal Navy had seemed so mighty it was impossible to imagine anyone standing against it. But on the far side of the Atlantic, the fleet did not seem so mighty against the vastness of the continent.

For the first time, he began to wonder if the colonists might not be beaten as easily as everyone thought.

This new country reminded him of Africa. It was not the climate, nor the smell coming off the land, but the untamed wildness of it. Along much of the coast, tangled forests came down to the shore. Long sand beaches stretched for miles. The villages and fishing towns that clung to the shore seemed no more significant than limpets crusted to a whale.

But for such a sparsely inhabited place, it generated an astonishing amount of trade. Every day, the *Perseus* intercepted at least two dozen vessels plying the waters: fishing boats heading for the Grand Banks; Nantucket whalers bound for the Southern Ocean; merchantmen carrying timber to the West Indies and rum to England. It seemed they would not let war disrupt the way of commerce.

Every ship the *Perseus* stopped flew a British ensign and swore allegiance to King George when challenged.

'So much loyalty, you wonder there are enough men to make a rebellion,' said Tew drily. 'I cannot believe they all love their king so much as they protest.'

'They love their profits,' said Coyningham. 'That is all these Yankees care for. When they see that war punches a hole in their purses, they will soon put a stop to it.'

A shout from the masthead cut off their conversation.

'Sail off the starboard bow!'

All the officers grabbed their spyglasses and hurried to the rail.

'A man-of-war,' said Tew, taking in the row of gunports. 'French, judging by her lines.'

As if to confirm it, the white pennant of France billowed out from her masthead.

'I count forty guns,' said the second officer, Lieutenant Verrier, who'd been studying her.

Every man in earshot looked at Tew. At that moment none of them, not even Coyningham, wanted to be in his shoes. If the French frigate had come from Europe, she would be carrying the latest news. If war had been declared between Britain and France since the *Perseus* left, the French captain could use that knowledge to devastating advantage.

'Have the men beat to quarters,' said Tew calmly. 'We will be ready to give a good account of ourselves if we must. But do not fire unless I give the command.'

The ship was cleared for action. Nets were strung above the deck to catch falling spars, while hammocks were stuffed in the side netting to provide shelter. On the gun-deck, partition screens were taken down and furniture stowed away. Boys sprinkled sawdust so the decks would not become slippery with blood. Powder was fetched from the magazine, the marine marksmen took their positions in the tops, and the gun crews loosed their tackles.

Tew timed their progress on his pocket watch. The process took seven minutes.

'What is the Frenchman doing?' Tew asked.

Midshipman Milnrow, stationed on the rail with a telescope, answered at once.

'She is holding her course, sir. She does not seem to be preparing for battle.'

The ships converged. Coming up from behind, the crew of the *Perseus* could now see the name written across the French ship's stern in shining gold letters: *Rapace*.

'It means "Predator" in French,' Verrier translated.

The *Rapace* shortened sail, letting the *Perseus* come up alongside her. There was no sign of unusual activity on her deck.

'If she has not cleared for action,' said Lieutenant Verrier, 'she is taking an awful risk.'

On the *Rapace*'s quarterdeck, a tall man in a cocked hat, wearing a commander's epaulette, took a speaking trumpet and hailed them across the water.

'*Bonjour*,' he said. And then, in lightly accented English: 'I hope you do not plan to start a war. When I left France, our countries were at peace.'

Along the deck, the men at the guns relaxed.

'Keep alert,' Tew barked. He picked up his own speaking trumpet. 'What is your business in these waters?'

'We escort a convoy en route to Martinique,' answered the Frenchman.

Tew took a long slow look across the horizon.

'I see no convoy.'

'There was a storm. We are separated. That is why we have come so far north.'

'If there had been a storm, we would have met it,' muttered Coyningham. 'We had the calmest crossing imaginable.'

Tew ignored him. 'Do you plan to enter port in America?'

'*Non*,' the French captain assured him. 'We sail south and try to find our ships.'

It was the first time Rob had seen Tew hesitate. He looked uncertainly at the circle of officers clustered around him.

'He is lying,' said Coyningham. 'We have the weather gage and our guns are loaded. We can dismast him with a single broadside, then board him and strike his colours before he knows what has happened.'

'That would be a black piece of infamy,' countered Verrier. 'To take advantage of a peaceable ship, when our nations are not at war. It would be little more than piracy.'

Coyningham sneered at him. 'Every man aboard would say that she fired first.'

He was probably right. Along the deck, a row of expectant faces looked to the captain. The sulphurous smell of a burning slow match tinged the air. All it needed was for one spark to fall on the touch hole.

Tew shook his head. 'We cannot start a war. Stand down.'

Steam hissed as the matches were doused in buckets of water. The helmsman turned the wheel, and the *Perseus* began to diverge from the *Rapace*'s course. The French captain raised an arm, half in salute and half in farewell. At that distance they were too far off to see his face, but it seemed to Rob that there was an arrogance in his stance, almost like a smirk.

'I hope that is the last we see of them,' he murmured to Angus.

Angus nodded. 'It doesn'ae sit right, having a Frenchman under our guns and letting him go. Like letting a wolf from a trap.'

A brittle mood prevailed on the ship that night, and the following morning. Routine tasks went uncompleted, petty officers snapped at the men, and the officers could barely restrain their tempers. Coyningham was in an especially black humour, cursing and threatening the men fit to start a mutiny.

'Is he so eager for battle?' Rob wondered. 'I took him for a coward.'

'It wouldn'a have been much of a fight when we had the Frenchie under our guns. And if we took her, he'd have been given command of the prize,' Angus explained. 'He'd have sailed her back to England a hero. Promotion, medals, maybe an audience with the King.'

'But we are not at war with France.'

Angus shrugged. 'Everyone knows it's coming. After the first shot, no one'll care who fired it.'

A chill went down Rob's spine. The day had gone dim; the coast had disappeared. Tendrils of fog were drifting over the gunwales, wrapping the ship in a blanket.

'Shorten sail,' came Tew's voice from aft. Rob had not noticed him come on deck, but the captain had an uncanny intuition for where and when he was most needed on his ship. 'We are too near shore for my liking, and there are treacherous reefs nearby. Put leadsmen in the chains, and lookouts on the bows. If there is a Yankee privateer about, she may well try to slip her anchorage in this fog.'

The men hurried to obey. The earlier lassitude was forgotten in an instant. No one wanted to be caught blind on a hostile, unfamiliar shore.

'You heard the captain!' shouted Coyningham, striding down the deck with the boatswain's mate in tow. 'Up that mast and reef the mainsail. The last man down will feel the taste of the lash.'

Thomas ran past Rob to the mainmast rigging. He was unrecognisable from the callow boy Rob had helped up to the crosstrees that first week at sea. Now he could swing himself out on the channels as lithely as any able seaman, racing his shipmates to the top.

But something was different this morning. His face was pale, his eyes downcast. He fumbled on the ratlines, climbing slowly as if he was carrying a great weight. The rest of the topmen were already far above.

It was the fog, Rob realised. He had trained the boy to overcome his fear of heights by looking at the horizon. Now that they were hemmed in by the fog, the horizon had disappeared. Thomas's terror had come racing back. He would be stuck halfway up the mast, just like the first time.

And Coyningham would make him pay.

The topmen had already finished furling the mainsail. They slid to the deck along the backstays, landing agile as cats. Thomas was left alone in the rigging.

'Get down here now,' Coyningham ordered.

One of the topmen moved to assist Thomas, but a bark from Coyningham stopped him dead.

'A dozen lashes to any man who helps him.'

Rob glanced back. Tew stood impassive on the quarterdeck, conferring with the sailing master. He must have seen what was happening, but he could not countermand his first lieutenant in front of the men.

Thomas climbed down slowly. Each step was agony, though he knew that was nothing to what he had coming. The moment he reached the deck, the boatswain's mate seized him. He tore off Thomas's shirt and bent him over a barrel. Two petty officers held Thomas's arms and legs, while the boatswain's mate pulled out his starter rope.

'Give that to me,' said Coyningham.

Rob could not believe his eyes. It was unheard of for an officer to flog a man – but Coyningham seemed to have abandoned reason. All his rage at being denied his prize yesterday was channelled into this.

And something else. As Coyningham raised the rope, he caught Rob's eye with a malevolent stare. *I cannot touch you*, he seemed to be saying, *but I can hurt you*.

Rob knew he shouldn't respond to the provocation. He knew it was what Coyningham wanted. If Rob went any further, he would lose all the protection of his rank.

Coyningham brought down his arm. The rope hummed in the air – then stopped so suddenly the end cracked an inch above Thomas's back.

Rob held the rope where he had grabbed it in mid-air. The first lieutenant had brought it down with astonishing force, but Rob was stronger. He gripped the rope so tightly Coyningham could not pull free.

Coyningham tugged against him with all his might. Rob held fast. The rope stretched taut between them.

Rob let go. Coyningham, caught off balance, stumbled backwards, tripped and fell hard on his backside. A few of the men laughed, but quickly thought better of it. A dangerous light had come into Coyningham's eyes.

He stood and dusted himself off.

'You will regret this,' he hissed. 'This is mutiny.'

Belatedly, Rob realised every man on deck was watching him.

'Marines!' Coyningham bellowed. 'Clap Mr Courtney in irons!'

Two scarlet-coated marines threaded their way across the deck. The sullen crew were in no mood to make way, but they could not protect Rob without risking a charge of insubordination.

Rob waited defiantly. What could he do? It had been madness, putting himself between Coyningham and Thomas. He had given Coyningham the excuse he wanted, and he would pay the price. But he could not have done anything else.

'Wait!'

Tew's voice rang across the deck. He strode towards Coyningham.

'What is the meaning of this?'

Coyningham froze. For a moment, Rob thought he might lash out at the captain. That was too much to hope for. There would be no comeback from striking Tew: Coyningham would be court-martialled.

And perhaps he might have done it. The deck was gripped in silence, waiting to see what would happen. The fog deadened sound, so that the slap of the waves on the hull beneath them seemed distant.

But the roar of a twelve-pound cannon carries through any-thing. The boom echoed out of the cloud and across the deck, dislocated by the fog so it seemed to come from everywhere at once.

No one moved as the sound rolled away. Then Tew snatched the rope from Coyningham's hand and threw it aside.

'Pull yourself together,' he said brusquely. 'And clear for action.'

The fog was beginning to lighten. The bowsprit speared through shreds of cloud as the *Perseus* moved forwards. All eyes peered out over the gunwales, scanning the mist for every shadow. The other ship must be close. They could hear the creak of timbers and cordage, rumbles that might be running feet – or guns being run out.

'What's that?' Angus pointed off the starboard bow, where a grey mass seemed to float through the fog. They stared, but it did not resolve itself. Instead, it faded away until they could not be sure it had ever been there.

'You are jumping at shadows,' Rob said.

Nonetheless, he watched closely where Angus had pointed. There was no sound. Angus must have imagined it.

Rob turned his attention to the port side.

'There.' Rob's sharp eyes picked it out before anyone else. Through the wisps of fog, something substantial. He punched Angus lightly on the shoulder. 'You were looking the wrong way.'

'I know what I saw,' Angus insisted.

But there was no time to argue. As the helmsman altered course, the other vessel came into definition. A brigantine, large for her type but smaller than the frigate. She was a mer-chant ship, or had been once. Now her sides had been pierced for guns. Rob counted eight, including two swivels mounted near the stern. The red-and-white striped flag of the rebel navy hung from her stern. A privateer.

She ran out her guns. It was raggedly executed, without precision. The crew must be volunteers, full of enthusiasm but lacking drill or discipline. The *Perseus* showed them how it should be done. On Tew's command, every gunport lifted as one. The men hauled on their tackles, and fourteen cannons ran out in perfect unison.

The men cheered. The brig would be easy prey, and then a payday for them in the prize courts.

'What is she thinking?' Rob wondered. 'She cannot hope to match guns with us.'

'She will not fire,' said Coyningham. His temper had improved as he contemplated the prize he would command. 'They are baring their teeth, so they can say they took on the mighty Royal Navy. They will not bite.'

The brig fired.

It was not the single overpowering broadside of a navy ship: the guns exploded erratically, like a string of fireworks igniting. It didn't matter. From a hundred yards off they could not miss. Eight cannonballs struck the *Perseus*. Some screamed through the rigging; others hit the gunwales, throwing off clouds of splinters.

'Fire,' ordered Tew.

The *Perseus*'s full broadside crashed out as one deafening blast. Flame spat from the guns. Smoke mingled with the remnants of the fog. Across the water, Rob saw devastation unleashed on the brig. She was lower in the water and the British gun crews had aimed their cannons with lethal accuracy. Great bites were gouged out of her side. One of her guns was overturned. Her mizzen yard was snapped in two and fell to the deck.

Her crew did not lack courage. Even in the face of the onslaught, they kept reloading. Once more, the British crews were faster and more efficient. They poured out another broadside before the Americans could fire again.

'Strike your colours!' Tew shouted across the water through his speaking trumpet. 'You cannot win.'

'You will sink me before I strike!' came the defiant reply, accompanied by half a dozen shots as the privateer finally readied her guns again.

'You cannot fault their bravery,' Tew conceded. 'But we will get no prize money for a sunken ship.' He searched out the second lieutenant. 'Mr Verrier! Prepare a boarding party.'

Rob, standing nearby, saw the fury on Coyningham's face. By rights, the first officer should have led the boarding party. Even in the chaos of battle, Tew had not forgotten Coyningham's treatment of Thomas. This was his punishment.

Verrier shouted orders. Rob ran to his side, handing out pikes and cutlasses to the men in his watch. The brig saw what they intended and tried to bear away, but the *Perseus* had the weather gage and followed her around. Their hulls inched closer.

'Keep down,' Rob called. 'She has not lost her teeth.'

The American guns were still firing, still dangerous. A marine reeled away with a splinter piercing his cheek into his mouth. A block was shot away. It fell from the rigging and cracked a man's skull. Rob crouched with his men behind the gunwale, Angus beside him, as the ships slowly closed together. They were so near that the brig's guns could hardly elevate high enough to shoot over the side of the frigate.

Seized by the glory of the moment, Midshipman Milnrow stood up, waving his sword like a lunatic.

'Prepare to be boarded, you damn Yankee bastards!' he shouted.

The cry was still echoing across the water when his body convulsed, struck from behind. A cannonball erupted through his stomach, tearing him in two. His head and torso were torn from his waist, cartwheeling through the air and over the side. His legs stayed upright for a moment, like a headless chicken, then toppled over, gushing blood across the deck.

The men stared. But worse than the horror they had witnessed was the realisation of what had happened. The cannonball that killed him had not been fired from the brig. It had come from behind, from the other side of the ship.

Forgetting the brig to port, all eyes turned to the starboard side.

Another ship had appeared. She had crept up behind them while they were distracted by the brig, hiding in the fog until she was almost upon them. Rob glimpsed the outstretched talons of her figurehead.

'The French frigate!' he cried.

É tienne de Bercheny had waited his whole life for this moment. He gripped the sword his mother had given him, with its gold handle and ivory inlay. He would make her proud today. He would kill Englishmen.

Through the fog, he glimpsed the striped flag of the Continental colours fluttering at his masthead. He grimaced. It was not glorious to sail into his first battle under false colours, but it was a necessary expedient.

A man sat beside him on a stool, sketching deft lines on a pad with a charcoal stick. His name was Jean, and he was an artist. Constance had paid for him to accompany Étienne. When they returned home, the pictures would be engraved and printed in all the newspapers to illustrate her son's triumphs.

'When you draw the ships, show us under the flag of King Louis,' Étienne ordered him. 'Maman will not want the Paris public to think me a coward.'

Obligingly, the artist smudged out the rebel flag and drew in a fleur-de-lis instead. The comtesse's instructions had been clear. He was here to burnish a legend, not to document fact.

Étienne nodded. Along the deck, his crew crouched by their guns, linstocks at the ready. Étienne assumed an heroic pose, chin up, eyes staring into the distance. Let the artist record that. He raised his sword, ready to spring the trap on the English frigate.

'*Pour le roi!*' he bellowed. The men cheered.

'Aim high,' he told them. 'We must have our prize in good condition to sail back to France.'

He swept his sword down.

The French frigate fired. So did the brig. The *Perseus* was smashed from both sides, caught in a vice of flying iron. A blizzard of metal and wooden splinters exploded at the men on deck from every direction, while blocks and cordage rained down from above.

'But we are not at war with France,' protested Verrier. He had the plaintive voice of a child, whose opponent had broken the rules of the game.

'She is not fighting for France,' said Rob grimly. He pointed to the frigate's masthead. Instead of the white flag of King Louis she had flown the day before, she now sported the same striped ensign as the brig.

'It is a trap,' said Tew. 'They planned the whole thing.' There was no time for recriminations. 'We cannot fight two ships at once. Lieutenant Verrier, take your men and board the brig.'

Verrier stared. The brig had veered away, putting clear water between herself and the *Perseus*. The boarding party would have to approach her in the ship's boats.

'That is madness.'

'It is an order,' said Tew. 'Even if you cannot take her, you will at least stop her from engaging us. I will make sail and try to come to terms with the Frenchman.'

It was a desperate plan. Even one on one with the *Rapace*, the *Perseus* would be downwind, outgunned and short of men. Added to that, she had already sustained heavy damage, while the French ship was fresh.

For the boarding party, the odds were worse. If they somehow got aboard the brig, they would be stranded on an enemy ship, outmanned and with no hope of reinforcement. The best they could hope for was to sell their lives dearly.

'What are you waiting for?' Rob shouted.

He vaulted over the side and slid down the ladder into the cutter. With cries of '*Perseus*' and 'King George', the rest of the men followed.

They were terribly exposed. The *Perseus*'s guns had fallen silent as Tew sent men aloft to make more sail, but the brig and the French frigate continued to batter her. Cannonballs from the brig screamed over the heads of the men in the boat. As the *Perseus* drew away, the cutter was left in open water between the two ships. A sitting duck.

'Pull,' Verrier commanded.

The men bent to the oars, speeding the cutter through the waves towards the brig's bow.

Cheers sounded from the American brig as the crew saw the *Perseus* draw off. They thought she was running away. Her captain crammed on sail to give chase. It bought the cutter vital moments while the Americans were distracted.

But the boat was not invisible. As the brig's men went aloft to loosen sails, they saw the cutter closing. Shouts alerted the men on deck. Rob saw them with rifles running up the ratlines to take position in the tops.

The marines in the cutter kneeled and tried to pick off the American marksmen. From the rocking boat, their inaccurate muskets had little hope of hitting their targets. The best they could do was worry the Americans, making it harder for them to aim.

It was not enough. One of the rowers fell from his oar, clutching his side. Rob took his place at once.

'Pull harder,' Rob urged his shipmates.

The brig was gathering speed. If she passed them, then the cutter would be left a spectator in the battle, while the brig would be able to cross the *Perseus*'s stern and rake her decks.

The men heaved, breaking their backs with the effort. Another man was hit in the shoulder by a musket ball. Lieutenant Verrier changed places with him, so that the officer rowed while the wounded man took the tiller with his one good arm.

Slowly, the cutter and the brig came together. The rifle fire from above ceased as the cutter came into the shadow of the hull. A man leaned over the side. Verrier raised his pistol and shot him in the face.

But they could not keep pace with the brig under full sail. The men at the oars were flagging.

'One last heave!' Rob shouted.

Leaving his oar, he clambered over the benches to the bow. A rope lay coiled in the bilge, with a grappling hook tied to one end. Balancing himself on the thwart, Rob took the rope and paid out a length. He swung it in the air, as he had many times back home slinging a lasso around his father's cattle, then let fly.

He had one chance, and he judged it perfectly. The grappling hook sailed through the air and caught on the chains below the brig's bowsprit. Rob fastened the rope end to a cleat on the cutter's bow, just as it jerked taut. The cutter bounded forwards as the brig took the strain.

Rob and Angus hauled in the rope until they came under the bowsprit. Behind them, marines and sailors readied their weapons. Rob waited for the command.

It didn't come. Rob looked back: every second they delayed increased their danger. What was Verrier thinking?

Verrier lay slumped over his oar, a dark bloodstain spreading around the small hole punched through his blue coat. Rob felt a pang of sorrow. The lieutenant had been a good man, brave, and a bulwark against Coyningham's brutality. But that did not matter now. If they waited any longer, they would all die.

He sought out the only other officer in the boat, a pimple-faced midshipman named Evans. He was younger than Rob and white with terror.

'Give the command,' Rob hissed.

The midshipman looked at him blankly.

'The order to board. The men look to their officers,' Rob added urgently. 'You are the senior officer aboard now.'

Evans swallowed hard and nodded. He stood, his knees shaking so badly Rob feared he would fall in the water.

'At 'em!' the midshipman shouted.

The men cheered and surged forwards. Rob tucked his cutlass in his belt and held his knife between his teeth. He grabbed the bow chains, swung himself up onto the cathead and then onto the deck.

An American sailor came at him with a pike. Rob had practised sword drills on the *Perseus*, but he had little formal training. Instinctively, he swung the cutlass at the pike and battered it aside. Strength, more than technique, saved him. The pike's point went wide of his shoulder and lodged in the bowsprit. The American tugged on it, but he had buried it so deep he could not get it free. Rob brought the cutlass down on his collarbone with a blow like chopping wood, so hard he almost cut through to the man's heart. The American collapsed.

Rob twisted the pike free from the bowsprit and reversed its point. This was a more familiar weapon, like an old friend. He had gone out in the bush many times hunting with sharpened sticks. His father's Qwabe herdsmen had delighted in teaching Rob the use of their *assegais*, the long light throwing spears of their tribe. Rob stabbed and jabbed it expertly, making space in the press of men the same way he had in the tangled forests of Africa. Beside him, Angus wielded a boarding axe with lethal effect, driving the Americans back.

Over the clash of steel, the shouting and screaming, Rob heard the dull boom of cannon fire like distant thunder. The *Perseus* must be engaging the French frigate. In the thick of battle, he could not see who was winning. But at least he was playing his part. Distracted by the boarders, the American crew could no longer handle the brig. She was bearing off downwind, away from the two other ships. That would level the odds for Captain Tew.

But for the *Perseus*'s men aboard the brig, the odds were grim. The American ship carried a big crew for her size, and the boarders were too few against them. They were hemmed in, a knot on the foredeck fighting for their lives. More than half lay dead or wounded already. The young midshipman was shouting bravely to keep fighting, but it was a lonely voice. If they could not break out, they would have to surrender or die.

Rob drove the pike into an American sailor's belly. Instead of pulling back, he kept hold of the shaft and drove forwards, ramming the weapon through his opponent. The point burst out of the man's back. He was pushed into the man behind him, who was skewered with his shipmate on the protruding point. Rob pushed on. Both men were driven backwards, knocking more of the brig's crew out of their way until they collapsed on the deck.

Rob let go of the pike. Before anyone could react, he ran into the space he had created, leaped up onto the gunwale and swung himself into the rigging, jackknifing his legs to avoid a cutlass thrust.

He ran up the ratlines towards the main top. The rigging shook under the feet of men chasing him, but he didn't look back. Halfway up, he saw a rope tackle dangling from a yard. He leaped for it. There was no room to miss, but he snatched it in mid-air and let his momentum carry him swinging over the main deck, almost to the mizzen mast. Not quite far enough. He grabbed a backstay, swung himself off it and managed to get hold of the mizzen shrouds.

In the chaos and the smoke, the men on deck lost sight of him. Rob climbed to the top, then edged along the gaff boom until he found the halyard that held the brig's flag in place.

He cut it with his knife. The rope slithered away as the rebel flag fell billowing to the quarterdeck. Below, Rob heard shouts of consternation, then a strange and sudden hush. To strike your flag was to surrender your ship. For a moment, the Americans wondered if the battle was lost.

A figure in a blue uniform coat strode from the quarterdeck, brandishing a pistol.

'Fight on!' he bellowed. 'We have victory in our grasp.'

The American captain levelled the pistol towards the bow. Rob saw it was aimed at Angus. While the Americans were confused, the Scot had broken out with a group of boarders, charging across the main deck. But he had not seen the gun aimed at him.

Rob let go of the yard and dropped. From that height, he would have snapped both his legs if he had hit the deck. But the captain broke his fall. Rob landed on top of him, knocking his pistol from his hand. Before the captain could recover, Rob stabbed him through the heart.

A swivel gun stood mounted on the side. Rob swung it around so that it pointed inboard, where the American sailors were gathered. As it pivoted, he felt something move inside the barrel. It was loaded. The gunner must have abandoned his station, or been killed, before he could fire it.

The swivel was fitted with a flintlock, like a rifle; and there was powder in the touch hole. Rob jerked the rope attached to it. The flint sparked; the flame ran through the touch hole and ignited the powder in the barrel. A hail of tiny shot spat from the cannon's mouth, reaping a terrible harvest on the main deck. Cut down from behind, the American crew faltered. It was all the encouragement the British sailors needed. With shouts of 'God save the King,' they charged forwards.

And suddenly the battle was over. Their colours had been struck; their captain was dead: the Americans had nothing left to fight for. As quickly as the battle had started, they threw down their weapons and surrendered to the boarders.

Angus ran aft to Rob.

'What are your orders, sir?'

Rob stared at him, dazed. 'My orders?' He looked down the length of the deck. Blood, bodies and broken limbs littered every inch. 'Midshipman Evans is in command.'

'The midshipman caught a bayonet. You are the senior officer.'

Rob stared at his friend blankly. He was not yet nineteen. There were men in the crew who had served at sea for thirty years or more. He felt their eyes on him. Bruised and blood-spattered, flushed with victory, they were looking to him.

How could he tell them what to do?

But instead of being distracted by their expectation, he found it gave him strength. Something stiffened inside him, like a sail filling with the wind and snapping taut.

'Lock the prisoners below,' he said.

The *Perseus*'s men had taken the ship, but they were still outnumbered by the American crew. He needed to secure the victory before the Americans recovered their morale.

A warm smile spread across Angus's face. He could see the mantle of command settling on Rob's shoulders as the boy came to terms with his responsibility. Men would follow him, Angus thought, wherever he led them.

They herded the Americans and locked them in the hold. Rob inspected the ship. She had taken heavy damage from the *Perseus*'s broadsides. Her mainsail had been shot away, and her boom dangled off the mizzen mast like a broken limb. Among the bodies and blood, her deck was littered with cordage and splintered timbers.

'Set parties to clear the deck and get some sail on her,' Rob ordered.

The wind had risen, a stiff onshore breeze blowing them towards land. Until they got steerage way, they would be helpless before it.

The wind had driven off the last of the fog so Rob could see clearly at last. Across the water, the two frigates, the *Perseus* and the *Rapace*, had drifted far away from the brig. With the naked eye, it was hard to tell how they had fared, and there were no telescopes to hand on the shattered quarterdeck. Both still had their colours aloft, and a haze of smoke over their decks where the cannons were firing. The *Perseus* seemed to have come off worse, but Tew was working her hard, using her superior speed to manoeuvre so the Frenchman's guns could not come to bear.

'We must help her,' said Rob. 'Together, we may be able to defeat the French.'

He saw doubtful faces around him. The men were exhausted. It would take all their strength to make the brig serviceable again. The prospect of having to re-enter the battle was enough to drive them to mutiny.

Rob forced himself to smile. In the heat of the moment, the words his men needed to hear seemed to come naturally.

'Are we not the most feared warriors on the ocean? Do we want the men we left behind getting all the glory when they capture the Frenchie frigate? Shall we leave them to spend the prize money? This is your chance to prove yourselves worthy of our flag – and make yourselves rich.'

It brought a ragged cheer from his men. They cleared the deck and sprang to their work: breaking open the sailmaker's locker to stitch canvas and splice lines that had been cut in the fight.

But it was taking too long. The wind blew them back, away from the frigates and into the mouth of the great bay that opened in the shore. The brig's hastily repaired sails and cordage could not take the strain of beating into the wind. Angus, manning the wheel, grimaced.

'Something's amiss,' he told Rob. 'Her rudder's not answering aright.'

'Her cables?' Rob asked in a low voice.

If the rudder cables had been shot away, it would take hours to repair. The vessel would be at the mercy of the wind and currents. And they were rushing ever closer to the rocky promontory at the mouth of the bay.

Angus shook his head. 'More likely blockage under her stern keeping the rudder from turning. We can steer her afore the wind. But if we try to put her hard over, it might snap.'

Rob made his face calm so that the men wouldn't divine his panic. Those nearest had already overheard too much, pausing in their tasks to look at him. He gazed at the line of white breakers foaming on the rocky headland. To be caught on a lee shore, with jury-rigged sails and a broken rudder, was any sailor's worst nightmare. If they could not turn into the wind, their only option was to sail into the bay and hope they could find a sheltered inlet to repair the damage.

Rob remembered the charts he had studied aboard the *Perseus*. The coast hereabouts was a treacherous maze of sandbars, shoals and reefs. But that was not the worst of it.

The land around Narragansett Bay was a stronghold of rebel sympathisers. And inside the bay was the harbour of New-port, where – according to Tew's reports – the rebel navy kept a flotilla. The moment the rebels saw the brig, and real-ised what had happened, they would seize her back. They would not be kind to the British sailors who had taken her.

Now Rob felt the loneliness of command, of having to choose between bleak options. Whatever he did, men might die. But if he delayed any longer, the sea would make his choice for him. They were already so close to shore he could hear the waves breaking on the rocks.

'Bear away downwind,' he ordered, with all the confidence he could summon. 'We will enter the bay.'

The men jumped to obey. The promontory slid past, barely a hundred yards off their beam, as the brig threaded her way through the channel between an island and the mainland. It reminded Rob of the entrance to Nativity Bay back home.

'Maybe put a leadsman in the chains,' Angus murmured in Rob's ear. 'Treacherous waters, hereabouts.'

Rob nodded, angry with himself for forgetting such an obvious precaution. How much a captain had to remember! Even when faced with the biggest decisions, he could not neglect the thousand other details necessary to keep a ship safely afloat.

Rob gave the order and promised himself he would do better next time.

Luckily, the wind was dead behind them. It drove them down the middle of the channel, away from the treacherous shallows at its edge. The breeze eased as they came in shelter of the land. Rob was confident enough to alter course a few points, looking for a cove where they could anchor.

Nothing looked promising. The rocky shore offered little protection, barely so much as an inlet. As they sailed further on into the bay, Rob began to worry that they would never get out. Even if the wind shifted in their favour, the French frigate was most likely out there. If she sailed in after them, they would be trapped.

'There,' said Angus. Rob looked up.

It was an anchorage. But not the quiet cove or deserted beach he had hoped for. As the brig came past a spit of land, the bay opened out to their right. Where Angus had pointed, was a complete harbour. It looked a prosperous place. The wharfs and cranes were built to accommodate transatlantic trade. Solid four-square houses lined the waterfront, extending some distance back, while along the coast shipyards supported vessels in various states of construction. It must be the town of Newport.

'We will get a warm reception there,' murmured Angus.

He handed Rob a spyglass he had found in the wreckage of the captain's quarters. Rob put it to his eye and scanned the ships at anchor in the harbour.

All of them carried the striped pennant of the rebel navy. It was not much of a fleet – half a dozen converted fishing boats and schooners – but they would make short work of the wounded brig.

Once again, Rob felt the claustrophobia of command closing around him. He had made his decision, and it had failed. Now he was trapped on the horns of a dilemma. If he tried to flee, the Americans would chase him down. If he held his course, he would sail into their arms. The only card he had to play was that the Americans did not yet know that the brig had been captured.

He stared through the spyglass, thinking furiously. As he surveyed the harbour, he noticed another ship he had not seen before. A frigate, so gleaming new she must just have been launched from the shipyard. Her masts were already stepped, her sails mostly rigged. Soon she would be ready for sea. Fully armed, she would be the most powerful ship in the American navy.

An idea formed in Rob's mind. A way to escape the poisoned choice he had. He gave Angus the telescope and pointed to the frigate.

'What do you make of her?'

His friend ran an expert eye over the ship.

'She's a big 'un. Pierced for forty guns, and you can see how stout her timbers are by how low she sits in the water. She'll fear nothing but a ship of the line when she's finished.'

'Then maybe we can do something.' Rob's eyes were bright with mischief. 'Open every scuttle and gunport and wedge them open. Bring up all the tar, cordage, sailcloth and wood you can find in the stores, and stack it on the main deck. I want this ship ready to burn like a bonfire.'

Angus looked astonished. 'A fire ship?'

'Even if we could beat out of this bay without breaking the rudder, we would never outrun those ships in the harbour. If we land, they will have us in chains in an instant. One way or another we cannot keep hold of this prize. At least we can put her to good use.'

'And how do we get away?'

'If we manage to sail the fire ship into that harbour, there'll be so much confusion and panic they will not see us escape.' Rob gestured aft, where they were towing the boat that had brought them from the *Perseus*. 'We can make our escape in the cutter.'

Angus gave Rob a look that was half admiration, half anxiety.

'They say command changes a man. But look at you. Half an hour ago you could hardly open your mouth to give an order. Now you are Sir Francis Drake.'

Angus had meant it as a compliment. But he saw Rob flinch at the words, as if he had opened an old wound. He could not know that the mention of Sir Francis Drake had reminded Rob of the Neptune sword, the magnificent gift that Drake had given his ancestor Sir Charles Courtney. Going into battle, in command of his own ship for the first time, Rob should be wearing it. He felt its absence like a hole in his side. Seven generations of Courtneys, and he had lost it.

Angus touched his forehead. 'Meaning no offence, sir.'

Rob recovered himself. He saw the concern on his friend's face and clapped him on the shoulder.

'You do not have to salute me yet. I have just got hold of my first ship, and now I am about to burn her to the waterline. I fear I will not be a captain for long.'

'Long enough.'

As Angus ran to supervise the preparations, Rob turned the telescope back on to the harbour. He could see a commotion around the quayside – men and women hurrying to watch the brig approach. They could see she had been in battle and were desperate for news. Was it a victory?

The thought that she might have been captured did not seem to have occurred to them. The bow hid the pile of kindling that was being tossed on the main deck around the mast. Fire was a seaman's greatest fear, but now they embraced it with devilish glee and ingenuity. They soaked sailcloth and hammocks in tar, dipped them in gunpowder and piled them over the wood around the foremast. Other men pulled apart rope ends and bound them with powder and splinters in paper packets. They would burn long enough to make sure the fire took good hold.

'How long will we have before the fire reaches the magazine?' Rob wondered.

'Five minutes,' Angus guessed.

Rob measured the distances with his eyes. They would have to sail right into the harbour before they fired her, to be sure that no one had time to get aboard and put out the fire.

'I hope the men are ready to row for their lives.'

A few small craft had set out from the harbour to intercept the brig. Rob watched them, his chest tightening.

'Run up the Yankee colours.'

The red-and-white striped jack broke from the masthead, where Rob had cut it down a short time before. A cheer rang out from shore.

It would not fool them for long. With her makeshift canvas, the brig was coming in too fast. She should be shortening sail, preparing her anchor cable. Instead, Rob had crammed on every scrap of speed he could extract from her.

Angus reappeared at his side. His face was grim.

'Begging your pardon—' he began.

'Not now,' Rob snapped. He was feeling the tension, the knife-edge he was walking. Set the fire too soon and it would give the Americans time to react. Too late, and his crew would burn with their ship.

'This cannot wait,' Angus insisted. 'What will you do with the prisoners?'

Rob froze. With so many decisions to make, so much danger, he had not thought of the brig's crew crammed captive in the hold. If he left them there, they would be burned alive.

Whatever the risks, he could not have that on his conscience.

'Lower the ship's boats,' he said. 'But take the oars out. Bring the prisoners up in groups and let them into the boats. They will make it to land eventually.'

'They will see on shore what we are doing.'

Rob shrugged. 'There is no choice.'

There was no time to lower the boats in orderly fashion. Rob's men pulled out the oars and added them to the pile of wood on deck, then launched the boats over the side with great plumes of spray. By the time the first one was in the water, a dozen prisoners had come up from the hold and been ushered over the gunwale at the point of a boarding pike. None tried to resist. One look at the tinder around the mainmast made them desperate to be off the brig.

Rob checked their progress again. The sight of men disembarking into the boats while the ship was under full sail had caused consternation on shore. Meanwhile, one of the small boats that had rowed out to greet them was off their bow.

A man dressed in fine clothes, with a blue cockade in his hat, stood unsteadily in the stern and hailed the brig.

'What news?'

'A great victory!' Rob shouted back, trying to mimic the flat vowels of the Americans. 'We gave King George a taste of his own medicine.'

Huzzahs sounded in the little boat. But the man in the back was frowning.

'If it was a victory, why are you abandoning ship?'

'We were holed below the waterline,' Rob said, though the brig was riding high. 'The pumps cannot keep up.'

But it was impossible to maintain the lie. The American sailors in the boats had overheard every word, and they started a furious protest.

'He's lying!' they shouted. 'The British took the ship. They mean to burn her.'

Rob had no more time. There were still twenty or thirty American sailors on deck, waiting to climb into the boats. If they took it into their heads to fight, now they were in sight of safe harbour, he might lose the ship.

'Throw the others overboard!' he shouted.

Without hesitation, the British sailors drove the Americans to the side. Any who hesitated were encouraged with a sharp kick to the backside, or the flat of a cutlass across their shoulders. Some shouted that they could not swim, but Rob didn't worry about that. They would find their way to the boats or be picked up by their comrades. His own men were in far greater danger. The Americans knew the brig had been taken. It would not take them long to launch an attack.

A shrill shriek drew his attention to the main deck. It sounded like a girl's voice.

'Is this the gallantry of British sailors, to throw a defenceless girl overboard?'

Three civilians had appeared on deck: two men, and a young woman of about seventeen wearing an emerald-green dress. She had lost her bonnet, so that her raven-black hair streamed around her shoulders.

Even in the midst of battle, surrounded by the enemy and with the ship primed to explode, she had a face to make every man on deck forget his work and stare at her.

'Where did these people come from?' Rob asked, astonished.

One of the sailors knuckled his forehead. 'I found 'em in one of the cabins below when we took the ship. Locked 'em in the hold with the others.'

Rob crossed the deck to the passengers.

'Who are you?'

The shorter of the two men drew himself to his full height. He barely stood five feet tall. He was enormously fat, with sagging jowls, a florid nose and a powdered wig which had slipped askew in the commotion.

'Thank God you are here,' he said. 'My niece and I feared these rebel vagabonds would cut our throats.'

Rob stared in surprise. The man had a strange accent, neither properly English nor American, but a sort of slurred drawl.

'You are not one of the Yankees?'

The man's face flushed with outrage. 'Indeed not. I am a loyal subject of King George. Hezekiah Bracewell is my name.' He indicated the other two. 'My niece, Miss Sophie Bracewell – and my clerk, Mr Crow.'

Rob glanced at the other man. Bracewell had called him a clerk, but he looked more like a bare-knuckle boxer than a sec-retary. His shoulders strained against his short jacket, his arm muscles bulged and he had a deep scar carved down one cheek. He caught Rob's gaze and returned it with a menacing stare.

'How did you come to be here?' Rob asked Bracewell.

'I was on my way to my estates in Jamaica when this brig overhauled my sloop and took us captive. I need not describe the horrors we apprehended at the hands of these ruffians, especially touching my niece's virtue.'

His niece, Sophie, averted her face, as if the horrors he alluded to were too great. For some reason, Rob had the feeling she wasn't frightened at all.

The last of the American sailors had entered the water with cries and splashes. The unexpected passengers were the only three remaining. Belatedly, Bracewell looked around and noticed their course, their speed, and the pile of combustibles stacked around the mast.

'What the devil is going on?' he demanded. 'What manner of rescue is this?'

'You are not yet out of danger,' said Rob. He could not afford to risk civilians in his plan. He turned to Angus. 'Put them over the side with the others.'

With a cry, the girl collapsed to her knees and threw her arm around Rob's legs. Her angelic face stared up at him imploringly.

'I beg you, sir, do not condemn us to such a fate.'

'They will not let you drown.' Rob did not sound as sure as he meant to. Her blue eyes had a hypnotic quality that cut through his defences. 'The sailors will take you to shore in their boats.'

'But if we fall into rebel hands, who knows what they will do to us? To *me*.'

Her hand clasped his thighs. Such was her distress, she didn't seem to realise how close her fingers reached towards the crotch of his trousers. Rob hoped her uncle hadn't noticed.

'I would do anything to be spared such a fate.'

Rob had no time to argue. Nor, he found, did he want to.

'Go to the stern.'

He pulled himself away from her grasp. While they spoke, the brig had continued bearing down towards the frigate in the harbour. No one on shore could doubt their intentions now. Rob could see the carpenters and riggers lined up on the frigate's side, staring at the ship rushing towards them. A few sailors on the anchored ships had climbed into the rigging to get a better view. None of them had thought to man their guns.

Rob stared at the harbour, the unfinished frigate and the water between them, constantly calculating speed and distance. It was time.

'Load the guns,' Rob said. 'Plenty of powder and double-shotted. Then set the fire and let us be away.'

The men did as he ordered. They lashed the brig's wheel in place, braced her sails and let down ropes over the stern into the cutter. Angus lit one of the bundles of kindling, threw it onto the pile of wood and ran aft. It smoked for a moment, then ignited with a puff of flame as the powder caught.

At the stern rail, Bracewell was staring aghast at the cutter in the water below.

'Do you expect my niece to climb down there like a common tar?' he demanded.

'Either that or burn.'

Smoke from the fire was blowing over them. Before Bracewell could react, Angus lifted Sophie by her waist and threw her over his shoulder. One-handed, he vaulted over the rail and let himself down by the rope into the cutter. Bracewell had no choice but to follow, puffing and cursing. He slid down heavily, skinning his hands. Crow the secretary followed, surprisingly nimble for such a heavy man.

One by one, the rest of the crew clambered into the cutter. Rob was the last to go. He took a final look at the brig and felt a pang of regret. He had only commanded her an hour or two, but she had been *his*. It would be hard to go back to being a master's mate aboard the *Perseus*, dodging Coyningham's traps and answering to pimple-faced midshipmen.

If you delay any longer, you will not have to worry about Coyningham ever again.

The flames were rising up the mast, catching the lower edge of the sail. Rob leaped off the rail and dropped heavily into the waiting cutter. The moment he landed, Angus gave the command and the men bent to their oars as if the Devil himself were lashing their backs. The cutter bounded through the water.

Rob took his place with the other men, working an oar as hard as any of them. Looking back, he saw panic overwhelm the harbour. Some of the ships were trying to get under way.

Others, too hasty, had cut their anchor cables and were drifting out of control.

None of them could stop the brig. Like a bright burning angel, she bore down on the harbour, straight at the unfinished frigate. The flames licked from her masts and yards, making a pyramid of fire two hundred feet in the air. Her sails had already turned to ash, but momentum carried her forwards. Booms sounded from within her hull as the fire touched the cannons Rob had primed. They fired as if manned by a ghostly crew, cutting random swathes through the nearby vessels and scattering the crowds on the quay.

She rammed the frigate so hard her bow collapsed with the impact. The new-built ship's timbers were dry, and her rigging dripped with fresh tar. Her deck was strewn with sawdust and rope-ends. She went up in flames like a beacon. The fire climbed still higher, burning so hot Rob could feel it from across the water.

'Keep rowing!' he yelled above the din of the conflagration. 'We are not safe yet. We must be away before the magazine blows.'

He had hoped for five minutes before the fire reached the powder magazine in the bowels of the ship. But he had not counted on the combined impact of two ships on fire. The shock of the collision had opened the brig's timbers all along her side. Air rushed through the gaps, feeding the flames to a greater frenzy.

The magazine exploded. The blast seemed to shake the sea itself. Thousands of pieces of burning debris were thrown into the air, falling in a rain of fire over the other ships. A sloop that had cut her anchor caught fire and drifted into another, setting it ablaze in the mouth of the harbour.

The men in the cutter whooped and cheered themselves hoarse. Rob could not stop grinning. They passed the boats they had dropped earlier with the American crew and sang raucous songs of victory. One of the men climbed up on the thwart and dropped his trousers to show them his bottom.

'You may kiss my arse, you Yankee scoundrels!' he shouted.

No one gave chase. There was not a ship left in Newport that could put to sea. Even if there had been, the approach to the harbour was blocked by burning vessels. It would be weeks before they could clear the hulks, months to replace all the shipping they had lost.

Rob ordered the crew to step the mast. The men stowed the oars and sat back as the wind filled the sail. The cutter heeled over eagerly, her hull skimming the surface like a racing yacht.

Men shifted aside as Hezekiah Bracewell and his niece made their way aft. Bracewell thumped down on the bench opposite Rob, while Sophie spread her skirts beneath her and perched daintily beside her uncle.

'Damn fine work,' Bracewell complimented Rob. 'Those rebel pirates will think twice before they cross swords with King George's navy again.'

The girl twisted a dark lock of hair around her finger. She shot Rob a radiant smile.

'My uncle and I are in your debt, Captain . . .?'

Rob shook his head. 'Not "captain", miss. Just plain Mr Courtney.'

His eyes met hers, and something seemed to tighten inside him. Her pale skin was unblemished, and her pert lips made a perfect Cupid's bow. Her eyes sparkled with suggestive energy.

'I am sure when they hear of your exploits in London, they will make you an admiral,' she declared.

Rob blushed. 'I only did my duty.'

'Then I trust you will be rewarded in some other fashion.'

She leaned forwards, making it difficult for Rob not to see down her cleavage. Her dress was cut low and tight, pushing her breasts up into two soft globes.

From three seats forward, Angus caught his eye.

'Steady,' he warned, trying to keep a straight face. 'You may find there's a bit of a swell.'

They had left the bay, and the waves had grown larger. Rob scanned the horizon, but there was no sign of either the *Perseus* or the *Rapace*. They were alone.

'What now?' asked Bracewell. Even his voice sounded small against the ocean.

'The nearest safe harbour is Boston, in Massachusetts colony,' said Rob. 'With the damage the *Perseus* took, that's where she'll head for. Especially if she has a prize in tow.'

He left it unsaid that the *Perseus* might have been sunk, or taken by the French frigate. It would be a hard enough journey without worrying about that.

Sophie clasped his hand in hers.

'I am glad we have you to steer us, Mr Courtney.'

They sailed into Boston three days later, aboard a sloop that had picked them up off the Rhode Island coast. The moment they entered the harbour, Rob scanned the shipping anxiously. His heart leaped. There was the *Perseus*, safely at anchor, her crew busy with hammers and paintbrushes repairing the scars the battle had left.

'She survived,' said Rob happily.

They took the cutter back to the *Perseus*. Their arrival caused an almighty commotion: a thousand questions shouted down, and joyful reunions from men who thought they had lost their shipmates forever. Only Coyningham soured the mood. He gave Rob a ferocious glare, as if he could not bear to see him alive, and took him aft to Tew's cabin at once.

Tew was standing in front of a mirror, adjusting his dress uniform in preparation for going ashore. He did not look surprised at the intrusion, but merely cocked an eyebrow and said, 'Mr Courtney. I did not think we would have the pleasure of your company again.'

'How did the fight with the Frenchman end?' Rob wanted to know. 'Did you capture her? Sir,' he remembered to add.

'We were damned lucky to escape,' said Tew. 'She had the better of us. If we had not got a lucky hit on her mainmast, we would not have been able to escape.'

Rob could see the frustration in his eyes. Tew was a brave and honourable officer: it must have hurt to break off the engagement without victory. But he had been short-handed, and his ship had taken a terrible punishment. Closing with the Frenchman would only have killed more of his crew, and probably they would still have lost.

It took a certain kind of courage to sail a ship into battle. Now Rob saw it took just as much to know when to withdraw.

Coyningham had less sympathy.

'We could have taken her, if you had not derelicted your duty,' he sneered. 'In the heat of battle, you sailed away and abandoned the fight.'

'The wind was against us, the ship was crippled and we were on a lee shore,' Rob said, more calmly than he felt. He had guessed Coyningham would hardly welcome his return, but he had not expected quite so much vitriol. 'We could not return to the battle.'

Tew drummed his fingers on the hilt of his sword.

'What of the second lieutenant? Or Midshipman Evans?'

'They died in battle, sir,' said Rob. 'I was in command. I take full responsibility for what happened.'

'And the prize?' said Coyningham. 'Since you returned with nothing more than our own cutter, I presume you contrived to lose her, too.' He jabbed his finger accusingly at Rob. 'You know what happens to a commander who loses his ship. You will take full responsibility for that, too.'

Rob tried to keep his temper.

'I lost the brig because I sailed her into Newport harbour and used her as a fire ship against the Americans. We must have burned a dozen or more of their ships, including a frigate they were building. So, yes, I do take full responsibility for that.'

Silence gripped the cabin. Coyningham and Tew stared at him with scarcely contained disbelief: one in fury, the other in wonder.

'So it is true,' murmured Tew.

'How do we know that?' Coyningham's face had gone red; he sounded almost deranged. 'We only have Courtney's word for it.'

'All the men aboard will swear to what we did.' Rob remembered the Bracewells. 'And the prisoners we rescued.'

'Of course it is true,' said Tew. 'We had the news from Newport yesterday. The reports are scarcely credible, but there can be no doubting the truth of it. The damage you have done to the rebels is incalculable.'

Rob was not sure if he was expected to respond. Tew was staring up at the skylight, lost in thought, while Coyningham glared at Rob.

'With Lieutenant Verrier dead, there is a vacancy to fill,' said Tew. 'I will need to speak to the admiral, of course, but I am confident he will approve my decision.'

Coyningham started to protest, but Tew silenced him with a withering look. He held out his hand. Rob shook it, not sure what it signified.

'Congratulations, Lieutenant Courtney.'

Even before the promotion was announced, the news spread through the ship. Rob's shipmates poured him double measures of grog, slapped his back and cheered him until their voices were hoarse.

Angus raised his mug. 'To Lieutenant Courtney,' he toasted. 'There's not many pressed men as earn an officer's commission.'

'I will not forget where I came from,' Rob promised.

Angus downed the last of his grog. 'Of course not. You'll need us watching your back when Coyningham comes for you.'

The men around them laughed, but Rob did not share in it. Through the haze of too much rum, he could feel an awkwardness spreading through him. This might be his last time with his messmates on the gun-deck. When his promotion was confirmed, he would move to the gunroom and an officer's cabin. He would dine from china plates, and drink claret instead of grog. If a sailor talked of mutiny, even in jest, Rob would have to see him flogged.

Angus misread his mood.

'Are you thinking of her? Miss Sophie Bracewell, the girl from the brig?'

Rob hadn't been thinking of her, but the moment Angus said her name he saw her in his mind as clear as day.

'She's hard to forget.'

'I suppose she's gone to Boston,' said Angus.

'Her uncle took her ashore the moment we anchored.'

'No doubt to stop her having her heart stolen by some dashing tar.' Angus winked at Rob. 'He probably saw the way you looked at her.'

'Me? What man didn't look at her?' Rob protested.

'Aye. But you were the only one she returned the look to.'

Rob tried to pretend he hadn't noticed. 'It does not matter. I doubt I will ever see her again. And her uncle would never let her consort with a common sailor.'

From over the side, Rob heard a sudden clamour. He scrambled to his feet. Every church bell in the city seemed to be ringing at once.

'Is there a fire? Are the Yankees attacking?'

Angus cuffed his ear. 'You chuckle-head,' he said. 'That's your victory they're ringing.'

He was right. The British army had endured months bottled up in Boston without a success to cheer. They celebrated Rob's exploits at Newport like parched men given the bottle. Salutes were fired, services of thanksgiving held, and a commemorative sword voted for Rob. The Commander-in-Chief, General Howe, invited Rob to a ball at his mansion where he would be the guest of honour.

The attention made Rob uneasy. He knew the only reason he was being feted as a hero was because the British were desperate. And in the back of his mind, he worried that news of his exploits might make their way back to his enemy in London. He might be thousands of miles away from Baron Dartmouth, but he had not forgotten him.

From aboard the *Perseus* as she carried out her repairs in the harbour, Boston seemed invincible. There were three ships of the line anchored nearby, and a dozen more men-of-war that could have sunk anything the rebels could set against them. Yet all their strength could not hide the fact that Boston was a city under siege. From the *Perseus*'s masthead, Rob could look out over the green rolling hills and see a great ring of earthworks and palisades scarring the landscape. The narrow neck which connected the city to the mainland had been barricaded at either end. No one could enter, but nor could they leave.

'It doesn't matter,' said Coyningham over dinner in the gunroom. 'While we command the ocean, we can resupply our troops until kingdom come. The Americans will rot in their trenches and die of the plague before they starve us out.'

'They could defeat us,' said Rob, 'if they put guns on that ridge to the south.'

He had seen it from the masthead – an eminence called Dorchester Heights that commanded the city. For some reason, neither the British nor the Americans had thought to occupy it.

'They could,' agreed Coyningham, 'if they had the guns.' Ever since Rob's promotion, he had maintained an icy politeness, laced with sarcasm and condescension. 'But there is no siege artillery for five hundred miles. We are quite safe.'

Rob thought of how bravely the Americans had fought off Newport – how the brigantine's commander had put his ship right under the *Perseus*'s guns as bait for the trap. He wondered if the British officers' confidence was misplaced.

But if fighting the colonists was unnerving, it was nothing to the terror of entering the governor's mansion for a ball in his honour, when the appointed evening came. Rob felt ridiculous. Worse than ridiculous – a fraud. The brand new uniform coat with its gold lace hung stiffly. The breeches were too tight, and the stockings bit into his calves. It felt like dressing up.

The moment he appeared the room fell silent. All eyes turned on Rob. The orchestra played a grand fanfare, that led on to the popular tune by Handel, 'See the Conquering Hero Comes'. The assembled guests sang the words lustily, so that the candles seemed to shake in their holders.

Rob froze. He might have run from the room, if Tew hadn't come up beside him, taken his arm and steered him through the watching crowd.

'Smile,' he whispered in Rob's ear. 'You are the hero. They expect you to look like one.'

Rob fixed his face in something like a smile and tried to acknowledge the applause as he walked uncertainly to the front of the room, where a raised dais had been erected. A round-faced man stood in the splendid uniform of a full general, with a golden epaulette and the star of the Order of the Garter sewn on his coat.

Rob managed to mount the steps without falling over.

'You look almost as comfortable as I feel,' said the general with a brisk nod.

Rob grinned. If a general felt self-conscious, he did not feel so bad.

'I shall not keep you long. But you have given us cheer in a dreary season, and the people must have the chance to salute their hero.'

A servant appeared at the general's elbow and gave him a velvet cushion. A sword rested on it.

'The loyal citizens of Boston took up a subscription and wish me to present this to you as a token of their admiration,' said the general.

Rob took it. It was superbly made, with gold chasing down the scabbard and a pommel wrought like a snarling lion. Yet when he drew the blade out a few inches to examine it, he saw it was no flimsy presentation sword. The steel was strong and supple, whetted to a keen edge.

'A proper weapon,' said the general, as if reading Rob's thoughts. 'I did not take you for a man who cared for trinkets and show.'

Rob bowed to the general. It was a bittersweet moment. The sword was perfect. He could feel the balance of the blade, the way it would move like an extension of his arm. It was beautifully made, and lethal. Yet it was not the sword he should be holding. That was thousands of miles away, in his enemies' hands.

But you earned this yourself, he told himself. It was not inherited from some dusty ancestor, echoing with past glories. This was a new blade with its future yet to be written.

He buckled it onto his belt. 'Thank you, sir. It is a generous gift.'

'If you use it to kill Yankee rebels and Frenchmen, then it will be money well spent.'

The general put a hand on Rob's shoulder and turned him around to face the assembly. The guests cheered again, and as the applause died away the orchestra struck up the first dance. Rob escaped gratefully from the podium, though there was no anonymity for him in the crowd. Everywhere he turned, men wanted to shake his hand and toast his health, while ladies blushed and giggled behind their fans.

'I feel like a fortress besieged on all sides,' he told Tew, during a momentary pause.

'Take refuge on the dance floor,' Tew told him. 'At least there they can only come at you one at a time.'

Rob took the advice. He was a good dancer. His grandmother had taught him some of the steps in Nativity Bay, while he had learned more modern figures with Hugo in London. He never wanted for partners. For each girl that spun away to the next set, another stepped prettily towards him. They swooped and sashayed in a blur of fine clothing and silky graciousness, like wheat fields in an undulating breeze. It was a young man's dream, but Rob did not enjoy it as much as he should have. He began to feel that his fame was something apart from him, a shiny trophy that interested the girls far more than Rob's true self. They offered little conversation, and when Rob tried to speak to them they only looked bored. He always let them go feeling he had been a disappointment.

The night wore on. The whirling on the dance floor, and the many toasts he had drunk, left him giddy and exhausted. All he wanted was to sink into his cot aboard the *Perseus*. He scanned the crowd for Tew, wondering whether the captain would rescue him. But before he could bow out, the orchestra had started the next tune, and there was another girl stepping towards him.

Still looking for Tew, Rob hardly noticed her.

'Have you forgotten me so quickly?'

He realised the girl was speaking to him. He looked down, and almost tripped over his own feet in his surprise as he took in her long raven hair, braided around her head, her red-bow mouth and those eyes sparkling with mischief.

'Miss Bracewell,' he said. The fog in his brain cleared instantly. 'I did not know you were here.'

'Where else would I be?' she retorted. 'There is no way in or out of this city.'

'I meant . . .'

She stepped away, pirouetting around while Rob stood leaden-footed. She moved forwards again and took his hand.

'Is your uncle here?' Rob asked.

'Over there.' Sophie nodded to a corner of the room, where Bracewell was in conversation with the admiral. 'Would you rather dance with him?'

'N-no,' Rob stammered.

'Good. I hear such terrible tales of what sailors get up to.'

Rob thought he must have misheard. He knew what unnatural vices some of the men practised aboard ship, but surely a lady could not have heard such scandalous rumours.

The dance had stopped. Sophie came towards Rob, so close he could feel the heat radiating from her skin.

'I am sure after so long confined aboard ship, with only those hairy men for company, you would relish a woman's touch.'

Before Rob could reply, one of her hands was resting lightly on the front of his breeches. To anyone watching, it would look as if she had her hands folded demurely in front of her. But in the cleft between them, her fingers gripped him through the cloth of his breeches, manipulating his pulsating manhood until it was all he could do not to gasp.

'I have a room upstairs,' she whispered. 'Follow me in two minutes.'

She stepped away, curtseying so low her mouth was almost level with his groin. Then, with a guileless smile, she rose and went out through a side door.

Rob's head was spinning. He had to lean forwards, so that the tails of his coat hid the unseemly bulge Sophie had encouraged, pressing out of his breeches like a bowsprit.

Another woman was approaching for the next dance, bearing down on Rob like a privateer intent on seizing its prey. Rob flashed her a smile.

'Excuse me,' he apologised, 'I am in need of refreshment.'

He followed Sophie through the side door and found himself in a hallway, with a grand staircase rising to the upper floor.

There were no lights, but a trail of yellow wax from the dance floor led up the stairs. Rob followed it.

The landing at the top was eerily quiet. The noise from the ballroom was a distant murmur. Rob padded down the corridor, following the spots of wax to a door that had been left ajar. A light glowed from the room within.

Rob opened the door and stopped in astonishment. It was a bedroom, with thick curtains drawn across the windows, a fire smouldering in the grate and a large canopied bed in its centre. Two flickering candles cast an intimate glow.

Sophie lay on the bed. She was naked. Her raven hair spilled across the pillows, her arms spread out. Her legs were parted slightly, revealing a small tuft of dark hair between her thighs. Her skin glowed as soft as a peach in the candlelight. She was touching herself intimately and moaning quietly.

In a swift movement she raised her head and whistled the first few bars of 'See the Conquering Hero Comes'.

'Are you just going to stare? Or are you going to wield that mighty sword you have been presented with.'

Rob felt himself stiffen as his senses took in her beauty. But he hesitated.

'What if someone finds us here?'

'It is my own room. My uncle and I are guests of General Howe.'

Rob shut the door and strode to the bed. He did not know how much he had wanted her until that moment; now the desire burst through him. The sword dropped forgotten to the floor as he undid his belt. A gold button popped from his new coat as he tore it off in his haste. He climbed onto the bed like a ravenous man before a feast.

Sophie rose to meet him, gasps coming from deep in her throat. There was strength in her slim white arms. She caught him off balance and rolled him on his back. She crouched over him on all fours, a wild look in her eyes. Her long hair hung down and brushed against his chest. Her breasts grazed his stomach as she moved her body from side to side.

'You do as I tell you,' she told him.

She was unlike any woman he had ever met. She knew what she wanted, guiding his hands to the places on her body where she would take the most pleasure. She tossed her head and writhed against him like an eel. She dug her fingers into his skin until her nails drew blood. She moaned with pleasure, so loud the servants in the hall must surely have heard it, but when Rob tried to cover her mouth with a kiss, she bit his lip and pinned him against the bed, stretching his body as taut as a rope. Rob thought he would explode, but she was an expert lover. He lost count of the times she brought him to the brink, only to ease away at the last minute, saving him up for herself.

At last, with a groan that must have echoed all the way back to the ship, she climaxed, cupping her breasts in her hands and squeezing her nipples until they were as engorged as ripe cherries. At the same she released Rob. He emptied himself into her with hard, shuddering thrusts that rocked the bed.

They lay naked together afterwards, tangled in each other's bodies and musk. Rob knew he should leave. Tew would wonder what had become of him. He was an officer, now: he should not be returning to his ship by slipping over the side, praying the night watch did not see him. But he was under Sophie's spell.

'Where did you learn such amazing lovemaking skills?' he asked, incredulous.

'Where did you?' she countered.

Robert had no answer. He could hardly bear now to think of his exploits in London's brothels with Hugo. The whores had been neither common nor cheap, but compared to Sophie they were half-shilling streetwalkers. They knew the right moves but didn't invest them with the wholehearted, body-shaking abandonment that Sophie had displayed. The pleasures they provided were physical transactions. Sophie was a magician in the arts of love.

He leaned across to kiss her, but she rolled away.

'You must go,' she rebuked him. 'My uncle is next door. If he finds you here, he will have you thrashed to within an inch of your life.'

The hot blood in Rob's veins cooled to ice. He thought of the noise they had made, so shameless and full-throated.

'What if he heard us?'

She shrugged her white shoulders. 'He has never caught me before.'

That did not console Rob – but he had no time to wonder how many other lovers Sophie might have taken this way, or to be jealous of them. He pulled on his breeches and buttoned the shirt as best he could.

'When can I see you again?' he asked.

At that moment, he would have quit the Royal Navy and thrown the gilded sword into the harbour if it let him spend one more night with her.

A smile played across her lips. But before she could answer, a thunderous boom sounded from outside. It was a cannon shot: not the distant barrage they were used to from the American lines, but deafeningly close. The windows rattled, and the ewer on the washstand jangled. Moments later, the house shook under an enormous impact. A glass fell off the dresser and shattered. A rumbling noise filled the room as the slates on the roof above started to tumble down and smash on the pavement below. Shrieks and shouts rang through the household.

Rob reacted at once. Still half-dressed, he threw himself onto Sophie. She squealed as he rolled her off the mattress, landed on the floor and slid under the bed. Just in time. It sounded as if an avalanche was going off over their heads. Dust filled the room. The bed creaked and groaned as rubble poured over it. Would it hold? Or would they be crushed to death?

Cal Courtney stood on the ridge of Dorchester Heights, looking down at the spires and wharves of Boston in the grey light before the dawn. It was as if he'd disturbed an ants' nest. A moment earlier the scene had been a picture of tranquillity, a city asleep despite the siege. Now, panicked figures crowded the streets. Church bells were ringing, windows were slammed open, and plumes of dust rose from the buildings where the cannonballs had struck. The bewildered inhabitants stared at the hill, unable to comprehend what was happening.

When the sun went down the night before, the hilltop had been empty. Now, it was a fortress. Walls had appeared, as if suddenly and inexplicably a genie had created them. Thousands of American soldiers were strung across the hillside. More despairingly, from between the breastworks poked the muzzles of two dozen huge siege guns, trained on the city and the British fleet at anchor.

Cal savoured the triumph. This was his victory. It had taken months, suffering unspeakable ordeals. Hauling those cannons over mountains and through blizzards, Cal had lost one finger to frostbite and another when his hand froze to a metal wheel rim and was crushed beneath it. Day after day, inch by inch, he had brought the great guns through five hundred miles of wilderness. When the winter thawed, he had dragged them through mire, and when it turned savage he had driven them through chest-deep snowdrifts.

Even when they arrived in Boston, the work was not complete. To reach the high ground, they had had to cross a neck of water controlled by the British, only a few hundred feet from the British sentries. They had chosen the night of the general's ball, when all the British officers had been away from their posts. In the dark, the Continental Army had manhandled the twenty-four great guns up a steep and frozen hill. The earth was too hard to dig trenches and emplacements, so they had brought wooden frames stuffed with twisted straw to make rudimentary ramparts. Barrels had been filled with stones to make breastworks. If the British attacked, the barrels would double as weapons to be rolled down the slopes and break their ranks.

Cal touched the gun and said a prayer for his little brother. This would not bring Aidan back. It would not avenge the hurt Cal had suffered. But it was the beginning.

He raised his sword again and looked down the line of cannons. *His* cannons. The gunners stood with lit matches behind them, awaiting his command.

'Fire!'

Rob didn't hear the guns' second shots. His ears were filled with dust and deafened by the barrage of beams and roof tiles cascading down over his head. It was too much for the bed to bear. One of its legs gave way. The bed collapsed towards the corner, pinning Sophie's foot. She screamed; she tried to pull her foot free, but it would not come. Still the rubble kept falling. Another bed leg snapped. The bed yawed like a ship's deck in a storm, a narrow lean-to barely high enough for them to breathe. If one more leg broke, they would be crushed. But Sophie still hadn't managed to free her foot.

The avalanche slowed. The torrent of rubble became an occasional piece of debris. The room went quiet, though the dust was thick. Rob pressed his hands and knees against the floor, and pushed up, taking the weight of the bed on his back. It was immensely heavy. He strained and heaved; he could barely lift it.

The bed moved a fraction, enough for Sophie to pull her foot free. They crawled out from under the collapsed bed and looked at the ruin of the bedroom.

The ceiling had disappeared, open to the grey morning sky through a lattice of broken beams. The ruins of the roof, and half a wall, lay piled across the room.

Sophie was still naked, her pale skin smeared with grime and blood that had combined with the sweat of her lovemaking. She picked her way through the carnage to the remains of her dresser and pulled out a plain white shift. She wriggled into it.

'Does this always happen when you take a lady to bed?' she asked.

Rob marvelled at her composure. She had nearly died, yet apart from a slight limp when she put weight on her left foot, she seemed unaffected. Through the dust that caked her face, her eyes were bright with defiance.

'Only you,' he told her.

Something gleamed among the rubble. The gilded scabbard of his new sword. He pulled it out from the stones. There was a dent in the guard, but the blade was still true. He dressed quickly and buckled on the sword.

The interior wall had half collapsed, but by some miracle the door frame remained standing. Rob opened it and stepped through into the corridor. There was less destruction but more noise. Every guest and servant in the house seemed to be scurrying about in panic. Many carried vessels filled with water: serving dishes, bed pans, chamber pots, anything they could find. Rob smelled smoke. A candle must have been knocked over by the impact and started a fire.

'Where is your uncle?' he asked Sophie.

She led him to the next room. Before Rob could touch the door, it burst open. Bracewell stood, fully dressed in coat, breeches and shoes. Mr Crow, his secretary, was behind him. Both men's eyes settled on Sophie.

'Thank God you are safe,' Bracewell said. In his panic, he didn't ask why Rob was with her, or in such a state of undress, though the leer on Crow's face suggested he guessed all too well. 'What the devil is going on?'

'The rebels,' said Rob. 'We must get out this instant.'

The smoke was thickening. The servants had vanished like rats from a sinking ship.

He took Bracewell's hand and dragged him towards the staircase. They had not gone three paces when an almighty crash sounded from the hall ahead. Sparks blew in on a blast of hot air, fanning flames around them. The smoke grew so thick he could hardly see.

'The staircase must have collapsed.'

Rob tugged Sophie and her uncle to the ground, where the smoke was thinner. He tore strips off his shirt and gave them to the others to hold over their mouths.

'What now?' said Sophie.

'Follow me.'

Crawling on the floor, he led them back to Sophie's room. The smoke rose through the hole in the roof like a chimney, letting more air into the room. Rob kept down low and found his way to the window. The glass had shattered. With a fallen brick, he hammered out the frame and swept away the shards of broken glass. He peered out, gulping in the fresh air outside.

It was too high to jump to the ground. But halfway down, the roof of the stable block joined to the rear of the house, creating a makeshift mezzanine level. It was the best they could do. The heat on Rob's back was gaining in intensity. The flames had entered the room. There was no time for anything else.

'But we will break our legs!' cried Bracewell.

'Better that than being burned alive.'

Rob tried to push Bracewell towards the window. But Bracewell stood his ground, his bulk so immense Rob could not move him.

'You go first,' Bracewell ordered Crow. 'See if it is safe.'

Crow gave his master a black look. But he was an obedient servant: he did as he was told. Rob watched him land on the stable roof, roll over and then leap down, unhurt, into the courtyard.

The heat was increasing. Rob lifted Sophie through the window, let her dangle as far as she could and then dropped her down. His heart was in his mouth until he saw her land safely.

'You next,' he said to Bracewell.

Bracewell clambered onto the window ledge. Then, suddenly, he paused.

'My purse,' he cried. 'It is in my room.'

'Leave it,' said Rob.'

Below, on the stable roof, Sophie looked up beseechingly.

'Jump, Uncle, before it is too late.'

Bracewell refused to move. A burning beam fell from the roof, passing inches from Sophie's head. The stables were filled with straw. When the fire reached them, they would ignite like a Roman candle. Sophie was in grave danger. But she would not leave without her uncle, and he would not go without his purse.

'I cannot. It is too valuable.'

'More valuable than your life?' Rob meant it rhetorically, but Bracewell nodded vigorously.

'You cannot—'

Rob cut him off with a mighty shove that dislodged Bracewell from the windowsill and sent him tumbling down onto the stable roof. His weight was too much for it. The roof collapsed, dropping Bracewell through. The straw inside must have broken his fall, for a moment later Rob saw him run out of the stable doors into the courtyard. Just in time. A moment later, the fire caught hold of the stable and set it ablaze.

It was spreading inside the house, too. Roof timbers crashed down in the room behind. Rob scrambled onto the window ledge. Scanning the courtyard, he saw a pile of straw heaped up in the middle of the courtyard. It was far enough from the stable that it had not yet caught fire, but it was also far from the window. Could he reach it?

He had no choice. He pushed off on the balls of his feet and leaped as far away from the building as he could. The ground rushed towards him. He braced himself.

Rob sailed through the air, over the yard, and landed on the pile of straw. It was thicker than he'd thought, cushioning the jarring impact. As his legs came up, he rolled away on his side so that the force of the landing dissipated through his shoulder, and came to rest.

He lay in the straw, testing his legs to see if he'd broken any bones. He had not realised that his shirt-tails were on fire. The straw smouldered underneath him, then burst into flame. Rob sprang up like a cat from a stove. He rolled on the cobblestones to try and put out the flames.

A cold, hard impact stung his body senseless. There was a hiss and a rush of steam. Rob opened his eyes and found himself lying soaked in a puddle. Sophie stood over him, holding a bucket. Her uncle stood beside her.

'We are not safe yet.'

Rob took Sophie's hand and led her through the gate with Bracewell and Crow. A crowd had gathered to watch the fire. Rob pushed through them and did not stop until they were a good distance away. The guns seemed to have ceased firing.

He was scorched, soaked, bruised and aching. But with Sophie's adoring eyes on him, he regretted very little of it.

'A night with you is a memorable experience,' he whispered to Sophie, as her uncle puffed up behind them.

'That is just the beginning,' she murmured in his ear, before putting on a demure face as her uncle arrived. He looked up at Rob admiringly.

'Well, Mr Courtney . . .'

'*Lieutenant* Courtney,' Sophie reminded him.

'This is the second occasion in as many weeks that you have saved me. That is quite a debt. I must find some way of repaying it soon, or the interest on it will ruin me.'

Sophie tapped her uncle's arm in mock indignation. 'You forget, Uncle, that Lieutenant Courtney has also saved *me* twice. I must find some way to reward our gallant lieutenant.'

Sophie smiled prettily. Rob felt himself blushing.

'The chance to be of service is its own best reward,' he said.

Sophie leaned in close to him. The scent of her perfume was strong, even above the smell of smoke and straw.

'I think we can do better than that.'

Cal Courtney was furious. When the guns opened fire that morning, it had been the sweetest moment of his life. The only happiness he had felt since Aidan died, a vindication of his death, and Moses', and everything Cal had done.

But after fifteen minutes, the artillery colonel had called a halt to the bombardment. They had knocked over a few walls, and the governor's house was burning, but otherwise they had barely touched the city's defences.

'We have made our point,' the colonel said. 'Now we will see how the British respond.'

Cal waited in a state of nervous anticipation. He desperately wanted the British to attack. Stumbling up that steep slope, with barrels full of stones rolling through them, they would be massacred. It would make the patriot victory complete.

But the British did not take the bait. They tried to bombard the ridge from their batteries across the bay, but their guns would not elevate high enough. The cannonballs struck harmlessly into the lower slopes, bouncing off the hard ground, and the attempt was quickly abandoned. A few scows filled with soldiers put out from Boston, but they returned when the wind rose. Otherwise, the British stayed within their defences.

'Let me put a few more shots into them, and see if that provokes them,' Cal begged. But his plea was ignored.

'General Washington does not wish to risk any more civilian deaths.'

'I did not drag these guns five hundred miles through bog and blizzard to see them sit idle!' Cal raged. He turned to his gunners. 'Open fire.'

'Belay that!' shouted the colonel. The gun crews stared uncertainly between the two officers. 'I will have you before the general for insubordination if you say one more word.'

'I will obey orders when Washington sends an officer fit to give them. You are nothing more than a well-connected stay maker.'

The colonel flushed. Before the war, he had been a *corsetier*, a maker of women's undergarments. He was mortified to be reminded of it.

'Apologise at once, or I will demand satisfaction.'

'I will give you more than satisfaction.'

Cal had no interest in the gentlemanly rules of duelling. In his anger, he would settle this the way the boys around the farm always had. He clenched his fist and drove it towards the colonel's jaw.

The colonel wasn't expecting it. He shied away, but that lowered his face, so instead of connecting with his jaw, the punch struck his nose. There was a crunch of cartilage, then a gush of warm blood over Cal's fist. It felt good. If he could not get at the British, at least he could take out his rage on the man who had stopped him. He drew back his fist for another blow.

Arms seized him from behind. However much the gunners sympathised with their captain, they could not stand by and let him beat a superior officer. Cal struggled against them, tearing out of their grasp. It took four men to hold him back.

The colonel rose, clutching a handkerchief to his face. Under the blood, his skin was chalk white. When he spoke, his voice was like a honking duck.

'At least on the duelling ground I would have given you a fair chance,' he said. 'Now it will be the hangman's noose.'

As Cal's anger cooled, he realised with sickening certainty that the colonel was right. General Washington loathed indiscipline. He would offer Cal no leniency for what he had done.

The colonel gestured to the men. 'Take him away.'

ob hired a waterman to row him out to the *Perseus*. He implored Bracewell and Sophie to come with him, for their own safety, but Bracewell refused.

'I must go to the general,' he said. 'I have urgent matters I must discuss with him.'

In the confusion of the morning, Rob hoped he would be able to slip aboard unnoticed. But Coyningham missed nothing. He was waiting for Rob at the top of the ladder.

'Lieutenant Courtney,' he sneered. 'Absent from your station once again when the battle starts. You should have returned much earlier, when the first shots were fired. What have you been up to? Wait until I inform Captain Tew.'

Rob controlled his temper. 'Tew gave me twenty-four hours' shore leave.'

'And did you use that time to become a chimney sweep?' Coyningham's eyes raked over Rob's appearance: his torn and charred clothes; no shoes or stockings; the soot that covered his face. 'Tew should have known better. You can make a man an officer, but you can never make him a gentleman.' He turned away. 'Wash yourself and change your clothes. If you were a common tar coming aboard in this state, I would give you a dozen lashes this instant.'

Rob cleaned himself up. He felt embarrassed at the way he had appeared in front of the men. He knew, as an officer, he should do better. Perhaps if he had been born to it, like Coyningham, he would have known what to do. At the same time, he had no regrets. He could still taste Sophie on his lips, feel the memory of his body inside hers.

'Who is she?' Angus asked, when they found themselves alone on deck.

Tew had been called to the flagship for a conference with the admiral, and the mood on the ship was anxious. Dorchester Heights was almost two miles away from the British anchorage, at the limit of the guns' range – but that did not stop the American gunners taking a few speculative shots at the fleet. Some balls fell in plumes of spray among the anchored ships. One shot a perfectly round hole through a sail that had been spread out to dry.

'Who is who?' Rob asked innocently.

Angus's face broke into a grin. 'You need to try better than that. I can smell the cunny on you. I bet the girls were lining up to feel the great hero's sword.'

Rob flushed. 'Even if I had, I would not tell—'

He broke off as a cry went up from the lookout. Tew's launch was returning from the flagship. His face was grim when he came aboard and summoned the officers to his cabin.

'The general has decided to abandon Boston,' he said without preamble. 'We cannot dislodge the Yankees from those heights, and we cannot defend the city against their guns. We will evacuate the troops and retreat to New York.'

Murmurs of dismay and disbelief sounded around the cabin. Boston was the most heavily fortified city in North America. If they could not hold it, nowhere was safe.

Rob's stomach clenched as he thought of Sophie. She had nowhere to go, and the American troops had besieged Boston for almost a year. He could imagine what they would do to her when they finally took possession of the city.

'What of the civilians?' he asked. 'There must be thousands of loyal subjects in Boston. What will happen to them?'

'We will do what we can,' said Tew curtly. 'We have an understanding with General Washington that he will allow us to retreat unmolested, if we leave the town intact. We will take as many loyalists as we can fit in our ships, once we have embarked the troops.'

Whatever the generals had agreed between themselves, the departing troops were in a savage mood, and they took it out on the city. The mood was near anarchy. The cannons were silent, but the city echoed with the sound of windows and doors being smashed, men shouting and women screaming. Homes were looted almost before the families had fled from them. The harbour was choked with the flotsam of items that had been discarded: furniture, barrels, barrows and clothes. Rob saw a gilded coach floating past like a half-sunk throne.

Every day, the long wharf was thronged with crowds desperate to get aboard the transports and men-of-war in the harbour. Winter had returned with a vengeance. Bitter winds whipped up the bay and lashed the refugees with stinging hail. Sometimes the guards had to push them back at the point of a bayonet. Safe aboard the *Perseus*, Rob felt like a coward. He scanned their faces through his telescope, afraid he would pick out Sophie among them yet also longing to see her. He could not bear to think of her in that chaos. Rob had given up on secrecy and told Angus about Sophie.

'She'll be fine,' said Angus. 'She's a girl that knows how to get looked after.'

But after a week with no word from Sophie, Rob could stand it no more. One night, under a half-moon, he stole on deck with a canvas bag filled with clothes. He stood on the gunwale, staring at the icy black water below. The ebbing tide pulled a river of junk past the hull.

'Cold night for a bath,' said Angus's voice behind him. Rob turned.

'I heard a knock against the hull. I thought it might be Yankees trying to cut us out.'

Angus put his hands on his hips. 'Is that so, sir?'

Rob dropped the pretence. 'I have to find her. I cannot stand thinking of her helpless in that city.'

'Six months ago, you were set fair to rot in a debtors' prison for the rest of your life. Now you are a lieutenant and a hero. Will you throw that away for a girl?'

'She is not just a girl,' said Rob angrily. 'I love her.'

It was a bold statement, but how else to explain why he could not stop thinking of her, dreaming of her; the way he trembled at the memory of her? He had only read about love in books, but he was sure this must be it.

'You're eighteen, Rob. What you ken about women . . .' Angus snorted. 'Maybe she gave you a night like no other. But that's your jock talking. You dinnae ken what real love is.'

'You have no idea how I feel for her.'

'Tender feelings won't save you from the noose if they hang you as a deserter. D'you want to give Coyningham that chance?'

Rob jumped onto the gunwale. In his anger, he would have leaped into the water that moment. But through the darkness, he heard the splash of oars, and a dim light approaching.

Instantly, he was on high alert.

'Who goes there?' he called.

'Ship ahoy,' came the reply. 'Boat from the flagship, with passengers for the *Perseus*.'

A small vessel came against the ship's side. The boatman held up his lantern, revealing three passengers huddled in boat cloaks in the prow. One was short and stout, his face covered by a broad-brimmed hat. The second was so stocky he looked like a mountain under his cloak. But the third was slender and poised, with a scarf tied over her long raven hair. She looked up, and their eyes met. Sophie.

Rob stared. 'Am I dreaming?' he said to Angus. 'The gods must be smiling on me.'

He looked up to the heavens and raised his arms as if in supplication.

Angus rubbed his eyes. 'That, or you have the luck of the Devil himself.'

'What is this?' Coyningham's voice broke the spell. He had arrived on deck unseen. Rob wondered if he ever slept. He had an unerring instinct for finding Rob, whatever the hour.

'Hezekiah Bracewell!' Sophie's father shouted up from the boat. 'We have orders from the admiral. We are to come aboard and take passage on your ship.'

Coyningham shot Rob a suspicious look, as if he suspected a plot. But he roused the watch and had them rig the boatswain's chair, a canvas seat suspended on ropes for those who would not brave climbing the ship's ladder.

They hoisted Bracewell aboard like a sack of potatoes.

'This is most irregular,' sniffed Coyningham. 'Stealing aboard in the dead of night.'

'Do you wish to consult with the admiral?' Bracewell retorted. 'Here are my credentials.'

He handed Coyningham an oilskin packet.

But Coyningham did not take it. At that moment, Sophie rose over the side of the ship. In her elegant white dress, hands folded in her lap and skin glowing gold in the lamplight, she looked like an angel hovering in mid-air.

Coyningham stared, his mouth open.

He shook himself and turned to the crew.

'Do not leave Miss Bracewell hanging there. Bring her aboard this instant or I will have the hide off your backs.'

The sailors hoisted the chair over the side and lowered Sophie to the deck. She stepped off, swaying as if she might faint with the unfamiliar rocking of the ship. Coyningham hurried to her and took her arm.

'Thank you, Lieutenant,' she said with a smile that tore Rob's heart.

'Let me show you to your quarters,' said Coyningham. 'You may have my cabin.'

'That will not be necessary,' said Bracewell. 'I am sure when the captain learns we are aboard he will insist on giving up his own cabin.'

Coyningham swallowed. 'Of course. I will inform him at once.'

He led Bracewell and Sophie aft, leaving Rob and Angus amid the baggage that was being hoisted aboard. For refugees fleeing an abandoned city, the Bracewells had brought a good pile of possessions.

Watching Coyningham take Sophie's elbow and steer her around a coiled rope on deck, Rob was tempted to grab a pike from the racks around the mast and run the first lieutenant through. He had spent a week dreaming of Sophie; been willing to risk everything for her. And now she was aboard and Coyningham had taken her out of his reach.

Sophie glanced back. The half-moon lit up her face, so Rob could see every detail of her exquisite features.

She caught his gaze and held it. She formed her lips in a silent kiss.

Rob started to breathe again. She still loved him. Sophie disappeared through the door, but he held the image of that last kiss like a portrait embedded in his mind.

'Don't get no ideas,' said a rough voice in his ear. Crow, Bracewell's clerk, had clambered aboard unnoticed. The look on his face said he had read Rob's thoughts all too clearly. 'Miss Sophie's not for the likes of you.'

Before Rob could respond, Crow spun away to supervise the stowing of Bracewell's baggage. Rob let him go. He would not be intimidated.

'There'll be trouble,' said Angus darkly. 'Do'nae go fighting the Bloodhound for Miss Sophie's affections.'

'She would never so much as look at him.'

Angus gave him a sideways glance. He was about to say something, and then changed his mind. For all his maturity and rank, Rob was still a teenager in the full flower of lust. There were some things he would not hear.

'Bad luck having a woman aboard ship,' was all Angus said.

The *Perseus* set sail next morning, peppered with sleet and hail. Bracewell, Sophie and Crow were the only passengers. Looking back as they sailed out of Boston harbour, Rob saw hundreds of wan figures still huddled on the docks, desperately hoping to be taken away before the rebels took the city. He wondered what power Bracewell had that he could persuade the admiral to let him commandeer the frigate, when the situation was so dire.

'We are sailing south,' Tew informed his officers.

He was in a bad humour. He was unimpressed by the new orders Bracewell had brought, and at having to give up his cabin to the new arrivals. Tew had moved into Coyningham's cabin, Coyningham into the second lieutenant's, and the second lieutenant – a jovial fellow named Fawcett – into the cabin that should have been Rob's. Rob, as the most junior officer, had been sent to mess with the midshipmen, a fact Coyningham had taken particular pleasure in. It put Rob further away from Sophie, while Coyningham slept beneath her.

'We are no longer heading for New York,' Tew continued. 'We are bound for Jamaica. It seems Mr Bracewell has an errand there which is of the utmost important to the war. The admiral has ordered me to put my ship at Mr Bracewell's disposal, and render him every assistance.' He didn't bother to hide the scepticism in his voice.

He spread a chart on the table, plotting the route they would take. Rob barely noticed. He was thinking of the voyage ahead. Eight weeks at sea, at least, aboard ship with Sophie. He was certain they would find some way to snatch a few moments away from her uncle, and from Coyningham's jealous eyes. Thinking about it made his loins stiffen in anticipation.

Tew rolled up the map and surveyed his officers.

'Let us hope for a calm and pleasant voyage.'

Standing outside a tent in the Continental Army's camp, Cal Courtney watched the frigate sail out past Governor's Island. He was surprised to see her leaving. The rest of the British fleet was still at anchor, still taking on passengers and supplies from the boats that bustled around the wharves. He wondered why this solitary ship had been allowed to leave so soon. Where would she go? Rumours were rife that the next British assault would fall on New York City. Cal desperately wanted to be there.

That was a foolish hope. The only action he would see now would be a court martial hearing, for striking a superior officer. The knowledge left a void inside him. He cursed himself for not being able to control his impulsive temper. His father had often warned him it would ruin him, and that stung even more.

How could he honour Aidan's memory if he could not fight?

A head poked out of the tent.

'The general will receive you.'

Two sentries escorted Cal. His hands chafed in the manacles he wore but he stood proud, more like a hero than a prisoner. He stared defiantly at the general sitting behind his desk.

The general studied him curiously. He had stern grey eyes, and grey hair tied back in a queue. He wore a simple blue coat, without any insignia of rank. He was a handsome man, though his jaw protruded slightly from the false teeth he wore.

'Mr Courtney,' he said in his soft Virginia drawl. 'The hero of the hour.'

He spoke so calmly, Cal could not be sure if he was being sarcastic. Cal said nothing.

'What am I to do with a man who can bring guns across a wilderness that all agreed was impassable, who opens up a city that everyone said was invincible, yet who cannot keep his discipline in the hour of his triumph?' the general mused.

'We Courtneys have always struggled with authority,' Cal told him.

'Indeed.'

Many times, Cal had seen the general stand as solid as a rock, but now he seemed uncharacteristically hesitant.

'This is not an easy army to lead. You may be an extreme case, Mr Courtney, but none of you New Englanders takes well to authority. Colonel Duffield insists I should cashier you, or every man in the Continental Army will think it is his right to assault his superiors.'

He rubbed his jaw, where his false teeth were uncomfortable.

'Why did you attack the colonel?'

'It was rank cowardice to stop the bombardment so soon,' said Cal. 'If we had continued, we could have sunk the British fleet, captured their army and won the war in an afternoon.'

The general smiled. 'If only it could be so. But we would have had to destroy Boston to achieve it. The British are dug in like termites – and they have many armies. I only have one with which to defend America. I cannot afford to waste thousands of lives in a vainglorious assault – or to antagonise the Massachusetts representatives in the Continental Congress.'

'I cannot agree, sir.'

'You hate the British.'

'They killed my brother.' Cal raised his hands, shaking the chains so they jangled. 'All I want is a chance to avenge him. Take off these manacles, give me a gun and I will risk any hardship for a chance.'

'So I see,' said the general.

He thought for a while.

'I cannot keep you here,' he said at last. 'We are trying to forge a professional army out of a rabble, and I cannot sanction indiscipline.'

Cal stiffened. He had half expected this – the general was a stern disciplinarian – but even so he felt betrayed.

'There cannot be a scandal,' the general went on.

'I will resign.'

Cal could go into the wilderness, maybe join some of the Indian tribes who were fighting with the rebels. But the general was shaking his head.

'I have a different task for you. One that will allow you to keep your rank, and maybe even burnish your laurels.'

Cal found himself daring to hope again.

'A French frigate, the *Rapace*, is patrolling off the coast. France has not yet entered the war, so she is sailing under a letter of marque, as a privateer. It is inconvenient to King Louis that a ship sailing under the American flag should be crewed entirely by Frenchmen. He wishes to maintain a pretence of neutrality, at least for the moment. He has asked for a representative from our army to go aboard as nominal commander and assist with their operations.'

He leaned forwards. 'However many sieges and battles we win, we will never defeat the British on land. While they control the seas, they will evacuate their armies, and move them to attack us in another place. We have to beat them at sea to win this war.'

Cal knew he was being offered a reprieve, but he could not be bothered to feign gratitude.

'I know nothing about fighting at sea,' he protested. 'I will not let you exile me to count seagulls in the middle of the ocean just to protect a colonel's dignity.'

The general pursed his lips. He was a patient man, but to those who defied his decisions he could be an implacable enemy.

'You will learn the style of fighting soon enough. A cannon fires just the same at sea. And if you think I am sending you away from the action, you are mistaken. The privateer is to sail on a mission of the utmost secrecy. If you succeed, you will turn this war decisively in our favour. You will have your fill of glory. You will also be entitled to a one-eighth share of all prize money for the vessels she captures.'

The general noted the light that came on in Cal's eyes when he mentioned the money. Honour and duty were all very well, but like any young man he needed to make his way in the world.

'This ship is a man-of-war in all but name. She will tear through the British shipping like a fox through a hen house. In six months, you could clear one hundred thousand pounds.'

Cal's cheeks had flushed red. He wasn't a mercenary man. He was doing this for his brother, and for the cause of liberty. Yet the thought of such a fortune kindled something different in him. The fight he had had with his father after Aidan's death still stung. His father had called him a traitor to the family; he had cut Cal off without a penny. How sweet it would be to return in triumph, driving up to the farmhouse in his own carriage. He had sacrificed so much: he deserved something in return.

'I will go,' he said.

The general allowed himself a smile. He was a shrewd judge of character, and he had the measure of his man now. He handed him a sealed letter.

'These are your orders. Do not open them until you are at sea. When you see the mission I am entrusting to you, and the opportunities it affords, you will thank me for it.'

'Yes, sir.'

The general stood. 'I have no doubt you will succeed, Mr Courtney. There is something inside you that will not let you fail.'

Cal rendezvoused with the frigate at Newport. The *Rapace* had anchored well outside the harbour, which was still blocked with the black skeletons of the burned fleet. From the launch that carried him out, Cal studied the ship intently. He was determined to master this new domain of war, and he wanted to understand everything about her.

The boat came alongside the frigate. The lieutenant in the launch gestured Cal to get in the boatswain's chair that was lowered. Cal pushed it away and started to climb the wooden rungs set in the ship's hull. He would not be hoisted aboard like cargo.

The crew were assembled on deck. Cal could hardly help staring. Everything about them looked as if it had been measured against a ruler. They stood in perfect rows, their backs as straight as the creases pressed into their trousers. Every uniform was spotless, nothing out of place. It made a change from the ragged Continental Army, where it was rare to find two men wearing the same colour coat.

A young officer stepped forwards and offered a crisp salute. He wore red stockings, red breeches, a red waistcoat and blue coat embroidered with anchors on the cuffs. Cal bristled with indignation. The boy was no older than he was. Was the captain trying to humiliate him by having this junior lieutenant greet him in front of all the men?

'Where is the captain?' he snapped.

The officer bowed stiffly; but his face was charged with anger.

'I am the Chevalier Étienne de Bercheny, and I have the honour to be the captain of this ship.'

'I was expecting someone older.'

'So was I,' answered Étienne.

Their eyes locked. Two young men with all the pride and arrogance of youth. Both fighters and killers, both used to having command, each jealous of his honour. Cal's hand moved instinctively to the pistol in his belt, while Étienne reached for the hilt of his sword. In that moment, it would only have taken a twitch of a muscle for them to call each other out to a duel.

But as they looked at each other, the tension changed. Apart from their height, they could hardly have looked more different. Cal, with his thick red hair and strong face; Étienne, blond-haired and pale skinned, with the fine features of an angel. Yet in Étienne's eyes, Cal saw something familiar, like meeting an old friend. And he could see from the change in Étienne's face that he had recognised it, too, in Cal. More than the kinship of two warriors, more than a common hatred of the British. Something profound, as if they had known each other in a past life.

Both men were too wary to drop their guard completely. But they relaxed fractionally. Cal offered his hand, and Étienne shook it.

'I think we have something in common,' he said, in heavily accented English.

'*Oui?*' A number of tutors had attempted to teach or beat French into Cal, but he had never had the patience for it. 'What is that?'

'We both like killing Englishmen.'

Cal gave a hearty laugh. 'Then we will get along famously.'

'Where shall we start?'

'I have orders.'

Cal took out the packet he'd been given. The general had told him not to unseal it until he was at sea, but Cal had been too impatient to wait. He'd torn it open the moment he got back to his tent. He had read it with mounting amazement, astonished by the audacity of the mission. By the time he finished, any doubts he'd had about accepting the assignment had vanished.

'We are to sail to the West Indies,' Cal told Étienne.

'But the British fleet is in Boston,' protested Étienne. 'If we go to the Caribbean, we will lose our chance to engage them.'

'In the Indies, we will hurt the British more than anything we could do here. Besides,' Cal added, 'not all the British ships are in Boston. Three days ago I saw a frigate slip away.'

Étienne's jaw tightened. 'Did you see her name?'

'The *Perseus*.'

'Three days,' Étienne mused. 'She could be anywhere by now.'

'She could,' Cal agreed, with a wolfish grin. 'But we have many spies in Boston. Now that the British are evacuating, suddenly everyone is a patriot. It is said that the *Perseus* carries information vital to the war. And she is bound for Jamaica.'

Étienne took a deep breath. The fight with the British frigate had been his first battle. The fact that his prey had escaped was an intolerable insult to his pride. Now he had the chance to avenge it.

'I shall set course for the West Indies at once, *monsieur*.'

The temperature rose as the *Perseus* travelled south. She had left Boston in a blizzard of hail and sailed into a three-day storm, but now she cruised under blue skies. Officers abandoned their coats and stood the watches in their shirtsleeves.

It was not just the sun that warmed the atmosphere aboard ship. Sophie Bracewell's presence had the men simmering. Captain Tew rigged an awning over the quarterdeck, so that Sophie and her uncle could sit out in the shade. Bracewell often kept to his cabin, but Sophie was out every morning, sitting in a chair with a book or her embroidery. The men on the ship could not take their eyes off her. Sophie seemed unaware. She sat quietly, her head tilted to one side, lips parted in concentration, a stray lock of hair hanging down over her cheek.

The men could look, and dream, but they knew she was out of their reach. It was different for Rob. He could not forget that night he had spent with her, the touch of her skin and the feeling of her body around his. Going about his duties on deck, watching every other man on the ship staring at her, was torment. Sometimes she would look up from her reading and catch his eye, with a smile, and then the desire would almost burst from him. Sometimes she ignored him, and Rob would descend into a black and sullen mood.

'You are like a dog in heat,' said Angus. 'You need to bend that wench over the capstan and have done with her, or you'll burst your breeches with lust.'

Rob's promotion had not changed their friendship. In front of the other men, Angus was a model of respect. In private, he was as forthright as ever.

'You do not understand,' said Rob.

He was certain it was love. But he also knew Angus had a point. He was young and impulsive, eager to taste again the forbidden fruits that Sophie offered him, driven by a craving he could barely contain. He had to find a way to get Sophie alone.

It was hard on a ship where you were never more than three feet away from another man. It was harder with Sophie sleeping in the great cabin with her uncle. Most difficult of all was their travelling companion, Crow. He was a menacing presence. Half his teeth were missing, and the rest were rotted black. He kept a cone of sugar in his pocket, from which he would snap off crumbs and crunch them noisily. He followed Sophie like a vulture stalking a wounded gazelle. When she came on deck, he took up position at the rail, glowering at any man who came close. When she went in, he padded after her. At night, he slept on deck in front of the cabin door like a faithful hound.

One day, he caught Rob stealing a glance at Sophie. The look he gave him was filled with such malice even Rob shivered. But he was determined to get past him.

A week out of Boston, Bracewell invited the officers to dinner. Tew was in a bad humour, being hosted in his own cabin; the rest of the officers were glad of the opportunity to talk and flirt with Sophie. Crow served the food.

'How do you find life aboard ship, Miss Bracewell?' asked Fawcett, the second lieutenant. 'We must seem terribly uncouth after Boston society.'

'Gentlemen bore me.' Sophie had arranged the seating so that she was next to Rob. 'I prefer the company of men of action.'

'I trust one can be both,' said Coyningham.

He was seated on Sophie's other side, sitting stiffly. He barely touched his food. It was plain to every man on the ship that he had set his heart on Sophie – and equally plain that she had no regard for him. He was almost pathetic to watch on the quarterdeck. If her handkerchief blew away, he would retrieve it; if she so much as mentioned the heat, he would fetch her a fan. Yet she rarely looked at him.

'May we enquire as to the nature of your errand in Jamaica?' asked one of the midshipmen, a fat youth named Brompton. 'Or is it confidential?'

'It is entirely confidential,' said Bracewell. Then he winked. 'But I may say it goes to the very heart of our campaign in America.'

'Then we are sailing the wrong way,' said Fawcett, to widespread mirth. He pointed through the stern windows, back at the *Perseus*'s wake. 'America is that way.'

'The war will not be won in America,' Bracewell told him. 'It will be won in the Caribbean.'

'There is no fighting in the Caribbean, so far as I have heard,' said Tew.

'Yet it is indispensable to the war.' Bracewell slapped the table, rattling the crockery and slopping wine from his glass. 'This ship – its sails and ropes, its guns, its timbers – d'you know where they came from?'

'Chatham dockyard,' said Tew.

'Sugar. This whole war is paid for with sugar. Every button on your uniform, every grain of gunpowder, every stitch of canvas on every ship.'

'I prefer to be paid in guineas,' said Brompton.

More laughter, but Bracewell did not join in.

'Do you know how much the government pays to keep even one ship afloat, or one battalion in the field? Now multiply that by all the ships in the navy, all the regiments in the army, and you have some idea of what it costs. No government can afford that from its revenues.'

'We still get paid,' said Fawcett.

'Because the government borrows the money,' Bracewell expounded, with the ardour of the true enthusiast. 'So long as the ministry can levy taxes on sugar imports to repay its debts, London's bankers will lend them almost unlimited funds.'

Rob shivered. He had not forgotten his own encounter with London's bankers. He knew at first hand how ready they were to advance money – and what they wanted in return.

'Surely that makes the government beholden to the bankers?'

Bracewell gave him an indulgent smile, baring his wine-stained lips.

'Every man is a creature of his creditors. That is the first rule of life.'

A question occurred to Rob.

'Is Baron Dartmouth part of the ministry?' he asked, as innocently as possible.

'Baron Dartmouth is a great friend of mine,' boasted Bracewell. 'He serves as President of the Board of Trade and Foreign Plantations.'

'Have you known him long?' Coyningham asked.

'Since he was plain Sir Christopher Courtney. He was a director of the East India Company, then governor-general in Calcutta. He made a fortune in India before returning to London. He has been a staunch ally of the sugar interest.'

'Courtney?' Sophie's ears had pricked up at the name. 'Why, do you think he can be related to our gallant Lieutenant Courtney?'

Amused laughter rippled around the table. Rob forced himself to join in, though inside his mind was racing.

'Was Dartmouth's father also eminent?'

'Indeed. He was Sir Guy Courtney, Consul General to the Orient.'

Rob had half expected it. Yet at the sound of that dreaded name, he flinched. His fork dropped out of his hand with a clatter, bounced off the plate and fell to the floor.

All eyes turned to him. Quickly, Rob bent down to pick up the fork. It gave him time to steady himself. Since his earliest childhood, Guy Courtney had been a name second only to the Devil in the terror and loathing it conjured, enough to give Rob nightmares. Guy had brought Zayn al-Din's murderous forces to Nativity Bay to attack Fort Auspice. Guy had held a dagger to Rob's father's throat when George was but three years old. And Baron Dartmouth, the author of all Rob's misfortunes, was his son.

Everything that had happened in London – the loan, the fire, the sword, the sense that Rob was in the grip of some invisible and implacable foe – suddenly made terrible sense.

By the time Rob straightened up, he had composed his emotions. But he found Bracewell giving him a ferocious look, staring at him with outright suspicion.

'You seem very interested in Baron Dartmouth. Are you certain you are not related.'

'He would hardly be drawing a lieutenant's pay if he were related to one of the richest men in England,' said Sophie.

The other officers laughed; the conversation moved on. Rob tried not to look at Bracewell. But he felt the man's gaze upon him under knitted eyebrows.

When the port had gone around, Bracewell wiped his mouth with his napkin.

'There is a matter I wish to raise with you, Captain. I believe our course will take us past the coast of the Carolinas?'

Tew nodded warily.

'There is an inlet on the coast of South Carolina, a place called Seabrook Bay. You know it?'

'I have seen it on the charts.'

'I would be obliged if you would call in there. I have an estate a little inland, and it is imperative I visit it to recover some valuable property.'

Tew frowned. 'My orders are to take you to Jamaica with all dispatch. We have already lost too much time.'

A day out of Boston, the *Perseus* had lost her topmast in a winter gale. It had taken the best part of three days to repair it.

'Your orders are to put your ship at my disposal.' Bracewell jabbed his finger at Tew, almost knocking over the decanter. His voice had turned ugly. 'I insist you do as I command.'

'It will delay our arrival in Jamaica,' Tew answered. 'And the South Carolina coast is in rebel hands, crawling with their privateers. Even if we reached the anchorage, there is no guarantee that you would get to your house safely.'

'Then it is lucky we have so many *men of action* aboard,' said Bracewell emphatically.

While they argued, Sophie's chair had slid imperceptibly towards Rob's. She opened her legs a little, so that her thigh pressed against his. Rob crooked his foot behind her ankle, working his way up her calf.

The port came around again. Rob had not forgotten the shock of the news about Baron Dartmouth. But Dartmouth was thousands of miles away in London. With a bellyful of wine, and Sophie's flesh warm against him, he had more immediate needs to satisfy.

'Very well.' At the end of the table, Tew had conceded defeat to Bracewell. 'I must obey your orders. But I will record in the logbook that it was against my better judgement.'

'I am not interested in your judgement,' said Bracewell. Too much wine had made him bilious. 'If you confine yourself to navigating me where I need to go, that will suffice.'

Tew coloured. All the officers, even Coyningham, stiffened. To insult a captain on his own ship, in his own cabin, was an unthinkable offence.

But there was nothing Tew could do. He stood.

'Thank you for your hospitality, Mr Bracewell.' He nodded to Sophie. 'Miss Bracewell. I bid you goodnight.'

The officers paid their respects and filed out after him. As Rob pushed back his chair, he felt something poking in his ribs. When he looked down, he saw that Sophie had jammed a small folded piece of paper into his waistcoat.

'Wait for me tonight,' he read, when he got back to his cabin.

When the midshipmen he bunked with were asleep in their cots, Rob stayed awake, fully dressed. He knew he should be thinking about Christopher Courtney, about what Bracewell's news meant and how he would get the Neptune sword back. Yet his thoughts always slid back to Sophie.

There was a knock at the door. Rob jumped up and opened it. Sophie was waiting impatiently in a thin nightgown and shawl.

She kissed him urgently, biting his lip so hard he tasted blood. She peered behind him at the snoring midshipmen.

'Is there somewhere more intimate we can go?'

There were not many private places on a hundred-foot ship, but Rob had given the problem considerable thought. Lighting their way with a lantern, he led her along the passage, down another ladder to the lower deck. Further forward, a small door opened into a space at the bow where they stored ropes. The heavy anchor cable lay in coils like a great sleeping serpent, while lesser lines were stacked neatly around it.

Rob spread the blanket he had brought on the planking.

'I thought this would be more comfortable.'

'Love does not always have to be comfortable.' Sophie looked at the coils of rope. 'I have heard in the navy you flog the men?'

'Sometimes it is necessary. But what has that to do with love?'

'Have you ever done it yourself?'

Rob shook his head. 'That is for the boatswain's mates.'

'But you have seen it done?'

Rob nodded.

'Show me,' she commanded.

She stretched up her arms and pulled her nightgown over her head. Underneath, she was naked. Her hair hung over her breasts, and her skin glowed in the lamplight. She ignored the blanket, but kneeled on the floor and leaned forwards, hugging her body against the thick hawser.

Uncertainly, Rob took a short rope from a bucket of stray ends. He slapped it gently across her back. Sophie barely flinched.

'Harder,' she commanded.

Rob tried again. This time, he left a pale red streak over her skin.

'Harder,' she said again. 'Hurt me.'

Rob did not understand. But there was a hypnotic tone in her voice that he could not disobey. Tensing his arm, he brought the rope down with force. A livid red welt rose across her back that made Sophie catch her breath. She gave a gasp, though Rob could not tell if it was pleasure or pain.

'Again.'

Rob obeyed. The harder he struck, the more Sophie seemed to delight in it. She moaned, softly at first but with ever greater intensity. She opened her mouth and bit down on the rope in front of her to muffle the noise. She arced her back, twisting this way and that. Soon there was a pattern of red welts crisscrossing her back, though Rob was careful not to break the skin. Her moans rose to a crescendo.

At last they died away to a whimper. Sophie raised herself and turned to him. Her breasts were covered in sweat, while the hair between her thighs glistened dewy wet.

She reached out and took the rope end from Rob. She swished it experimentally through the air.

'Undress,' she ordered him.

Rob did as he was told. She reached out with her free hand, cupping his manhood, teasing and stretching it. She leaned in close, letting her nipples rub against his chest as she reached behind him.

He felt the tickle of the rope end as she ran it down his back. The candlelight reflected two flames in her eyes.

'Now it is my turn.'

Rob woke late next morning. The welts Sophie had left throbbed on his back. He had to wait until the midshipmen had gone on deck before he rolled out of his cot for fear they would see the marks. He pulled on his shirt quickly, still smarting with the memory of it. Yet when he went on deck, Sophie was in her usual seat under the awning, working at her embroidery under Crow's watchful gaze. Rob tipped his hat to her but she pretended not to notice.

'What does she mean by it?' he thought in anguish. Angus noticed it, too.

'Have you done something to upset Miss Bracewell?'

Rob tried to keep an impassive face, but he was not old enough to keep from blushing. Angus saw it in an instant.

'You had her,' Angus deduced. 'You canny devil.'

'But this morning she will not look at me.'

Angus burst into laughter at the sorry look on Rob's face.

'She's testing you,' he explained. 'She does not want you to think you can have her too easy.'

Two can play at that game, Rob thought.

For the rest of the morning, he acted as if Sophie did not exist. He kept his attention on his men, taking unusual interest in their work. When he had to cross the quarterdeck, he gave Sophie a wide berth. It took an enormous effort of will not to look at her. Visions of the night before kept forcing themselves in front of his eyes. He didn't dare glance to see if his behaviour was having an effect on her. He knew her catlike instinct would catch him in an instant.

A warm breeze came up in the afternoon. Sophie's nimble hands worked deftly at her embroidery. Suddenly, she gave a cry. She had pricked her finger on her needle, and in her surprise she had let go of the embroidery. The wind lifted it from her lap and blew it over the rail.

Before it disappeared into the ocean, a firm hand snatched it out of mid-air. Coyningham crossed the deck and handed it back to Sophie. He bowed.

Sophie looked at him, eyes shining with gratitude. She held the fabric to her bosom.

'Thank you,' she breathed. 'I have spent so many hours at this, I would have been quite desolate to lose it now. Truly, love conquers all.'

Coyningham flushed. 'I beg your pardon?'

Sophie smoothed out the embroidery and held it up. Stitched across the centre was the Latin motto *Amor Vincit Omnia*: Love conquers all.

A sickly smile spread over Coyningham's face.

'I am glad I could be of service.'

There was still a drop of blood on Sophie's finger. She put it in her mouth and sucked the fingertip, rolling it around between her moist lips.

'You can be sure of my gratitude, Lieutenant.'

Tew's voice interrupted their moment. 'If you are finished, Lieutenant, it is past time for exercising the guns.'

Coyningham tipped his hat and bowed again. As he passed Rob, he shot him a look of triumph.

'Do not get ideas above your station,' he said.

That night, Rob went to the rope store again. He did not know if Sophie would come, but his body was so hungry for her he would have tried anything. He waited an age, while the lamp burned low. Lustful thoughts of Sophie and jealous thoughts of Coyningham mingled in his head until they almost drove him mad. What if she had rejected Rob? What if she was even now in Coyningham's cabin, squeezing him between those exquisite thighs. What if—?

He snapped out of his reverie as he heard the light tread of feet on the planks outside. Sophie crept in, dressed in her thin nightdress. Rob marvelled at her ability to creep about the ship, past Crow, without being detected. He wondered where she had learned such skills.

He went to embrace her. But Sophie pulled back and gave him a stinging slap across his cheek.

'What were you doing today?' she demanded. 'You did not look at me once. Did you think that now you have had me, you could treat me like a common whore?'

'Me?' said Rob, astonished. 'You treated me as if I did not exist.'

Tears came into her eyes. 'How could I? Do you think it is easy, sitting there every day with Crow watching like a jailer? Do you know what my uncle would have him do to me, if he knew what we have done?'

Rob felt a stir of guilt. 'What about your conversation with Coyningham?'

'Coyningham means nothing to me. He is so forlorn, so hopeless. I took pity on him. Will you hate me for that?' She stamped her foot in frustration. 'But you! If I gave one inkling of my feelings for you . . .'

She buried her head in her hands, her dark hair falling over her face.

'I am sorry,' said Rob. 'I will not do it again.'

She looked up. She was smiling. Her eyes gleamed in the light of the little horn lantern that burned behind the glass.

'I forgive you,' she said, pulling her nightdress over her head.

'Thank you.'

'But you will still have to be punished.'

The next day, Tew posted double lookouts at the mast-heads, and rotated them every two hours. Once, there was a rumour of a sail on the horizon, but it did not appear again. Every man was on edge. The crew could see the captain did not like this detour to South Carolina, playing Bracewell's errand boy, and his mood infected them all.

The heat rose further as they approached the Carolina shore. The sun had disappeared. Grey clouds pressed down on them, making the atmosphere hot and clammy. It reminded Rob of Christmas time at home in Nativity Bay, the humidity building as they waited for the January rains. At his first sight of land, the memory became more vivid still. The low-lying shore, fringed with mangrove swamps and muddy islets, could have been Africa. It made him think of his family. What were they doing now? Would they be down on the beach, skimming stones over the bay and watching for Rob's return? Had they forgiven him?

He wanted to go back. He wanted to take Sophie, to introduce her to his sister and show her off to his father. He wanted her to understand where he had come from, the soil of Africa where he was rooted.

But he could not go back without the Neptune sword. Now that he knew who Baron Dartmouth really was, he was more determined than ever to get it back.

'Penny for your thoughts, sir?' murmured Angus beside him.

Rob smiled sheepishly. 'I was thinking of home.'

'Mr Courtney.' Tew's voice carried the length of the ship, summoning him to the quarterdeck. 'A word, if you please.'

Rob joined him by the chart table. All the officers were assembled. Bracewell was there, but Sophie had kept to her cabin that morning. Rob wondered if she was aching as much as he was.

'Seabrook Bay is a maze of islets and swamps,' said Tew, sweeping his hand over the chart. 'Even at high tide, we will struggle to get close to shore. At low tide, we risk running aground.'

'If we were stranded, we would be sitting ducks for any rebels in the area,' said Fawcett, the second lieutenant.

Tew nodded. 'Precisely. We will enter the bay as the tide is rising. From then, Mr Bracewell, you will have six hours to reach your house, retrieve your property and return to the ship before we weigh anchor.'

'What is the nature of this property?' asked Rob. 'Is it heavy?'

'A strongbox,' said Bracewell. 'Also, some servants of mine will be returning.'

Tew's face flashed with annoyance at the thought of more passengers being brought aboard his ship. He knew better than to argue with Bracewell.

'I will lead the expedition,' Rob volunteered.

He was hungry for action, and eager to prove himself again to Sophie and her uncle.

'Lieutenant Courtney, always eager to hog the glory,' sneered Coyningham. 'As first lieutenant, I should have the command.'

'Indeed,' said Tew. 'However, Lieutenant Courtney will go as second in command.'

'Is that necessary?' protested Coyningham. 'Surely you will need Lieutenant Courtney aboard ship.'

'My decision is final.'

'My secretary, Crow, will accompany you,' said Bracewell. 'He can show you the way.'

There was a loud crack behind them as Crow bit off a piece of sugar. Rob hadn't heard him arrive. He crunched the sugar between his few remaining teeth, spittle running down his chin. With a brace of pistols tucked into his belt, he could have been taken for a pirate.

As they made the final preparations, Tew took Rob to one side.

'You know that the governor has issued a proclamation to free any loyal slaves?' He handed Rob a stack of papers. 'These are certificates which vouch for their freedom. Give them to any slave you see.'

Rob looked at his captain in surprise. This was not part of their orders.

'Why, sir?'

Tew looked almost embarrassed. 'Slavery is abhorrent,' he said simply. He turned away, as if afraid of letting Rob see his emotion. 'If there is anything we can do to help those poor souls, we should.'

'You can rely on me, sir.'

They set out in two boats, Coyningham in one and Rob in the other. Crow directed them through the shoals and mudbanks, into the mouth of a river that disgorged into the bay. It was an eerie place. In the distance, a few fishermen dug in the mud for shellfish. Through the trees that lined the riverbank, Rob caught glimpses of grand houses standing among green lawns. Sometimes the forest gave way to great open rice fields, connected to the river by sluice gates. Yet no one was at work, and weeds sprouted in the fields.

'What has happened?' Rob wondered.

Crow gave him an evil grin. 'The governor said the slaves could go free if they'd fight for England. Half of 'em ran, and them what stayed was locked up so they couldn't follow the others.'

Rob tried to make sense of it.

'So the rebels who are fighting for liberty wish to keep slaves – and the British king who they claim will enslave them has actually freed the slaves.'

Crow looked confused. 'Man's got a liberty to keep slaves,' he said. 'Or what's the world come to?'

Before Rob could reply, Crow pointed to a wooden landing stage protruding from the riverbank.

'This is the place.'

They rowed in and tied up the boats. Rob checked the pocket watch he had borrowed from Fawcett. Two hours had passed already.

'How far to the house?'

'Four miles,' said Crow.

An hour there, an hour back. It would be close.

'We have no time to lose.'

They set off at a fast pace down a track through the forest. The men bunched close to each other. On land, sailors and marines were like fish out of water. They looked around uneasily, brandishing their weapons at every sound.

Bushes rustled in the road to their right. Instinctively, one of the marines raised his musket and fired. There was a scream. To Rob's horror, three black women stumbled out of the undergrowth. They raised their hands in surrender.

'Don't shoot,' they pleaded. 'We loyal. We loyal.'

Crow drew his pistol and aimed it at them.

'Like hell you are. Runaways, more like.'

Their leader dropped to her knees. She wore a short white shift, torn and stained by the forest.

'We ain't runaways. King George set us free.'

'King George has no interest in you,' said Coyningham curtly. 'And we do not have time to delay.' He turned to the marine lieutenant. 'March on.'

Before he could move, the woman threw her arms around his legs.

'Please, sir,' she begged. 'We gonna starve in the forest. An' there's rebel troops up that road, horses and guns and everything.'

Coyningham kicked her aside. 'Get out of my way.'

'Wait.' Rob crouched beside her. He gave her his handkerchief to wipe her face. 'Is it true there are rebel forces ahead?'

She nodded, her eyes round and white with fear. 'Hundreds of 'em, on the march from Charleston.'

'And they have cannon?'

'Yes, sir.'

'Where are they?'

She raised her hand and pointed up the track. Then, slowly, she swept her arm around in an almost complete circle.

'Everywhere?'

She nodded.

Rob lifted her to her feet.

'Go down to the bay,' he told her. 'There is an English ship there. If you can reach it, her captain will give you shelter.' He turned to Coyningham. 'We must go back,' he said. 'If we continue, we will be cut off from the ship.'

Crow growled, 'Mr Bracewell needs his property.'

'Of course he does,' Coyningham agreed. 'You are a greater fool than I thought if you believe the word of a darkie,' he told Rob. 'More probably the rebels put her there to frighten us. I doubt there are more than half a dozen of them, if there are any at all. One glimpse of our bayonets will send them fleeing.' He laughed. 'Once again, it seems you wish to run at the first hint of danger.'

'It's wrong to risk the men,' Rob insisted. 'They volunteered to serve the King – not Mr Bracewell.'

'If you wish to go back to the *Perseus* and tell Mr Bracewell you did not have the stomach for it, you have my permission. Then his niece would see what manner of hero you truly are. But I am in command. We go on.'

Rob had no choice. He could not return alone, and he would not abandon the men. But his worries deepened as they went on. The land around them was forest and thick swamps, perfect for an ambush. A dozen men could block the road completely. If they had a cannon, the *Perseus*'s men would be cut down like corn.

The forest ended at a stone wall and an iron gate across the road. Stone sphinxes peered down from the gateposts. Beyond, a carriage drive led across lawns to a handsome red-brick house surrounded by a cluster of buildings. It had the forlorn atmosphere of an abandoned property.

'Wait outside,' Crow told the sailors. 'I'll be ten minutes.'

'I will join you,' said Coyningham. 'Miss Bracewell asked me to retrieve a few of her personal effects.'

Rob felt a flash of jealousy. Why had Sophie not asked him? What could she possibly want? He forced himself to stay impassive.

The two men disappeared into the house. Rob and his men waited at the foot of the steps. Every second that passed, he felt the danger of the situation pressing in on them. The rebels could not be far off.

Was it his imagination, or could he hear voices?

'Search the outbuildings,' he told Angus. 'Make sure there is no-one spying on us.'

Angus gave him a crooked look. 'If this is a trap, we're already in it.'

He took two men and hurried across to the cluster of store-houses on the far side of the lawn. They checked inside two of the smaller huts, then approached a larger barn with a bar across its doors. Rob saw Angus stoop and peer through a crack in the boards, then hastily lift the bar.

The doors burst open. Rob had been right – they were not alone – but it was not rebels he had heard. They were black people, men women and children who flooded out of the barn and ran towards the house shouting questions.

'What is happening?'

'Is massa coming?'

'Where are the rebels?'

Rob watched them in shock. Growing up at Nativity Bay, he was used to being among black people. But at home they had been proud and free, laughing and chattering as they worked. They could hunt and fight as well as anyone. The men and women here were different. They moved slowly, eyes downcast and backs stooped. Even the children clutching their mothers' hands looked frightened, as if the spirit had been taken out of them.

How long were they locked in that barn?

Not all of them had been broken. One in particular caught Rob's attention, a young woman of about eighteen. She wore a pretty calico dress, rather than the work clothes of the other slaves, and her slim arms had not been bulked up by labouring in the fields. She wore her hair pulled back from her face in a yellow scarf, emphasising her soft round features, her almond eyes and golden-brown skin.

She was young, but despite her youth she had a poise and a maturity beyond her years. Rob could see women twice her age looking to her for guidance, while little girls hugged themselves against her skirts.

Rob didn't realise he'd been staring at her until she caught his eye. She didn't flinch but held his gaze until Rob began to blush. There was defiance in her look, a strength that said no man could possess her. Unaccountably, Rob felt ashamed.

He remembered Tew's errand. He reached into his cartridge pouch, pulled out the certificates the captain had given him, and held them in the air.

'I have an announcement to make,' he said awkwardly.

Fifty pairs of eyes stared dully at him.

'The governor has decreed that any slave who will fight for the King shall have his freedom.'

He peered at them, wondering if they had understood. There was no great joy on their faces. Some of them looked suspicious. One man, heavily tattooed with tribal markings, looked almost angry.

'What trickery is this?' he cried. 'You think you can steal us?'

'No trickery.' Rob showed them the papers. 'You see this stamp? That is the seal of King George. He will not betray you.'

He read from the paper. '"I do hereby declare free all Indentured Servants, Negroes, or others that are able and willing to bear arms, they joining His Majesty's troops as soon as may be, for the more speedily reducing this colony to a more proper sense of their duty."' He looked up. 'Who will join us?'

No one moved. Rob stepped down and approached the nearest slave, a man of about sixty with dark scars criss-crossing his back. Rob pressed one of the certificates into his hand.

'You are free.'

The man stumbled. One by one, Rob handed out certificates to all the slaves. They stared at the papers as if they could not comprehend their freedom.

'Go down to the bay,' said Rob. 'There is a ship there that will give you safe passage.'

He worried for a moment that the ship would be overloaded, but he couldn't concern himself with that now. He trusted Tew to honour the king's promise.

None of the freed slaves made for the gates.

'Go,' Rob repeated. 'Before the rebels come.'

But they were not listening to Rob. They were looking to the man with the tattoos Rob had noticed earlier. He was not much older than Rob, but even in his slave rags he had a natural air of command. He frowned, considering, like a lion sniffing out the hunter's hide. Wary of a trap.

At last he spoke, in an African language that Rob could not understand. The others nodded. To Rob's surprise, they began trooping back to the slave quarters to the rear of the mansion.

'What did you tell them?' he cried. 'Would you condemn them to a life of servitude?'

The big slave gave him a scornful look. 'I tell them bring what they have. We are going.'

'What is your name?' Rob asked.

'Scipio.'

'Where are you from?'

His eyes narrowed in an expression that said, without words, *Why do you care?*

'I was born in Africa,' said Rob.

For the first time, he saw he'd penetrated the slave's guard. Hostility gave way to curiosity.

'I am Ebo tribe.'

'And born to a noble house,' Rob guessed. The elaborate designs down the man's back marked him as a prince, as surely as Rob's tattoo showed him to be a sailor.

Scipio straightened and stretched out his arms. Muscles rippled along his naked torso, making the designs move like scale armour.

'I am a prince from the line of Eri,' he declared, and in that moment he looked every inch of it. 'The *mzungu* steal me and bring me here.'

'And now I have come to free you,' said Rob. 'Perhaps, when it is over, we will sail back to Africa together.'

Scipio stared at him. His scarred face was a battlefield of emotions, suspicion and distrust warring with hope.

'Who are you?' he asked softly.

'My name is Robert Courtney.'

The slaves returned from their quarters, carrying bundles of various sizes wrapped up in blankets and kerchiefs. Inside, Rob could see pots and pans, mirrors, a few hand tools and bright pieces of cloth. Everything these people owned in the world. It reminded him of the loyalists abandoning Boston, but they had been kings compared with this.

The slaves made a pitiful sight. Yet there was dignity, too. The despair Rob had seen earlier had gone, replaced with quiet determination. They all looked at Rob, waiting for his command.

Rob felt something stir inside him. Under their gaze, he began to sense their pain. Torn from their homes and families, transported across the ocean to be worked like animals. And now they were looking to him.

He cleared his throat. 'I will not let you down,' he promised.

To Rob's surprise, their faces fell. A second later, he realised why.

'The hell you doing?'

Crow and Coyningham had emerged from the front door of the house onto the steps behind Rob. Coyningham seemed to have a pile of petticoats in his arms, while behind him four sailors carried a sturdy strongbox.

Crow surveyed the slaves with a curl of his lip.

'Who said for you to muster the slaves?'

'I am taking them back to the ship.'

'Of course,' said Crow. 'But they don't need them goods where they're going.'

Rob wondered what he meant. Then a cry went up from the slaves, shots were fired and he forgot all about it.

The rebels had arrived.

Cal knew nothing about seamanship, but he could recognise skill when he saw it. Étienne's handling of the *Rapace* had been superb. They had caught up with the *Perseus* much sooner than expected, thanks to a winter storm that had blown up from the Atlantic. The British frigate had taken the brunt of it, while the *Rapace* sat it out in a sheltered harbour. Since then, the *Rapace* had shadowed her prey for almost a thousand miles, lurking just below the horizon.

'It is not hard,' Étienne said, when Cal complimented him on his ability to track her. 'We know she is sailing for Jamaica.'

Then the *Perseus* turned west towards the coast of South Carolina. That confused her pursuers, until Cal looked at a chart.

'According to the intelligence the general gave me,' Cal said, 'there is a man called Hezekiah Bracewell aboard that ship. He owns an estate here.' He put his finger on a spot on the map marked Seabrook Bay. 'I'll wager all my prize money that is where they are going.'

They had devised a plan. Cal had disembarked at Charleston to make contact with Continental forces in the area. Étienne had taken the *Rapace* to follow the *Perseus*.

'We will rendezvous at Seabrook Bay, by sea and by land.' Étienne closed his hands, interlocking the fingers like the jaws of a trap. 'Then we will have the British at our mercy.'

Cal had no trouble raising a company at Charleston. The city was a patriot stronghold, filled with young hotheads bursting for a crack at the British. Cal's name was already famous from his exploits in bringing the cannons to Boston. In no time, Cal had the men and guns he needed.

But he had not been quick enough. He should have reached Seabrook Bay before the *Perseus* could put men ashore. Instead, news had come on the road from Charleston that a British detachment had already reached the plantation. Cursing, Cal had raced on, leaving his field guns to catch up later.

Now he crouched behind a gatepost, reloading his rifle. As an officer, he wasn't supposed to carry a rifle, but he was too impatient to wait until he got into pistol range. And he was a better shot than most of his men.

He drew a bead on a black slave, a tall man covered in scars. He tightened his finger on the trigger, then thought better of it. There was no point wasting bullets on Negroes when there were British sailors to kill. He switched his aim to a marine corporal, and fired.

The moment the rebels opened fire, everything turned to pandemonium. The marine corporal sank to his knees as the bullet entered his eye socket and exited the back of his head, blood geysering. Slaves threw themselves to the ground. Children screamed. The *Perseus*'s men ran for cover wherever they could find it.

Rob ducked behind a carved statue of a lion and peered out over its back. Puffs of smoke blossomed from the forest at the far edge of the estate. Bullets rattled against the house, chipping flakes off the brickwork. One hit the lion's face and smashed off its snout.

The rebels were advancing. Already they were spilling over the estate fences and running across the lawns, kneeling to fire, then moving on while their comrades covered them.

'Back to the boats!' screeched Coyningham. He cowered in the shelter of the mansion's doorway, clutching a handful of petticoats he had brought out. 'Back to the boats before they cut us off.'

'What about the slaves?' said Rob.

Coyningham looked at him as if he was mad. 'What are you talking about? Leave them, you fool.'

'The rebels will put them back in chains if they catch them.'

'They will hang us if they catch us.' Coyningham ran down the steps, hurling himself unceremoniously to the ground. 'The Negroes will only slow us down. They are not our concern.'

'They're volunteers for the King.' Rob pointed to the certificates that the freed slaves were clinging on to. 'They're fighting for the King.'

'Half of them are women and children, and the rest are cripples.'

Coyningham turned to the men. The colonial infantry were working their way around the property towards the back gate. If they reached it, there would be no escape.

'To me!' Coyningham shouted. 'Give them one volley and go.'

'Belay that,' Rob countered. 'If we run, the Negroes will be massacred.'

Coyingham's face turned purple. 'You disobey a direct order? This is mutiny!'

Crouching on the ground, the two officers stared at each other like a pair of snarling dogs. Shots flew all around them. If they did not resolve this, more men would die.

'You go to the ship,' said Rob. 'Take Crow and half the men. I will stay behind to delay the rebels. Sir,' he added, between gritted teeth.

He saw the calculation in Coyningham's face.

'I will leave you ten men. If you can find any who are willing.'

Looking around, Rob could see there was no shortage of volunteers. He picked out ten of the best – Angus, Hargrave, Thomas among them – and wished he could take more.

'I will see you back at the ship, sir.'

'We will not wait for you,' said Coyningham. 'The tide is already on the ebb.'

He turned and ran, not slowing to keep pace with the men who were carrying the strongbox after him. Rob's detachment kept firing, covering the retreat until all Coyningham's party had reached the safety of the forest.

'Now what?' said Angus. 'There's at least a hundred of those Yankees. Not good odds.'

'You forget these freed slaves have enlisted with King George.' Rob turned to Scipio. 'Does Bracewell keep weapons here?'

Scipio nodded.

'Show me where they are. Then take your people and follow Lieutenant Coyningham to the bay. Leave a dozen of your stoutest fellows. We will hold the house to slow the Yankees down.'

'No,' said Scipio. 'I stay and fight. Phoebe take our people.'

He pointed to the woman wearing the yellow headscarf that Rob had noticed earlier. Evidently she was Phoebe. Rob noted the possessive look Scipio gave her, the way his eyes found her automatically. He guessed they must be husband and wife.

Unaccountably, he felt something like jealousy. He dismissed it. The attackers had reached the outbuildings. Musket balls peppered the walls. Women lay over their whimpering children to protect them. They could no longer risk staying out in the open.

'Go,' he told Phoebe. '*Perseus* men, fall back to the house.'

They ran inside. The house was opulently decorated, with crystal chandeliers and embossed wallpaper that must have come from England.

'Smash out the windows. Put men on all sides of the house so the rebels cannot take us by surprise.' Rob turned to Scipio. 'Where does Bracewell keep his guns?'

There was a strongroom at the back of the house. The door was made of thick oak planks bonded with iron bands and fastened with an enormous lock. Rob looked at it doubtfully.

'We will never break that open.'

With a grin, Scipio produced the key.

'No secrets for master from slaves,' he said, as the lock snapped open.

Bracewell must have lived in terror of his slaves, Rob thought, as he peered into the gunroom. It was almost as well stocked as the *Perseus*'s armoury. One wall was lined with hunting rifles, fowling pieces and shotguns; the other held a dozen muskets. Shelves held bags of musket balls, lead and moulds for casting, and boxes of paper cartridges. On the floor at the back there were two small kegs of gunpowder.

'This is enough to withstand a siege for a year,' said Rob.

His eye was drawn to one weapon in particular, something he had never seen before. It had two barrels set one on top of the other, mounted on a pivot so their positions could be swapped around. The stock was made of beautifully carved maple, fitted with gold chasing. Rob lifted it down from its rack and examined it. One barrel was rifled, the other a smooth-bore shotgun. A catch rotated them to allow the choice of which one to fire.

Rob shouldered the gun and took a rifle for good measure. Scipio passed out muskets, powder and shot to the Negroes who had stayed behind. They followed Rob up a grand staircase to the first floor, where the *Perseus*'s men were already mounting a brisk defence.

Rob was glad Sophie wasn't there to see what had happened to her home. Windows had been broken, rugs trampled, and priceless furniture overturned to form makeshift barricades. Musket balls whizzed in from outside. One hit a porcelain vase on a shelf and shattered it. Another put a round hole through the centre of a large gilt-framed portrait.

Rob peered over a mahogany dining table that had been pushed in front of a window. Angus and his men had managed to check the Americans' advance. The freed slaves had made their way across the rear lawn and reached the back gate into the forest. He saw a flash of Phoebe's yellow turban as she ushered the last stragglers out.

But they had not gone unnoticed. Two American soldiers edged out from behind the rice mill and gave chase, probably thinking of the bounty to be had for captured slaves. Rob raised his rifle, sighted and fired. The first man went down. The second checked his run, glanced at the house, then scrambled back to shelter.

Phoebe looked up. Rob felt a jolt go through him as their gazes met. She raised a hand in thanks. Then she disappeared into the trees.

The rebels could not follow unless they could get past the house. That would not be easy. Musket balls were ineffective against the solid brick walls, and Rob's men were keeping up a steady fire to keep the rebels back. With Bracewell's arsenal, they could hold out for some considerable time.

Unless the rebels brought up artillery.

Rob ran from room to room, encouraging the men and watching for danger. The sailors had shown the freed slaves how to use the guns, and they had proved swift learners. The hope of freedom gave them all the motivation they needed: they fought as fiercely as any of the sailors. It made Rob wonder how any man could enslave another on account of the colour of his skin.

But though his men held the attackers back, more rebels were arriving all the time. They worked their way around the house, using the outbuildings as cover. The defenders could not stop them.

'They'll surround us if we do'nae go now,' warned Angus.

'No,' said Rob stubbornly. 'We must give the women and children more time.'

He remembered the looks on their faces, the way they had trusted him. If they were recaptured by the rebels, it would be worse than if they had never escaped. Rob had to make sure they got away.

He found Scipio in a panelled drawing room, crouching behind silk-upholstered sofas, coolly taking potshots at the American soldiers. A group of them had found Bracewell's carriage in the coach house and were pushing it towards the house, using it as cover for their approach.

'Is there any other way to the sea?' Rob asked. He knew they would have to leave soon. But if they took the road they had come by, they would draw the rebels after the fleeing slaves.

'Yes.'

Scipio loosed off another shot. It hit the rear corner of the carriage, throwing up a storm of splinters. One of the men behind stumbled into view, clutching his face where the splinters had struck it. Nonchalantly, Scipio reloaded his gun and shot him dead.

'How?'

Scipio paused reloading again and pointed with the ramrod to the north of the property.

'There.'

Rob peered out of the window. 'But it's swamp.'

'There is a path.'

Rob glanced at his borrowed watch. He did not want to leave. But if he waited much longer, they would miss the tide. Tew would sail without them, and they would be trapped between the sea and the rebel army.

Rob crossed the hall to the other side of the house. Angus and three of the sailors were in a grand bedroom. They had pulled the mattress off the bed and propped it up in the bay window that overlooked the garden, using it as a shield.

'They're all over us like flies!' Angus shouted, over the din of musket fire.

Looking outside, Rob could see rebel troops massing among the slave quarters. Yet their fire had slacked off. What were they planning?

A deep boom drowned out the crack of musketry. A second later, the house shook to its foundations. Pictures fell off walls. From downstairs, Rob heard an almighty crash as a complete dinner service toppled off its shelf and smashed.

'They have artillery,' said Angus in dismay.

'Time to go,' said Rob.

'It's too late,' said Angus. 'We're surrounded.'

'We will create a diversion.' Rob looked around the room, the beginnings of a desperate plan forming. 'Tip that mattress out of the window. Then help me with this chest of drawers.' He searched out Hargrave. 'Fetch a powder keg from Bracewell's store.'

The men pushed the mattress through the shattered window. Rob unbuckled his sword. He and Angus went to a long rosewood chest standing against the wall. Between them, they dragged it to the window. With a mighty heave, they lifted it and threw it into a flower bed. It rolled once and came to rest on its side in front of the mattress.

'After it!' cried Rob.

He and Angus followed the chest through the window. They landed on the mattress, just as a hail of bullets chewed splinters out of the chest in front of them. The stout timber stopped the bullets as effectively as a sheet of iron.

Rob checked his gun. Both barrels were loaded. He could hear the rebel soldiers from the other side of the chest, barely twenty feet away. He caught Angus's eye, held up three fingers and counted down. On three, the men rose as one, discharged their rifles and dropped behind the defence before their enemies could fire back.

Rob heard whoops from the other side as the rebels charged. They knew they could reach them before they had time to reload. Calmly, Rob poured powder from his horn into the flash pan. He thumbed the catch on the gun and spun the barrels around so that the shotgun clicked into place, then stood.

The rebel soldiers were too close to raise their guns. One or two slowed, thinking he meant to surrender. The others came on, ready to gut him on their bayonets.

Rob fired the shotgun. At that range, he could not miss. A cone of birdshot sprayed from the muzzle, felling the oncoming soldiers in an instant. One took a ball in the eye; another took three shots through his throat.

Rob and Angus vaulted over the chest of drawers and ran into the midst of the fallen soldiers. Rob tugged a rifle from one man's hand, reversed it, and impaled him on his own bayonet. One man tried to climb to his feet. Angus clubbed him with the butt of his rifle until he stopped moving.

There were no enemy soldiers alive on this side of the house. Rob looked up to the window, where Hargrave's face peered down.

'Throw me the powder keg.'

Hargrave dropped it carefully into Rob's arms. Small fires were already smouldering in the grass where wadding and discarded cartridge papers had fallen. Cradling the keg, Rob ran to a small whitewashed building that the Americans had been using as a redoubt, a hundred yards from the main house.

He gave Angus the double-barrelled gun.

'Go back to the mansion. Muster the men by the north entrance.'

He could see Angus did not like to leave him. But Rob was an officer, and in the heat of battle the Scotsman could not disobey an order. He did as he was told.

Rob pulled the bung out of the keg and poured out a thin trail of gunpowder as he covered the last few paces to the outbuilding. An overwhelming stench hit him as he opened the door, so strong he almost dropped the barrel. He had been expecting a storehouse, or maybe an animal pen. This was something different: the stench of human filth and blood and rotting flesh, and beneath that, something more primal. The smell of fear and despair. Even a whiff of it made Rob want to turn and run, like a horse scenting fire.

The horror deepened as his eyes adjusted to the gloom inside. Blood splashed the walls almost waist high. Hooks hung from a thick beam across the ceiling, and shackles were bolted to the walls. An assortment of wicked implements hung on leather thongs from pegs: curved knives, billhooks, cleavers, branding irons and hammers.

It must be a slaughterhouse, Rob told himself, though he remembered the smell of butchered animals well enough from Nativity Bay to know this was different. But he had no time to delay. Outside, he heard the cannon fire again, making the knives jangle on their pegs. Rob stooped to put the powder keg down.

As he did so, his hand knocked something on the floor. It rolled away and came to rest in a square of sunlight that came through the window grille in the far wall.

Rob stared at it. It stared back. It was a human eyeball. There was no mistaking it: a brown iris, the pupil an empty hole still staring in terror. It trailed a string of nerves from the back where it had been ripped out of its skull.

The four walls seemed to close in on him. Rob felt an overwhelming urge to vomit. He had to get away.

He left the keg in the room and ran for the door, gulping lungsfull of fresh air. After the dark room, the sunlight dazzled him. He squinted at the ground, following the dark thread of the powder trail he had laid.

Discarded wadding was still burning in the dry grass. If he was not quick, the powder would catch before he could get to safety. He drew his pistol, primed it and aimed at the start of the fuse.

A shadow fell across the grass at his feet. Rob looked up, but not in time. A man crashed into him, knocking him off his feet. As Rob fell, his fingers clenched around the trigger. The pistol fired into the air.

The two men landed heavily on the grass, rolling away from the powder fuse. Everything was blur and shadows. Rob tried to batter his enemy with the pistol barrel, but the man ripped it out of his grasp and threw it aside. He had the strength of a tiger.

They wrestled on the ground. They were well matched, both young and strong. Locked together, neither could land a telling blow. But with every second that passed, Rob's defeat became inevitable. More rebel troops would come up. Angus and the others in the house would be cut off. The *Perseus* would sail, and they would be abandoned.

Rob lay on his back, fending off the blows that his opponent rained on him. Their faces were so close that sweat from the man's hair dripped into Rob's eyes. Rob had an impression of vivid red hair, and green eyes mad with the frenzy of battle.

As long as he was on his back, he would lose. He wriggled an arm free and managed to grasp a clutch of thick hair at the back of the man's head, holding it still. Before his opponent could break free, Rob tensed his neck muscles and headbutted the man with all his strength.

The green eyes blinked. His grip loosened. Rob pushed from the ground, rolling his opponent off him. The knock Rob had given him would have stunned an ox, but his enemy was already moving again. Both men sprang to their feet at the same moment and stared at each other, bloodied and breathing hard.

Rob felt for his sword. It was not there: he had left it in the house. He was unarmed.

Rob's opponent drew a long, curved knife from a concealed sheath in his boot. Behind him, Rob could see a dozen or more rebel soldiers running towards them.

'You have no escape,' said the American. 'Will you surrender?'

'No.'

'You are a brave man.' He was squinting, as if something about Rob troubled him – or seemed familiar. 'Have we crossed paths before?'

'I doubt it.'

For a moment longer those green eyes looked puzzled. Then he shrugged it off.

'In any event, I suppose this will be the last time we meet.'

He raised the knife. Sunlight bowed off the blade – then suddenly vanished. The sun had disappeared, blocked out by the almighty cloud of smoke and dust that had shot into the air where the blockhouse had been. At the same time, a roar blasted Rob like a burning hurricane, hitting him with a hail of debris and throwing him onto the ground. He buried his head in his arms to protect himself as stones rained down.

While they fought, the fires in the grass had ignited the powder trail. Peering back through the smoke, Rob saw the torture house had been levelled to its foundations. Near him, the man he had fought lay prone, the back of his head bleeding where a piece of rubble had struck it hard.

Rob pushed himself up. The American's knife lay on the ground. Perhaps it would have been wise to stick it in its owner, but Rob did not have time. The man was probably already dead.

Rob ran to the mansion and crashed through a ground-floor window into what had once been a formal dining room.

Scipio was waiting for him. He did not ask about the explosion, but beckoned him on.

'Come.'

He brought Rob through to the other side of the house and opened a side door. All their men had assembled. Rob counted them off. A few had been grazed by bullets, and one man's arm hung limp, but otherwise they had come off lightly.

'Are you hurt?' said Angus.

'I was lucky.'

Angus returned the double-barrelled gun.

'Here's hoping we keep lucky.'

No one saw them as they left the house to the north and raced across the lawn. Many of the rebels had been killed or stunned by the blast. The rest had rushed to help their comrades. The way was momentarily clear.

The lawn ended at a rail fence. Beyond it, the land dipped into a soggy morass of mud and long grass, studded with small shrubs and gnarled trees. It looked impassable.

Shots and shouts rang out behind them as the Americans realised what was happening. Scipio lifted a loose rail in the fence and stepped through. Rob followed. His foot sank into the mud up to his ankle.

'Are you sure there is a path?'

Scipio nodded impatiently. 'Yes.'

'Doesn'ae matter if there's not,' said Angus. 'We'll be dead either way.'

Cal opened his eyes. He didn't know how long he'd been unconscious, but it couldn't have been long. His ears were ringing, and dust was settling from the explosion behind him. A bruise the size of Bunker Hill had started to swell up on the back of his head where the stone had smashed it.

He had been fortunate. The men who'd been coming to help him lay strewn across the grass like branches after a storm. Those closest to the blockhouse had been torn in two by the force of the explosion. Others looked as if they'd been crushed by a giant fist. None of them were moving.

Cal pulled himself to his feet, gritting his teeth against the pain. He looked up, and promptly threw himself to the ground again as he remembered the British marksmen in the mansion. He crawled across the grass and took cover behind a rosewood chest of drawers that had been thrown into a flower bed. He peered over it.

No one fired at him. Scanning the windows, he saw no movement behind the shattered panes. The house was empty.

Running footsteps approached as his men came up.

'Are you hurt, sir?' said a young lieutenant.

He mopped at the blood matted into the back of Cal's head, but Cal shook him off. In that instant, he understood everything that had happened.

'It was a ruse.'

With the lieutenant and his men following, Cal ran around the house and found a trail of flattened grass across the lawn, ending in a broken fence at the edge of the property. He reached it in time to see the British disappearing into the low scrub of the swamp.

He grabbed a rifle from one of his men and sighted it on the back of the last man fleeing. Before he could fire, the man ran behind a bald cypress. It was too far anyway. Cal threw the rifle aside.

The lieutenant stared at the swamp. Whatever tracks the British had left, the wet ground had closed over them, leaving no hint of the path they had taken.

'Do we follow them?'

Cal rubbed the dust from his eyes. 'Can they get to Seabrook Bay that way?'

'No, sir.'

'Then leave them.' Heavy wheels rumbled on the carriage drive as the field guns rolled past. 'We have bigger game to hunt.'

Scipio led the way through the swamp, moving as nimbly as the insects that buzzed about their feet. Even when his foot splashed in water, he would unerringly find firm ground an inch below the surface. Rob wondered how he did it. To his eyes, the landscape was featureless.

Rob tried to step where Scipio did, but he always seemed to end up soaked. He moved a fraction to the right to avoid a thorn bush and sank waist deep in swamp water. Several times it was only a tug on his elbow from Scipio that stopped him falling deep into the mire.

Scipio tapped his forehead, indicating that Rob should concentrate. It was hard. The tangled vegetation hid them from sight, and the wide, open landscape played tricks with sound. There could have been rebels ten feet behind them, or two miles away, and they couldn't have known the difference.

The dull boom of a cannon echoed over the marsh. A flock of ducks was startled into flight.

'They cannot possibly see us,' said Rob. 'Are they shooting at shadows?'

Angus shook his head. 'That was not a field piece. It was a ship's gun.'

'Maybe the *Perseus* is signalling she is leaving.'

'Maybe.'

They hurried on. The ground became wetter, then firmer again. They came to a small island in the middle of the swamp. Rob saw lean-to shelters made of branches fixed to the trees, the remains of campfires. And tied to a stump, on a thin finger of clear water, was a pair of flat-bottomed canoes.

'You came here before?' Rob asked Scipio. The African nodded. 'Why didn't you run away? Surely they couldn't have found you here?'

Scipio frowned. 'Phoebe,' he said shortly. 'I could not leave.'

Rob wondered about the girl in the yellow headscarf. He pushed the thoughts aside as he scrambled into the low boat and cast off. With eight men in each canoe, the water almost came over the low sides. There were carved planks to use as makeshift paddles, while Scipio crouched in the stern on the balls of his feet, using a long sapling pole to steer them through narrow channels in the reeds and grass. The channels made a labyrinth of water, and the clouds hid the sun so it was impossible to find a bearing. Rob marvelled that anyone could navigate his way.

Rob looked at Scipio. 'Where does this come out? Seabrook Bay?'

'Fremont Bay.'

Rob had seen the name on the chart. It was north of where the *Perseus* had anchored, separated from it by a thick neck of land. They would have to paddle out into the open sea, and then south and back around, to arrive where they had started. The *Perseus* would not wait that long, even if the overloaded canoes could survive the ocean surf.

But there was nothing else to do.

The channel widened. They joined a river, the current tugging them on towards the bay. The tide was ebbing fast: Rob could see the water level dropping against the stalks of the reeds. He checked his watch and prayed Tew would hold station off the coast.

They were so low in the water, and the reed banks so high, they didn't see the bay until they came around a bend to the mouth of the river. Clear water stretched in front of them: a muddy bay fringed with palmettos and twisted mangroves. A small, thickly forested islet guarded the mouth of the bay.

Rob looked at the low spit of land that separated them from the next bay. If he stood up, he should be able to see the *Perseus*'s topmasts.

'Is there a channel between the bays?' he asked Scipio hopefully.

Scipio didn't answer. He was staring in the opposite direction, over the larboard side. Rob followed his gaze. The shore had opened out further, so they could see deeper into the bay. A sloop sat at anchor, floating as innocently as a fishing boat. But her sides were pierced for gunports, and the red-and-white stripes of the American ensign flapped from her stern.

There was nowhere to hide on the flat water of the bay. She would see them in an instant, if she had not already. And one shot from those cannons would sink them all.

'Quick,' Rob hissed to Scipio. 'Swap places with me.'

There was so little room, they almost capsized trying to manoeuvre around each other. Rob took the pole. It was hard to keep his balance, let alone steer the tiny craft, but he managed to bring her bow around so they were heading towards the sloop.

'What are you doing?' hissed Angus in front of him.

'Ready your weapons,' Rob answered. Angus handed him the double-barrelled gun Rob had taken from the plantation. 'We are going to board her.'

A man wearing a straw hat appeared at the sloop's side. He looked surprised to see the two canoes approaching so boldly. He shouted something unintelligible. More men appeared alongside him.

Lined up like ducks, thought Rob. It was the men he couldn't see that worried him.

'Sloop ahoy?' he called.

'Who are y'all?' came the challenge, from the man in the straw hat.

'Robert Courtney.' He didn't bother to give a false name. He waved his pole at the freedmen in the boat. 'We caught these slaves running away from Mr Bracewell's plantation. Thought we'd bring them to you.'

The men on the sloop conferred. Rob had come so close he could hear what they were saying. He heard his own name repeated several times, and he wondered why that should be.

The men on the sloop reached a decision.

'These slaves of yours,' said the man in the straw hat. 'We share the bounty. Fifty-fifty.'

'Seventy-thirty,' Rob countered. 'We caught them.'

'And we'll bring 'em back to market. Sixty-forty.'

'Done,' said Rob, smiling to mask his disgust that men could barter so casually over human lives.

The canoe bumped up against the sloop. The man in the straw hat tossed down a line and made them fast. Rob gestured Scipio to go first.

'And don't give no trouble,' he added with a wink.

Scipio climbed the ladder, followed by the other freed slaves. Rob watched them disappear over the side, one by one. Then it was his turn. Only six rungs, but it felt like the longest climb of his life with his men below and the American crew above.

He came over the side and took in the scene at a glance. Scipio and the others had been herded against the mast. Four sailors guarded them with boarding axes. A dozen other men loitered around the deck, watching. On such a small vessel, Rob was counting on the fact there would be no one below.

The man in the straw hat grinned at Rob.

'Mr Courtney. A relative of Major Courtney's, I presume?'

Rob didn't know what he meant. He gave a vague nod.

'Fine work taking the fugitives. But you should have bound them. Slaves is like wild dogs. You can't never let 'em off the leash or they'll bite.'

'Very true,' said Rob.

In one motion, he swung the double-barrelled gun off his shoulder and fired. The American's head exploded like a melon under a hail of point-blank shot. Before the crew could react, Rob had flipped the barrels and fired again. One of the men guarding the slaves dropped to the deck. The other three had barely begun to move when Scipio and his men launched into them with the knives they had hidden in their trousers. They wrestled the axes from their captors' hands and butchered them.

A few of the remaining crew tried to fight. They had no chance. The rest jumped over the side. By that time, all of Rob's men had gained the deck. They took potshots at the men in the water to hurry them along, while Rob and Angus made a search below decks.

All the crew were accounted for. The ship was theirs.

The men cheered – but there was little time for celebration. The tide was slipping out. They would have to be quick to rendezvous with the *Perseus*.

While the men unbrailed the sails, Rob kicked off his muddy shoes and ran up the rigging to the masthead. It was not nearly as high as he was used to on the *Perseus*, but the land around was so flat he could see for miles: over the neck of land and into the next bay.

His hopes soared. There was the *Perseus*, still in Seabrook Bay. But what was she doing? Her anchor was raised and her topsails set, but she was making little headway. Was Tew still waiting for him? Surely the tide was too far out for the captain to risk his ship like that?

Rob noticed something moving at the mouth of the bay.

Another ship.

She had been hidden behind the wooded island, but now she sailed out from its lee like a wolf breaking cover. A frigate flying American colours, her gunports raised and her cannons run out. That gave Rob his second shock. He recognised her. She was the *Rapace*, the ship they had fought off Newport. How on earth could she have come to be here?

Now he understood Tew's manoeuvres. With the wind against him, Tew couldn't leave the bay without sailing under the privateer's guns and being blown to pieces. He was trapped.

Rob slid down the backstay so fast he burned the skin off his palms. He told Angus and Scipio what he'd seen.

'So there's a stalemate,' said Angus. 'The Frenchie doesn't dare sail into the bay to engage, and Tew can't sail out.'

'The French ship doesn't have to come in,' said Rob. 'If the *Perseus* stays much longer she'll be stranded by the tide. The Yankees can bring down their guns on shore, and they'll blast her until she surrenders.' He balled his fists so tight his nails bit into his palms. 'We have to help Tew.'

'We're in the wrong place.'

Angus pointed to the spit of land that divided the two bays, curving around far to the north. It would take hours to beat up to the mouth of the bay, and hours more to sail back down to where the privateer was stationed.

'If only there were a way through,' groaned Rob.

Scipio had listened to everything they said. Rob was not sure how much he understood, but now he pointed towards the spit of land.

'There,' said Scipio.

Rob looked. All he saw was a solid green wall of waving reeds and seagrass.

'How can a boat get through there?' he asked.

'There is a way.'

'Even with the tide so low?'

Mudflats were already appearing around the edge of the bay. Soon there would be barely enough water to float a cork.

Scipio nodded.

'How can you be sure?' asked Angus. 'Were you not kept on the plantation?'

'I was boatman.'

'We must try it,' said Rob urgently. 'It is our only hope of getting there in time.'

'And if we run aground?' pressed Angus. 'We'll just be another target for the privateer to batter at her pleasure. We'll lose the ship.'

Rob grinned. 'It was never ours to start with.'

'Aye,' said Angus. 'But one day I'd like to collect a wee bit of prize money for all these ships we capture.'

The crew ran to their stations. The freed slaves did not know how to work a ship, but they could haul a line as well as any man. Under Angus's direction, they soon had the sail smartly set. Rob took the wheel, while Scipio stood in the shrouds calling out directions.

Rob searched out Thomas on deck. Since his first run-in with Coyningham, the boy had become a capable seaman. He still did not like going aloft, but Rob made sure to give him deck work as often as he could. Thomas repaid him with staunch loyalty.

'They must have a lead line aboard this ship,' Rob told Thomas. 'Find it and go to the bow. I want to know to the inch how much water we have beneath our hull.'

Thomas ran to obey. From the rigging, Scipio gave Rob a bemused look.

'You do not need it,' he told Rob.

Rob bridled at being told how to captain his ship.

'If we are in dangerous shallows, I must know.'

'Danger everywhere.' Scipio shook his head impatiently. 'Now you know.'

Thomas's voice rang out from the bows. 'Two fathoms.'

Rob flinched. The shore was barely two hundred yards ahead, and still he could not see the channel Scipio had promised. He was putting a lot of faith in the freed slave.

'One fathom six,' called Thomas.

'For God's sake,' muttered Angus. 'That's not so much as a whore's cunny-hair under our keel.'

Rob hardly heard him. He was concentrating on Scipio, who pointed the way like a compass needle. Rob coaxed the wheel gently – infinitesimal movements, as if he were guiding a frightened horse.

Something scraped the side of the ship.

'What was that?'

'Sunken tree,' said Angus.

From the corner of his eye, Rob saw reeds and trees sliding past. He had not realised they had entered the channel. It was so narrow, he could not see the water off their side. It looked as if the ship were gliding over the land.

'Set topsails, and every scrap of canvas you can find,' he said to Angus.

'Sir?'

They both knew that the faster the ship sailed, the harder the impact if they struck the bottom. They might split open the hull.

'If we strike bottom, then we are lost. But if we run aground in the mud, an extra few knots of speed might carry us over the bar.'

'One fathom,' called Thomas.

'Christ help us.'

Rob glanced at Scipio. The former slave was rigid, eyes fixed ahead in an expression of implacable concentration. The only part of him that moved was his arm, directing the way forwards.

A shudder went through the hull. Rob clutched the wheel for balance, and almost turned them into a thicket of trees. He straightened up in time. The ship was still moving, her keel slithering over the muddy bottom with a terrible rasping noise.

Every man aboard held his breath, waiting for the sloop to grind to a halt. She kept going, slower and slower as the mud fought her momentum. Foot by foot, inch by inch.

Rob wondered if he should have thrown the cannons overboard to lighten her load. But if by some miracle they did get through, he would need every gun he had to take a sloop up against a frigate.

The sloop came to a standstill. For a moment Rob felt weightless, as if his body had not caught up. Then the first wave of despair crashed over him. He had failed.

A gust of wind snapped the sails. With a creak of her timbers, the ship rocked forwards again. On deck, no one dared move. Slowly, she tilted on her keel and slid into the water so gently she barely made a ripple. The mud was left behind. The sloop gathered pace as the wind stiffened. Rob could see water on either side as the channel widened at last.

'Two fathoms five,' called Thomas.

Scipio gave one last gesture ahead and dropped down out of the rigging. Rob was so relieved he embraced him.

'That was a tight squeeze.'

'I tell you we go through.'

'You did.'

Now that Rob no longer had to concentrate on his course, he could see they had come across the spit of land into Seabrook Bay. To his right was the *Perseus*, tacking this way and that like a caged animal as Tew tried to keep her in deep water. Dead ahead, he saw the stern of the privateer.

From this distance, it was obvious how badly outmatched the sloop was. The frigate towered over Rob's small vessel.

'She won't know if we're friend or foe,' said Angus.

'Then let us remove all doubt.'

Rob hauled down the American flag. He slit the fabric with his knife, cutting out the Union flag in the corner so that it was all that remained.

'Run up our colours. Then clear for action.'

'She'll come at us with all she's got,' warned Angus.

'Of course. We need to distract her so *Perseus* can get out of the bay.'

The response from the *Rapace* was immediate. The privateer's sails braced around as she altered course, trying to train her broadside on the sloop. Rob gripped the wheel again, barking orders to keep the sails trimmed as he followed the frigate. As long as he stayed behind her, she could not bring her guns to bear.

He looked over at the *Perseus*. Tew had seen what was happening. He could not know that Rob was aboard the sloop, but he had seen the flag. The *Perseus* was coming about, ready to sail out of the bay to attack the privateer. If Rob could keep the French ship off her station long enough, the *Perseus* and the *Rapace* would be able to engage on equal terms.

The frigate fired a shot from her stern chaser. The ball landed with a splash barely ten yards off their beam. Rob had not meant to come so close. The freed slaves worked with a mighty will, but they were inexperienced sailors. Their only time at sea had been packed in the hold of a slave ship. They could not work the ropes and sails as well as a trained crew.

'Steady,' he murmured.

The frigate was coming around again. If Rob could not bring the sloop past her stern in time, they would be doomed.

'The *Perseus*!' cried Angus. The shock in his voice made Rob look up.

The *Perseus* had stopped. She sat in the middle of the bay, riding high in the water, rocking on her beam ends. The wind filled her sails, but her hull didn't move.

'She's run aground,' Rob realised in horror.

The tide had moved out faster than the ship could escape. She was helpless.

A cannon sounded, deafeningly close. In the moments that Rob had been distracted by the *Perseus*, the privateer had come about and was now bearing down on them. Her bow chasers were already in range. In a minute they would be facing her broadside.

The tables had turned. They were trapped between the privateer and the shore, and the *Perseus* could do nothing to save them.

Rob put the wheel over.

'Ready about,' he called. 'We'll make for shore.

'Against this tide?' said Angus doubtfully. 'We'll end up stranded like the *Perseus*.'

Rob handed him the wheel. 'Hold our course until we can go no further.'

It had become a question of who blinked first. The privateer had a deeper draught; the sloop was in shallower water. Whoever turned would be left vulnerable. Whoever did not would end up as helpless as the *Perseus*.

Étienne had studied every manual of tactics and naval theory until he could recite them by heart, but nothing in their pages had prepared him for this. Surely it must be witchcraft: how else to explain it? The sloop had sailed across dry land, and now she was heading for the shore as if hell-bent on her own destruction. He half expected her to rise out of the sea and fly.

'Monsieur?' said the first lieutenant. His face was drenched with sweat. 'We cannot follow. Do we come about?'

Maybe it was sorcery. Maybe Étienne was bewitched. Taking a frigate under full sail hard up against a lee shore, in unfamiliar waters and in the teeth of an ebbing tide, was madness. If she struck bottom, her keel would be ripped out. Her masts would topple like dominoes. Étienne's beautiful ship would become a hulk.

He knew the lieutenant was right. He had to come about or lose his ship. He readied to give the order – but somehow, the words would not come. From his mother, he had learned a ruthless and dispassionate single-mindedness, that when in sight of a target all that was required was willpower to conquer it. It was a simple matter – winning was all. Glory and adulation and his mother's approval would follow. Changing course would be admitting defeat. He could not do that.

'Fire our bow chasers.'

The first lieutenant swallowed nervously. 'The guns will not depress enough. At this range, the shot would fly over the target.'

'Fire them anyway!' Étienne raged.

The world had gone dark. He barely noticed the men around him, the ship beneath his feet or the shore ahead. Like a falcon fixed on its prey, all he saw was the sloop as a single bright point.

Something knocked the hull, a thud that sent vibrations ringing through the ship. Every man on deck froze as they waited to see what it meant. They stared at each other uncertainly. Étienne kept rigid discipline on his ship and to disobey an order was inconceivable. But the most loyal man was starting to think that if they did not take matters into their own hands, Étienne would drive them to destruction.

The ship surged on. The knock might have been a sandbar, or it might have been a piece of flotsam in the water. It might even have been a gunner dropping a cannonball on deck. It did not slow the *Rapace*.

The sound had shaken Étienne out of his trance. The pupils of his eyes dilated from pinpricks to wide open pools as he took in the shore rushing towards them. He had not realised how close they had come. The water was shallow and he could see the bottom over the rail. If they did not turn now, they would drown. He had to give the order.

Still, he could not utter the words.

The first lieutenant glanced at Étienne. His hand closed around the hilt of his sword. Did he have the courage to use it on his own captain?

'Shall I give the order, *mon Capitaine*?'

Étienne did not move. Then, almost imperceptibly, he nodded.

'**S**he's going about,' cried Thomas.

'Thank God,' said Rob.

The privateer had left it perilously late. She heeled over so hard Rob could see the weed trailing off the bottom of her hull.

'Hard alee!' he called.

He had left it late, too. He heard the keel scrape the bottom as the sloop came about. If she hadn't been tilted so far over by the sudden manoeuvre, she might have stuck fast. The boom thumped over; the freed slaves raced to brace the sails. Then they were moving again, away from the shore and towards the safer water in the middle of the bay, with the French frigate dead ahead.

The hunter had become the hunted. The sloop was chasing the *Rapace* out of the shallows. Rob had the advantage, and he would make it tell.

'Take us across her stern,' he ordered. 'We will rake her.'

The sloop's brass six-pounders were not big cannons. The frigate would be armed with eighteen- or even twenty-four-pounders. But against the privateer's unprotected stern, the sloop's guns would be enough. At that distance, the cannon-balls would smash through the windows and fly the length of the gun-deck, taking out any man or gun in their path. A single broadside would wreak devastating damage.

Angus organised the men into makeshift gun crews. He did not have enough to service all the guns, so he had them load and aim each gun in turn under his direction.

'Fire,' said Rob.

The deck shook as Angus touched the linstock's flame to the first cannon. Then again, as he moved down the line, and again, and again. Each gun fired in turn as the sloop crossed the privateer's wake. By the time the last shot died away, the frigate's stern was a tangle of twisted wreckage. The ruin in the tight confines of the deck would be much worse.

Rob had no illusions he was safe. Even wounded, the frigate had the strength to land a mortal blow on the sloop.

'Come about,' he ordered. 'We will repeat the attack.'

They did not have to reload. Turning about brought the starboard guns into action for the first time. Again Angus fired the cannons in turn. The shot tore through the gaping wound at the back of the ship. The hole was so big Rob could see through to the deck within, glimpse upended guns, smashed timbers and broken men. He had no sympathy.

'Reload the larboard guns. We will come about for another go.'

He was determined that the French frigate would become nothing but a heap of splinters. He had wrested the advantage, and he would make it tell.

Angus and Hargrave supervised the reloading, while Scipio directed the men on the braces.

'Keep us close behind her,' Rob warned. 'If we give her space to come about, she will blast us out of the water.'

He could see the gap between the two ships widening. The frigate was gaining headway. Soon she would have room to turn and bring her guns to bear on the sloop.

But there were no men on the frigate's guns. They had left them, climbing into what was left of the rigging to put on more sail. Rob waited for her to turn, but she never did.

'She's heading out to sea,' said Angus in disbelief. 'We've chased her off.'

The raking fire that Rob had poured down her decks must have done even worse damage than he'd hoped. Altering course only to avoid a sandbar, the frigate gained the mouth of the bay under full canvas. For a moment, Rob thought about giving chase. Then sense took hold. In the shallow waters of the bay, the sloop's manoeuvrability gave her an advantage. Out on the open ocean, the frigate would have the space she needed to make her armament deadly. And Rob had to consider the *Perseus*.

'Make fast the guns,' he ordered. He summoned Scipio and gave him the wheel. 'Take us as close to the *Perseus* as you can.'

He realised the men were watching him, expectant. The battle had ended so suddenly, they were unsure what had happened.

'We won,' he told them. He forced himself to forget his cares for a second, so the crew could see his delight. He owed them this moment. 'The pride of the Yankee navy, and we sent her away with her tail between her legs.'

The men cheered. Black and white alike embraced each other, shouting huzzahs and taunts after the fleeing frigate. Rob sought out Scipio and clasped his hand.

'You saved us all,' he said. 'I am glad we fought together.' He looked around the bay that hugged them close. The frigate might have gone, but there were other enemies nearby. 'We are not safe yet.'

Across the bay, the *Perseus* was still stuck fast in the mud. The crew had started to throw provisions overboard to lighten the ship. Rob sailed the sloop as near as he dared and dropped anchor amid a stream of casks and spare timber bobbing away from the frigate.

Rob took the canoes across to the *Perseus*, with Scipio and his men. The freed slaves scanned the frigate's decks anxiously, hoping that their wives, sisters and children might have escaped aboard. There was no sign of them, though Coyningham's party had evidently come back unscathed. Bracewell's strongbox stood on deck by the mainmast.

Rob remembered the tall slave girl, Phoebe, and hoped she was safe.

Something Hugo Lyall had said about slaves ran through his head.

It is the best life they could hope for. If we did not feed and clothe them, and direct their labour, they would starve to death.

It had rung false then, but Rob had been unable to argue. Now that he had seen the reality of life on a plantation, it sickened him to think that Hugo could have lied so blatantly, that all their high living in London had been paid for by such cruelty. Did he really believe it? Did Sophie believe it, too? He could see her on the *Perseus*'s deck, her hair blowing in the breeze. Surely she did not know what torture was meted out on her uncle's plantation. How could he tell her?

Tew pushed through the crowd of cheering men to greet Rob.

'Lieutenant Courtney,' he said, and even his composure could not hide the true emotion in his voice. 'Once again, you show a most remarkable talent. Seeing you fend off that frigate in a mere sloop is a sight I shall not soon forget. Like watching a terrier savage a mastiff. The Admiralty will not credit it when I put it in my despatches.'

Rob blushed. Once again, he found the hardship of battle much easier to handle than the glory that came with it.

'We would not have managed without the men from the plantation.' He found Scipio, lurking by the rail, and tugged him forwards. 'This man showed us the hidden channels through the swamps so we could reach you in time.'

Tew thrust out his arm and shook Scipio's hand, though there was unease in his manner that Rob did not understand. There were three Negroes in the *Perseus*'s crew, and Rob had never seen Tew treat them differently from any other man. 'I am in your debt, sir. If you wish to volunteer, it would be an honour to have you join my crew. I am sure Mr Bracewell would not begrudge it.'

'Mr Bracewell has nothing to do with it,' Rob said. 'I distributed the governor's certificates, as you ordered me. Scipio and the others are free men.'

Tew looked uncomfortable. Perhaps he had not told Bracewell about the certificates. Scipio spoke first.

'My family,' said Scipio. 'Women, children. They come?'

'A group of Negroes from the plantation reached the bay. We were able to bring them aboard before the frigate arrived.'

Scipio arched his eyebrows. 'Where?'

'They are below,' said Tew. 'But I must tell you—'

'Deck there!' a lookout interrupted from the masthead. 'Rebels on shore.'

Whatever Tew meant to say was forgotten as every man rushed to the side. The beach, which a moment earlier had been empty, was now filled with rebel soldiers forming up.

'Their muskets are out of range,' said Coyningham complacently.

'They have more than muskets.'

Rob pointed. A team of horses had emerged from the forest, pulling a field gun on a carriage. Another team followed, then more and more. The crews unharnessed them and began to dig the cannons into position on the beach.

The *Perseus* was bow-on to the beach. Apart from her two bow chasers, she could not bring her guns to bear against the American cannons. Stuck on the sandbar, she would be at their mercy.

'We could try to storm the beach,' suggested Rob. 'Drive them back before they entrench the guns.'

Tew shook his head. 'There are too many of them. They would slaughter us before we got out of the boats.' He raised his voice. 'Back the sails. Throw the guns overboard.'

'We will want the cannon when we get out of the bay, if the French frigate is still there,' muttered Coyningham.

'We will not need them if those rebel guns start firing,' retorted Tew.

'I will have the sloop try to pull us off,' said Rob.

The men ran to their tasks. Rob fastened a hawser to the frigate's stern and had his men run it back to the sloop. Hargrave and Angus manned the *Perseus*'s bow chasers and peppered the beach with shot. Using blocks and tackles, the rest of the crew lifted the spare anchor out of the hold and jettisoned it, along with every scrap of furniture aboard. The yards were braced around to catch the wind and drive the ship backwards, while the sloop set all her canvas to try and haul the frigate away.

It was not enough. The sails filled, but the *Perseus* did not budge.

A sudden crunch from behind Rob made him start. He turned, to see Crow two feet away. He did nothing to help, but stood watching while he chewed on his cone of sugar.

'If you wants to lighten the load some more, you could throw the darkies overboard.' He spat a wad of brown saliva onto the deck. ''Course, Mr Bracewell'd have somethin' to say about the loss. Terrible dear, those slaves was.'

Rob needed a moment to control his emotions so he did not knock Crow to the deck.

'They are free men, now.'

Crow raised an eyebrow. 'That's not what I heard.'

A gun boomed from the bow, followed by a cheer from the men on deck. On the beach, one of the American guns was now a smashed pile of wood and metal. Hargrave had scored a direct hit.

'That will buy us a little time,' said Tew.

Hargrave fired again. But the Americans were wise to the threat. They moved their guns where the bow chasers could not reach them.

'Lower the boats,' said Tew. 'They can help pull us.'

'We do not have enough men to man them,' objected Coyningham.

'Then we will use the freed slaves.'

'But Mr Bracewell said—'

'If Bracewell wishes to object, he will find himself in the water along with the other dead weight.' Tew called down the companionway. 'We need more hands. Every man, woman or child who is strong enough to pull an oar, come on deck now.'

The freed slaves emerged, blinking into the sunlight. Rob divided them between the *Perseus's* boats, seasoning each group with a core of sailors who could show the others what to do. He watched them with a lump in his throat. Some were no bigger than his sister Susan, six or seven years old; others were older than his grandmother. But they took their seats in the boats and listened as the coxswains told them what to do. Many looked frightened, but there was a fierce determination in every face as they gripped the oars.

He glimpsed Phoebe in her yellow headdress taking her place with the others. She looked up at the ship and caught Rob's eye. He turned away hurriedly.

More lines were attached from the boats to the stern. The boats fanned out like a team of horses trying to pull a dead weight. The rowers leaned on their oars. Their dark skins shone with sweat, the muscles honed by years of back-breaking toil. A woman in the bows started a song: a low chant in a language Rob could not understand. The others joined in, pulling together as they sang the response. Even in their rags, there was majesty in the sight.

A gust of wind blew off the mainland. The *Perseus*'s sails, already taut, bulged tighter. At the end of the hawser, the sloop strained like a dog on a leash. The men and women in the boats dug their oars into the water.

Rob felt the deck tremble beneath his feet.

The *Perseus* had moved.

The cannon fired, but the ball flew overhead. In their haste to fire, the American gunners had misjudged their elevation, though their aim was true. The ball struck the end of the mainsail yardarm and snapped it off. A sailor who had been working there, a man named Rudston, fell screaming into the water.

'Heave!' Rob shouted to the crews in the boats.

Freed slaves and sailors alike bent their backs to the oars. There was a splash from the side as another cannon went overboard. For a moment, it seemed it still might not be enough.

With another gust of wind, he heard the keel rasp against the mud as the ship slid back. This time, she did not stop. Water gurgled under her hull. The tide had turned, giving her the crucial inches of clearance she needed. The wind and the sweat of the rowers kept dragging her back, further and further. Rob thanked God and the Admiralty for the copper sheathing, which smoothed her hull and let her glide more easily over the bottom.

The song from the boats sounded louder. The sailors had joined in the slave chant. They did not know what the words meant, but they sang out lustily. The *Perseus* gathered pace.

The Americans were determined they would not let her get away. Two more cannons fired from the shore. One ball went wide, but the other smashed through the gunwales. Men ran to cut away the wreckage.

'What is this?'

Bracewell had come on deck. Rob noted neither he nor Crow had lifted a finger to help, though both men were stronger than most of the freed slaves in the boats. Bracewell did not look pleased at their deliverance. His face was almost purple with rage.

'Who sent my people into the boats?'

'They went of their own free will,' said Rob. 'If they had not, we would still be beached on that sandbar.'

The deck rocked as the ship came free and moved into clear water. No one cheered. They were not out of danger yet. The rebels were reloading.

'Bring them back this instant!' screeched Bracewell. 'You do not know what they are capable of. They will use those boats to escape.'

'What if they do? They are free men and women.'

'They are my property. And if you abet their escape, you are complicit in an act of theft.'

'Can property steal itself?' Rob asked.

If Bracewell answered, his reply was drowned by the report of another cannon from shore. Every man instinctively ducked, but there was no danger. The gunners had not managed to adjust their aim for the *Perseus*'s movement.

And now she had reached deep enough water that she no longer needed to be pulled. Her bow came around, and the sails were set on a course out of the bay. Rob called in the boats. The freed slaves scrambled aboard, their clothes soaked with sweat but their faces radiant with success.

Then they saw Bracewell and Crow. A murmur ran through them; their heads dropped. Many drew back, cowering as if they expected to be beaten.

'Get below,' hissed Bracewell.

Scipio stepped forwards.

'No,' he said firmly. 'We free now.'

'If you say that again, I will have Crow whip the hide off you,' said Bracewell. 'Get down, the lot of you.'

Scipio unfolded his certificate. 'We free,' he said again.

Bracewell snatched it from his hands. 'What is this nonsense? Who gave you this?'

'I did,' said Tew. 'The governor signed them himself.'

'And I have told you already that I have a dispensation, from the President of the Board of Trade and Foreign Plantations.' Crow opened the strongbox that Coyningham had brought from the plantation house. Bracewell pulled out a large piece of paper, with a wax seal hanging from the bottom. 'The governor's proclamation does not apply to me. That is the law.'

The two men faced each other: the owner and the captain, with Scipio between them. A gun fired from shore again; Rob heard the tinkle of glass as it broke the stern cabin windows, but no one seemed to notice.

'I promised them they would go free,' Rob murmured – more to himself than to anyone else, but the words seemed to have a galvanising effect on Tew. He put his hand on the hilt of his sword.

'These people are aboard my ship,' he said. 'I am the final arbiter of the law here, and I say they are free.'

'You are making a mistake,' Bracewell warned Tew.

Coyningham looked appalled. 'Is it worth your reputation for these darkies, sir?'

'It is worth it for these *men and women*,' said Tew evenly.

'The moment we reach port, any court will affirm that the slaves are my property,' Bracewell insisted.

'Not if we dock in London. The courts have determined that as soon as a slave sets foot on English ground, he is free.'

The rebels fired again. One ball went wide, the other struck near the transom. The crew ran to attend to the damage, but Bracewell, Tew and Rob hardly noticed it. They were locked in their own battle of wills.

'Will you sail these wretches halfway around the world just so they can call themselves free? Will they be better off dumped on the docks of London like so much cargo, homeless and impoverished and with no means of supporting themselves? Is this what you call mercy?' Bracewell leaned in close. 'That property is worth a great deal of money to me. I would be willing to make a certain contribution to ensure their safe return.'

'Is that so?' said Tew.

'To you personally, you understand. In recognition of the great hazards you braved to rescue the property, I would be willing to offer, say . . . two hundred pounds.'

Rob gasped. That was as much as a captain would earn in a year. Even Tew looked impressed.

'That is a tidy sum.'

'And another hundred pounds to be shared among the brave tars of this ship who rescued my property from the rebellion.' Bracewell had raised his voice so that the men on deck could hear. 'That will buy you a fair few tumbles when you go ashore.'

A murmur went around the deck. The crew looked to their captain. From the other side of the ship, the freed slaves whose destiny was being decided watched anxiously. Tew bowed his head. Rob wondered that he didn't break under the weight of the decision.

'No,' he said. 'It is not enough.'

The thunder of guns rumbled around the bay. A spout of water rose astern where the ball landed. With the wind filling her sails, the *Perseus* was outrunning the rebel cannons.

'Three hundred pounds, then,' said Bracewell. 'And I assure you, that is almost as much as those rascals are worth.'

'You mistake me,' said Tew. 'What I meant is that there is no sum that will buy a human life. Keep your money, tainted as it is with the blood of the men and women who earn it for you. I would not take a penny of it.'

A few of the crew looked angry, but more were nodding in approval of their captain. Bracewell had turned so red Rob thought he would explode with fury.

'I will write to London,' spluttered Bracewell. 'I will see you cashiered and drummed out of the navy. By the time I have finished dragging you through the mud, your own mother will not admit to knowing you. I will destroy you.'

Crow's hand went to the pistol he kept inside his coat. Tew saw the motion, as did Rob. He snatched a pike from the rack on the mast and levelled it at Crow's throat.

'If you touch your firearm, I will run you through,' he warned.

Crow went still. Tew sought out one of the boatswain's mates among the crowd.

'Mr Leake,' he called, 'escort Mr Crow and Mr Bracewell below. They should not be on deck in the midst of battle.'

The burly boatswain's mate hesitated to approach Bracewell in his rage. Bracewell did not wait: he stormed towards the companionway. Crow followed.

'I will make you pay,' Bracewell warned at the top of the ladder.

The moment he had disappeared below, Rob felt the mood on deck lift. The freed slaves broke out in laughter and excited chatter. Even Scipio could not keep a smile from his stern face.

'Thank you,' he said simply.

Tew looked embarrassed. 'You do not need to thank me. You should never have been deprived of your freedom in the first place.'

They were approaching the mouth of the bay. Behind them, low bangs and puffs of smoke told that the gunners on the beach had not given up, but it was more from frustration than hope. The *Perseus* was out of range.

But the rebels would not quit. They added more powder to the guns, to increase their range, and fired one last salvo. A shot struck the gunwale, throwing up a cloud of splinters. The ball bounced across the deck and came to rest near the foot of the mast.

'With your permission, sir,' Rob said to Tew, 'I will go aboard the sloop with Scipio and lead the way. There may be more uncharted shallows to avoid before we get out of the bay.'

Tew didn't answer. Rob turned. The captain was not where he had stood a moment ago.

He lay on the deck, his blood-soaked hands clutching his face. A foot-long splinter had impaled his right eye. The hands gripped the splinter, but there was no life in them. The splinter had gone into his brain and killed him instantly. The movement must have been instinct, the last reflexive jerk of his body before he died.

Rob kneeled beside his captain, his heart pounding. He tugged the splinter free, though it made no difference. He folded Tew's hands over his breast, and closed his one remaining eye. He cradled the captain in his lap. Hot tears ran down his cheek, but he was not ashamed. Most of the men around him were weeping, too.

A shadow fell over Tew's body as Coyningham stepped forwards. Rob looked up, and felt his grief harden to anger as he saw the gleam of triumph that the first lieutenant could hardly contain.

'Take him to the sick berth until we are ready to bury him,' said Coyningham. He sought out the boatswain's mate. 'Mr Leake. Take Mr Bracewell's property below and lock them in the hold.' He considered the freed slaves: some cowering, others balling their fists ready to fight. 'Bind them with whatever you can find. I do not know that we will have enough manacles for all of them.'

Over his shoulder, Rob saw that Bracewell and Crow had reappeared from the companionway, drawn to the calamity like vultures to a carcass. Crow bit off a piece of sugar and chewed it, like a spectator at a hanging. Bracewell's eyes narrowed at his unexpected advantage.

Rob could not bear the sight of them.

'No!' he cried. 'The Negroes are free.'

'They are Mr Bracewell's property,' said Coyningham.

Rob stood. 'The last thing Captain Tew did was to set them free. Will you undo his order while his body is still warm?'

'Enough!' barked Coyningham.

The mood on deck was ugly. Surrounded by the wreckage of battle, their captain's body laid out on the planking, the crew did not know how to react. When the boatswain's men approached Scipio, he threw them off. Angry muttering sounded among the crew.

Coyningham knew he was in danger of losing the ship. He drew a pistol from his belt and cocked the hammer.

'I am in command!' he shouted. 'Any man who defies me, I will hang as a mutineer this very afternoon.' He jerked the pistol towards Rob. 'That includes you, Mr Courtney.' The pistol swung towards Scipio. 'As for you, you black filth, I will throw you overboard – women and children all – if you resist.'

Afterwards, Rob wondered what would have happened if he had acted that instant. Between the sailors loyal to him, and Scipio's men, he might have deposed Coyningham, seized the ship and secured the slaves' freedom. For an instant, their fates hung in the balance.

But the habits of naval discipline were too deeply ingrained. The men were in shock from the loss of their captain, exhausted from saving the ship, and reluctant to throw away their lives for a group of dark-skinned strangers.

As for the freed slaves, there were too many women and children among them. If they made a fight of it, there would be a massacre.

Scipio let the boatswain's mate clap on a heavy pair of manacles and lead him to the ladder. Crow spat in his face as he passed, but Scipio did not flinch. One by one the others followed, heads bowed.

Coyningham still had the pistol in his hand. He swung it lazily back towards Rob.

'Is there anything you wish to say, Lieutenant Courtney?' His voice was dangerous, his finger curling around the trigger. He knew how close he had come to losing the crew.

Rob fought the urge to punch him. Coyningham would shoot him dead without a second thought: Rob could see the bloodlust in the man's eyes. He had to stay alive and out of Coyningham's clutches. It was the only way he would be able to help the crew, Scipio, Phoebe and all the souls who were now at the mercy of Coyningham's whims.

'I will see Captain Tew is taken below,' he said tightly.

'*Mr* Tew,' Coyningham corrected him. '*I* am the captain now.'

Étienne de Bercheny watched the British frigate sail away in company with the sloop. Anger boiled up inside him. He slammed his fist on the rail, so hard that the battered wood snapped under the blow.

'This is your fault!' he shouted at Cal. 'If you had brought your guns to the beach in time, we would have destroyed the frigate.'

'If you had attacked right away, and not dallied out at sea, you could have done it yourself,' Cal answered.

A boat had brought him out to the *Rapace* as soon as the British ships had cleared the headland. He had a bandage wrapped around his head, and a deep gash on his arm from the battle at the house, but he barely noticed them.

'Do you accuse me of cowardice?'

'Do you accuse me of dereliction of duty?'

Each man was as furious as the other. Battle-weary, exhausted, and their pride dented. They had not been defeated, but letting their adversary escape made their hearts boil.

'If you insult me,' said Étienne, 'I will have no choice but to demand satisfaction.'.

He wanted to fight someone, and he did not care who it was. He let himself imagine how good it would be to feel his rapier point slide through the American's guts after the frustration of the battle.

Cal knew he was strong, but he was not a trained swordsman. Étienne had studied with the greatest fencing masters Paris had to offer. The Frenchman would bait him like a bull and turn him inside out. That would be a poor way to pay his debt to Aidan.

'Duelling among ourselves benefits only our enemies,' he said, with all the self-control he could manage.

Étienne's hand was already on his sword. He paused, surprised and disappointed.

Reluctantly he let go of his sword and offered Cal his hand.

'We could not have destroyed her,' Cal reminded him. 'That was not our mission. We had to let her go.'

Étienne grimaced. What Cal said was true, but it still pricked his honour. Where was the glory in allowing a ship to escape?

'Even so, we should have done more damage.'

'We will have another opportunity,' Cal consoled Étienne. 'And next time, there will be no escape for her.'

'*Vraiment*,' said Étienne. In his current mood, he would have pursued the British ship to the mouth of Hell if he could. But even he could not take his ship to sea with half its gun-deck shot away. 'Now we must make repairs. We will anchor in the bay. Your guns will shelter us while we mend the damage.'

As they sailed back into the bay, something in the water caught Cal's eye – a piece of the *Perseus*'s gunwale that had been shot away. But there was movement. A man, half-submerged, was clinging to the wreckage. He must have fallen overboard from the British frigate in the heat of the battle. He was kicking out, trying to steer the makeshift raft towards land, but he was no match for the tide. Soon he would be swept out to sea. From his frantic splashing, Cal guessed he couldn't swim.

Cal found a coiled rope amid the carnage on the *Rapace*'s deck. He tied a bowline in one end, whirled it over his head and let it fly towards the man in the water. It was a trick he had practised often, roping livestock on his father's farm. The line flew true, landing so close to its target it almost looped over the man's shoulders.

The sailor took it gratefully. A choice between being a prisoner of war and drowning at sea was no choice at all. Cal hauled on the rope, pulling the man to the ship until he could grab the ladder.

The crew paused in their work as the castaway came aboard. They were in no mood to be forgiving. The prisoner eyed them fearfully. As he took in their vicious looks, it began to cross his mind that there might be worse fates than drowning.

'What is your name?' Cal asked.

'Rudston.'

'And your ship, the *Perseus*. Who is her commander?'

'Captain Tew,' said Rudston, unaware that Tew was dead. He had gone overboard before the final cannonball hit the vessel.

'I would like to meet Captain Tew,' said Étienne. 'Twice now he has fought off my ship. The third time will be to the death.'

'Was he the man who led your men to the plantation?' Cal put in. He remembered the man he had wrestled with outside the house, the strange feeling of familiarity as he had looked in his eyes.

'That was Lieutenant Courtney,' said Rudston. 'Between him and Captain Tew, you'll not find two braver men in the navy.'

'Courtney?'

At the sound of the name, an electric shock went down Cal's spine. He felt, with a certainty beyond reason, that there must be a connection. He knew his father had had a sister, and he never spoke of her. What if this was her son, or some other branch of the family tree?

Of course it was fanciful. What were the chances of him encountering such a person here? And yet . . . there had been something so familiar in that face it had gone to the core of his being.

Étienne laughed. 'It is a coincidence, *non*?'

'Probably,' said Cal doubtfully.

He wanted to know more, to ask Rudston everything he knew about his mysterious namesake until he could be sure there was no connection. But Étienne had other ideas.

'These impudent British are as slippery as eels. It is time we make an example.'

A smile spread across his pale face. He barked an order to the boatswain in French. The boatswain blanched. He stammered a reply, but a curt word from Étienne cut him short. With a salute, he disappeared towards the rope locker at the bow.

'What are you doing?' said Cal. 'This man is a prisoner of war. We should confine him until we can arrange an exchange.'

Étienne ignored him. 'Do you know what the Dutch do to punish a man? They call it *kielhalen*. In English I think you say "keelhauling".'

Cal had heard tales of such punishments from his father. As strong as his stomach was, he had squirmed every time, while his mother tried to cover Aidan's ears.

'I thought that was outlawed long ago.'

'The old ways have their place.'

'Please, sirs.' Rudston had gone pale with fear. He dropped to his knees on the deck. 'That's a death sentence.'

Étienne pretended to consider that seriously.

'I think a man can survive. It will be interesting to find out.'

His men seized Rudston. The Englishman writhed and squirmed in desperation; he tried to bite the men who held him, but there were too many. They manacled his feet together, attaching a length of chain shot to the fetters to weigh him down. Meanwhile, other men passed a rope through blocks on the ends of the mainsail yardarms. With some difficulty, they looped it under the ship's bow and worked it back amidships so that it passed under the keel, from one side to the other.

They tied one end of the rope to Rudston's hands, and the other to his chained feet. Now he was part of the loop. He screamed and struggled, but he was tied fast. There was no escape.

Cal watched with growing disgust. In his father's stories, it was never the heroes who keelhauled their victims. As much as he longed to fight the British, this was sheer cruelty.

'What do we gain by this?'

Étienne shot him a dismissive look. 'We strike terror into our enemies.'

'Please,' Rudston begged, almost frothing at the mouth with fear. 'I'll tell you anything you want.'

'Such as?'

'The *Perseus* is bound for Jamaica,' Rudston babbled. 'There's a man aboard, very important. Planter, name of Bracewell. We was taking him to his plantation.'

'I know this already,' said Étienne. 'There is nothing you can tell us that is of interest.' He turned to the crew. 'Lift him up.'

Étienne's men hauled on the rope tied to Rudston's feet. They lifted him off the deck, so that he dangled upside down like a piece of meat. Rudston's terror redoubled.

'Let me down,' he pleaded. 'I can tell you more.'

Étienne put his mouth close to Rudston's ear. 'You have nothing to give me except the pleasure of watching you die.'

The sailors laughed. They swung Rudston over the side, then lowered him towards the water. On the other side of the ship, another team hauled on the rope that was tied to his hands. Rudston bucked and jerked, but he was stretched between the two ropes like a prisoner on the rack. Cal felt sick. He desperately wanted to cut him free, but in front of Étienne and his crew he was powerless.

Rudston's screams rose to a fever pitch, then choked off as his head went underwater. Cal peered over the side and saw a pair of pale white feet disappear into the depths.

'How long will it take?'

Étienne shrugged. 'We will see.'

A strange silence gripped the deck. Now that the prisoner was submerged, all the crew could do was imagine what he was suffering beneath their feet. The *Rapace* did not have copper sheathing to smooth her bottom like the *Perseus*. Every mile she sailed, barnacles and other shellfish would have fastened themselves to her hull, forming a crust like a thousand razors. Rudston was being dragged over it, while simultaneously drowning.

'Keep it tight,' Étienne ordered.

If the rope went slack, the man would sink away from the hull and be spared the ordeal. Cal thought of him down in the depths, his mouth open in soundless screams that would flood his lungs with water. Drowning would be a mercy.

The men hauled on the rope. Pieces of weed started appearing on it. The rest of the crew crossed to the far side and looked down, waiting for the prisoner to emerge. They took bets on how long it would be before his body broke the surface, and whether he would have survived.

There was a cry as he broke the water. Cal heard the body slithering up the side of the ship, a thud as it bumped against an open gunport. There were no screams now.

The bound hands came up over the gunwale, clasped together as if in prayer. Rudston's body followed. The seawater ran red off his skin with the blood of a thousand cuts. His nose had been torn away, and one eye dangled from its socket.

There was a reason he wasn't screaming. His neck had been sliced open, so deep his head hung on a thin flap of flesh, lolling back.

Étienne looked at the dangling figure, like a surgeon studying a cadaver. He seemed disappointed.

'Are you not satisfied with the punishment?' asked Cal.

'I wanted to make him do it again.' Étienne pouted, then shook his head. 'Cut the rope,' he ordered, 'and let the sharks have him. We have delayed long enough.'

'Indeed,' said Cal.

It was a relief to see the body drop into the water and vanish. The horror of what he had seen disgusted him. This was not why he had joined the patriotic cause. His ears roared with his father's voice saying, 'See what kind of men you have thrown in your lot with?' He gritted his teeth and tried to ignore it. This was war.

'We should not let the English frigate get too far ahead of us,' he said.

Better to concentrate on the task at hand.

Étienne nodded. 'As soon as we have repaired the ship, we will set our heading for Jamaica.'

And perhaps when they caught the *Perseus*, Cal thought, he would find out the truth about the mysterious Lieutenant Courtney.

As an officer, Tew should have been buried on land. Coyningham refused.

'There is nowhere we could sail within a thousand miles that the rebels do not hold,' he told Rob. 'And by the time we reach Jamaica, the body will be nothing but a hive of flies.'

He smiled, enjoying Rob's distress.

'My orders are to take Mr Bracewell and his niece to Jamaica with all despatch. We cannot afford to waste any more time.'

Tew was buried at sea, like a common sailor. They wrapped his body in a sheet of canvas, his sword on his chest and two cannonballs at his feet to weigh him down. The ship's ensign flag was stretched over him, and the bundle laid on a grating propped up on trestles at the side of the ship. The quartermaster rang the ship's bell to summon the crew. The officers lined up at the front of the quarterdeck, while the crew stood in solemn lines on deck.

There was no chaplain aboard the *Perseus*. Coyningham conducted the service.

'I am the resurrection and the life, saith the Lord . . .' he intoned.

Rob thought of the book he had seen in Tew's cabin, the childish inscription on the flyleaf: 'To Daddy, Come back safely, Love Edward'. Tew had rarely spoken of his family but Rob knew he had left a wife and a young son at home in Hampshire. It would be months before they knew what had happened. They would not even have a grave to visit. The best they could hope for were the rough coordinates Rob had scribbled down, a position to be plotted in the midst of the ocean.

'We therefore commit his body to the deep, to be turned into corruption, looking for the resurrection of the body, when the sea shall give up her dead.'

The flag was raised off the shroud. Two gunner's mates lifted the grating and tipped it up. The body slid forwards.

Perhaps this was right, Rob told himself. Tew had been a man without pretensions, a true sailor. He had loved the sea and the Royal Navy.

'Amen.'

The body dropped into the water with a splash and disappeared beneath the grey waves.

Rob was now the second lieutenant. Fawcett became first lieutenant. Rob should have been given command of the sloop they had captured, but Coyningham claimed he could not spare him. When they met with a seventy-four sailing north, they handed over the prize to be taken to New York and sold.

'Another prize you couldn'ae keep,' said Angus dolefully.

Coyningham did not appoint a new third lieutenant at once. He told the midshipmen he would promote one of them when they reached Jamaica, prompting a furious competition among them to win his favour. Rob knew they would report every word of gossip to the captain in an effort to gain the advantage. In a day, Coyningham had turned a collegiate gunroom into a den of snakes.

It didn't take long for the mood to spread to every corner of the ship. From the cabin boys to the officers' table, the division was plain. Many men accepted Coyningham's command as the natural order of things. The captain possessed the authority, for better or worse; they would try to keep out of trouble, and earn his favour as they could. But there were others who cherished the memory of Captain Tew and feared for their futures. They looked to Rob as their leader, though he did not encourage them.

'There's a fair few of 'em sayin' you should be captain instead of the Bloodhound,' said Angus.

It was two bells of the middle watch – one o'clock in the morning – and they were up on deck, one of the few times they could speak openly without fear of Coyningham overhearing.

Even then, there were some things that were too dangerous to say aloud. Rob silenced him with a glare and glanced over his shoulder.

'Coyningham is in command,' he said neutrally.

Angus would not be silenced. Rob could smell the rum on his breath.

'The way he runs this ship, he'll have a mutiny on his hands afore we reach Jamaica. He's turned us from the finest ship in the navy, to nothing more than a damned slaver.'

It was true. The temperature was rising as they sailed south. With fifty slaves locked in the hold, a stench had arisen from the ship's bowels: human sweat, blood and excrement. The howls and wails that emanated from within made the *Perseus* sound like a ghost ship. Every cry of pain was like a needle in Rob's heart. He had promised them they would be free. He had brought them aboard. And now they were worse off than if they'd stayed at the plantation.

'And the way he fawns on Mr Bracewell,' Angus went on. 'Like it's Mr Bracewell's ship, and not the King's.'

'He has designs on Bracewell's fortune.'

'Designs on his niece, you mean.' Angus saw the look on Rob's face. 'Don't say you didn'ae see it. I know you're sweet on her, but Coyningham follows her like a lost dog. And he has the captain's stripes on his sleeve.'

Rob had barely looked at Sophie since he returned from the plantation. His body still burned with desire for her. But his mind recoiled from the barbaric conditions he had seen at her uncle's house, and the way Bracewell had betrayed the freed slaves.

'Be careful,' Angus warned him. 'She may look like a lamb, but underneath she is a tiger.'

Rob thought of the stripes she had left down his back and nodded ruefully.

'That she is.'

A light appeared on deck as the cabin door swung open. A figure wrapped in a yellow shawl stepped onto the deck in her bare feet. She looked around, then crossed to Rob and Angus.

It was Phoebe. She was Sophie's maid, so – alone of the slaves – she was given the run of the ship. The lamplight gleamed off her golden brown skin.

'Lieutenant Courtney.' She curtsied. 'Miss Sophie said she was expecting to see you.'

Her voice was soft. Working as a maid, she had learned to speak good English, though modulated by the warm vowels and sensuous rhythms of her native language. It reminded Rob of the family servants and farm workers at Nativity Bay.

Angus gave Rob a hard stare. 'I didn't know you had other plans for this evening.'

'I didn't.'

Rob looked away. He did not mind Angus knowing about his affair with Sophie – his friend knew too much of what had gone on already. But he was embarrassed that Phoebe had become Sophie's go-between. He didn't want her to know.

Phoebe waited for his response, hands folded in front of her. But as Rob looked up, he saw her eyes quickly turn away, averting her gaze. Had she been looking at him? What could she think? Surely she must blame him for what had happened to Scipio and the others.

'Tell your mistress I am needed on deck this evening. Captain Coyningham is particular about keeping the watch.'

She nodded and made to leave. But Rob suddenly found he wanted her to stay.

'Where are you from?' he asked.

She stopped in surprise. She wasn't used to people speaking to her except to give orders or scold her.

'Me?'

'You,' said Rob.

'It is many thousands of miles away, across the ocean.' Her voice was tight with longing and sadness. 'You would not know it.'

'Tell me.'

'I am of the Qwabe.'

'On the east coast of Africa? Where the mountains meet the sea?'

She stared at him as if he had performed an act of magic.

'How can you know that?'

'I was born on the banks of the Umgeni river.'

'But . . .' Her face was a mask of astonishment. 'You are *mzungu*. A white man.'

'I am a wanderer,' said Rob, using the literal meaning of *mzungu*. 'My ancestors wandered to Africa. And now I have wandered here.'

She looked sad. 'You are teasing me.'

'Never. Do you remember the smell of the thorn trees after the rains?'

Even saying it took Rob back there . . . the vanilla-sweet scent in the air. He could see in her eyes she remembered it, too.

'The red dust . . .' she murmured.

'The air so clear you can see to the end of the world . . .'

'The thunder of the rivers after the rains . . .'

'How did you come to be here?' he asked.

Her eyes clouded with sorrow. 'You do not want to hear my story.'

'There is nothing I would want more,' Rob insisted.

And it was true. He wanted to listen to her voice, to keep looking into those eyes which seemed to reflect everything in the world he longed for.

Angus rose. 'I ought to check on the forestays.'

He retreated towards the bow of the ship.

Rob gestured to Phoebe to be seated.

'You will have to sit on a cannon,' he said. 'I'm afraid we have no more comfortable seating on deck.'

He thought he had frightened her, that she would fly away back to her cabin. But after a moment, she smoothed her skirts and perched on the twelve-pounder.

'My story is like all the others,' she said. 'I was taken.'

He could see the memory pained her. 'You do not have to tell me if it saddens you.'

But she wanted to tell him. 'We were in the fields with my mother, my sister and I, when we saw a great ship anchored off the coast. We had never seen one so close before, so we went down to the beach.

'There were white men. We had never seen them, either. They had come for water. They gave us shiny beads, and a mirror. We showed them a spring to fill their barrels.'

She paused, trembling with the memory. 'One of them had a beard. I remember how it roughed my cheek when he picked me up. His breath smelled of aniseed. His name was Don Pedro. He was Portuguese, though of course I did not know that then. He asked if I wanted to see aboard the ship. My mother said no, but I begged her. The white men, they were all so friendly. They laughed and smiled and gave my mother brandy from a bottle. So she said yes.

'I was excited. Even the little rowing boat that took us out astonished me. We were not a seagoing people – I had never been in a boat before. The waves sparkled like glass. When I put my hand in the water, I shrieked because I thought it would bite me.'

She bowed her head. Without thinking, Rob reached out and took her hands in his.

'The moment we went aboard, they grabbed us. They put us in chains, and threw us in the hold. The man with the beard was the captain. He took my mother to his cabin, and even in the bottom of the ship we could hear her screams. I was young, but old enough to know what he did to her.'

A tear escaped her eye. She looked surprised. Rob guessed she had long since wept herself dry over this story.

'The hold was full – they did not need more slaves. Slavers had never come to our country before. They only came because they needed water, and they took us because we were there.' She shuddered. 'They stacked us like firewood, on top of each other, chained together in our own filth.'

Rob remembered the conditions in the press room aboard the hulk in London. He tried to imagine living in those conditions for months, crossing the oceans, with not dozens but hundreds of other bodies crammed in together.

'I think they wanted to take us to Brazil. But there was a storm, and they were driven far north. The ship almost sank. Many died.'

'Your mother?'

Phoebe shook her head. 'She died before we left Cape Town.'

Rob thought of the story Tawny Cornish had told, of seeing the slave ship in Cape Town throwing dead captives overboard to the sharks. To think it might have been Phoebe's mother . . .

'The ship arrived in Jamaica. The Portuguese decided to sell us, so they could repair their ship. They took us to the slave market like animals. Bracewell found us there. He said he couldn't use a child, but the slavers offered me for free if he would take twelve other slaves. So he took me. He gave me to his niece as a plaything.'

'A playmate?'

'A play*thing*. She did what she liked with me – like a doll. She dressed me up and undressed me, she braided my hair, she fed me titbits from her table and took me into bed with her. And when she was angry, she beat me and tried to twist my arms off.'

Rob thought of the way Sophie took pleasure in inflicting pain. It excited her. He had thought it was part of a game. Now, imagining her having that power over a human being, to do exactly as she wanted, he could see it was no game at all. It chilled him to his core.

He felt a surge of shame and anger.

'I wish I could have saved you.'

'You were not there.'

There was no bitterness in her voice, no blame. Only surprise that Rob might think he had had a chance to change things. He took no comfort from it. He burned with the injustice of the world, longing to prove her wrong.

There was one other question he had to ask.

'And Scipio? Is he your husband?'

Phoebe eyed him curiously. 'Scipio is not my husband. Miss Sophie would never let me marry.'

'I meant . . .' Rob tried to find words that would not be crude or insulting. 'Like a husband.'

She could see his embarrassment. She laughed. A low, husky sound he instantly wanted to hear again.

'He is nothing like a husband. He is my brother.'

'But he is Ebo and you are Qwabe. Your homes are thousands of miles apart.'

'He was married to my sister.'

'Your brother-*in-law*?'

'Yes. She died two years ago.'

Rob felt he had been holding his breath for a very long time, like swimming underwater, and had finally broken the surface. He felt dizzy, dazed by a rush of conflicting thoughts. Against the terrible suffering Phoebe had endured, what did it matter if she had a husband or not? It was the height of selfishness to let his desire intrude on her tragedy. And even if he dared name what he felt for her, in what world could he ever act on it?

Yet from the moment he had seen her, he could not take his eyes off her. When she spoke, all he wanted was to listen. He knew nothing, except that he had to be with her.

Phoebe was still watching him.

'Why do you care if I am married?'

Rob did not know what to say. And because he was young and foolish and ignorant, and there were no other words, he said, 'Because I love you.'

He knew he was being impulsive, his emotions spilling over like a drunk unable to hold his glass of ale. He did not regret it. After Boston, he had thought he loved Sophie Bracewell, but now he saw that had been nothing more than lust, an animal hunger that overrode all reason. What he felt for Phoebe was entirely different, a sort of inner radiance that she drew out of his soul. All he wanted was to be close to her.

She started to laugh again, then stopped as she saw the awkwardness on his face.

'Do not say such things. Even if I . . .' She shook her head, as if trying to clear it of a dream. 'It is impossible.'

'I could buy your freedom.' He couldn't hold back.

'Miss Sophie would never sell her favourite toy.'

'Steal you away, then. I could work my passage to Cape Town, then find a ship to take us up the coast to Nativity Bay. We would be back where we belonged. We could walk in the thorn trees, and graze cattle by the river. You would be free.'

The hope on her face was almost too painful to see. She stared at him, but in her eyes she was looking at the landscape of her childhood, her home.

'It is impossible,' she said again, but less certainly.

Rob barely knew her. How could he make such reckless promises? Yet he meant them from the depths of his soul.

As if an invisible hand had taken hold of him, he leaned forwards to kiss her. She didn't resist. His lips met hers, as soft as the peaches that Louisa grew in the garden at Fort Auspice. He breathed in her scent.

Rapt in her story, in her face, he did not see the cabin door open behind her. Angus rose from where he had been sitting in the bow, carving a piece of scrimshaw. He opened his mouth to warn Rob.

Rob had already sensed the movement, but too late. He pulled back from Phoebe, to see Sophie striding across the deck, wrapped in her gown. He had never imagined such a pretty face could twist itself into such an ugly fury. With her hair blowing loose, her mouth contorted in a snarl, she looked like one of the Gorgons his grandmother used to tell him stories about, who could turn men to stone with a look.

'Get back to your place, you little *whore*,' she hissed at Phoebe. 'And you,' she said, turning to Rob. 'You tasted the sweetest fruit. If you prefer the company of slave *trash*, I will arrange it so you spend the rest of your days with them. A few weeks in the cane fields and your skin will be as black as theirs.'

Rob rose. 'I am not one of your slaves to command,' he said. 'I am an officer of His Majesty's Navy. And as soon as we reach port, I will lodge a petition with the governor for the release of Phoebe, and all the other slaves, under the terms of the certificates we gave them at Seabrook Bay.'

Sophie laughed. 'And after the governor has dined with my uncle, his great friend, what do you think he will do with your petition?' She tossed her head. 'You are so naive.'

'You are a monster,' said Rob. 'Like your uncle.'

Sophie grabbed Phoebe and pulled her off the cannon so she fell on the deck. She grasped a fistful of Phoebe's hair and started dragging her across the planking. Phoebe screamed with pain. Rob leaped up, took hold of Sophie's arm and tugged it away. Her hand ripped off a clump of Phoebe's hair.

'If you touch Miss Sophie again, I'll put a bullet through yer heart and drop you over the side like old Captain Tew,' said a voice from near the mizzen mast.

It was Crow. The glowing bowl of a pipe jutted from his mouth, and the steel barrel of a pistol glimmered in his hand, trained on Rob.

The barrel moved a fraction. 'Or I might make you watch yer darkie whore die first.'

Rob let go of Sophie.

Sophie stepped away, then landed a stinging slap across Rob's cheek. Rob didn't flinch.

'You will pay for this,' she hissed.

She dragged Phoebe back to her cabin. Crow waited until she had gone. He took a lump of sugar from his pocket and crunched it noisily, but the pistol in his hand never wavered. Rob didn't doubt that if he moved, Crow would put a bullet through him.

When Sophie and Phoebe had gone inside, Crow moved back towards the cabin. But he did not enter. He sat on the deck by the door, his hat pulled low and the gun in his hand.

Rob and Angus retreated towards the bow. Angus peered at Rob's face, as if expecting to see a bruise spreading.

'For a wee slip of a thing, she hits like a prizefighter,' he observed.

Rob touched his cheek. He remembered all the other bruises and scratches and bites Sophie had left on his body. He'd thought that was a sign of her love, an uncontrollable passion. Now he saw there was no love in her heart, only infinite cruelty.

'She'll get her revenge,' Angus said. 'You're not safe, Rob. Her and Coyningham, they're cut from the same black cloth. You've seen the way he follows her, cock in his hand. If she whispers in his ear, he'll break you back to a fo'c's'le hand and have you flogged down to your bones.'

'I am an officer.' Rob was trying to listen to his friend, but thoughts of Phoebe kept crowding his mind. 'There are limits to what he can do to me.'

Angus shook his head. 'Take my word, they will find some way to hurt you. Her and him both.'

A groan rose from the slaves in the hold, as if the ship itself was warning them.

The weather grew warmer, but the sun did not shine. Long clouds scudded across the sky, blown by a thick, sticky breeze that was worse than no wind at all. It left the men sweltering in their shirts. The stench from the hold grew worse every day, like a rotting corpse. Among the officers, only Coyningham kept his coat on. He had the sailmaker sew a strip of white lace on the sleeve, to give him a commander's rank. He touched it frequently, his fingers rubbing the lace as he paced the deck.

'He'll wear a hole in it, if he's not careful,' muttered Rob.

Sophie Bracewell kept her place in her chair under the awning on the quarterdeck, still the centre of every man's attention. But the midshipmen no longer found excuses to talk to her about the weather, and the warrant officers did not try to engage her on the pretext of explaining some point of seamanship. They feared Coyningham. He stood beside Sophie as often as he could, glaring at any man who glanced in her direction. He had his steward provide her lunch, and drinks. If she mentioned her book was in her cabin, or her fan, or her needlework, Coyningham would order them delivered.

Sophie kept Phoebe in attendance, standing behind her so she was out of the shade of the awning. Phoebe wore a thin white dress and no corset. The damp fabric clung to her body in the heat, so that her dark flesh was visible through the gauzy material. Every curve and swelling was on display. She might as well have been naked.

There was a raw, savage atmosphere aboard ship. Some looked at Sophie with such hunger Rob feared for her safety.

It was Sophie's revenge – laying Phoebe out like a piece of meat before a pack of slavering dogs. Standing hour after hour in the blazing tropical sun stripped her of all dignity. Rob feared Phoebe would faint. But her head never lowered. She stared ahead, meeting the men's gazes with defiance so that many of them were forced to look away, ashamed.

Rob sensed how much she must be suffering. He hated himself for being the cause of it. In the mid-afternoon, he filled a cup of water from the open cask by the mainmast, and carried it aft. Sophie looked up from her needlework and flashed him a razor-sharp smile.

'For me? How kind. I declare, in this heat I am absolutely *parched*.'

'It is for Phoebe,' said Rob.

Sophie's face hardened. 'I forbid it.'

'She is thirsty.'

'She will have to get used to standing in the sun where she is going, and working a great deal harder than this. When she is cutting cane in high summer, there will be no *gallants* to bring her water.' Sophie giggled. 'Of course, she has been a house servant all her life, so it will not be what she is used to. Her dainty hands will take some adjusting to heavy labour. But I am sure the overseers' lash on her back will encourage her.'

Rob wanted to throw the water in her face. He turned and offered the cup to Phoebe.

'I'm sorry,' he mouthed.

Phoebe reached for the cup. Her hand closed around it, clinging on so that her fingers were wound around Rob's.

Water splashed onto the deck as the cup was dashed from their hands. Phoebe pulled back with a cry. Crow stepped between them.

'Miss Bracewell said you're not to go near the girl,' he growled.

Rob met Crow's eyes in a fury. He wanted to knock him down. But there was a pistol in Crow's belt, and he could feel Coyningham's gaze hot on his back. Rob was the second lieutenant, but he was powerless.

He nodded to Phoebe. 'My apologies, miss.'

'One day, I will make Crow pay for what he does,' Rob said to Angus when they were out of earshot.

'He only does what Miss Sophie tells him,' said Angus. 'She's the one to watch for. Be thankful she has done nothing worse to get her revenge.'

Rob thought of Phoebe in a cane field, bent double, hands bleeding, the overseers' whips raining down blows on her naked back. He had to save her before that happened. For now he agreed with Angus. It was best not to make things worse.

But he had underestimated Sophie.

Next day, as usual, she was sitting in her chair on the quarterdeck. Rob was inspecting the starboard guns when he heard her say to Coyningham, 'So many men in such a tight space. Do you not fear for your life?'

'Discipline is the key, miss. We keep them on a short leash. If any are tempted to impertinent thoughts, a taste of the lash brings them to heel.'

Sophie's eyes sparkled. Her glossy lips parted. She put a hand to her chest, her fingers cupping her breast.

'Is it very painful?'

'We must make it so,' said Coyningham. 'To teach them their lesson.'

'Indeed,' said Sophie. 'There is nothing like pain to stiffen a man's sinews.'

Her eyes flicked to Rob. She smiled as she caught him watching her.

'Wouldn't you agree, Lieutenant Courtney?'

'I find praise and a kind word usually serves better to motivate the men,' he said. 'Pain can make a man fear you, but it is heart you need when it comes to a battle.'

'We shall see about that, Lieutenant.' She turned to Coyningham. 'There is a small yellow purse in my cabin. It has my prayer book in it . . .'

'Of course.'

Coyningham went below at once. But when he returned, he was empty-handed, flushed and confused.

'I could not find the purse,' he apologised.

'But I left it on my bed,' said Sophie. 'I am certain of it. You could not fail to see it.'

'It is not there now,' Coyningham assured her.

'Where could it have gone?' Her mouth made an *O* of surprise. 'That prayer book was a gift from my poor late mother. It is all I have to remember her by.'

'I will find it,' said Coyningham.

Sophie looked at him over the top of her fan.

'I do hope . . . No – it is too terrible to contemplate.'

'What?'

'You do not think that perhaps . . .?' She paused, collecting herself. 'I kept a sum of money in that purse. I hope one of your men was not . . . *tempted* by it.'

Coyningham's face went dark.

'By God, if they have . . . Mr Leake!'

The boatswain's mate came scuttling up.

'Search the ship for Miss Bracewell's purse,' Coyningham ordered him. 'If any man has taken it, there will be two dozen lashes with the cat.'

'So few?' said Sophie. 'For such an outrage?'

'Four dozen,' Coyningham corrected himself.

The men assembled on deck, angry and bewildered. It was the dog watch, and most of them had been off duty. They did not care to have their leisure time interrupted. Bangs and crashes echoed out of the hatchway as Leake and his mates carried out a thorough search of their sea chests.

Rob looked at Sophie. A curious smile played over her lips.

What mischief have you planned? Rob wondered.

Suddenly there were shouts from below. Leake came up the ladder, clutching a yellow silk bag in his fist. He presented it to Coyningham.

'One of the men had took it. We found it in his things.'

The crew on deck went silent. Four dozen lashes was close to what a man could endure.

Coyningham gave the purse to Sophie with a bow. She clasped it to her chest.

'Thank you,' she said, favouring Coyningham with a golden smile.

Her mouth hardened. 'Who was the vile thief who stole it?'

Leake surveyed the assembled men. Most bowed their heads, praying his glance would not settle on them. A few, confident of their innocence, stared back. Leake raised a hand, moving it over the crowd.

'Him.'

His finger pointed accusingly. Rob felt as if he'd been punched in the stomach. At last he fathomed the depths of Sophie's revenge.

Leake was pointing at Angus. The sailors around him shrank back, as Leake's assistants seized him. Angus remained calm.

'I didn'ae do it,' he said, loud enough to carry to the quarter-deck. 'Someone's done this to bugger me.'

'Silence,' roared Coyningham. 'Put up the grating. Strip him down and assemble all hands to witness punishment.'

Sophie sat up, her lips parted. Rob sidled close to her.

'Please do not do this,' he said in a low voice.

'This is the captain's decision. I cannot change his mind.'

'A word from you and Coyningham will call it off. You know he is infatuated with you.'

'I am glad not every man thinks me more loathsome than some darkie whore.'

'If you wish to hurt me, I will take any punishment you choose. But do not take it out on my friends.'

She looked at him over the top of her fan. Her eyes were hard as diamonds.

'This *is* your punishment.'

On the main deck, the grating had been lifted off the hatch-way and leaned against the front of the quarterdeck. The marine drummer boys beat a staccato tattoo. Leake's men brought Angus to the grating. They stripped him to his waist, spread-eagled him and tied his wrists fast with the seizings.

Rob lined up with the other officers. He thought about forc-ing his way through, cutting Angus down and putting a blade to Coyningham's throat. It was impossible. Even if the men doubted Angus's guilt, or flinched at the harsh sentence, the bonds of discipline bound them to obedience. And there were the marine sentries, muskets loaded and tipped with bayonets, standing along the quarterdeck rail. They would stay loyal to Coyningham.

Angus turned to Rob. He shook his head the merest fraction.

'We'll need you later!' he called, loud enough that Rob could hear.

The drum roll reached a crescendo and stopped. Leake took the cat out of its baize bag. The knots rattled on the deck as the nine long tails fell loose. Rob heard a gasp behind him. Sophie had risen from her seat and come to the quarterdeck rail to watch.

'You should not witness this,' said Coyningham. 'It is not suitable for a lady.'

'No,' said Sophie. 'The crime was against me. I must see him punished.'

Coyningham nodded. The drummer tapped a single beat on his drumhead. Leake flexed his arm.

'One,' said Coyningham.

The whip lashed into Angus's bare back. The tight knots left a line of livid red weals in the skin.

Sophie gasped as if she were about to faint. She slipped one hand into Coyningham's arm, clinging on. The other hand rested on her dress, below her belly.

Watching the punishment was the hardest thing Rob had ever done. Sailing into the bay at Newport, or facing down the French frigate at Seabrook, had been child's play in comparison. He wanted to close his eyes, but he owed it to Angus to bear witness to every stroke. It was all his fault.

Coyningham was observing, mesmerised. Rob remembered the pleasure he had taken seeing men flogged before. He remembered also what Angus had said about Coyningham and Sophie. *They're cut from the same black cloth.*

Rob had witnessed many floggings aboard the *Perseus*. It was a fact of navy life. The men hated to see them, but if they thought the man was guilty, they accepted the punishment as part of the order of things. Now, the mood was darker than it had ever been. They started to get agitated. They had joined the Royal Navy for honour and glory. With the taste of blood on their lips, and the stench of the slave hold rising through the air, they wondered what they had become.

After twenty-four lashes, the surgeon examined Angus and pronounced him fit to continue being punished. Angus was almost unconscious. He slumped against the grating, with barely enough energy to flinch when he was struck.

'Forty-eight.'

By the time the final stroke came down, Angus's back was a mess of blood and torn flesh.

'Dismiss the men,' Coyningham ordered brusquely.

He scanned the watching crowd, shrinking slightly as he saw the hostility boiling off the men.

'Let that be a lesson to all who think they may make free with Mr and Miss Bracewell's property.'

They cut Angus down. Rob, Thomas and Hargrave went to his aid. Rob held his head and poured brandy in his mouth, while Hargrave sluiced his wounds. Angus clenched his teeth so hard when the salt water hit, Rob thought he might bite his tongue off. But he made no sound. He would not give Coyningham the satisfaction.

A shadow fell over them from the quarterdeck. Rob could see the polished toes of Coyningham's riding boots, almost level with his face. Sophie's feet, in her gold-braided slippers, stood close beside.

'Leave that man,' drawled Coyningham. 'The next man who helps him will get a dozen lashes himself.'

The crew stared. After such a flogging, a man needed days to recover. Usually he was left to recuperate in the sick bay. It was unheard of to deny the flogged man even basic care.

Something snapped inside Rob. He stood and squared up to Coyningham, his fists poised to strike. Coyningham was so surprised he could not speak. His mouth flapped open like a fish.

'Stop,' cried a feeble voice. It was Angus. 'Don't do it,' he gasped. He spat out the words, accompanied by flecks of blood. 'If you touch him, he'll hang you from the yardarm and never have to answer for it. You'll get your chance,' he added, more softly, so that only Rob could hear.

Rob backed away, casting his eyes downwards so he did not have to see the triumph flooding Coyningham's face.

'Have a care, Mr Courtney,' he hissed. 'Your time will come.'

Rob nodded. 'It will indeed. And when it does, you can be sure I will be ready.'

Coyningham blanched. Rob enjoyed the shadow of doubt he had cast in the brute's mind, though he could not enjoy it for more than a fleeting moment.

The agony Angus had suffered had really been meant for Rob. Sophie tormented Phoebe every day to punish him. What other ways would they find of hurting him?

'*Lieutenant Courtney!*'

Rob woke to someone calling his name. By now, the navy had got him used to being turned out of bed at all hours, alert at once to any shift in wind or tide. This time, it took a moment longer to surface. He had been dreaming of Nativity Bay, of his grandmother Louisa. In his dream, he had been back on the beach the night he left. The moon had made a great silver reflection on the water. Louisa had waded into the bay, her hair luminous in the moonlight. Rob had called at her to stop, but she had carried on, deeper and deeper until the reflected moon swallowed her.

'Lieutenant Courtney?'

Hargrave's voice brought him back to where he was, crammed in his cot in a stifling cabin. Hargrave peered through the open door, ducking his head against the low timbers. He carried no light, but Rob could hear other men in the passage behind him.

'Is something wrong?'

'We need to talk. Quiet, like.'

Rob dressed and followed them up on deck. The tropical stars burned large and bright in the sky, while a crescent moon glimmered on the horizon. A low, sad song rose from the captives in the hold. It reminded him of Africa, taking him back to his dream and the strange ache in his heart. What would Louisa say if she could see him now?

Half a dozen men had gathered on the foredeck. Thomas, and three or four others from their watch. Even Angus had staggered out of his sick bed, sitting stiff-backed by the rail. He must still be in great pain: two of his shipmates sat beside him to steady him if he faltered.

'What is this?' Rob said, though he guessed the answer.

'We can'nae let Coyningham go on this way,' said Angus. 'We need to stop him.'

'He will not listen to me,' Rob replied. 'You know that.'

'It's past time for talking,' said Hargrave. 'We need action.'

Rob looked around the group. Every man's face was grim with purpose.

'You mean—'

'Mutiny,' said Angus.

Rob glanced down the length of the ship in case anyone had overheard.

'That's a word no man should ever even think. Just for saying it aloud, you'd get a flogging to make what you had before look like a rap on the knuckles.'

'I doo'nae fear the lash. I fear what'll come of us if we don't do it.' Angus leaned forwards, wincing as his shirt tightened against the weeping scars on his back. 'It'll feel more proper with an officer to lead us. More men'll join. The question is – are you with us?'

Rob's mind raced. His conscience was torn in two. Courtneys had served in the Royal Navy since Sir Charles Courtney served with Francis Drake. To turn mutineer would put a stain on the family honour that would never be expunged.

But what use was honour if it left men like Angus at the mercy of tyrants like Coyningham? If it meant that brave men like Scipio could be cheated of their liberty and locked in the hold like cargo? If a monster like Sophie could use naval discipline to extract cruel revenge on innocent sailors?

Rob thought of all the men who had carried the Neptune sword before him – down to his great-grandfather Tom, and Jim. What would they have done?

'Where would you go?' he asked.

The men shuffled uneasily. This was not a well-crafted plan, Rob saw: it was a counsel of desperation.

'I would like to go home,' said Thomas, in a small voice that reminded Rob he was still a child.

'Do you think you could sail up the Thames and drop anchor in the Pool of London, you ninny?' asked Hargrave. 'If we do this, we can never go home.'

No one answered. The men had fixed upon mutiny as a desperate remedy for their situation, but they had not thought through the consequences.

'If you do this, you will all be hunted men,' Rob warned. 'The Royal Navy's reach stretches around the world, and they will not forgive the theft of one of their finest ships. There will be no port on earth where you could be safe.'

Hargrave looked disappointed. 'Does that mean you'll not do it?'

'I ken it's hard for you,' said Angus, 'being an officer and all. But you was one of us before you was one of them, and I hope you've nae forgot it.'

Rob shook his head. 'I have not forgotten it.'

Down in the bowels of the ship, he heard a rattle of chains and a moan. One of the captives must have stirred in their sleep, disturbing all the others around them. Perhaps they had wakened from a bad dream, only to find themselves in a worse nightmare.

Rob made up his mind.

'If you are still set on this course, then I am with you.'

He knew as soon as he spoke the words that it was the right choice. A feeling of relief brightened through him. The men felt it, too. A ripple of gratitude ran through them; they began to look more hopeful.

'But we must be careful. If Coyningham hears a word of this, he will have us swinging from the yardarms.'

The men's faces hardened. None of them underestimated the stakes, or the consequences if they failed.

'How many of the crew would stay loyal to Coyningham?'

Angus counted on his fingers.

'The boatswain's mates. The midshipmen. The marines. Maybe half the petty officers. A dozen others that're tight with him.'

'And who would join us?'

Angus sucked his teeth. 'Most of the rest.'

'I say do it now,' growled Hargrave. 'While we're on the open ocean. Once we get close to Jamaica there'll be other British warships about.'

'And what'll we do with them that don't join us?'

'Put 'em adrift in an open boat.'

'They'd die.'

'It's more'n they'd do for us.'

'No,' said Rob. He had studied the charts that afternoon. 'If we set them adrift in the ocean, their lives would be on our conscience. We must wait until we are among the islands. Then we can put Coyningham ashore in a deserted spot, with any men who want to stay with him, and trust that a passing vessel will rescue them in due course.'

There were murmurs of dissent, but Rob quashed them with a look.

'Also, we will need to take on water and provisions for our voyage.'

Angus saw the intent in his eye. 'Where d'ye have a mind to go?'

'To Africa.'

'Africa?' cried Thomas. So far as he was concerned, it might as well be the moon. 'But we will all die there.'

'I know a place we can go,' said Rob. 'A place the navy will never find us.'

The men were chattering again, some in favour of Africa, others unhappy. Rob could see they were unsure. If it came to a vote, it would be hard to know which side would win.

'If you want me to lead you, then we go to Africa.' He had his own interests in mind as well as his mates. This could be a homecoming in many ways, rest for his conscience as well as his soul. 'Otherwise, you are on your own.'

They conceded. Mutineers they might be, but they could not imagine life at sea without an officer to command them. And Rob was one of the few men aboard who could read the charts and navigate their position.

'When's it to be?' asked Angus.

The next days were torture for Rob, as the *Perseus* slowly made her way south. He had lit the touchpaper but did not know when the explosion would occur. Every day increased the chances they would be discovered. You could not keep a secret on a ship the size of the *Perseus*. Angus and his friends had to sound out the crew, looking for allies. If they misjudged even one man, word would get back to Coyningham. And then they would be dead men.

The temperature rose and the air grew sticky. When the crew swabbed the decks, the water boiled off in clouds of steam. The moans of the slaves in the hold grew more desperate. Rob tried to arrange for them to be given extra water, and to be brought out on deck for air, but every time Coyningham countermanded the order.

At last, they sighted land: low, lush islands that barely broke the sea. Further to the horizon, they could see the larger masses of Cuba and Saint-Domingue. It added to the febrile atmosphere. One island belonged to Spain, and the other to France. Although Britain was not at war with either country, both had previously been enemies and no doubt would be again soon. There was not a man aboard who felt comfortable sailing between the two territories.

'We must go tonight,' Rob decided. 'It's a full moon. And once we are past Cuba, we will be a day's sail from Jamaica.'

Angus nodded. The wounds on his back had closed, though he still grimaced when he walked.

'Then let's be on with it.'

Rob could not sleep that night. He lay awake in his cot, fully dressed, listening to the ship and imagining all the ways the plan could go wrong. He tried to put the thoughts out of his head. It was too late now.

He heard the ship's bell strike two bells of the first watch. A moment later, he heard a soft tap on his door. Hargrave, Thomas and Angus were waiting in the passage.

None of them spoke. They had gone over what they would do so many times, each knew the plan by heart. Rob led Hargrave and Thomas to Coyningham's cabin, while Angus went to the weapons store. Rob's heart pounded. The seriousness of what they were doing weighed heavily on him, but he knew it was the right thing. His spirits rose as he imagined the look on Coyningham's face, the outrage of knowing he had lost his command.

He halted outside the first lieutenant's room, which Coyningham still occupied while the Bracewells were in the great cabin. He was about to open it, when he heard a strange knocking coming from within. Was Coyningham having a restless night?

Rob would not take any chances if the captain was awake. He drew his pistol.

'On my word,' he told the others. 'One, two . . .'

The lookout's voice drifted down through the open hatchway.

'Deck there. Sail off the starboard bow.'

Rob froze. A sail could mean two things, either of them disastrous. If she was friendly, they could not let her come alongside while they were in the act of mutiny. But if she was an enemy, they would not be able to fight her off with one half of the crew at war with the other.

Everyone was looking at him.

'What do we do?' whispered Thomas.

'Wait here.'

Rob went on deck, seized a spyglass from the rack and ran up the shrouds, surprising the lookout on the crosstrees. The man pointed out the vessel he had seen.

Rob cursed. The ship had crept up close on them while the moon was behind the clouds. Now, with the moon out, he could see her plainly with the naked eye, barely three leagues distant. She moved serenely across the silver sea, her sails glowing in the moonlight like a ghost ship.

It was a calm night. Any commotion aboard the *Perseus* would easily carry across the water. But was she friend or foe? Rob aimed the telescope at her prow.

He stiffened. The shadow was deep under her bowsprit, but a little moonlight reflected off the white foam surging around her bow. Enough to make out the shape of her figurehead: a dark bird, beak outstretched and wings curving back down the sides of the ship.

Was it the *Rapace*? Had she followed them? How could she have repaired the damage so fast? There was no flag, and the low moon silhouetted her so he could not see if there were gunports down her side, or how many. Whoever it was, she had seen the *Perseus*. She altered course, turning her nose so that she would intercept the frigate.

Rob had an instant to decide what to do. There were over two hundred men aboard his ship, most of them asleep. At the speed with which the other ship had come up, she would overhaul them soon. If Rob didn't warn the crew now, and the ship turned out to be an enemy, they would die in their hammocks.

He slid down the stay. Angus loomed out of the gloom carrying an armful of cutlasses.

'Is she against us?'

'I cannot say.'

'Then what do we do?'

Rob clenched his teeth. It felt unfair that all the burden of this decision had fallen to him – it would be much easier not to have to make it. The injustice of it almost paralysed him, but he knew he could not shirk it.

'I will wake Captain Coyningham.' They were the bitterest words he had ever spoken.

'If you do that, we'll lose our chance,' Angus warned him. 'It's only one more day to Jamaica. Bracewell will put those slaves to work on his plantation or sell them off. Would you condemn them to that?'

Rob felt the pressure mounting inside him, almost fit to crack his skull. He shook his head.

'Better they live than we all die. We will find another way.'

'There is no time,' said Angus. 'It's now or never.'

Rob could not look his friend in the eye.

'Have our men stow their weapons. It will not do if Coyningham comes on deck and finds them armed to the teeth.'

He hurried below to the first lieutenant's cabin. He was readying to knock, when a strange mewling noise came from inside, an urgent muttering and a crack like a piece of wood snapping.

Rob opened the door but it struck something on the floor. There was a low yelp of pain, and a high-pitched cry of surprise. Rob peered in.

At first he thought the mutiny had begun already. Coyningham lay spread-eagled on the floor. He was face down, naked, his hands tied behind his back and his nose bleeding where the door had hit it. He was not alone. Sophie sat astride him, also naked, with a riding crop in one hand and a feather in the other.

Coyningham's eyes widened in outrage. He tried to speak, but his words were muffled by the gag Sophie had tied across his mouth.

Sophie smiled at him. She was glistening in a sheen of sweat, her nipples engorged.

'Have you come to join us?' she said. 'I have always been curious to try such an arrangement. I believe in France they call it a *ménage à trois*.' There was a sly look in her eyes. 'Or perhaps you want to take your gallant captain all for yourself?' She parted Coyningham's buttocks with the riding crop. 'I think he would like that.'

Rob felt no jealousy. If anything, he was stirred to shame to think that he'd once thought he loved this woman. But it was not the time to dwell on his own feelings.

Rob pulled the gag off.

'We've sighted a sail,' he said, before Coyningham could speak. 'She may be hostile. Shall I order the men to clear for action?'

Coyningham nodded.

'I will leave you to get dressed.'

On deck, the guns had already been loaded. The other ship was closing fast. She had seen the *Perseus* clearing for action. Hastily, she ran up her own flag. The white ensign of a British merchantman.

'It could be a feint,' said Rob. 'We've seen privateers hoist false colours before.'

But watching her approach, he did not feel the tremor of danger he had felt when he saw the *Rapace*. A thin cloud had veiled the moon, making it hard to see clearly, but there was none of the activity on her deck that would tell of a ship getting ready to fight. And although he had only seen the *Rapace* in the heat of battle, there were aspects that did not seem right. There were too few men on her deck. Too few guns. None of the splashes of fresh paintwork that told of recent repairs that the *Rapace* would have to have made.

She shortened sail as she came alongside the *Perseus*, a musket shot away. The moon came out and her bow moved around and Rob could see the figurehead plainly at last.

It was not a screaming, rapacious hawk. It was a placid brown bird, like the quails that Rob had often seen running about his feet at Fort Auspice.

He should have felt relieved. Instead, he tasted bitter bile in his throat. He had had the chance to save Phoebe, free Scipio and avenge Angus, and he had missed it.

'What ship?' he called across the narrow gap of water.

'The *Corncrake*,' came the reply. 'Out of Bristol, bound for Port Royal. We have orders for you.'

She was nothing more than a merchantman.

R ob told himself the mutiny had been doomed the moment the sail appeared. They could never have seized the *Perseus* with another vessel bearing down on them. In his heart, he knew it wasn't true. The plot had been well planned. They could have taken the ship, and if the *Corncrake* had tried to intervene a shot across her bows would have sent her away.

Rob had made the wrong decision. He replayed the events of the night before in his head a thousand times. What was the real reason for his decision? Why had he not taken his chance? Was there an ugly flaw in his mettle, his ability to face up to the ultimate test? Lurking in the back of his mind was the cruellest question of all.

Was he a coward?

Angus had not spoken to him since. The other men who had been in on the plot refused to meet his eye. They were tardy and disobedient, slow to follow his orders. Those who hadn't known about the plot could tell something was up. They watched him suspiciously, as if they could smell the failure on him.

At least Coyningham stayed in his cabin. He assumed that by now every man in the ship must know what Rob had seen him doing with Sophie. He could not step on deck without drawing a hundred furtive glances and sniggering whispers. He could not flog every man aboard, so he stayed below, nursing his battered dignity.

The only time Rob saw him was when he summoned the officers to the great cabin to relay the orders the *Corncrake* had brought. Coyningham looked awkward when Rob walked in, poring over the chart table so that he would not have to meet Rob's eye.

The other officers crowded around. Bracewell was present, having graciously allowed them to use the great cabin. Sophie was absent.

'This is our position,' said Coyningham, pointing to the channel between Cuba and Saint-Domingue. 'From here, we have a clear run south to Jamaica.'

Jamaica stretched across the map like an extended thumb. Bracewell planted a finger on the north-west corner of the island, far from any of the towns and ports that were marked.

'Thebes Plantation, my estate, is here.'

'The *Corncrake* has brought further orders,' said Coyningham. 'A supply convoy from England is approaching Jamaica. It is bringing powder and ammunition for the Caribbean garrisons, a year's supply.' He looked around gravely. 'There is enough powder and shot aboard that convoy to start a war.'

The officers nodded.

'Then we had best make sure it reaches its destination,' said Fawcett, the first lieutenant.

'Precisely,' said Coyningham. 'A squadron of warships has escorted her this far, but they will now sail to join the war in America. As soon as we have delivered Mr Bracewell and his niece to their home, we will rendezvous with the convoy and escort it to Port Royal, which is here –' he pointed on the map – 'at the mouth of the Kingston Harbour in south-eastern Jamaica.'

The officers' faces fell. For a ship like the *Perseus*, convoy duty was like yoking a racehorse to a hay wagon. Slow sailing, endless chivvying of the cumbersome merchantmen, and no prospect of battle or prizes.

'Are there no other ships that could do this?' asked Fawcett, speaking for all of them.

Coyningham shook his head. 'We will be the only escort.'

'If the convoy's as valuable as you say,' Rob said, 'surely it needs more protection.'

'As ever, Lieutenant Courtney blanches at the first sign of danger,' said Coyningham.

Several of the midshipman laughed sycophantically.

'The seas around Jamaica are safe,' Bracewell assured them. 'Once the convoy is in sight of land, there is no danger of attack.' He pointed to the far western end of the island. 'The only danger is here. There is a shoal where many ships have grounded, and a strong current runs around the cape. You must keep close to the shore here.'

'We will do as you say,' said Coyningham.

'It would be safer to keep away from land,' argued Rob. 'If the convoy is close to a lee shore, an attack even by a single privateer could wreak carnage.'

'You heard Mr Bracewell's advice. We will set our course close to shore.'

'Mr Bracewell knows nothing of navigation,' Rob persisted.

Coyningham coloured. 'Do you presume to question my orders?' A dangerous edge came into his voice. 'That would be insubordination.'

Rob held his tongue. There was no point giving Coyningham another pretext to discipline him.

Coyningham turned away. 'If that is all, you may return to your duties. With a fair wind, we should raise Jamaica tomorrow.'

There was nothing more to be said. But as Rob filed out with the other officers, he noticed Bracewell examining the map, a smile spreading across his face.

They saw Jamaica from afar: hazy blue mountain peaks rising towards the clouds, higher than anything Rob had seen since he left Africa. Their steep slopes were thickly wooded, laced with strands of white cloud. Below, everything was lush and green.

'Looks like Eden,' said one of the men.

'Aye,' said Angus. 'And full of serpents, too, I'll wager.'

He shot a look at Bracewell and Sophie, who had come on deck as soon as they heard the lookout announce the sighting of Jamaica. With her raven hair bound neatly under her bonnet, a long green dress and a pair of white gloves, Sophie looked a picture of modesty. Phoebe stood behind her, holding a parasol over her mistress's head.

From the charts, Rob knew that most of the settlements in Jamaica were in the south-east of the island, around Kingston and Port Royal. The *Perseus* sailed clear of those harbours, making instead for the north-west coast. A spyglass confirmed what the maps had indicated: it was a wild, remote country. Villages were few and distant; the mountains came down close to the shore, leaving a narrow strip along the coast which was thick with mangrove swamps.

'There,' said Bracewell, steadying himself on the rail as he peered through a telescope. 'Thebes Plantation.'

The estate stood on an eminence above a sandy bay. A vast white house towered bright on a promontory against the green cane fields. Beyond it clustered groups of small cottages, storehouses and tall stone windmills, their red sails turning in the breeze. Further away the forest rose quickly to the mountains.

'It must be lonely, living here,' said Coyningham, who had emerged from his cabin.

'Indeed.' Sophie spoke politely, as if she were at a tea party in a Hampshire drawing room – as if the events in Coyningham's cabin had never happened. 'We are quite cut off from society at the Thebes Plantation. But my uncle prefers his solitude.'

Rob imagined Bracewell on his estate, a virtual monarch. He shuddered to think what a man like Bracewell would do with unchecked power like that.

'I hope you do not feel removed from agreeable company,' Coyningham persisted.

Sophie smiled at him. 'Never when you are present, Captain. You are always most stimulating.'

Coyningham glanced at Bracewell to see if he had noticed the saucy tone in her voice. But Bracewell's attention was on his estate.

'She is worth fifty thousand a year,' he announced. 'One thousand hogsheads of sugar, and rum besides.'

'And how many slaves?' Rob asked.

'Near four hundred.' Bracewell put down the telescope. He had not forgotten their confrontation at Seabrook Bay. 'There will be a few more, of course, with the people you brought from South Carolina.'

Rob did not dare look at Phoebe. The guilt was intolerable.

Before they dropped anchor in the bay, boats had set out from the wooden jetty that served the estate. Rows of bare-chested slaves manned the oars, lashed by the overseers who stood in the stern. As they came alongside, Rob saw that every man was chained to his oar. If the boat flipped in the surf, they would all drown.

Coyningham summoned the marines on deck, fully armed, making a phalanx around the hatchways. Then he opened the hold. The stench was almost unbreathable. The slaves were brought up one by one and forced into the boats. Rob could see from the disgust on some of the marines' faces that they did not like this duty, but Coyningham gave them no choice. He was desperate to curry favour with the Bracewells.

'You must dine with us tonight, Captain,' said Bracewell. His luggage had been loaded into the last of the boats, and he was ready to disembark. 'And your officers, too. We owe you a debt of thanks for bringing us safely home.'

'I would be honoured,' said Coyningham.

'Lieutenant Courtney must come, too,' added Sophie.

Rob and Coyningham both started in surprise, though a second later Rob realised he should have expected it. Sophie was like a cat, licking her claws as she toyed with the mice she had trapped. She didn't want Rob's company, except perhaps to flaunt herself. She wanted him there to prick Coyningham's lust, to put them in competition like two cocks in a ring. She didn't care who won. The sport was what she lived for.

Coyningham looked so downcast Rob almost felt sorry for him, until he glanced out to the water, and saw the boats taking Scipio and the other slaves ashore. Lust was no excuse for what Coyningham had done.

'Alas, Miss Bracewell,' Coyningham said, 'Mr Courtney must stay aboard ship to keep watch.'

'Quite right,' said Bracewell, who had no desire to bring Rob to his plantation. Behind him, Crow looked appalled. But Sophie was undeterred.

'Have you forgotten, Uncle, how Lieutenant Courtney rescued us from Newport? And saved our property in South Carolina. He must join us. I insist on it.'

'Very well,' said Bracewell. 'If Captain Coyningham agrees.'

Coyningham bowed stiffly. 'You know I can deny you nothing.'

Sophie lowered her voice. 'I do hope not, Captain.'

Rob and Coyningham went ashore in the middle of the afternoon. Fawcett and three of the midshipmen accompanied them, buoyant with excitement and high spirits. Rob and Coyningham sat awkwardly in the stern of the boat, saying nothing to each other.

From the jetty, stone steps led up the hill through terraced gardens. Vivid colours exploded all around them – pinks and oranges and blues and yellows of flowers Rob had never seen before. Marble statues watched from among the plants, barebreasted goddesses and priapic gods. The scent of the flowers was lush and thick around them. Everything was rich and sensual.

Yet Rob could not forget what underpinned it all. Through the trees at the top of the slope, he could see the ugly silhouette of a gibbet. A mournful chant sounded from beyond, a low wail like a funeral song.

A man was waiting for them at the top of the steps, silhouetted against the sky like a bird on a tree. Crow. He bared his blackened teeth as he saw them approach.

'Welcome to Thebes Plantation,' he drawled.

Bracewell's mansion loomed on the clifftop away to their right. But Crow led them inland towards the cluster of buildings beyond the palm trees.

'Mr Bracewell said to give you a tour of the estate before dinner,' Crow explained as they arrived at the stables.

Half a dozen horses were saddled and waiting for them. Crow's grin broadened as he watched the naval officers' ungainly attempts to mount, assisted by the black grooms and stable boys.

'Is the estate so large that we cannot walk?' asked Coyningham, clinging to the unfamiliar saddle.

'Even on horseback we'd need a full day to cover the whole plantation,' Crow answered. 'This is but a taste.'

He led them on horseback to a cluster of buildings about half a mile away. They stood downwind from the big house, and as Rob approached he understood why. The smell of rum hung over everything. Even in the *Perseus*'s hold, where the packed rum casks sometimes split open, Rob had never smelled anything like it. Just breathing in the saturated air made him feel tipsy.

They dismounted in front of a complex of buildings. At its heart was a tall octagonal windmill, built of stone and tapering to a high point. The red sails turned briskly in the breeze. A large, barn-like shed stood next door, and a succession of other outbuildings. The air was hot with an alcoholic steam that made Rob's eyes weep rum-flavoured tears.

'Sugar works,' said Crow.

As he spoke, a gang of slaves appeared, pulling a cart stacked high with cane stalks. They unloaded them and carried the stems in great armfuls into the mill. Crow and the officers followed.

Inside, the mill was dim, stifling and deafening. Cogs and axles descended from the ceiling, transmitting the sails' revolutions into a contraption where copper-covered rollers turned in parallel, parted slightly like the lips of a disembodied mouth. The slaves fed the cane into the voracious maw, their hands inches from the spinning cylinders. As each stalk entered, it was crushed as thin as paper and spat out the other side.

'You would not want to catch your arm in there,' said Fawcett.

'Perhaps that is what makes the sugar brown,' said Coyningham.

The others laughed, though it was no joke. It would be easy for a limb to get stuck in the mechanism, especially for the tired slaves. They looked half dead, their shoulders slumped and their eyes dulled almost past living.

'Harvest season,' Crow explained. 'We work the crop every hour of the day and all the night through.'

The rollers squeezed the brown cane juice from the stalks. The liquid dribbled out and collected into a channel below, which carried it away through an opening in the side of the mill. The party from the *Perseus* followed it outside and into the next building.

The moment they entered, the heat hit the officers like a body blow. Slaves worked stripped almost naked, ladling the liquid between a series of iron kettles, while children fed the fires burning beneath with the crushed stalks and cane trash.

'Boiling house,' said Crow.

As the cane liquid progressed from one kettle to the next, it became thicker and more viscous, until finally it was taken to the next building and decanted into large clay funnels set over jars.

'In a month, it'll be ready to put in your tea,' said Crow.

'What is the jar underneath for?' asked one of the midshipmen.

'Molasses,' said Crow. 'It runs out down the funnel. We turns that into rum in the still house.'

They went back outside and remounted their horses. There was another building, a squat shed set apart from the others, but Crow did not take them there. A chill went through Rob's heart as they passed it. It was the twin of the punishment hut he had seen at Bracewell's plantation in South Carolina. Even the slaves bringing in carts of fresh cane went out of their way to avoid it.

The *Perseus*'s officers passed the thatched slave cottages, surrounded by vegetable plots, and rode down a narrow track between the cane fields. Slaves ran ahead of them to open the gates that fenced off the different fields, or 'cane pieces', as Crow called them. They waited until the party had passed through, closed the gate, then raced ahead again. Crow kept a brisk pace with his horse, so that the slaves had to sprint to reach the next gate in time.

Rob could hardly believe how far the plantation stretched. They rode for almost a quarter of an hour between the rustling cane thickets before they reached a place where a gang of slaves were working. All were dressed in white calico, shirts and trousers for the men, blouses and skirts for the women. They slashed the cane with long, curved knives, topping off the fronds and stripping the leaves before putting them in the carts. They didn't glance up at the new arrivals. They knew if they slacked their work for a moment, they would feel the lash of the overseer who paced the rows behind them. Four more men armed with rifles and pistols stood guard at the corners of the field.

Rob recognised a couple of the faces working the cane – men who had fought beside him at Seabrook Bay. Bracewell had wasted no time making use of them. Rob felt relief that they did not look at him – he could not have stood the rebuke – then felt ashamed of himself. What was his guilt next to the torments these men would suffer?

He looked for Scipio, but did not see him.

Fawcett glanced nervously around. The sight of thirty Negroes, all wielding the viciously sharp cane knives, left him uncomfortable.

'Are the guards for our protection?'

Crow winked at him. 'Gallant officers like yourselves don't need no protectin'. These are to stop the runaways.'

'But where can they go?' asked Midshipman Brompton. The fat youth gestured to the mountain rampart towering in the distance over the cane. 'You are surrounded by impenetrable cliffs and forests.'

Crow lowered his voice. 'They go to the Maroons.'

Half a dozen blank faces looked at him.

'Who are the Maroons?' asked Rob.

'Escaped slaves. Been living in the mountains for years. Mostly they keeps to themselves.'

'And you let them run free?' said Coyningham.

'Them mountains is near impossible to get into. We got an understandin'. We leaves them in peace, and they brings back the runaways for the bounties we give 'em.'

'Then why do your slaves flee to them, if they know they will be returned?' asked Rob.

Crow shrugged. 'Man has to hope for somethin'.'

'They betray their own kind?' said Fawcett.

'Set a thief to catch a thief.' Crow glanced at the sun. 'Best get back. Mr Bracewell will be wanting you soon enough at the big house.'

Everything about Bracewell's mansion was monumental. It stood like a mountain at the top of the cliff overlooking the bay, four storeys high and built of stone. Dark arches opened into the ground floor, while the windows above were small and tight. A house built to intimidate, not welcome. A long stepped walkway led up to it, lined with stone fish ponds and shaded by tamarind and palm trees. At the top, a stone obelisk thrust to the sky, almost as high as the house.

They were sweating and out of breath when they reached the end of the walkway. The sun was still hot, yet as they stepped into the shadow of the great obelisk Rob felt a chill go through him.

Bracewell's corpulent frame leaned over the iron railings on the first-storey balcony. He looked down on them, a smile playing over his lips.

'Captain, lieutenants, gentlemen – welcome to Thebes Plantation.'

The moment they stepped inside, Rob felt he had passed through a magic curtain to a different world. As brutally austere as the outside of the house had been, the inside was opulent to the point of madness. The floors were marble, the rooms lined with fluted columns painted in gold leaf. Huge gilded mirrors hung on every wall, so that each room seemed to stretch away to infinity. Rob and his companions were reflected back on every side, from every angle. It gave him the disconcerting feeling of being surrounded.

Serving girls emerged from behind the pillars, bringing champagne in crystal goblets on silver trays. The men from the *Perseus* stared at the slaves with the lust of men who had spent weeks cramped aboard ship. The women wore gold collars around their necks and flimsy white loincloths tied across their hips. They were bare-breasted, their eyes downcast as they served the drinks. Rob scanned them to see if Phoebe was among them but he did not see her.

Midshipman Brompton saw Rob looking around.

'Sight for sore eyes, eh?' he said in a loud voice.

He had not yet emptied his glass and he was already slurring his words. Rob guessed he had been drinking before they left the ship.

'Which one d'you like best?' Brompton asked. 'Me, I'm taking that one.' He pointed to a statuesque, high-breasted woman with copper-coloured skin. 'Tits like a pair of twenty-four pound cannonballs.'

Rob gave him a look that could have cut steel. Brompton, oblivious, continued.

'Mr Bracewell said we could have whichever we liked after supper.'

Rob considered the women with new pity. None of them appeared older than him, and many were younger. When one caught his gaze for a second, he saw abject terror in her eyes.

'They're slaves, see,' said Brompton. 'You can do what you like with them.'

Whatever else he might have said was drowned out. A muscular male slave, also wearing nothing but a loincloth, struck a bronze dinner gong that made the mirrors tremble in their heavy frames.

'Dinner is served,' said Sophie.

Rob hadn't seen her enter. As soon as he saw her, he wondered how he could have missed her. Her dark hair was piled up in ringlets, her eyes were rimmed with kohl and her lips had been painted a seductive red. She wore a yellow silk dress that shimmered in the candlelight, cut so low and tight across the front that she was one loose stitch away from being as exposed as the slave girls.

She smiled at Rob, then linked her arm in Coyningham's and led him to the dining room. Rob followed, hating every second. The garish gold trappings made him feel dizzy. The plight of the slave girls, knowing what was to happen to them later, sickened him. But he had to stay, if only for the chance of seeing Phoebe.

The dining room was at the back of the house, overlooking the bay. It looked like a Roman emperor's palace. Soaring columns formed a double colonnade down the sides of the room, painted with gold and blue bands. The walls were decorated with scenes of bare-breasted maidens delivering tribute to a god on a throne. Life-size statues of Bacchic figures watched from alcoves, with grotesque animal heads and enormous erect phalluses. The candlesticks were shaped like snakes, strangely lifelike, twisting upwards, with the candles protruding out of the serpents' mouths like mice being devoured.

A long dining table ran the length of the room. Bracewell took his place at the head of the table, in a mahogany chair big enough for three men to sit in. Through the arched windows behind him, the anchored *Perseus* looked no bigger than a child's toy. Bracewell seated Coyningham on his right, with Sophie beside Coyningham. Rob tried to find a place further down the table, but Sophie indicated the seat opposite her and called out, 'Do join us, Lieutenant.'

Rob obeyed. The evening felt like a sadistic punishment: he feared where it would end. But he knew if he resisted her, she would find still crueller ways of making him pay.

The champagne was exquisite, and miraculously cold. Rob sipped it as if it were poison. The servants brought the food. Even in his wildest nights with Hugo in London, Rob had never seen such a meal. There were hot and cold meats, stewed and fried and grilled; pickled fish and plain fish; pepper-pot, cassava bread, pineapples and other tropical fruits. A turtle soup was brought in a huge silver tureen. There were glasses of hock, bumpers of claret and tumblers full of Madeira.

Rob enjoyed none of it. He listened as the voices became louder and coarser. He watched how the junior officers treated the semi-naked serving girls, the way their hands crept possessively inside the loincloths to fondle the girls' thighs or grab their buttocks. They moved their glasses out of the way, so the girls had to bend low over the table to refill them, their breasts hanging in front of the officers like ripe fruit. Rob saw Midshipman Brompton grab a girl's breast and twist her nipple until she gasped with pain. Sophie chattered happily as if she had not noticed. Her uncle presided over the table with a complaisant smile on his face, enjoying the sight of his guests debauching themselves.

Rob tried not to drink too much. He had to keep his wits about him – and his temper. He knew Sophie would find a way to provoke him, and he could not risk losing control. But there was little else to do. He did not participate in the conversation. He drained one glass, then several more. He began to slide lower in his chair, wishing he could disappear under the table.

'What did you make of the plantation, Mr Coyningham,' said Sophie.

'Very interesting,' said Coyningham, attacking a chicken leg with his knife and fork. 'Clearly you have a deuce of a job getting those Negroes to work.'

'They are as devious as children,' said Sophie, 'and as idle. But a bite of the whip usually makes them sit up and do their duty. Do you not find the same, Captain?'

Coyningham choked on his wine. 'I hope you are not comparing British tars to your darkies?'

Sophie flashed a smile that showed all her teeth.

'There is a clergyman in London who says that beneath their dark skins and horrid faces, the Negroes are no different to you and I.'

'Is that so?' Coyningham gave up with the knife and fork. He picked up the chicken leg and started ripping at it with his teeth. 'What an outlandish notion.'

'You must be thirsty.'

Sophie beckoned a slave to refill Coyningham's glass. The girl's breasts brushed his shoulder as she leaned in. He squirmed with embarrassment.

Sophie turned to Rob.

'And you, Lieutenant? What do you think of our methods?'

'I think the Devil himself would recoil from them,' said Rob.

Sophie laughed, as if he had made a fine joke. But Bracewell, who had been listening to the conversation from his throne, said, 'You disappoint me, Lieutenant. I would have thought a man of action would not be so delicate in matters of discipline. Negroes are feeble creatures.'

'What about the Maroons?' said Rob.

'What of them?'

'If the Negroes are as feeble as you say, how are the Maroons able to escape and live free in the mountains?'

'Hogs live wild in the mountains, too.' A dribble of blood from the meat ran down Bracewell's chin and dripped on the table. 'But that does not mean we cannot run them to ground when we choose to go hunting.'

'Is the sport good on the island?' asked Coyningham.

Bracewell started to lecture him about the quality of the island's game, but Rob had stopped listening. A door had opened behind one of the columns, letting in a procession of slaves bearing plates of jellies and sweets in exotic shapes. And there, among them, was Phoebe. Rob's stomach knotted to see her. She was dressed like the others, bare-breasted, wearing only the gold choker around her neck and the thin loincloth that covered almost nothing.

She stood next to Sophie and placed a jelly on the table. Rob stared at her, trying to make eye contact, but Phoebe kept her face turned down.

Sophie missed nothing.

'Look at your handsome suitor,' she commanded. 'Lieutenant Courtney is eager to admire your beauty.'

Phoebe raised her head. Rob gasped. The skin around both eyes was bruised black, with more bruising around her neck as if someone had tried to throttle her. There were scars on her cheek that looked as if they'd been made by burning hot iron.

Rob's fury boiled over. 'What have you done?' he hissed.

The jelly Phoebe had brought was in the mould of a sphinx, sitting on a bed of whipped cream. Sophie scooped up a handful and sucked it off the end of her finger.

'You must not worry,' said Sophie carelessly. 'If I break her, I can always buy another.'

The serving girls had departed. Phoebe made to go but a gesture from Sophie stilled her.

'Stay here.'

Without taking her eyes off Rob, she slipped her hand into Phoebe's loincloth, working her fingers up the inside of her leg. Phoebe stood motionless, only the slightest tremor betraying her.

'Is this what you wanted?' Sophie asked Rob.

She squeezed Phoebe's thigh. Her hand rose higher, pushing back the cloth to reveal the tops of Phoebe's thighs, the inward line of her hips and the small triangle of black hair where her belly curved in.

A drunken argument had started at the other end of the table. The officers were braying loudly, their faces smeared with cream and wine and jelly. Next to Sophie, Coyningham was deep in conversation with Bracewell, listening to him talk about sugar prices. No one else noticed Sophie as, with her finger and thumb, she pried apart the lips of Phoebe's womanhood.

'Let her be,' whispered Rob, gripping the table so hard his knuckles turned white.

Sophie jerked her hand. Phoebe gasped with pain as Sophie's fingers thrust into her. A tear budded in her eye and rolled down her cheek. Rob gripped his dinner knife and imagined driving the point through Sophie's flawless breast, into whatever passed for a heart beneath.

But Crow was standing behind Sophie, leaning against one of the pillars. His coat was unbuttoned, so Rob could see the walnut butt of a pistol gleaming against his shirt. Crow rested his hand on it, ready to draw and fire before Rob could act.

Rob opened his mouth to speak, but Sophie reached across the table and pressed a finger to his lips. He could smell Phoebe on her skin.

'Think carefully before you say anything,' said Sophie. 'In the house, I only play with my servants. You have seen what we do to them in the fields.'

Bracewell stood and clapped his hands. 'It is time we gentlemen retired to the lounge. I have some entertainment there that I believe you will find most agreeable.'

'But not Mr Courtney,' said Sophie smoothly. 'He is required at the ship to keep watch. Is that not so, Captain?'

Coyningham's face lit up at the prospect of getting rid of Rob. 'Indeed, Miss Bracewell.'

The other officers had started making for the drawing room. Their laughter echoed down the passage, crude and raucous. Rob did not have to guess what kind of entertainment Bracewell had planned. He wanted no part of it.

But the one thing worse than being there would be leaving Phoebe to face it alone.

'The jollyboat will not be returning for another three hours,' Rob objected.

'There is a lamp down at the jetty,' said Coyningham. 'When you get there, signal the *Pegasus* to send the boat. Return to the ship, and then send the jollyboat back to await the rest of us.'

The serving girls followed the officers out. As Phoebe disappeared through the door, she cast a look at Rob. His heart lurched. He wanted to run after her, to pull her back and save her from Bracewell's debauchery. She saw the intention in his eyes and shook her head a fraction.

A heavy hand descended on Rob's shoulder. Crow had stepped away from his pillar.

'Best be getting you away, Lieutenant,' he said with mock courtesy, his hand still on the butt of his pistol. 'Afore there's any trouble.'

The drawing room door closed behind Phoebe. Rob listened to the shouts and laughter coming from behind it, the sounds of men ready to take their pleasure. He wanted to murder someone.

The doorbell clanged.

'Who the devil can be calling at this time of night?' Bracewell motioned to the doorman, a slave in red livery standing still as a statue. 'Open it, damn you.'

The door swung in. The visitor stepped into the brightly lit hallway. His clothes were worn and travel-stained, his face haggard with fatigue. He was clutching a letter in his hands, bound with many knots and seals. As soon as he had crossed the threshold, he made straight for Bracewell.

Crow jabbed his fist into the small of Rob's back to push him through the open door. Evidently Bracewell wanted to be left alone with his new guest. Rob stumbled forwards, jostling into the new arrival as they crossed in the middle of the hallway.

The visitor looked up in annoyance. His eyes met Rob's, and Rob saw the last person he ever expected to see.

Hugo Lyall.

Hugo stared as if he had seen a ghost. He had cursed Rob's name every day for the last three months, every mile of his miserable journey to this godforsaken spot. And now he had arrived, there was Rob waiting like the arms of Nemesis. It was impossible.

Before Hugo could speak, Bracewell's ugly-looking manservant hustled Rob into the night. The slave closed the door, leaving Hugo to wonder if he had imagined it.

Bracewell snatched the letter out of his hands. He examined the seals carefully while Hugo waited, sipping the wine that a servant brought him. It sounded as if there was an orgy going on in the drawing room – Hugo could hear full-throated moans and ecstatic cries. To his disappointment, Bracewell took him past the drawing room and into his study.

Bracewell slit open the packet and read the letter. Everything was Rob's fault, Hugo thought bitterly. If he hadn't met Rob, he would never have crossed paths with Baron Dartmouth, would never have been drawn into whatever feud Dartmouth carried against the Courtneys.

A week after the fire at the warehouse, the confrontation at the docks and Rob's escape with the Royal Navy, Dartmouth had summoned Hugo to his chambers once again. Hugo had needed most of a bottle of wine to gather the courage to go, though he knew he had no choice. A word from Dartmouth to his father could still see him cut off without a penny.

Rob's sword lay on Dartmouth's desk, like a relic on an altar. Dartmouth stroked his golden hand over the blade, metal rasping on metal.

'I have an errand for you,' he said, without pleasantries.

The throbbing of the wine in Hugo's head intensified. The guilt of what he had done to Rob had eaten away at him: the prospect of having to do more was intolerable.

'Have I not done enough for you?'

'You have done nothing.' Dartmouth spat the words. 'Robert Courtney is still alive.'

'I hope you do not expect me to join the Royal Navy to go after him,' said Hugo, trying to lighten the mood.

'That will not be necessary.'

'Thank God.'

'I require you to go to Jamaica.'

Hugo's mouth dropped in horror. 'Jamaica?'

'Your father has estates there, does he not?'

'Indeed, sir. But . . .'

It hardly needed to be said that the reason for owning sugar estates was to earn enough money to leave them as far behind as possible. The only men who stayed in the West Indies were those who could not leave, either because they were too poor to afford it, or because they were slaves.

'The climate is disagreeable,' Hugo said.

'I lived the first fifty years of my life in India,' snapped Dartmouth. 'For disease, heat and murderous blacks, I assure you India makes Jamaica seem as pleasant as Surrey.' His fingers closed around the hilt of the sword. 'Unless you wish me to speak to your father.'

Hugo swallowed. 'I am at your service.'

'I have a letter.' Dartmouth picked up a packet on his desk, bound in oilskin cloth and sealed in many places. 'It touches on a matter of the utmost sensitivity. It must be delivered to Mr Hezekiah Bracewell, at Thebes Plantation. You know it?'

'Every man on Jamaica knows Thebes. It is the richest plantation in the Indies.'

'See the letter is placed in his hands, and no other.'

'You may rely on me, sir.'

Dartmouth leaned forwards across the desk.

'I know I can. Otherwise, I will come to the West Indies myself and use this fine blade to skin you alive, inch by inch.'

That was how Hugo had found himself sweating in a tiny cabin sailing west. Six long weeks he had festered at sea. Then a chaise from Port Royal, over the most abominable roads imaginable. And now he was here.

Bracewell placed the letter face down on the table. He examined the packet. It had been carefully bound with so much string and sealing wax, it was hard to imagine anyone opening it undetected.

But Hugo would have had plenty of time during his weeks at sea to allow his curiosity to run free. A cunning man might have found a way to open the packet, and rework the seals almost invisibly. Bracewell did not think Hugo was so cunning – but he was not a man to take chances.

He waved the letter at Hugo.

'You know what this concerns?'

'Baron Dartmouth did not confide in me.'

Bracewell allowed himself a conspiratorial smile. 'But you are a resourceful young man. When I was your age, I could not have resisted trying to discover the nature of my secret mission.'

'I gave Baron Dartmouth my word I would deliver the letter unopened.'

'Of course you did.' Bracewell winked. 'But he is far away in London. You may be candid with me. Were you not tempted to pry open the seals on your letter?'

Hugo looked affronted. 'Certainly not. Dartmouth chose me because he knew he could trust me.'

Bracewell studied Hugo, his gaze so penetrating Hugo had to look away. Then Bracewell clapped him on the shoulder.

'Dartmouth chose well. I cannot reveal the purpose of your errand yet, but rest assured you have rendered our nation the highest service.'

'I hope you will give a favourable report of me to Baron Dartmouth. And my father.' Hugo took a gulp of his wine. 'But there is another matter I must raise with you. As I arrived, I saw one of your guests departing. A man named Robert Courtney.'

'You are acquainted with him?' Bracewell looked astonished. 'I thought he emerged from the gutter. He was a common seaman, until his fool of a captain promoted him beyond his station.'

'I met him in London.' Hugo's finger picked at the gold edging on his coat, worrying it looser. 'But you must know that Baron Dartmouth loathes Courtney. He would stop at nothing to . . .' He trailed off.

'To do what?' Bracewell leaned forward like a vulture. 'What does Dartmouth want with Courtney?'

'He wants him dead.'

Bracewell digested the news. From the adjoining room, sounds of laughter, screams and banging came through the wall, but in the study all that moved was dust.

'What is Dartmouth's quarrel with Courtney?'

'I cannot fathom it. It must be some great enormity. I have never seen a man so implacable in his hatred.'

But Bracewell was beginning to guess. He knew something of the illustrious name of Courtney, the great sailors and merchants of the previous century of whom Baron Dartmouth was the last surviving scion. He had never thought to connect it with the *Perseus*'s lieutenant, a jumped-up sailor with no manners or breeding. But the Courtney family must have been a far-spreading tree. Rob might be from some mongrel branch, forgotten and obscure. If there was an ancient feud between them, or if they had offended Baron Dartmouth, or if it was simply that their existence embarrassed him – Dartmouth was not a man to tolerate it. He would want the issue removed, permanently.

'Robert Courtney has been a thorn in my side too long,' Bracewell said. 'He insults my niece and foments rebellion among my slaves. I shall be as glad to be rid of him as Baron Dartmouth.'

By now, Hugo had picked at his hem so much he had pulled loose a good six inches of the trim. He wrapped the ribbon around his finger, pulling it until the tip went white. It felt like the only thing he had to cling on to. He did not know what to think. He had travelled across the ocean on this terrible errand, only to walk into the man who had caused it all, a man he never expected to see again. And now they were discussing murdering him.

He took another gulp of his drink. It settled his nerves and calmed his thoughts. He had not forgotten that he and Rob had been friends, once. But everything that had happened since had corrupted the memory until it became a tumour. Rob was the seed from which all his misfortunes had grown. He had taken him into his home, funded his pleasures, and all he had got in return was misery.

If Rob was killed, Dartmouth would be delighted. He would reward Hugo; he would convince his father that Hugo was not a dissolute wastrel. Hugo's allowance would not be cut off; it might even be increased. He could return to London, and sink back into the life of peace and pleasure he had enjoyed until Rob Courtney arrived on his doorstep.

He would give anything for that.

'Where is Rob now?'

'He is returning to his ship. I will send my men after him.'

'He is resourceful,' Hugo warned.

'So am I.' Bracewell rang a bell on the side table. 'You will want to rest after your journey. I will have someone show you to your quarters.'

Crow appeared noiselessly, a dark presence in the shadow of the doorway.

'I have decided that we have had quite enough of Mr Courtney,' said Bracewell. 'Take four men and see if you can apprehend him before he reaches the landing. After that, you may show Mr Lyall to the room we have prepared for him. He has suffered a long voyage. Ensure nothing disturbs his rest.'

Crow nodded. He held the door for Lyall, then padded after him.

When they had gone, Bracewell picked up the letter and studied it again. Robert Courtney was an intriguing problem, but he was a footnote to the real business. The contents of the letter were what mattered.

He ran his finger over the richly embossed paper. In the bottom right corner, his nail touched a bead of black wax. By sight, it was impossible to tell it from a drop of ink. Anyone who handled it would think it had dripped from a candle, or a stick of sealing wax.

But it was not there by accident. It was a prearranged sign. When the letter was folded, the wax stuck the paper together. Someone who unfolded the paper would break the internal seal without noticing it.

Bracewell had seen it. When he opened the letter, the wax had been unstuck.

In the candlelight, he reread the postscript written in Dartmouth's angry, crippled scrawl.

The boy who brought this letter is not to be trusted. If you suspect he has become privy to our secret, I rely on you to ensure he is never able to reveal it.

When Rob left the house he did not go far. His head was swimming, his whole body trembling. He felt sick to his stomach. Sophie's cruel heart had concocted an exquisite punishment. Phoebe was in that room as a plaything for men who did not even recognise her as human, while all he could do was stand outside. The windows on the great house were elevated, so he could not see in, but the noises that emerged painted a vivid picture of what was happening.

And then there was Hugo Lyall. True, Rob had only seen him for a moment: he could almost convince himself he had imagined it. A trick of the light, or the effects of the wine. But that would be a dangerous delusion. In his heart, there was no doubt.

He could not imagine what devilry had brought Hugo there. But Hugo had betrayed Rob once before, and Rob was certain he would do it again. Bracewell and Baron Dartmouth were friends: Bracewell had boasted of it. If Hugo told him that Dartmouth wanted Rob dead, Bracewell would not hesitate. Coyningham would happily accept whatever story he concocted to explain Rob's disappearance. Sophie would have her revenge.

Rob did not have a single ally on the island.

A wild plan began to unfold in his mind. He would go back to the ship, rouse the crew and seize her. With Coyningham and the officers ashore, there would be no one to lead resistance to the mutiny. Then he could bring some trusted men ashore and sack the plantation, free Phoebe and Scipio and make their escape.

He knew it was a desperate plan. Probably, there were a hundred reasons it would not work. But he had no time to think and he did not want to know. He had already waited too long.

He started down the long path from the house, back past the silent fish ponds, towards the steps that led down to the shore.

He had not gone more than a hundred paces when the door to the main house burst open. Looking back, Rob saw Crow's unmistakable silhouette, followed by four more men spilling out of the house.

The moon was just past full, but still more than bright enough. The men saw him at once. They called out to Rob to stop, but Rob did not wait. He broke into a run.

With shouts, the men chased after him. Glancing over his shoulder, Rob saw moonlight gleaming on the pistols and cane knives they carried, while Crow stood watching from the doorway. He had unleashed his dogs, and now he would wait for them to bring Rob to bay.

Rob reached the steps and began to descend towards the beach as fast as he dared. Less moonlight penetrated the thick vegetation; it was harder to see his footing. Plunging down, three stairs at a time, he missed a step and pitched forwards, almost breaking his neck. He rolled down three more steps, sprang to his feet and went on. The sound of hobnailed boots rang behind him, ever closer.

Pale sand glimmered as he came through the trees. Surf rippled over the beach. In the distance, he could see the *Perseus*'s masts silhouetted against the rising moon, but she was too far away. The boat crew had returned to the ship, awaiting a signal to fetch the officers back after Bracewell's dinner. Even if Rob could find a lantern, they would never come in time.

It was already too late. The men came out on the beach and fanned out around him, keeping a wary distance. They were white men, overseers from the plantation fields. Men for whom violence came as easily as breathing.

One, evidently the leader, jerked his gun at Rob.

'Come with us.'

They meant to murder him – Rob had no doubt of that. But they would not want to do it on the beach, in plain view of all the men aboard the *Perseus*. They would want to take him back up to the estate, perhaps to the hut that the slaves kept away from, where they would have hooks and chains and could work him over at their leisure. Perhaps they would ask him questions, though Rob had no idea what he could tell them. Perhaps Sophie would want to come and watch.

If Rob fought them there, he might have witnesses to his death – but he would still be dead. The men had spread out around him so it was impossible for him to fight them all. Better to stay alive as long as possible.

He let his shoulders slump and looked at the ground, giving every impression of a man defeated.

'It seems I have no choice.'

They searched Rob to be sure he was unarmed, then fell in around him, two in front and two behind. Rob did not resist. He walked between them, back towards the steps.

Suddenly he slowed, so quickly that the two men behind walked into him. Rob targeted the smaller of the two, the man on his left. He stamped on the overseer's foot and grabbed his wrist. Before the man could react, Rob had prised the cane knife out of his hand. Rob raised it, just as one of the men in front swung at him with his own knife. The blades clashed. Rob beat the blade away, spun inside the man's guard and threw a left-handed punch into the man's face. The man's nose collapsed into his skull; his knees buckled. Rob grabbed his shirt front and threw him into the man behind. They both went down.

Rob turned, in time to see the third overseer coming for him. He ducked under the blade and lunged at him, driving his shoulder into the man's stomach.

The fourth man hung back. The overseers were brutish men. They were used to violence. But they used their whips more than their fists – and they did not expect their victims to fight back. Faced with Rob's ferocity, they hesitated.

But they had more options. While the others nursed their bruises and staggered to their feet, the last man drew his pistol and levelled it at Rob.

'Drop the knife.' He had a strange, sing-song accent, almost like the way the slaves talked.

'You cannot kill a British officer,' said Rob. They were still on the beach, still in sight of the *Perseus*, if anyone was watching. 'You would be hanged for murder.'

The man wavered. 'Put down the knife,' he said again.

Rob obeyed. He threw the knife on the ground, faster than the overseer expected. His eyes flitted to it, drawn by the movement. At the same time, Rob kicked a spray of sand into the man's eyes.

Instinctively, the overseer's finger tightened around the pistol's trigger. A burst of flame lit up the night. Though he was firing blind, the pistol was pointed at Rob.

Except Rob had dropped to the ground. As the bullet passed over him, he rolled forwards and snatched the knife where he had thrown it. A scream sounded behind him as the bullet that had missed him hit one of the other men. Rob ignored it. In a single motion, he rolled out of his crouch and drove the blade into the overseer's belly. With the sand stinging his eyes, his victim didn't see the blade until it was buried inside him.

The overseer sank to his knees. Rob braced his foot against the man's shoulder and tugged the knife free. He considered his situation.

Four men had escorted Rob from the house. One was bleeding his guts out behind him. Another lay unconscious with a broken nose. The third writhed on the ground, clutching his hip where the pistol ball had struck it. Rob guessed it must have shattered the bone.

The last man stared, horrified, at Rob. Then he turned and ran.

Rob snatched a pistol from one of the fallen men and fired. But the fight must have shaken most of the powder out of it. The pan sparked feebly; the bullet barely carried twenty yards. The overseer disappeared around a bend in the path.

Rob gathered weapons from the men he had felled – two cane knives, three pistols and an ammunition pouch. He reloaded the pistols and stuffed two in his belt, keeping one handy. He wished he had his men here, Angus and Hargrave and the others, but they were waiting on the *Perseus*. Rob had no lantern with which to signal them, and no time to find one. The man who had got away would already be halfway back to the house to fetch reinforcements.

Rob fired two of the pistols in the air, hoping that the sound would bring men from the *Perseus*. He knew he should wait for them, but he had no patience. He was operating on instinct, not thinking about the consequences. Now that his enemies had shown themselves, he had thrown off the shackles of naval discipline. He was free to fight.

And if he was no longer bound by duty, he was free to rescue Phoebe. It was not only her beauty that had bewitched Rob. She represented a wild spirit entrapped, like a lioness in a cage. And he loved her. He had to set her free.

He set off back up the steps to the estate. He had not gone halfway when he saw lights coming towards him, a group of men shouting and jostling in their haste. He pressed himself into the undergrowth at the side of the path and hid behind a palm tree as they passed – a dozen or so men with Crow in the lead. They carried on down to the beach without seeing him.

As soon as they were out of sight, Rob continued up the path. At the top, he paused, listening for danger. From the house, he could hear the tinkle of glassware and laughter. Otherwise, the only sound was crickets, and tree frogs chattering in the undergrowth.

He crept the long flight of stairs to the main house, moving as quickly as he could. It would not be long before Crow found the overseers' bodies, and once he saw Rob was not on the beach, it would be obvious where he must have gone. Rob had little time to find Phoebe. He avoided the main door, in case it was guarded, and climbed onto the iron railings that ringed the house. He worked his way along them until he was underneath a large side window. Carefully, he raised his head to peer in.

The window was open. Inside was the drawing room, almost as opulent as the dining room. Thick Persian carpets covered the floors. Glasses and decanters were strewn over surfaces, many of them knocked over. On the walls, Oriental paintings showed naked women reclining in the throes of pleasure. But they were portraits of saints compared to the scene below.

Even in his worst debauches with Hugo, Rob had never seen anything so obscene. The *Perseus*'s officers lay sprawled on the sofas and chaises. Some had lost their breeches or their shirts; others were entirely naked. Every man had at least one woman on him. Fawcett had two: one kneeling between his knees and sucking his cock, while the other squatted over him and rubbed herself against his face. In a corner, Midshipman Brompton was receiving the attentions of a young slave boy.

Rob was no prude. Yet this sickened him. Some of the men had spent themselves too quickly and were lolling in a stupor. Others thrust away like sailors servicing their guns, ramming themselves in and out of their partners. The slave women lay on their backs or knees or bellies, passionless and blank. They did not scream or cry out; they waited for the ordeal to be over. Rob guessed this was not the first time they had been used this way.

His eyes swept the room and picked out Phoebe. She had her back to him, but he recognised her at once. She kneeled on the floor beside Coyningham, who slumped on the sofa with his breeches around his ankles. He lay back, evidently the worse for alcohol, while Phoebe grasped his manhood in her hand and pumped away.

A red mist descended on Rob. He reached for the pistol he had taken from the overseers. He was too angry to think clearly. All he wanted was to put a ball through Coyningham's forehead, never mind the consequences that would follow. He levelled the weapon, fighting to keep his hand steady. If his aim was a fraction low, he might hit Phoebe.

A movement at the edge of the room caught his eye. It was someone he had not noticed before, watching from the shadows.

The figure moved forwards a step, so the lamplight caught the curve of a flawlessly white cheek and a glittering eye. Skirts rustled. Rob gaped, the pistol forgotten. It was Sophie. She must have stolen into the room once the men were distracted. She did not participate but hung back in the darkness, her lips parted, her right hand rubbing herself between her thighs.

Rob finally understood her. It was not pleasure she loved, or men, or even women. It was power. In that room, the women had been broken and the men debased to the level of animals. Sophie alone stood detached, undetected, all-seeing. And to her, that was the most erotic sensation of all.

Rob lowered the gun. The sight of Sophie brought him back to earth. If he killed Coyningham, he would gain a moment's satisfaction – but he would condemn Phoebe to a lifetime of Sophie's cruelties. He could not let that happen.

Phoebe turned her head towards the window. Whether it was a sixth sense – or perhaps a confluence of spirits, of need and consolation, like a child groping in its distress into the night – Rob did not know. But as she searched the darkness outside, her eyes met his. Her mouth widened in surprise to see Rob, though the hand pleasuring Coyningham never stopped moving.

Rob put his finger to his lips and nodded towards the door. Phoebe understood. She whispered something in Coyningham's ear.

'More wine!' Coyningham slurred his words so badly they were almost unintelligible. He was struggling to keep his eyes open.

Phoebe rose and curtsied. Sophie did not stop her as she left the room. Coyningham barely noticed she'd gone. He slumped on the sofa, his trousers around his knees, his member slowly deflating, and started snoring.

Rob went to the front of the house as the door opened. Phoebe stole out, still dressed in nothing but her loincloth. Heedless of their danger, Rob hugged her to him and kissed the top of her head.

'Are you all right?' he said. 'I will kill them for what they made you do.'

She gave him a look so bleak it cut through to his soul.

'I have known worse. He was so drunk, he could barely rouse himself to touch me. I would have been there all night trying to finish him off.'

Shouts sounded from the path from the beach. Bracewell's men had found the overseers Rob had killed and maimed.

'We must go,' said Phoebe. 'If they find me . . .'

'Or me,' said Rob. 'I am under a death sentence now.'

He glanced at the hills, ragged shadows against the starry sky. His only hope was to flee there and hope that Bracewell's men could not track him.

But he could not leave yet.

'We must free the others. Where is Scipio?'

He would not forget his debt. At Seabrook Bay, the Ebo warrior and his men had saved Rob's life, along with the *Perseus* and all her crew. Rob had promised them their freedom; instead, they had been chained up like dogs in the hold and brought to this evil place. Rob had to make it right.

Phoebe led him at a run towards the sugar works. The mill's sails creaked as they spun freely in the night breeze. Next to it, firelight glowed in the boiling house where the work of processing sugar continued unabated. And beyond that, as dark as a tomb, the square white punishment house Rob had seen earlier.

A breath of wind brought the smell of it to him. He knew the scent. It was the same stench of suffering and despair he had encountered in the torture room at Bracewell's South Carolina plantation.

Phoebe had paused. She pointed, trembling, to the punishment house.

'Scipio?' Rob guessed.

'He tried to run as soon as we came ashore. Crow put him in there.'

'Go and find the others,' Rob told her. He could not bear to let her see what might be inside that place. 'I will free Scipio and meet you at the slave grounds.'

Phoebe ran off. The smell of the punishment house grew worse as Rob approached, then hit him with all its force as he opened the door. He stepped in – and almost went sprawling onto his face as his boot caught something on the floor. It was soft and warm, but motionless. Rob knew what it was even before he looked.

It was a human body, lying face down. Rob kneeled and turned it over, terrified of what he would see. Was he too late? Had Crow murdered Scipio already?

The dead man's face was pale in the moonlight that flooded through the door. It wasn't Scipio. It was Hugo Lyall.

A livid red line circled his neck, oozing blood. His windpipe was crushed. He must have been garrotted. Rob wondered why. He had no reason to love Hugo, but he would not have wished this lonely, brutal death on anyone.

He remembered Hugo's last words to him in London.

'I did not want it to end this way.'

A groan sounded from deeper in the room. Rob peered forwards. As his eyes adjusted, he made out a figure with arms spread-eagled, hanging between two chains attached to the ceiling. His head seemed to have grown to twice its natural size, bobbing about like a balloon.

It was Scipio. Rob ran to him and saw the full horror of his torture. What had looked like an enormous, distended head was in fact a huge iron collar clamped around his neck. The inside of the collar had a ring of sharp spikes pointing inwards. If the prisoner let his head drop, even for a moment, the weight of the collar would force the spikes through his neck.

There were bloody scars on Scipio's back, and more blood running down his neck and over his chest where the collar's spikes had pricked the skin. He looked half-crazed, fighting to stay awake through the pain and fatigue so that the collar would not slip.

Rob put down the pistol he held. He felt for the bolts that held the collar and the shackles in place. They were locked.

'Where are the keys?'

Scipio's eyes opened wide, white in the darkness. He cursed and spat, defiant even in extremis.

'Go to Hell, and burn forever,' he groaned.

'It's me,' said Rob. 'I am going to get you out of here.'

Slowly, recognition dawned on Scipio. He mumbled something that Rob couldn't make out. Rob leaned in closer. Scipio's cries became more urgent.

'Crow,' he said.

'Crow has the keys?'

A flash of pain exploded like lightning through Rob's head, just as he realised Scipio had been trying to warn him. He dropped to his knees, but a hand grabbed his collar, hauled him up and spun him around. Rob saw Crow's snarling face before a fist smashed into his jaw and sent him clattering against the wall.

'Thought I'd get you here,' said Crow in triumph. 'So sweet on the darkies, you is, I knew you couldn't keep your hands off him.'

The blow to Rob's head had stunned him. He fumbled for one of the pistols in his belt, but he was too slow. Crow kicked his hand away, then pulled both pistols out and threw them away to the dark corners of the room.

'I'm going to kill you slow,' he told Rob. 'Slow like a darkie, while your friend watches.'

'I'm a British officer,' Rob mumbled.

'You're a deserter. A traitor. A thief.' Crow punctuated each insult with a blow, sharp jabs to Rob's ribs and sides that sent spasms of pain through his body.

'I know what you done with Miss Sophie on the ship,' he said conversationally. Another punch, this time to Rob's jaw. 'I was watchin' you every time, through a knothole in the door.' Cane juice ran down his chin. 'Filthy, you was.'

He hit Rob hard in his stomach. Vomit rose in Rob's throat and spilled over his shirt front. He doubled over.

'What you want with some flea-bitten darkie whore, when you could have a prime piece of cunny like Miss Sophie, I don't know.'

Crow completed his assessment of Rob's shortcomings with three more swift punches that left Rob reeling. Before he could gather himself, Crow swept Rob's legs from under him and dropped him to the floor.

He gave Rob a keen glance. He saw a broken man doubled over in agony. It satisfied him. He turned away to take a knife from the rack on the wall.

'Now I've tendered you up, time for some carving.'

But Rob was not as helpless as he had let Crow think. Crow's onslaught had bruised him, but Rob's body was young and hard. The moment Crow turned away, Rob sprang to his feet.

Crow was quick. He spun around, a knife gleaming in his hand. Rob could not fight him – but he did not intend to. He ran for the door, hurdled Hugo's prone body and disappeared outside.

Footsteps pounded the yard behind him, though Crow's short, squat physique could not match Rob's long legs for speed. Rob ran past the boiling house and the curing house. By the time he rounded the corner of the mill, he had a few valuable seconds' lead. He ducked inside the mill's open door.

The noise of the machinery was deafening. Half a dozen slaves were at work, feeding fresh stalks into the relentlessly spinning rollers of the cane press. They paused and stared wide-eyed at Rob as he burst through the door.

'Help me,' he begged.

They looked uncertainly at him. None of them knew him. The only time they had seen him was riding through the estate in Crow's company, like one of the overseers. Perhaps they had heard that Rob had tricked the South Carolina slaves back into bondage. None of it made them willing to trust him.

The door banged open again. It had not taken Crow long to find him. He strode into the mill, rolling the butcher's knife in his hand.

'Get out,' he told the slaves.

The mill workers knew what Crow could do to them. They fled. Rob and Crow faced each other across the mill. The empty rollers rumbled and hissed.

'You think the darkies'd help you?' sneered Crow. He advanced towards Rob, shaping two deft cuts through the air with his knife. 'They won't help a dead man.'

He jabbed the knife at Rob's stomach. For a big man, he struck as quick as a snake. If Rob had so much as blinked, he would have been stuck like a pig. He reacted just in time, knocking the knife aside with his bare arm. Not without cost. The sharp blade opened a wide gash in his forearm.

Crow gave him no respite. He came at Rob again, and Rob had no defence. All he could do was retreat, leaving a trail of blood across the floor. Behind him, he heard the whirring of the cane press. Balling a fist, gritting his teeth against the pain in his arm, he managed to land a punch on Crow's shoulder. Crow shook it off and drove at Rob again. Rob leaped back without looking where he would land. His foot landed on a pile of dry cane trash that the slaves had left on the floor. The husks skidded from under him, and he could not keep his balance. He fell heavily on the floor, so close to the crusher he could feel drops of cane juice spraying against his skin.

Crow stood over him.

'When I'm finished with you,' he promised, 'even my dogs won't want to—'

He broke off, jerking backwards. A hand had seized him from behind. Crow raised the knife, but before he could turn it on his assailant the hand pushed him away. Crow stumbled forwards.

He tripped on Rob's outstretched legs, and instinctively threw out his arms.

His reactions were fast. He broke his fall. But it was only as he gathered himself that he realised what had stopped him. His hands had landed flat on the cane press.

His eyes widened in horror. He tried to snatch his hands away, but the sweet juice made the rollers tacky.

The rollers spun. Before Crow could even scream, his hands were dragged between them. He tried to pull himself free, but the remorseless machine tugged him in. Rob rolled away from under his feet as Crow was jerked forwards like a dog on a lead. In confusion, Rob saw Angus standing where Crow had been, but he had no time to wonder how his friend had got there.

Crow had found his voice. He screamed in such torment Rob would never forget the sound of the strangled screech. It did him no good. An ounce of juice was a pound of profit, and the heavy rollers had been built to squeeze every drop from fat bundles of sugar cane. They made short work of flesh and bone. They crushed Crow's hands, then his arms. His elbows gave the rollers a moment's pause, then those snapped with a terrible crack like green wood splitting and were fed through the mill. He was wedged up to his shoulders.

'Cut me free,' Crow pleaded, a gurgling mash of speech that was barely human.

He was trapped against the machine, held fast by the rollers. They spun against his face, stripping off the skin like ripping bark off a tree, so that his face became a mask of blood.

Rob didn't want him to die like this, but there was nothing he could do. Crow's knife had gone through the rollers and been shattered. There were no other blades in the mill, and Rob could not pull him out of the rollers. There was no way he could put Crow out of his misery.

Angus looked up. An iron hook hung on a chain from a beam, probably for hauling bundles of cane. Angus grabbed it. In a single motion, like a fisherman baiting a line, he hooked it into Crow's mouth and pulled the chain taut.

The sharpened point dug through the top of Crow's palate and into the soft tissue of his brain. Crow spasmed, then went still. He dangled grotesquely on the end of the chain, the tip of the hook protruding through the top of his skull, while the rollers continued to spin over his mangled arms. Blood ran into the trough below and flowed away with the cane juice.

Angus kneeled beside Rob and saw the gash Crow's knife had left.

'How's your arm?'

Rob looked at Crow. 'Better than his.' His mind was clearer, though he still had an electric pain throbbing between his temples. He stood, unsteadily. He noticed that Angus was dripping wet. 'How in God's name did you come to be here?'

'I guessed there was trouble when I saw lights on the beach. Then I heard gunshots. The boatswain wouldn't let us send the boat, so I swam ashore.'

Rob knew the scars from the flogging had still not fully healed. He tried not to think how much it must have hurt Angus, the effort of swimming so far and the salt water stinging his wounds. 'You should not have come.'

'No more should you.'

'I was already a condemned man. Coyningham will hang you if he catches you.'

'Then we are in the same boat.' Angus looked to the door. 'So where next?'

'We must rescue Scipio.'

There was a ring of keys hanging from Crow's belt. Rob unhooked them and led Angus back to the punishment house. Scipio was dangling in his chains, struggling against the weight of the infernal iron collar. Rob held him up, while Angus undid the locks with Crow's keys. As he was released, Scipio collapsed into Rob's arms.

They took Scipio between them, hoisting him on their shoulders, and made for the door. They crossed the threshold and stepped over Hugo Lyall's dead body again.

'Who was he?' Angus asked.

Rob was too tired to explain. He still could not imagine what strange fate had brought Hugo to the plantation.

'Another one of Bracewell's guests.'

'I'm beginning to get a sense of Mr Bracewell's hospitality,' said Angus.

Rob nodded. 'We should be away before we enjoy any more of it.'

They walked away from the sugar works, the fresh air beginning to revive Scipio. He hoisted himself off them and stood free, rubbing his wrists where the manacles had bitten deep into the flesh.

'I am in your debt,' he said.

'It was my fault,' said Rob. 'I had to set you free.'

'And Phoebe?'

'She is safe. She is waiting for us over there.'

Rob pointed through the trees to the slave quarters. He could see lights kindled, and a crowd gathered in the open space between the houses. He hurried towards them.

Though it was past midnight, it seemed every slave had been roused, even the youngest child. Sleeping babies cuddled in their mothers' arms, oblivious to the noise around them. Phoebe stood at the front, dressed in a white shift she had found. She smiled with relief when she saw Rob and Scipio were safe – but it did not last long.

'They do not want to go,' she said. 'They say Bracewell will hunt them down with dogs, or else the Maroons will sell them back to him. You know what happens to runaway slaves.'

Rob surveyed the sea of faces. Some were hopeful, some confused. Many were openly hostile. He remembered how the slaves in South Carolina had behaved in a similar manner, so brutalised they couldn't trust the offer of freedom. Rob had persuaded them otherwise. He had promised them liberty, but all he had led them to was more chains. Looking out at the crowd, he recognised the faces of those who had been brought with the *Perseus*. Like Scipio, some had fought beside him aboard the sloop, risking their lives to save the ship that then became their prison.

Why should they trust him now?

He stepped up onto a stone.

'Some of you were with me at the plantation in South Carolina,' he said. 'I said you would have your freedom. I was wrong.'

A murmur went through the crowd. Those who had been there had not forgotten. The others had already heard the story.

'This time I promise you nothing. You know, in every scar and wound you carry on your bodies, what Bracewell will do if you try to escape and get caught. You also know what will happen if you stay. You must make your own decisions.

'But I am the same as you. If Bracewell finds me, he will kill me. So I am going into the mountains.'

'And after that?' asked Angus softly.

Rob shrugged. Jamaica was a large island: a man might be able to live undetected in those mountains. Or he might manage to steal a boat and sail back to England or Africa. At this moment, all that mattered was staying alive.

'I have not thought further than surviving tonight,' he whispered.

He jumped down into the throng of slaves. Many were engaged in heated arguments; some were in tears.

'Why do they hesitate?' Angus wondered. 'It is a choice between slavery and liberty.'

'Liberty?' said Scipio scornfully. He gave Angus a dark look. 'They want to know how they stay alive.'

'So do I.'

There was no more time for talking. The roar of the cane mill would have drowned out Crow's death, but with the overseers dead or wounded on the beach, it would also not be long before someone noticed the disturbance in the slave quarters. The slaves made their choices. Some, too old or frightened, or calculating the odds against them, slipped back into their houses, but most stayed. They broke open the tool store and armed themselves with cane knives, mattocks and hoes. Some gathered their possessions in blankets. There was no order or organisation. In the dark, they ran as they could, in small groups or families.

Rob, Angus, Scipio and Phoebe followed the crowd along a track between the cane breaks. Leaves rustled in the darkness either side of them, while the air was ripe with the sweet aroma of sugar. A stone wall marked the plantation boundary, though it was not well maintained. Some of the escaping slaves had already pulled down a section when they tried to climb it. Rob and the others clambered over the rubble and squeezed through the gap. On the far side, the jungle thronged at once, dense and dark. Rob and Angus took the lead, using their cane knives to cut through the undergrowth. Phoebe followed, helping Scipio, who was limping badly.

'I make you slow,' he complained. 'Go.'

'It's the jungle making us slow,' panted Rob. 'And the mountain.'

But it was obvious Scipio could not go much further. Phoebe almost had to drag him up the slope, and she was tiring quickly. From below, they heard the sound of dogs barking.

Rob thrust his cane knife into Phoebe's hand.

'Take this.'

He hoisted Scipio onto his shoulders. His legs buckled under the big man's weight, but he found his footing and forced himself onwards.

Everyone was struggling. Phoebe had been a housemaid, not a field slave. Soon her hands were blistered, and her arm ached from swinging the cane knife at the thick forest. The blade grew dull. Angus could not make much of a dent in the undergrowth. The forest clawed and tore and tripped them.

Rob staggered on, his legs burning, his lungs bursting. The dogs sounded closer.

'Do you have a plan, Rob?' asked Angus in a low voice.

Rob shook his head, too tired to speak. There must be other escaped slaves in the forest nearby, but he would never find them. There might be cliffs on the mountain where they could mount a defence, but he did not know where they were. All he could do was head on.

He heard a trickle of water to his right and followed the sound to a small stream running down the mountain. They splashed through it to try and put the dogs off their scent, but Rob could not stay in the water long. The stones were too slippery, and with Scipio's weight on his shoulders the current almost upended him. They clambered out the other side and carried on up the slope.

Dawn was breaking. Light suffused the forest, though it hardly helped them see their way. The wall of green surrounding them was getting thicker.

They could still hear barking, but it sounded further off. Perhaps the dogs had lost the trail in the stream after all. As the urgency ebbed, Rob felt Scipio's weight heavier than ever.

Suddenly, without warning, Rob's body gave up. He sat down, rolling Scipio off his shoulder so that the Ebo lay flat on the ground. Rob's mouth was parched with thirst. He pulled a fistful of moss off a tree and sucked the moisture out of it like a sponge.

Angus and Phoebe threw themselves onto the forest floor. Stripes of blood darkened the back of Angus's shirt where his scars had split open.

'We cannae stop long,' said Angus. 'Bracewell will call out the militia. We've not gone as far from the plantation as we think.'

No one had breath to answer. The stillness was as heavy and melancholy as a graveyard. Time itself seemed to have come to a halt.

The silence was broken by the ratchet click of a musket's hammer being cocked into place.

Rob looked up in despair. Half a dozen of Bracewell's men had emerged into the clearing, guns raised. Ugly men, scarred by fights and the pox, their beards ragged and their hair wild. There was no chance of fighting them off. Before Rob could move, they had tied his hands behind his back. Angus made to resist, but a gun at his temple and a knife at Rob's throat left him little choice. Soon all four of them were bound.

One of the men uncoiled a long rope he carried over his shoulder and threw it over a tree branch, about ten feet off the ground. With practised hands, he tied a noose in the other end. Two of his companions grabbed Scipio and held him while the noose was placed over his head. They pulled it snug.

'What about her?' asked the hangman, gesturing at Phoebe.

'Orders was only to bring the white fellas back alive,' said the leader, a stocky brute with matted red hair.

The hangman put the barrel of his rifle under Phoebe's skirt and lifted it until it was above her thighs.

'Might as well taste the goods.'

The redhead nodded. 'We'll string him up,' he said, pointing to Scipio. 'But easy like. Keep him alive a little so he can watch us take turns.'

It took three men to hoist Scipio into the air, laughing and jeering as they did. Rob could barely watch. His friend's eyes bulged out of their sockets, white and round. He choked and gasped, spluttering for air.

Then the overseers turned their attentions to Phoebe.

The redhead slit open her dress from the hem to the neck and tore it off. He threw her to the ground and spread her legs. She did not make so much as a whimper.

'A quiet one, eh? I'll soon get you singing.'

He undid his belt and dropped his breeches. His cock stood erect, livid and engorged. Three of his men stood guard around the edge of the clearing, while the other two held Phoebe's legs.

She didn't struggle. Probably, Rob thought, sickened, it had happened to her before.

Rob tugged against his bonds, but the overseers knew their work and had tied the knots fast. Dangling from the tree, Scipio was still alive. He choked and jerked hopelessly. He had spun about in a half-circle so he could not see Phoebe's debasement. But he could imagine it from the sounds he could hear.

The redhead went down on his knees between Phoebe's legs. He seized her thighs and dug his fingers deep into her flesh. He licked his lips.

With a gurgling cry, one of his men staggered forwards from the trees and crashed to the ground. The redhead flinched, angry to be interrupted. The shout died on his lips as he saw the knife buried to its hilt in the man's back.

The men spun around, muskets raised, pointing them this way and that. There was no one to aim at. The jungle surrounding them was a wall of green.

A branch rustled. The men were spooked, their fingers already curled tight around their triggers. One curled so tight it fired the musket. It was all the others needed to follow suit. A crescendo of smoke and flame erupted as an uneven volley went blind into the forest.

The echo of the shots died away. The silence was so profound, leaves and twigs could be heard fluttering to the ground where the bullets had passed through. The men looked around, staring at one another.

Hope dawned to terror as they realised they no longer had a single loaded gun between them. Frantically, they began fumbling with ramrods and cartridges. In their haste, they hardly saw the figures who flitted out of the trees like shadows. A dozen men and women, all armed. Some carried cane knives, others axes and tomahawks, and one a naval regulation-issue cutlass. They were quick, effective and brutal. The overseers had no defence. Rob watched as they were hacked to pieces in moments.

One of the overseers' knives lay on the ground. While the butchering went on, Rob shuffled over to it and cut through the bonds that tied his wrists. As soon as he was free he ran to the rope that held Scipio. He could not get enough slack on it to untie the knot. He cut it with a cane knife, cursing the blunt blade as it reluctantly parted the thick fibres. Scipio had stopped moving. His dark skin had turned a grey-blue.

The last strand was severed. The rope broke. Rob was too exhausted to grab the loose end. Scipio's body dropped in a heap to the ground and lay there unmoving. Phoebe ran to him. She threw her arms around him and put her ear to his lips.

'He is breathing.'

Rob's relief was short-lived as he considered their unlikely saviours. Were they protectors? They clearly weren't plantation slaves, or hadn't been for some time. They must be Maroons, the slaves who had escaped and lived free in the wild interior of the mountains.

He remembered Crow saying that the Maroons sometimes brought back escaped slaves to their masters for a ransom. Why, then, had they killed the overseers? The laws of the jungle were infinitely perplexing.

He noticed that the Maroons had taken the guns from the dead overseers and were pointing them at Rob and Angus.

Rob raised his hands.

'Friend,' he croaked. 'I am a friend.'

Their leader, a tall and handsome black man with a string of red beads around his throat, stared at Rob. He glanced at Phoebe and said something in a language neither Rob nor Phoebe could understand. But Scipio could. He raised himself on his elbow and gave a low, short answer.

The Maroon leader looked surprised. He conferred with his men. He spoke more with Scipio. He nodded.

'You come with us.'

Rob was not sure if he was a prisoner or a fugitive. He was so tired his bones felt ready to collapse inside him. He did not think he could take another step. Yet the Maroons led him on relentlessly, forcing a brisk pace through the forest. Rob, Phoebe, Angus and Scipio stumbled along as best they could. They climbed high up the mountain, following twisting trails that seemed impossible to divine. The sun rose, the forest began to steam. The Maroons handed out pieces of raw sugar cane. Rob chewed on the fibrous stalk until he had sucked out every drop of the sweet juice within. It gave him a modicum of strength.

They passed through a narrow defile between high cliffs. A river ran through it, foaming between the huge rocks which littered the ravine. Looking up, Rob could see more boulders poised on the edge of the clifftops. Dark figures peered down from the heights.

'If we were enemies, they could crush us flat as canvas,' muttered Angus. 'No one could force this passage in a thousand years.'

There was no path here. They had to climb from boulder to boulder, slipping and gasping as they came within inches of the surging water. Rob lost count of the times his weary limbs nearly failed him, when he almost drowned. He was ready to topple where he stood and never rise again, when suddenly the river grew calmer, and the ravine opened out in a wide bowl in the hills. On either side of the river stood a village, wooden huts surrounded by vegetable gardens and small agricultural plots. Chickens and guinea fowl wandered freely, pecking the ground. A pig rootled in the earth.

Their escorts took them to an empty hut. There were mattresses stuffed with coconut fibre on the floor. Rob, Angus, Scipio and Phoebe fell onto them as if they were feather beds and dropped dead asleep.

The *Perseus* sailed away from Thebes Plantation the following morning. Only one man aboard was happy, and that was Midshipman Brompton, newly promoted to acting lieutenant following Rob Courtney's desertion. Coyningham was dismayed to be leaving Sophie. Any satisfaction he felt at having got rid of Rob was tempered by the devastation Rob had wreaked at Thebes. Bracewell's secretary Crow was dead, his overseers maimed or killed, and more than half his slaves had escaped into the forest. Bracewell had been in a towering fury, and Coyningham – as Rob's superior officer – had not escaped his anger. It was not the impression he had wanted to make on the guardian of his potential future wife.

The men were unhappy, too. Angus was a popular shipmate, and Rob had been the last bulwark protecting them from Coyningham's cruelty. Lieutenant Fawcett was weak, and Brompton too eager to make a good impression on the captain. Now they feared for the future.

Coyningham laid out the chart and summoned all his officers.

'We will rendezvous with the convoy in two days' time, and then escort it back along the Jamaica coast. I expect everything to be done with perfect precision. Any man who falters in his duty can expect a taste of the cat.'

The *Perseus* set her course to the north-east and beat away from Thebes Plantation. There was a fine breeze, and with her clean copper she made good progress. Soon, she was little more than a dot in the far distance.

But her sails had hardly slipped over the horizon when another ship appeared to the north. On a broad reach, she scudded before the wind, bearing down on the island like a bird of prey. All afternoon she grew in the distance, until at last she dropped anchor in almost the same place that the *Perseus* had been a few hours earlier.

The striped ensign of the rebel colonies flew from her mast-head, while below her bowsprit stretched an eagle with golden talons outstretched.

A boat put ashore. A small group of officers climbed the stairs to the great mansion. A black butler greeted them with chilled glasses of white wine and ushered them into the drawing room. The visiting officers seated themselves on the sofas which bore no trace of the orgy that had occurred forty-eight hours before. The cushions had been plumped up and the fabric scrubbed clean.

Bracewell entered with Sophie behind him.

'My apologies for the delay,' he said. 'An outrage was perpetrated yesterday. A damn British officer ran off with half my Negroes.'

The French captain – Étienne, resplendent in his white uniform coat – looked around cautiously.

'I hope this British officer is not still here?'

'He ran into the jungle. You need not worry about Lieutenant Courtney.'

To Bracewell's surprise, a sudden silence enveloped the room.

'What is it? You know this man?'

Étienne pointed to Cal, sitting on his right in the uniform of the Continental Army.

'This is Major Caleb Courtney.'

Bracewell gave him a penetrating stare. There was no obvious physical resemblance, except that both were about the same age, young and powerful. Yet even so, there was something indefinably familiar about the aura of the youth.

Bracewell shook off the notion. 'It seems you are not the only Courtney on this island. If you can be as much a hindrance to our enemies as Robert Courtney has been to me, you will do famously.'

Cal said nothing. Since the moment the Bracewells entered, he had been staring at Sophie with eyes like a wolf. Even Sophie, no stranger to adoring men's gazes, had blushed and looked away.

Cal realised they were waiting for him to speak.

'This Robert Courtney – did he sail on the *Perseus*?'

'Yes.'

'We have already crossed swords with him. Twice he managed to escape the traps we had set for him.'

It was clear from his voice he ached for revenge.

'I have sent men after him, with orders to bring him back alive,' said Bracewell. 'I think you and I would enjoy the chance to give this Courtney his due.' Not for the first time, he mourned Crow's death. Crow had been a true artist when it came to inflicting pain. 'Though you had better hope my men catch him before those bastard Maroons do. They kill any white man they find.'

Cal nodded. 'I would welcome the chance for an intimate conversation with this Robert Courtney.'

Étienne coughed. 'You speak of harming our enemies, Monsieur Bracewell,' he said. 'Can we be clear we are fighting on the same side?'

'My enemies are your enemies,' said Bracewell. 'The British government.'

'But you yourself are a subject of King George.'

'So was George Washington,' said Bracewell. 'We must adapt to the times.'

'Indeed,' said Étienne. 'But how can I be sure I can trust you?'

'You have seen the island,' said Bracewell. 'All we grow here is sugar and slaves. Everything else – every piece of furniture and clothing, every piece of iron and timber, our food and live-stock and wine, down to the last mustard spoon – is imported. And the greatest part of that trade comes from America. If America wins the war and the colonies cut themselves off from the British Empire, these islands will be impoverished.' He thumped his fist on the table. 'I will lose money!'

He recovered himself.

'Also, the British are taxing us outrageously. Our only choice is to throw off rule from London and ally ourselves with the Americans.'

'And this does not trouble you?' said Étienne.

'All that troubles me is failing to turn a profit from my estates.'

'You said "our only choice",' noted Cal. 'Who else is with you?'

'All the most significant landowners in the Caribbean. We are few in number, but together we control the lion's share of land and men across the West Indies. We are all sworn to this purpose. We have been planning it for months. Now is the time to strike.'

'If you rebel against the King,' said Étienne, 'he will send his army and navy to crush you.'

'His army is already overstretched in America. And we have an advocate in London. A very highly placed member of the government, who is sympathetic to our cause. He will work behind the scenes to ensure that the ministry does not declare war on us, but instead negotiates a peaceful separation.'

'A member of the government who is willing to trade away Britain's empire?' said Étienne drily.

'We have made it an attractive proposition for him.'

Bracewell winced to think of the colossal amount of money it had taken to bribe a man as rich as Baron Dartmouth. But it was an investment. When Bracewell controlled the sugar exports of the entire Caribbean, his money would be returned a thousandfold.

And he would also have kept safe all the capital he had invested in his slaves. In 1772 the courts had already ruled that slavery was unsupported by common law in England and Wales, and now the government had offered to free the slaves in America. What if they extended emancipation to the other colonies? The thought of his slaves going free was enough to give him nightmares. But in alliance with America, his slaves would be safe. A revolution led by men such as George Washington, Thomas Jefferson and James Madison – slave-holders all – would respect his property rights.

Étienne gave a chill smile. He had set out from France not knowing he would become part of this scheme. It was only when Cal Courtney came aboard in Boston that he had got wind of it. Yet now, he had the opportunity to surpass his mother's wildest dreams. If the Caribbean islands won their independence, Britain's sugar profits would disappear. The war in America would end in a week. And when the next year's sugar convoy set sail for Europe, it would be bound not for London, but for France.

'The first order of business is to cut off the British garrisons in these islands,' said Bracewell. He led Étienne and Cal to a mahogany table where a large chart of the Caribbean lay spread out. 'Every year, Britain sends ships to supply their garrisons in the West Indies. This year, because of the risk from privateers, the Admiralty has put a year's worth of supplies into one convoy. It is your job, gentlemen, to intercept it.'

'If the convoy is so valuable, it will be heavily guarded,' said Cal.

'Once they reach Jamaican waters, they will think they are safe. The naval escorts will leave the convoy and sail north to join the American war. The only ship guarding the convoy will be a lone frigate, the *Perseus*.'

'Are you sure?'

'I was in the room when they made these plans.'

'Why did you not sabotage the plans when you had the opportunity?' said Étienne.

'Are you quite mad? It is obvious to anyone who has the merest grasp of subterfuge and business. I could not reveal my hand to the rapacious British too soon.'

Bracewell's face was puce with frustration. He took a gulp of air and composed himself. He tapped the map at a point near the end of the island, a few miles along the coast from Thebes Plantation.

'This is where you will intercept them.'

Étienne studied the map thoughtfully.

'Even so, the British merchants will carry some guns of their own. Against the frigate alone, my ship would win easily. Against the frigate and an armed convoy, it is more difficult.'

Bracewell bared his teeth. 'You will not be fighting alone. When you engage the *Perseus*, you will be leading her into a trap.'

The ground wasn't moving when Rob woke, which confused him. He was so used to waking in his cot, the ship rocking him, that he did not know where he was. He lay still for a while, getting his bearings. The air was warm. The mattress he lay on was soft. Dappled sunlight shimmered through the coconut matting that made a roof above him.

Every muscle in his body ached, like his first day in the navy but much worse. Slowly, memories of the night before returned. The dinner with Bracewell. The fight with Crow. Freeing the slaves, and the flight from the plantation. He remembered Phoebe . . .

She was there. She lay curled against him, wrapped into the curves of his body like a musket ball in a mould. Her skin was so silky, he had barely felt her touch. She had the remains of her torn dress wrapped around her hips, but otherwise she was naked. Looking over her shoulder, Rob saw her breasts rising and falling with the slow breaths of sleep.

He reached over to hug her closer, laying his hand across her smooth belly. She stirred, snuggling herself into him. Her buttocks wriggled against his hips. To his embarrassment, he felt himself swell up hard at her touch. He tried to pull away, but she pressed herself more firmly against him.

Her eyes flickered open. She looked around and saw him.

She lifted his hand off her belly and moved it to her breast. She cupped his hand around the softness, and her hand around his. He brushed his fingers over her engorged nipple and she gasped.

She rolled over so that they came face to face.

'Do you want me?' she asked. She was not being provocative. There was something hesitant in her voice, almost afraid.

Angus and Scipio had disappeared. They were alone in the hut.

Rob leaned forwards and kissed her. Her lips parted. They were moist, sweet with the remains of the sugar cane they had sucked on their march. Rob ran his tongue over her lips and pressed into them. He wrapped his hands around her and pulled her body against him.

He slid inside her. His sailor's body began to move with the natural rhythm of a ship in a swell. He rolled on top of her, so he could look down into her wide-open eyes.

A memory of Sophie Bracewell flitted through his mind before he could push it away. With her, sex had been a game of violence, lust and power. With Phoebe, he felt an infinite tenderness. He wanted to hold her forever, to be one with her, to fill every inch of her body with joy and pleasure.

They climaxed in unison. Phoebe's whole body shivered. She closed her eyes, arched her back and pressed herself against him, making small mewing noises like a kitten while Rob emptied himself into her with great shuddering thrusts.

Afterwards, they lay in each other's arms, drenched in sweat.

'I have never done it like that before,' she said shyly. 'I did not know it could be so . . . nice.'

Rob squeezed her so tightly he thought he might crush her ribs.

'I have never done it like that before either,' he told her. 'And I never want to do it any other way again, except with you.'

A thump sounded above them, as a stone struck the roof, rolled down and dropped to the ground. Footsteps approached, accompanied by whistling. Rob rolled away, pulling on his breeches, while Phoebe snatched up her dress to cover herself.

Angus's voice sounded outside the hut.

'I hope you slept well, Lieutenant. Not too sore from your exertions, sir.'

Rob grinned. 'Just stretching out my aches and pains. And I am no longer a lieutenant. You do not have to call me "sir".'

'Aye. A proper lieutenant would still be sleeping.'

Rob looked at the sun. It was still climbing in the sky, about mid-morning.

'I only went to bed at sunrise.' Though for having only had a few hours of sleep, he felt marvellously refreshed, he realised. 'Was that only this morning?'

'It was not this morning,' said Angus. 'It was yesterday morning. You've slept a full day and a night since we arrived.'

Rob had never slept so long in his life. He felt disorientated. The day he had slept through felt like a hole in his memory.

'Has anything happened? What of the *Perseus*? What of Bracewell's men?'

'Kojo's men say the *Perseus* sailed this morning. To rendezvous with the convoy, most likely. As for Bracewell's overseers . . .' He drew his finger across his throat and his voice turned serious. 'Kojo's people didn'ae treat them kindly.'

Rob rubbed his eyes. 'Who is Kojo?'

'The king of these people.'

'I must see him.'

'Funny enough, that's just what he said.'

Angus led them through the village. It was almost like a town, with over a hundred huts, neatly built of wattle and daub and thatch. Everywhere Rob looked, the Maroons were at work. Women hoed vegetable plots, ground maize into flour or washed clothes in the stream. In one open hut, men were butchering the carcasses of wild pigs they had brought back and curing the meat over a fire.

Strangely, of all the places he had been on his travels, this reminded him most of home. The simple dwellings, the sense of men and women working hard but freely. No shouting or saluting, no overseers or boatswain's mates with whips. The happy feeling of shared industry.

At the centre of the village, earth had been heaped up to make a raised circular platform. It had been pounded hard and flat by the stamping of many feet. Rob blinked at the unexpected sight.

'It is a dancing ground,' he thought.

It was so familiar. He had seen similar spaces in the Qwabe villages around Fort Auspice, a place where the local people gathered for their ceremonial dances and to worship their gods.

Behind the platform, at the top of the slope, was a large building. It had stone foundations, and stout wooden timbers that made it more solid than any other structure in the village, though that was not what caught Rob's eye. A row of human skulls stood on posts around its perimeter.

In front of the house, a man sat under a palm-mat awning, on a seat so large it could only be called a throne. He was dressed in the most outlandish garb Rob had ever seen. He had a ruffled shirt and puffed-out breeches like some Tudor pirate; a broadcloth coat with scarlet facings and gold buttons; a black tricorne hat with three parrot feathers stuck in the band; and two cross belts which held a full armoury of knives and pistols. He was barefoot. His skin was greyish brown, with fine cheekbones and narrow, penetrating eyes which barely deigned to look at Rob. On his cheek, he bore the deep impression of a brand in the shape of a broad arrow.

Scipio was with him. A dark bruise around his throat showed where the overseers' noose had bitten deep, but otherwise he seemed much recovered from his ordeal.

'Kojo,' said Angus. 'He is the king here.'

Not sure what to do, Rob gave a small bow. Kojo gave him a dismissive look.

'No white man ever come here,' he said.

'Then I thank you. Your men saved our lives.'

Kojo didn't acknowledge his thanks. He studied Rob, like a farmer examining livestock at auction. When he spoke, he had lapsed back into his native language.

'He say his men not save you for kindness,' Scipio translated. 'They save you because they think Bracewell want you. Maybe reward, bring you back.'

Rob waited.

'Bracewell want you dead.'

Kojo nodded vigorously, giving a high-pitched laugh that echoed around the clearing.

'Bracewell wants Kojo dead, too,' Rob pointed out. 'Our interests are aligned.'

Kojo evidently understood more English than he let on. Before Scipio could translate, he launched into a long tirade, drawing a pistol from his belt and waving it in the air.

'I fight with the white man before!' he shouted. 'For the white King George in his great ships.'

Rob thought he must have misunderstood.

'You were in the navy?'

In answer, Kojo stripped off his coat and shirt. He flexed the muscle so that his bicep bulged up. The skin stretched taut, and printed on it in blue ink that was almost invisible against the dark skin, was a tattoo of an anchor wound with a length of rope.

Rob pulled off his shirt and showed Kojo his almost identical tattoo, in almost the same place.

'How did you end up here?'

The answer was long, complicated and delivered in two languages with much use of the pistol for emphasis. Between Scipio's translation, the fragments he understood, and Kojo's expressive gestures, Rob pieced together the story.

Kojo had grown up on the west coast of Africa, not far from where Scipio was born. Their tribes were part of the same loose confederacy and shared a common language. One day, a British man-of-war had anchored in the bay to take on water. Kojo had been fascinated by the vessel, the strange men who crewed it and the great guns she carried. He had gone aboard and volunteered to join the Royal Navy. The ship's crew had been decimated by fever, so the captain was glad to accept him.

Kojo's career in the navy had been successful. He had worked hard, learned quickly, and worked his way up to become a gunner. He had visited Cape Town, Bombay, London and New York.

Then he had come to Jamaica. He had gone out on shore leave, been separated from his shipmates, and got blind drunk on rum with a group of men in a tavern. Probably, they had done it deliberately. When he woke, his ship had sailed and he was in chains. His new friends turned him in to the authorities as an escaped slave.

Because Kojo was not a runaway, no planter came forward to claim him. But Kojo's captors had an accomplice at the naval dockyard in Port Royal. He claimed Kojo as a dockyard slave, and then shared the recapture bounty with the men who had kidnapped him. So Kojo worked for the Royal Navy again, but now as a slave rather than a free man.

Kojo pointed to the scar on his cheek. Rob realised now what it was – the broad-arrow mark of the Royal Navy. He had seen it countless times aboard ship, stamped on casks and chests. As a slave, Kojo had been another piece of government property to be branded in case of loss or theft.

Kojo had nursed his grievance. He arranged to work in the victualling depot. He travelled all over the island with the storekeeper arranging to buy provisions. Piece by piece, in whispered conversations behind the overseers' backs, he forged friendships and laid his plans.

One night, the island erupted. Slaves on twenty plantations rebelled at the same time. The night was as bright as day with the light of cane pieces and plantation houses burning. Every soldier and militiaman in Port Royal was sent to quell the revolt – at which point, the dockyard slaves made their escape. Kojo joined the other fleeing slaves and led them into the mountains.

What followed was all-out war. Kojo had committed the unforgivable sin of exposing the precarious foundations of the planters' control. In revenge, they terrorised the island. Any slave suspected of defiance was hanged. Any fugitives they caught were burned alive. Babies were slaughtered in front of their mothers, women gang-raped before their husbands. Rewards were offered to anyone who would betray Kojo: fifty pounds, then two hundred and fifty, and on up until the bounty finally reached a thousand.

They never caught him. Kojo and his followers melted into the deep forests and impenetrable mountains in the interior.

Those who had grown up in Africa knew how to fight in the jungle. Those who had been born in chains were soon taught. Whatever losses they suffered, they inflicted ten times more on their enemies. The militia learned to hate the forests. Insects devoured them, disease ravaged them and however deep they went they never found any Maroons. Then, just as they convinced themselves they were on a wild goose chase, gunshots would ring out as if from nowhere and white men would fall dead. You could follow their paths through the jungle by the trail of corpses they left.

Then something extraordinary happened. The planters gave up the fight. They sent a delegation to Kojo and sued for peace. Kojo suspected a trap, but the planters were in earnest. They were sick of this unwinnable war. They offered him what they had never offered any black man: freedom, and peace. And, by and large, they stuck to their agreement.

But he would never trust a white man again.

Kojo stared down at Rob and Angus. 'Everything you say about the white man is true,' said Rob.

Kojo nodded, surprised by Rob's honesty.

'But also true about the black man.'

Anger flashed across Kojo's face, a warning that needed no translation. Rob was not intimidated. He turned to Scipio.

'Who made you a slave? Did the white men come to your home themselves? Did they fight their own battles to make you a prisoner? Or were you sold by your own kind?'

Scipio nodded. 'It is what you say. It was the Aro tribe. They take me to the sea and they sell me to the white man.'

'And you?' Rob rounded on Kojo. 'You suffered as a slave, but when fugitives come here now you sell them back to the white man. How does that make you any better than the white men who bought and sold you?'

'Careful, Rob,' Angus whispered.

But it was too late. Kojo rose from his throne, shaking with anger.

'This is my peace!' he bellowed. 'I protect my people. Me!' He stamped his foot, gesticulating wildly with his pistol. 'If all the slaves come to me, the white man will follow.'

He carried on, but in his agitation he switched back to his native language.

'Sometimes you must feed the lion your cattle, so he does not eat your family,' Scipio translated.

'I meant no disrespect,' Rob said, trying to calm the situation. 'I only meant that a man is not what he is here.' He pinched the skin on his arm, showing its colour. Then he thumped his chest. 'A man is this – what is in his heart.'

While they'd been speaking, a crowd had gathered around them: almost all the Maroons in the village. Hundreds of them, yet they barely made a sound as they looked at Kojo to see how he would react.

Kojo surveyed the four captives before him. Rob, Scipio, Angus and Phoebe: two black, two white. His fingers played impatiently over the handle of his pistol.

He spoke, suddenly and quickly, in the language he shared with Scipio. Rob had the uncomfortable feeling of standing helpless while another man decided whether he would live or die. There was nothing he could do but wait.

At last Kojo looked to Rob.

'Scipio say you save his life.'

'As your men saved mine.'

'Yes,' said Kojo, pleased. 'Yes. I save your life.'

He seemed to reach a decision.

'I do not kill you,' he pronounced.

Rob tried not to sag with relief.

'But you not stay here. You, and you.' Kojo turned to Angus. 'You go.'

'Where is there that we can go?' Angus asked.

'Away,' said Kojo dismissively.

Rob tugged his friend's sleeve. 'There is no gain arguing. We will find a way.'

Kojo pointed to Phoebe and Scipio. 'You stay.'

Rob felt a pang at the thought of losing them, though at least they would be safe. He felt sure Kojo was not planning to sell them to a plantation owner. But—

'No.' Phoebe took Rob's hand. 'Wherever you go, I will go, too.'

'You cannot,' said Rob. 'There is no safe place for me on this island. I will live every day like a hunted animal.'

'Then that is how I will live, too,' she said. 'However many days you have left in your life, I want to live every one with you. And none without you. No one has shown me the true care that you have. I want to be by your side forever. I wish only for your happiness.'

'I, too, will protect you,' said Scipio, in a voice that brooked no argument. 'You are a good man. I owe you my life, I will repay you with my undying loyalty.'

Rob did not know what to say. Tears pricked his eyes, but he could not show weakness in front of the crowd. From the throne, Kojo was staring at them with something like incredulity. Rob wondered if he was having second thoughts about his decision.

'If we are no longer welcome here, we had best be off.'

He felt Kojo's gaze on their backs all the way to the end of the village. But Kojo was a man of his word. Perhaps he was glad to be rid of these interlopers. His men led them back down the gorge, the river swollen with rain. It foamed and roared around them as they leaped from boulder to boulder, Rob always ready at Phoebe's side in case she slipped.

At the mouth of the gorge, Kojo's guards gave them a sack filled with provisions and left them. Rob, Phoebe, Scipio and Angus trooped down a narrow path, barely wider than a goat track. Rob led them, though he did not know where he was going. The rains came again, lashing so hard the trees were no protection. Soon all of them were soaked to the skin.

'What now?' asked Scipio.

They had paused for refreshments, huddled under a thicket of bamboo for shelter. Rob chewed the tough smoked pork.

Even this one small meal had used up a good portion of the rations Kojo had given them.

'We could try to find another plantation,' Angus mused. 'Maybe they do'nae ken what happened at Bracewell's place. They might have a boat.'

'That would not work,' countered Rob. 'Even if they would help you and me, they would seize Scipio and Phoebe as runaway slaves.'

'Not if they thought they were our slaves.'

A growl from Scipio said what he thought of that plan.

'I die before I am a slave again.' There was a murderous look in his eye that brooked no argument.

'Maybe we can steal a boat,' said Phoebe.

'And go where?' said Angus. 'Every island for five hundred miles has slaves.'

'Canada,' said Phoebe. 'I heard Mr Bracewell talking about it. The slaves that are being freed in the American colonies are being taken to Canada.'

'Do you even know where Canada is?' said Angus incredulously. 'Who would sail a ship so far? You?'

'You have another plan?' Scipio challenged him, quick to defend Phoebe.

'Aye. And if you'd not been so jealous of your dignity, we could've tried it.'

Their voices had risen. Both men were on their feet, legs planted wide, arms crossed, like two bulls facing each other down.

'Enough!' cried Rob. He could see their tempers fraying. Hungry, wet, tired and alone, none of them had the strength for conflict.

Scipio and Angus fell silent, glaring at each other. In the sudden quiet that followed, Rob thought he could hear every water drop in the forest.

And there was another sound. Not far off, the bray of a mule and then a man's voice shouting angrily '*Merde!*'

In an instant, Scipio and Angus forgot their quarrel. All four of them dropped into the undergrowth and went still. Rob waited, rain dribbling down his neck, his mind racing.

The voice had spoken French.

Rob raised his head and peered over a rotting tree stump.

A man came into sight. He was about twenty yards down the hill, moving across the slope on a path that was hidden by the foliage. He wore a soldier's uniform, a tricorne hat and a white coat with red facings, though both were so spattered with mud the colours were hardly visible. A mule trotted along behind him, loaded with small barrels. Even from that distance, Rob could make out the sulphurous smell of gunpowder. They were powder kegs.

The uniform, like the swearing, was French. How on earth could a French soldier be alone in the jungle of a British island, leading a mule loaded with gunpowder?

He was not alone. As he progressed along the path, another soldier appeared behind him, leading another mule. Then more men, and more mules. With their heads bowed against the rain, their eyes watching the treacherous footing on the muddy path, none of them noticed Rob watching.

By the time they had all passed, Rob had counted thirty mules and nearly forty men.

'It makes no sense,' he said, when the French were a safe distance away. 'They cannot have invaded Jamaica overnight. And why would they be here, when the British forces are concentrated at Port Royal and Kingston?'

'There's an easy way to find out,' said Angus. 'Follow them.'

Rob made Angus stay behind with Phoebe, while he and Scipio followed the French column. Rob did not want to put Phoebe in danger if the French caught them, and Angus needed to rest his back, which was still sore from his wounds. It was not hard to find the trail. So many men and their heavy-laden beasts had churned the wet ground to a quagmire. Rob and Scipio could keep well back, without fear of losing their quarry.

They tracked them for hours. Rob began to worry about finding their way back in the dark, and what might have happened to Angus and Phoebe. But he did not turn around. If there were French troops present, they could only have arrived by ship. Perhaps that would be his way to escape from the island.

They must have walked many miles, when suddenly they came around a rocky outcrop and the forest fell away. The rain had eased. The setting sun burned in front of them, a bright orange disc sinking below the clouds. They were on a headland at the western tip of the island. Cliffs descended below them, towards a sea that sparkled gold in the evening light. The smell of roasting meat tinged the air and made his empty stomach flip over with hunger.

Rob flattened himself to the ground and crawled forwards, following the mule track to where it disappeared over the cliff. He peered down.

The cliff was not as steep as it had looked from behind. The track zigzagged down the slope, to a flat shelf about halfway down where a military camp had been established. The mules were tethered, munching on the wild grasses that grew there. Nearby, half a dozen white tents had been pitched against the cliff. Soldiers sat around campfires, boiling kettles and cooking pigs on spits.

The camp was efficiently run. It must have been there some time. The tracks between the tents were well worn, and the soldiers moved with the easy confidence of men who were used to their surroundings. They had been busy. At the cliff edge, they had moved rocks and boulders to create a low flat parapet. Wooden frames supported an awning of woven palm fronds to shade the ground below. A crane stood at the far end, ready to hoist supplies from the sea.

And against the parapet, lined up as if on a man-of-war, were a dozen long cannons.

Rob stared, trying to understand it. The guns made no sense as part of an invasion: they were pointing towards the sea. Any British force that attacked the battery by land could overwhelm it at once. What were the French doing?

Rob felt Scipio's hand on his shoulder.

'We go. Before they find us.'

Rob nodded. The French might have pickets, or they might send out patrols at night. He and Scipio retreated into cover, then turned for the long walk back.

The tropical darkness fell swiftly, before they had covered more than a couple of miles. Rather than risk losing their way, they spent the night huddled in a makeshift shelter between two boulders, then set off again at first light. They moved carefully, wary in case they met anyone else coming down the path.

The return seemed longer than the outward journey. The sun was past noon when they reached the spot where they had left Angus and Phoebe.

Neither of them were there.

'Is this the place?' Rob wondered, though he was certain it was. There was a rock shaped like a pig's snout, and Angus had cut a broad-arrow blaze onto the trunk of a tree.

A brown mammee apple flew out of the forest and hit him on the cheek. Angus rose grinning from the bushes at the side of the path.

'You took your sweet time,' he said.

'We went to the end of the island,' Rob told him. 'There are French troops. They have built a battery that commands the western channel.'

Rob saw Phoebe coming down behind Angus, carrying the food bag. He felt faint with hunger. He delved into the bag and started chewing ravenously on a piece of smoked pork.

Phoebe drew Rob away. She whispered in his ear. Rob took a step backwards and raised his arms, shaking his head. Phoebe held him by his shoulders, spoke quickly and urgently. Then she turned and disappeared into the forest.

'What was that about?' said Angus.

'She has a plan,' said Rob.

'That's as may be, but there's something you need to see.'

Rob tore off a piece of pork in his teeth.

'I have not eaten since I left you yesterday.'

'It's important.'

The note of urgency in Angus's voice cut through Rob's hunger. He followed his friend up the slope to where a rocky outcrop thrust from the side of the mountain. They scrambled onto the summit.

The rock raised them above the trees, giving a panoramic view down the mountain to the coast. To the west, Rob saw the island tapering to the point where he and Scipio had found the French battery. He swept his eyes over the miles of jungle that they had traversed, marvelling how small it looked from this height.

But that was not where Angus was pointing. He steered Rob's gaze north, to where the forest gave way to the dark green squares of the cane-brakes of Thebes Plantation. Rob could see the sails of the windmills, brought to a standstill with no slaves to man them; the slave cottages; the great house on its eminence above the sea.

And beyond it, a ship. A landsman's inexpert eye might have mistaken her for the *Perseus*. She was a frigate, anchored in the same place, with similar lines and armament. But Rob and Angus knew their ship as a child knows its mother – and this was not her.

From that distance, they could not see her figurehead, but the American flag hanging from her masthead confirmed what they had known at once.

'The privateer,' said Rob. Instinctively, he crouched down, though he could not be seen from so far away. 'But what can she be doing there?'

'Nothing good,' said Angus. 'And what mischief does Bracewell plan with her?'

Far to the north-west, a sail broke the distant horizon. Rob, trained by many hours at the masthead, spotted it at once.

'The convoy,' he said.

And suddenly he saw it laid out before him as if on a map. The *Perseus* would escort the convoy along the Jamaica coast. She would see the French frigate, and Coyningham would give chase. He would follow the *Rapace* to the headland and sail right under the guns the French had placed there. The *Perseus* would be at their mercy. The rest of the convoy would be left defence-less, and they would all be taken.

'But why?' he murmured.

'Bracewell must be in league with the French,' said Angus. 'Mebbe he means to make himself king of Jamaica.'

Rob remembered what Coyningham had said. *There is enough powder and shot aboard that convoy to start a war.* If Bracewell was working with the French, they would be able to take Jamaica. The other Caribbean islands had tiny garrisons. A well-equipped force would sweep them aside in a matter of weeks. Britain's sugar empire would collapse.

Rob had little loyalty to King George. He did not care if the Union flag flew over Jamaica, if merchants in London grew fat on sugar profits, or if the American colonies won their independence. Those were questions for ministers and generals.

But he had a duty to his shipmates on the *Perseus*. He could not let them be massacred under the French guns. Nor could he forget the slaves who toiled on Bracewell's plantation, and the thousands of others in bondage on the other plantations across the Caribbean. As miserable as they were, if the islands became Bracewell's private kingdom the slaves would exist in permanent torture, with no hope of salvation.

Down in the bay by the plantation house, seamen ran up the *Rapace*'s rigging and began to set sail. The crew hauled on her anchor. In the surf on the beach, a boat was being made ready. The ship was preparing to leave.

'We must stop them,' said Rob.

'Aye,' said Angus. 'But how?'

The *Rapace*'s boatmen held the launch steady as Bracewell clambered in. They had pulled it high up the beach so he would not get his feet wet. It would not be easy sliding it back into the water with his great bulk weighing it down.

Two slaves hoisted in a large iron strongbox. It added to the weight. Bracewell fussed with it until it was safely stowed under the thwart. He clamped it between his feet, as if afraid someone might try to break it open from under him.

Sophie stood at the water's edge. 'Why can't I come, Uncle?'

Bracewell shook his head. His chins wobbled. 'There will be fighting, my dear. You will be safe in the house.'

'But there is nobody in the house to protect me. And so many of our Negroes are in the forest. Think what those black brutes would do if they captured me.'

She shuddered. Her face went so pale she started to swoon. She might have fallen, if Cal Courtney had not been there to catch her in his arms.

'You should take her aboard,' said Cal. 'You can keep her out of the way when the battle starts. With our guns on the clifftop, the British frigate will barely have time to run out her guns before she is smashed to pieces.'

'What does the captain say?' said Bracewell.

'*Je m'en fous*,' said Étienne. 'But decide quickly. The convoy will be safely docked in Port Royal if we are always arguing.'

'Very well,' grunted Bracewell. He leaned forwards, double-checking that the lock on his strongbox was secure. 'You may come if you wish, my dear.'

'You may have my cabin,' said Cal.

'You are too kind.' Sophie gave him a beaming smile. Her gloved fingers slipped between his as he offered her his hand to help her into the boat. 'But where will you sleep?'

'I will not be aboard the ship. I will be commanding our guns on the clifftop.' He could not hide the regret in his voice.

'Then I wish you all success,' said Sophie. 'I hope that after the battle we can enjoy the fruits of the victory together.'

'That would be my greatest pleasure.'

Sophie seated herself on the bench beside her uncle. The rowers heaved the boat into the water and struck out for the *Rapace*. Cal turned to the cliff.

He did not know which excited him more. The promise of Sophie's favours, or the thought of having a British fleet under his guns.

Rob, Scipio and Angus ran through the rustling cane pieces, past the still windmills and down to the bay. With the slaves having deserted, the plantation felt ghostly empty.

They ran onto the wooden pier that jutted into the bay. Rum barrels stood stacked ready for export. The sun had opened their seams, and the air was thick with the smell of the liquor that had seeped through the cracks and evaporated.

Half a dozen boats lay moored to the jetty. Rob ran an expert eye over them. Most were wide, flat-bottomed barges built for rowing hogsheads of sugar to merchant ships. But one caught his attention. A long pinnace, with a mast and canvas laid across her thwarts ready to be mounted. She had clean lines, and a sharp prow. With a fair wind, she would make good speed across the water.

Scipio and Angus had seen her, too. Without waiting for Rob, they leaped into the pinnace and began stepping the mast. Rob cast off the line and took the tiller. Soon they were away from the shore, gathering speed as they came out of the shelter of the bay and caught the full brunt of the wind on the open sea.

Rob squinted at the ships further out. In the time it had taken him to get down from the forest, the convoy and the *Perseus* had made good progress. The *Perseus* was almost dead ahead, the convoy behind her and the privateer a few miles off her bow. They looked close but Rob knew that was an illusion. He wished he had a spyglass.

The *Perseus* had already seen the *Rapace* and taken the bait. She ran up her colours and crowded on sail. Rob watched the crew running up the rigging. Those tiny figures, ant-like against the blue sky, were his friends. Thomas would be up there some- where, swallowing his fear. Hargrave would be checking the guns, making sure they were primed. Men Rob had eaten, slept, joked and fought with for months. He had to save them.

The pinnace had the wind off her quarter, and a gaff rig. The *Perseus* was sailing before the wind. Her square-rigged sails would act as a brake on her speed, as the headwinds created by her speed pushed her back. That gave Rob hope the pinnace could catch her.

Scipio watched the mainsail like a hawk, constantly loosening and tightening the canvas by the tiniest fractions, like an expert rider twitching the reins to coax every inch of speed from his mount. Angus worked the jib, while Rob steered the little boat to catch all the wind he could.

The pinnace flew across the water. The gap to the frigate closed, but agonisingly slowly. The waves were bigger out in the deep water, harder for the pinnace to overcome. Some of the waves broke over her bow, so that Angus had to let go of the jib sheet and bale out the bilge.

Rob looked at the ribbon tied to his masthead. The wind was coming round. That would help the *Perseus* and slow the pinnace.

'Can we signal her?'

Angus shook his head. 'No flags.'

The *Perseus* was pulling away. The French frigate had slowed her speed, drawing her prey closer. Coyningham would think he was outsailing her, not realising he was hastening into the trap. The pinnace was being left behind.

'Is there nothing we can do?'

Rob swore. They had travelled several miles along the coast. He could see the headland where the French guns were waiting, not far off their larboard bow.

For an instant, Rob was transported back to the morning at the warehouse in London – the feeling in the pit of his stomach as he saw his entire fortune gone up in smoke. He was powerless. He had failed. And this time, men would die.

A cannon fired. Rob looked to the land, expecting to see smoke rising from the shore battery. But they were still out of range. The shot had come from the *Rapace*'s stern chasers.

'They're trying to goad the Bloodhound,' said Angus.

'No,' said Scipio. 'They shoot the sail.'

He was right. A round hole had appeared clean in the middle of the *Perseus*'s mainsail. It was perfectly placed. The full force of the wind was driving against the sail, concentrating in the single point of effort in its centre. Now, the canvas could not take the strain. The fabric tore open, streaming from the yards like laundry on a line.

'They have winged her!' cried Rob.

The French were taking no chances. They meant to cut down the *Perseus*'s steerage way, so she couldn't escape when the main battery opened fire.

But it had given Rob a chance. With her mainsail in ribbons, the *Perseus* slowed sharply. She lost more speed as the men left their stations to clear the broken canvas from the yards.

The gap between the pinnace and the frigate began to close. It was their last chance, and all three men knew it. The boat heeled over as she gathered pace. Scipio had pulled the sail so tight Rob feared it would snap. All three men hooked their legs under the thwarts and leaned out over the side to counterbalance the angle. Spray dashed against them. The boat was going so fast she no longer hit the waves bow-on, but planed over them from crest to crest. The water slapped against her bottom, almost bouncing Rob into the sea. He clung on.

A second shot flashed from the *Rapace*. It hit the foresail yardarm. The corner of the sail flapped loose, spilling wind and slowing the ship's momentum even more.

They were so close that Rob could hear the shouts of the men on deck. In the frenzy of the chase, few men noticed the pinnace coming up off her beam, but a few of the gun crews saw the boat approaching. They peered over the gunwale.

'It is a trap!' Rob shouted, trying desperately to make his voice carry over the wind and water. 'You are sailing into an ambush!'

The men looked uncertainly down at him. One or two glanced over their shoulders. But they did not relay the message. Coyningham had managed to reset his sails. The ship started to surge forwards again. At the same time, the pinnace came into the big ship's wind shadow and started to lose headway.

'Take the tiller,' Rob told Scipio.

He ran to the front of the boat and found the anchor rope coiled in the bow. He cut the anchor free, weighted the line in his hand and cast it across the water to the *Perseus*.

The rope arced through the air, uncoiling as it flew. Rob's stomach clenched as he thought it would fall short. But it was a good throw. The rope end struck the ship's side. For a moment Rob feared it would drop back into the sea.

Then a strong hand reached out through a gunport and grabbed it. The rope went taut as the men aboard the *Perseus* took the strain. Slowly, they hauled in the pinnace alongside. As soon as they were close enough, Rob leaped across the gap between the vessels, grabbed on to the frigate's hull and raced up the ladder.

The ship was cleared for action. The marines were in the tops, while on deck the men crouched by their guns and the young powder monkeys waited by the companionways to fetch more gunpowder. They stared at Rob as if he were a ghost.

'It is a trap,' said Rob, gabbling the words in his haste. 'The French have a battery on the headland. The privateer means to draw you under their guns and then annihilate you.'

Lieutenant Fawcett, standing by the mainmast, looked incredulous.

'A French battery? On Jamaica?'

'They are in league with Bracewell.' Rob pointed to the *Rapace*, only half a mile distant. 'I saw him board that ship this afternoon. He has betrayed you all.'

Fawcett gaped. Then he disappeared from sight, as a tall figure in a cocked hat stepped in front of him. Captain's lace gleamed on the cuff of his coat.

'Mr Courtney,' said Coyningham. 'I wonder that you dare show your face aboard this ship again.'

'Forget our quarrel,' Rob pleaded. 'You are sailing into a trap.' From the corner of his eye, he could see the headland drawing closer. They had minutes at most before the guns opened fire. 'I beg you, sir.'

Coyningham's face split wide in triumph.

'I do not know what game you are playing, Mr Courtney – but you have lost.'

He turned to the marines who had come down from the quarterdeck and formed a ring around Rob.

'If we were not about to sail into battle, I would hang you from the yardarm this instant. As it is, I will have that pleasure to look forward to once our victory is secured.' He turned to Angus and Scipio, both hedged in by the marines' bayonets. 'MacNeil will hang alongside Mr Courtney. As for you . . .' He jabbed a finger at Scipio. 'I will return Mr Bracewell his rightful property when I invite him aboard to witness the executions. When he hears the lies you have told about him, I am certain he will wish to see justice served. As will Miss Bracewell.'

'I am not lying,' said Rob. He had to make them understand. 'It is the truth. Bracewell has betrayed you all. If you do not change course, you will all die!'

He was still shouting as the marines seized him. They pulled him down the companion ladder so hard he almost broke his neck, then down another ladder to the orlop deck.

They brought in Scipio and Angus. They shackled the men's legs, passing the chains through iron rings on the floor. If the ship sank, they would be dragged down with her.

'For God's sake listen to me,' pleaded Rob. 'Even if Coyning-ham will not change course, at least signal the convoy to stand away from that headland. Otherwise they will be sheep to the slaughter.'

The marines didn't listen. They bolted the door and left the prisoners alone in the darkness.

Deep in the ship, Rob could hear the water sluicing against the hull, only a few inches away. In the past he had found the noise of a ship in her element comforting. Now it was the sound of the *Perseus* racing to her own destruction.

'What now?' asked Angus.

Rob tugged on his chains, but the bolt was sunk deep in the ship's timbers. He would not work that out in a hurry.

'Either we'll be sunk by the French or hanged by Coyningham.'

'If that's the choice, I hope the French make it quick. I wouldn'ae give Coyningham the satisfaction.'

A low sound rose from the darkness, so deep Rob thought it must be the rumble of the guns coming through the deck. Then he realised Scipio was singing. There was profound sadness in the song, but also an unshakeable defiance. As Rob listened, he found it gave him strength.

'What is that?' Rob asked, as the final notes died away.

'A song to the ancestors,' Scipio answered.

'Asking them for help?'

'For revenge.'

Rob admired the man's spirit. 'We will need all your ancestors and mine if we are to have any chance of that.'

The planks shuddered beneath them. The room seemed to reverberate. Rob heard muted shouts from on deck. The battery must have opened fire.

'Cover your ears,' Rob called, a moment before a shattering roar shook the ship. The *Perseus* had fired her own broadside.

'They would have been better saving their powder,' said Rob. 'They cannot hope to hit the shore battery.'

Locked in the dark room, Rob was deprived of every sense except hearing. He could hear thumping as the crews moved their guns, the rumble of the trucks as the men hauled on the tackles to run out the cannons once more, and then the thunder of the broadside.

But . . .

'Can you hear that?' said Rob. 'The sails.'

There was a silence in the room as all three men listened intently.

'I do'nae hear a thing,' said Angus.

'Exactly.

There was no creak of rope or timbers from the frigate changing her point of sail. No change to the sound of the water rushing past the hull.

'Why are we not altering course? Coyningham is not trying to get away from the guns.'

'Maybe they shot away the rudder. Or one of the masts.'

'We would have heard it.'

More cannons fired – on both sides. Rob flinched as the hull shuddered again under the impact of the enemy iron. It was no consolation that he was probably the safest man on the ship. He wanted to be on deck, fighting with his men however hopeless the cause.

The noise of the battle was becoming more ragged. In the face of an onslaught they could not resist, the crew's discipline was crumbling.

'Why doesn't Coyningham show them our stern?' Rob wondered. 'At least then we would make a smaller target.'

His ears were attuned to every bump and rattle on the ship. Above the clamour, he heard footsteps rushing down the ladder outside. Bolts rasped, and the door was flung open. Thomas peered in. His face was black with powder scorches, and he had a cut below his right eye. He looked terrified.

'You cannot desert your post, Thomas,' said Rob.

He remembered the boy's fear climbing the mast. How much worse must it be facing this invincible enemy in battle?

But Thomas shook his head.

'It's the captain, sir.'

'Is he dead?' asked Angus hopefully.

'No – but he won't do nothing.'

'What do you mean?'

'He's stood on the quarterdeck. Won't move, won't speak. Just fiddles with the buttons on his coat.'

'What about the first lieutenant?'

'Mr Fawcett says if he takes command it's mutiny.' Thomas peered at Rob. 'The men are saying you're the only one who'll know what to do.'

Rob shook his chains. 'I cannot do anything while I am bound up like this.'

Thomas produced a key. 'I took this off Mr Leake.'

'That was very accommodating of Mr Leake.'

'He didn't argue. Not after I'd laid him out flat on the deck.'

'You are learning fast, Thomas. We'll make a sailor of you yet.'

Thomas unlocked the shackles. Rob climbed to his feet. His ankles were stiff from the iron cuffs, but he had no time to waste. He ran up the ladder as quickly as he could.

The battle had not gone on long, but the damage was already calamitous. Several of the guns had been smashed. The ship had lost her fore-topmast, and part of her mizzen boom. Several more sails flapped loose where their fastenings had been shot away. Some of the crew still worked their guns, particularly near the bow where Hargrave was marshalling them with ferocious energy. But many more milled around in shock, unsure what to do. The wounded lay untended in the scuppers, while wreckage that should have been cleared away hung from the rigging like shattered limbs.

In the midst of the carnage, Coyningham stood as still as the eye of a storm. He stared down the deck, stiff-backed, his face as ghostly white as his hair. The only movement was the tic of his finger, worrying at the brass buttons on his coat like a stain he could not remove.

Rob remembered his first experience of command, aboard the brig in Narragansett Bay, off the town of Newport. How he had forgotten to put a leadsman in the bow to check the depth, because of the thousand other details and decisions he was trying to hold in his head at once. Perhaps that was what had frozen Coyningham – so many decisions they had jammed his mind like rocks clogging a pipe.

For a rare moment, Rob felt sympathy for Coyningham, the loneliness of command that could never be shared. Then Coyningham saw Rob.

Battle, the massacre of his crew and the imminent prospect of losing his ship had not shaken Coyningham out of his panic. But the sight of Rob, walking freely across his quarter-deck, shocked him out of his stupor. His face twisted. His hand stopped fiddling with the button. He drew his sword.

'You!' he cried. He advanced towards Rob, sword outstretched. 'You mutinous, cowardly, upstart *rat*.' The sword sliced through the air, inches from Rob's face. 'Now that I am ruined, you think you can take my command from me?' There was another swipe of the sword. Rob stepped back. 'I will see you hang.'

The crew paused in their work to watch this confrontation between the officers which could decide their fate. But every delay meant more men would die. Rob could not allow it to drag out.

A belaying pin lay on the deck where it had been knocked loose. Rob stooped and grabbed it; as Coyningham lunged at him again, he beat the sword aside. Before the captain could riposte, Rob stepped inside Coyningham's guard. He wrapped his fist around the belaying's pin's handle and punched Coyningham in the face.

Rob had imagined doing that many times since he stepped aboard the *Perseus*. Yet now he had done it, he felt no joy. Too many men had died already because of Coyningham's malice and cowardice.

Coyningham staggered backwards. Angus and Scipio grabbed his arms and held him fast. Rob's blow had not knocked him out. If anything, it had driven him to new depths of madness.

'This is mutiny!' he screamed. Blood and spittle sprayed from his mouth, together with a tooth that Rob had punched out. More blood flowed from his nose so that his face became a gory mask, Coyningham a raving monster. 'Seize him! Seize them all!'

None of the crew obeyed. Coyningham's frenzied eyes found the boatswain's mate standing on the main deck. Leake sported a huge purple bruise on his temple where Thomas had felled him, but even he did not move.

'Mr Leake?' screeched Coyningham. 'Surely you have not joined the mutineers?'

'I wants to stay alive,' said Leake. He spoke for the whole crew. They knew Rob was their only chance of survival.

'Take him below,' Rob ordered. Angus and Scipio dragged Coyningham down the ladder to the brig. 'You will find the manacles already prepared for him.'

Lieutenant Fawcett had been watching the conversation from a distance. He stepped forward hesitantly.

'If the captain has been relieved, as first lieutenant I should be in command.'

The French guns had slacked off for a few moments. Now they opened fire again, hotter than ever. A dozen balls smashed through the *Perseus*'s bulwarks, scything across the deck. Smoke rose where they landed.

'Heated shot!' went up the cry, as the sailors frantically worked to douse the red-hot balls. Rob remembered the cannonball he had found in Nativity Bay, the day that Cornish arrived and his life had changed for ever. He remembered the stories of what red-hot cannonballs had done to Zayn al-Din's ships, all those years ago. If the *Perseus* did not move smartly, she would suffer a similar fate.

'I am in command,' he said, in a voice that silenced Fawcett and settled the matter. 'If you cannot accept that, you may go below.'

'I will not desert my post,' said Fawcett.

'Good man.'

Thomas had disappeared into the hold, but now he reappeared carrying a sword in a gilded scabbard. So much had happened, it took Rob a moment to recognise it. It was the sword General Howe had presented to him in Boston, after his victory at Newport.

'I kept this safe for you,' said Thomas. 'You should wear it.' He buckled it onto Rob's belt. 'Now you look a true captain, sir.'

'Thank you,' said Rob gravely.

But there were other matters to see to. He climbed into the shrouds to view the carnage on deck. The *Perseus* was in front of the French guns, about a mile off shore. She was broadside on, though her guns could not elevate high enough to reach the battery on the cliff.

But where was the *Rapace*?

Étienne stood on his quarterdeck and watched the stricken British frigate. Cal's guns had mauled her so badly she barely had a scrap of canvas that was not carried away or shot through with holes like a sieve. Her sides were smashed to pieces.

Beside him, Bracewell said confidently, 'Our plan has worked to perfection.'

'Poor Lieutenant Coyningham,' said Sophie, fingering the gold necklace at her throat. Étienne had ordered her below when the battle started, but she had refused. 'He was so devoted to me.'

'I hope you are not feeling squeamish,' said Bracewell.

'It is almost a kindness to put him out of his misery. Like a field hand who can no longer work the cane.'

Étienne moved away to consult the binnacle. He did not like having civilians aboard his ship. Bracewell was a necessary ally, but he was still an Englishman.

'Bring us about,' he ordered the sailing master. 'We will put a broadside in the frigate as we pass, and then see to the convoy.'

His first lieutenant started. 'You do not intend to board her?'

It was a simple question, but the look on his face spoke volumes. To seize a frigate was glorious. There was no renown in rounding up merchantmen.

The pleasure Étienne had taken from the *Perseus*'s distress soured. He knew the first officer was right. He glanced at Jean, the artist his mother had commissioned. He sat on a stool, sketching the battered English frigate. This was his chance to be immortalised.

'The convoy is what matters,' said Bracewell. Like a jackal sniffing wounded prey, he had homed in on Étienne's doubt. 'We need that powder and shot to drive the British out of the West Indies.'

Étienne gave a nod. 'As you say. We cannot spare the men to board the frigate now. We will come back for her once we have dealt with the convoy.'

The blast of artillery echoed across the water. Cal's guns had gone quiet, but now they opened fire with renewed ferocity.

'What is he doing?' said Étienne. 'The frigate is crippled. If he puts any more iron into her she will sink.'

That would not do. A hero of France needed a worthy prize. His mother would not forgive him if he sailed back without the British frigate. It was a matter of honour. The *Perseus* had fought him off at Newport and Seabrook Bay. He would not be satisfied until he stood on her quarterdeck and accepted her captain's surrender.

The *Rapace* had come about, sailing towards the frigate and the convoy in the distance beyond. Her course would take her past the battery on the cliff.

'If he does not stop firing, he will risk hitting us,' said the first officer, cursing under his breath. Jean, the artist, looked up anxiously from his sketchbook.

Étienne took a telescope and trained it on the *Perseus*. Wisps of smoke rose from her deck. Through the glass, he saw men with buckets and swabs, trying to put out the fires that had started to burn on the deck.

'*Mon dieu*,' he swore. Impotent rage seized him. 'Why is Major Courtney using heated shot?'

Cal was soaked with sweat. His shirt clung to his skin, so that the lettering embroidered on the fabric – Liberty or Death – stood out like a tattoo. The tropical sun was high overhead, and the palm trees shook with the reverberation of the guns. Yet for a moment he was taken back to a wintry afternoon on the heights above Boston. Looking down the barrels of his cannons, the enemy at his mercy, and being told by a jumped-up corset-maker that he could not fire. He remembered touching his guns that day, as icy cold as the ground.

Today there was no one to give him orders. He was in command. His guns were running so hot they charred skin that came into contact with them. The crews had to tip buckets of water over the barrels so they did not ignite the powder charges the moment they were rammed home. Cal would keep them going until the barrels split open if he had to.

He knew Étienne wanted the prize. He did not care. One frigate would not win the war. Étienne would get the convoy, and the convoy's supplies would ensure the wider victory. The British frigate was for Cal. He would shatter her timbers and burn her to ashes.

He tried not to think of the men aboard, simple sailors who probably loved their freedom the same as any American. Many of them would have been pressed against their will. Destroying them gave Cal no pleasure, but he felt compelled to do it, like a drunkard who could not feel the alcohol but still reached for the bottle. He had to do this, so that Aidan would not have died in vain. To prove his father wrong.

One of his gunners lifted a ball from the brazier and loaded it into the gun. Steam hissed from the cannon's mouth. The crew held their breaths as the ball rolled down the long barrel. They had soaked the wadding, to prevent the ball igniting the powder charge at once, but if they had not damped it down enough the cannon would explode and kill them all.

The ball was rammed home. The crew stepped back and covered their ears. The gunner touched the linstock to the touch hole.

For a split second, everything was still, except for the fizz of powder in the touch hole. Then the gun roared.

Another red-hot cannonball thudded into the *Perseus*'s hull. Steam hissed as the sailors rushed to douse it.

From the shrouds, Rob scanned the waters until he found the frigate. To his surprise, she had come about and was sailing towards them.

She means to sail to windward, he thought. *She will put a broadside in us.*

The *Perseus* would be caught between the shore battery and the privateer. With her canvas shot to pieces, the *Perseus* was barely moving. If she did not get out of range, it was only a matter of time before she was destroyed.

'Bend on more sail,' Rob ordered.

'That'll make a bonny great target for the French,' warned Angus. 'If the canvas catches fire, there'll be no stopping it.'

'We will burn anyway if we do not get away from those guns.'

The men hauled on the halyards, and the yard rattled up the mainmast, unfurling the fresh sail. It caught the wind as it rose and filled out. Rob felt the power transmitted into the deck at his feet. The ship began to move.

Hope flared on the men's faces. Rob moved to the wheel so the helmsman could hear his orders.

'We must put the privateer between us and the guns on shore,' he explained.

It was a dangerous gambit. The French ship was bearing down on them, and the *Perseus* only had her one sail. She had to cross the privateer's bows in time.

'If we do not pass her, we will be fucked like a whore from both ends' Angus warned.

'Then get more sail bent on,' snapped Rob.

The tension was beginning to tell on him. This was the true, terrifying isolation of the captain, when every choice seemed to lead to death.

The ship gathered speed. The fo'c's'le crew had managed to jury-rig another sail. It was an ugly, ungainly thing, but the *Perseus* had a thoroughbred's instincts and responded to every puff of wind.

But it was not enough. The French ship was moving too fast. She would cut them off. And on the cliffs, the gunners were reloading.

Cal watched the *Rapace* moving in for the kill. He knew he could not risk hitting her: they needed Étienne's ship to capture the convoy, if they were to realise the full scope of their plan.

In the midst of that steaming, tropical battlefield, he was suddenly transported back to the headquarters in icy, winter-bound Boston, listening to the general lay out his audacious mission. He remembered the elation he had felt at the thought that he, Cal Courtney, could end the war at a stroke. That would avenge Aidan's death, and show his father he had been right.

Now the moment had come. Everything had happened exactly as planned. The *Perseus* was almost gone, and the convoy lay helpless. He had achieved more than he could have dreamed of.

It should have been the proudest moment of his life. Yet now that he had victory in front of him, he did not feel filled with triumph, or delight, as he had imagined. A desperate emptiness yawned inside him. Ships, guns, wars, nations: what did they matter? All he wanted was his brother back, and his father welcoming him into the old Massachusetts farmhouse. He wanted Theo's arms around him, and to feel the warmth of a father's pride in his son.

A burning piece of wadding blew over the ground, trailing sparks. The smell in his nostrils reminded him of that terrible night at the arsenal, the powder cart's explosion. Had Aidan died for nothing?

He could not let that happen. This was the path he had chosen, and he must follow it to the end.

'Reload,' he told his gunners. 'Double-shotted and extra powder.'

'The *Rapace* is too close,' the gunnery sergeant protested.

'We still have time for one last shot.' Cal clapped him on the shoulder. 'I have faith in your aim.'

The gun crews swabbed out the cannons carefully. The heat of the barrels and the balls, and the quantity of powder, meant there was no margin for error. Artillerymen fetched the ammunition. They wore leather gloves and aprons, holding the iron balls with tongs as far from their bodies as possible. They flinched at the heat. These were the balls that had been sitting at the bottom of the furnace, and they glowed like coals. They had to work quickly. Between the powder charge and the burning balls was a wad of wet cloth. As soon as that dried, it would burst into flame and ignite the powder prematurely.

'Make every shot count,' said Cal.

He kneeled so he could take a sighting along the cannon's barrel at the British frigate. She had turned away, like a rabbit fleeing a fox, but she could not outrun his guns. There was no escape.

He closed his eyes again, trying to summon the faintest crumb of satisfaction. This should be his moment, but all he felt inside was void.

A cry sounded behind him.

Cal's eyes snapped open. He thought one of the gunners must have touched the hot metal, but he knew it could not be true. The sound had come from the jungle. There were no guns there.

Above the gun emplacements, the slope rose across stony ground to the treeline. Cal had few men to spare – the gun crews were all he had been able to smuggle ashore – but he had posted two sentries to the rear, on the principle that he wanted someone watching his back. It was one of those men who had screamed – and was screaming still. He had dropped to his knees, clutching a bamboo spear that protruded from his shoulder blades. His companion lay dead beside him. Around them, an army of black men was pouring out of the forests. They looked a rabble, half-naked, armed with cane knives and axes. They were nothing compared with the great guns of the French battery.

But the guns were pointing the other way.

'*Monsieur!*' The artillery sergeant had come up and was screaming at Cal. '*Monsieur! The guns!*'

Cal remembered the cannonballs smouldering inside the guns.

'Fire!' he shouted.

But he had waited too long. The balls had burned through the wadding. With the barrels angled upwards for range, the balls had rolled backwards and touched the bags of powder in the chamber. The scorching iron had burned through the sackcloth in an instant. Then it met the powder.

One touch was enough. The powder exploded. But it had ignited from the wrong end. The blasts ran backwards up the barrels, seeking the path of least resistance. They erupted through the touch holes in gouts of flame that roasted the men crouched around the guns. The power of the explosions, channelled into those narrow holes, forced the metal apart. The guns split open like nutshells.

Some of the force rebounded out of the muzzles. One gunner was still reloading: the blast fired the ramrod through his body, followed by two cannonballs so hot they cauterised the wound even as they passed through his belly.

For a moment, the gunner stared in astonishment at the mass of gore that had appeared in his stomach. His comrades looked in horror. They could see through him like a telescope, to the sea and the ships on the other side.

The gunner took one step backwards, teetering on the edge of the cliff. No one went to save him. By the time he fell, his comrades had forgotten him. They were fighting for their lives.

Scores of black fighters emerged from the jungle. Kojo led the way, cutlasses in both hands. Phoebe came behind him, armed with a bamboo spear which she used to push back any Frenchman who tried to escape.

The outnumbered French gunners stood no chance. Half the men were already maimed or dead from the exploding cannons; the rest put up no defence, and the Maroons showed no mercy. One Frenchman wandered dazed through the melee, eyes glazed, blood streaming from his ears. He was cut down. The rest were put to death, or driven over the cliff.

A handful escaped. A steep path led down the cliff to a rocky cove. They had landed the guns at the point, winching them up the cliff on cranes. There was a small ketch moored in the cove, hidden by rocks. A few of the gunners, with their wits about them and no interest in dying for the King of France, had fled there the moment they saw Kojo's men attack.

Cal followed them, struggling down the slope. He had been standing next to one of the guns when it exploded. The shock wave had thrown him onto his back a split second before the gun disintegrated into a lethal cloud of metal. The shards had killed men who were further away: Cal had been lucky, but he had not escaped unscathed. The flame had burned off half his face. Blood poured from his nose, his ears, and an open wound on his leg where a piece of iron had nearly severed it in two. He knew it would need to be amputated. He hobbled down the cliff using a ramrod for a crutch, stumbling on the rocky path.

'Wait!' he called after the men fleeing ahead of him. 'Help me!'

But either they were deafened by the explosion, or else they did not care about an American officer. They only wanted to save themselves. Before he was halfway down the cliff, they had reached the cove. Cal saw them untying the boat, pushing it into the bay. They would leave without him.

He glanced back. Kojo's men had not spotted the path. But they would find it soon enough, and then he would be trapped in the cove. He would be butchered like the rest.

He pushed harder – and tripped and fell. When he tried to lift himself, a stabbing pain told him he had broken his arm. Gritting his teeth, he forced himself up. His damaged leg took his weight, and he screamed. The leg buckled; he pitched forwards onto the ground.

Standing was impossible. But he would not give up. He crawled on his hands and knees, every moment agony. He had to reach the boat.

The *Rapace* and the *Perseus* bore down on each other like two knights in a medieval joust.

Étienne saw the *Perseus*'s plan. She meant to cross the *Rapace*'s bows, rake her from stem to stern, and then position herself so that the French ship was between her and the shore guns. It was not a bad plan, but it relied on her being able to sail upwind of the *Rapace*.

In that, she would fail. Even with her copper sheathing, she did not have the speed to complete the manoeuvre in time. Rob's crew had worked miracles getting their canvas back up, but it was not enough. The *Rapace* carried all her canvas, and she had the weather gage. It was just a matter of playing out the endgame.

The guns on the cliff had fallen silent. That pleased Étienne. It was outrageous that Cal had even attempted to use heated shot. He might have destroyed the frigate and robbed Étienne of his prize. Étienne would have stern words with him afterwards. If tempers flared, he would not hesitate to call him out to a duel. He would choose swords, of course. He had been schooled in fencing since he was five years old, the best pupil his teachers had ever seen. More than one fencing master had been sent away from his precocious pupil with his arm or cheek bleeding. One, whom Étienne particularly disliked, had lost an eye.

Étienne was still thinking about it when the battery on the cliff exploded. Instead of sharp tongues of flame spitting from the cannons' mouths, Étienne saw fireballs erupting along the clifftop. He grabbed a telescope, but by the time he had raised it the battery had been engulfed in a huge cloud of smoke.

Five hundred yards off his bow, a few cannonballs splashed harmlessly into the sea. What was happening? Even when the wind began to clear the smoke it left a gauzy haze, like a veil over the true scale of the carnage. Étienne had to squint to focus on the scene.

The stone parapet that had supported the battery was blown to rubble. Almost all the guns had been destroyed, and the crews lay strewn about. That was not the worst of it. There were Negroes. Half-naked Negroes armed with knives and hatchets. They had overrun the position. They were massacring Frenchmen!

Étienne brought the telescope down on the rail, so hard that the glass shattered. Those men had been specially chosen for this mission, the pride of French artillery. How could they have been defeated by a rabble of slaves? What had Cal done now?

'*Monsieur?*' His first lieutenant was keeping a safe distance, frightened of his captain's temper. 'The enemy is nearly upon us.'

Étienne had forgotten the *Perseus*. He raised the telescope again, saw the broken glass and tossed the instrument into the sea. He did not need it. The *Perseus* was so close he could see every detail with his naked eye.

She had come up faster than he expected. He had never seen sailors bend on fresh sails so quickly, let alone in the midst of a battle. She sailed as if the very Devil himself was in command. Even that would not be enough. The *Rapace* had the sea room to manoeuvre upwind and sail past her without engaging.

But Étienne hesitated before giving the order. Temptation nagged at him. Clearly the frigate was not as crippled as he'd thought. What if she made her escape while the *Rapace* mopped up the convoy? Where would be the glory?

It is for the greater good, he told himself.

The convoy was what mattered. He must not lose sight of that.

The greater good.

From the *Perseus's* quarterdeck, Rob knew he was beaten. When the guns on the cliff exploded, he had been as astonished as everyone else. Only when he saw the Maroons coming out of the forest did he realise what had happened.

Phoebe must have persuaded Kojo to attack the French, he thought.

It was the plan she had whispered in his ear, though he had never expected it would work. But it was too soon to celebrate. Even with the battery out of action, the wounded *Perseus* still was no match for the French frigate. His only hope had been to cross her bows, but he could see it was impossible. The privateer was bearing off, widening the gap. In a moment, she would be past the *Perseus*, and then she would have both the frigate and the convoy at her mercy.

A final, desperate idea struck him.

'Alter course to larboard,' he ordered.

'But that will put us broadside to broadside,' said Fawcett, horrified. He gestured along the deck. 'We barely have four guns on the starboard battery we can bring to bear.'

'Then load them,' snapped Rob.

'You mean to take her on?'

'I mean to bloody her nose. If she takes the bait, it will buy the convoy more time.'

'Aye,' said Angus. 'But that makes us the bait.'

For the second time that afternoon, Étienne suffered a nasty shock to his strategy. He had worked his ship so he would be able to rake the *Perseus* – but now the British frigate was changing course. She was running out her guns. Did her captain mean to challenge him? How could he hope to win with two makeshift sails and less than half her cannons operational? It was the height of impudence.

Étienne would teach her a lesson. The ships were almost parallel, barely a cable length apart.

'Aim high,' he said. He did not want to destroy the ship. He wanted her dismasted, so he could come back and seize her at his leisure. 'Run out our guns.'

Twenty twenty-four pounders rolled forwards to the gunwale. The crew crouched in their positions, faces bright, uniforms immaculate.

Étienne raised his sword. 'On the uproll—'

Guns fired. But they were not his. A split second before Étienne gave the command, the *Perseus* fired. Four cannonballs ploughed into the French frigate. Wood splintered, ropes frayed, and blood spattered her holystoned deck.

Étienne was outraged. How dare she draw first blood? For a moment he couldn't move for anger. Then he brought his sword down so hard the blade struck the deck and dug into the planking.

'*Fire!*'

The world shook as the cannons roared in unison. At that range, they could not miss. The cannonballs tore through what was left of the *Perseus*'s masts and rigging. Her foremast was struck a direct hit and snapped. The boom that held her makeshift mainsail was carried away.

The nets that had been strung to protect the men on deck were long gone. The crew had no cover against the ropes, blocks, battens and broken wood that rained down over them.

Men fought to escape from under the mainsail. Some were knocked unconscious. One was snared by a line trailing from the topmast and dragged overboard as it fell in the water. Everything was chaos.

Étienne surveyed the carnage. It would be hours before the British frigate could get on any more sail. She was helpless.

He noticed Jean. The artist was cowering on the deck, terrified by the noise of the guns.

'Stand up,' Étienne barked at him. 'I want you to see every detail of that ship, so you can paint her destruction.'

Jean did as he was told. He rose, sketchbook in hand, and peered over the side. Then he threw himself back to the deck as a cannonball flew by, inches from his head.

Étienne started. Somehow, near the *Perseus*'s stern, one gun was still operating. He could see her crew sponging it out, reloading. Why were they still fighting?

It was too much. If they did not know when they were beaten, Étienne would teach them. He lunged for the wheel, ripped it out of the helmsman's hands and spun it hard over. The ship shuddered. The rigging creaked in protest at the sudden change in course, the new strains it put on the ropes and sails. The *Rapace*'s bow came around towards the British frigate.

'What are you doing, *Monsieur*?' asked the first officer in surprise.

'We will board her.' Étienne glanced up and noticed the striped American flag flapping from the masthead. 'And take down that rebel rag. We will fight under our true colours today.'

Rob watched the *Rapace* haul down the rebel flag. The white banner of France embossed with golden fleurs-de-lis rose crisply to her masthead, snapping out defiantly in the breeze.

'Good,' said Rob. 'No more false pretences.'

The two ships were closing quickly. The *Perseus* was a virtually dismasted hulk; the *Rapace* strutted with her sails set and only a few scars on her gleaming paintwork to show she had been in battle.

Yet there seemed to be some confusion on her deck. Her crew were not prepared. They scurried about, fetching weapons and finding their stations. The order to board looked to have taken them by surprise.

Rob surveyed his own men. Bloody faces, torn clothes, but armed and ready for the final confrontation.

'Sell your lives dearly,' Rob told them.

A musket ball struck the deck six inches away from him. The French ship had marines in her tops, peppering them with musket fire. Rob did not flinch. He could not show fear in front of his men. The French muskets were poor weapons. At that range, the shooters would be trusting more to luck than skill.

The ships were a few yards apart. Rob checked the primings on the pistols Angus had fetched him. He rattled his sword in its scabbard to be sure there was no obstruction. He said a prayer for himself, and asked God to protect his men. He had no illusions about the odds. They were outnumbered and outgunned, their ship almost destroyed. The best he could hope for was to delay the *Rapace*, and give the convoy time to escape.

He was not afraid. This was what he had dreamed of all his life: to go into battle with a stout ship beneath him and a sword in his hand, as his ancestors had done since the days of Sir Francis Drake. This was his destiny.

The ships came alongside each other, barely ten feet apart. Rob had to crouch behind what was left of the gunwale. On the deck of the *Rapace*, the French crew had gathered their weapons and were turning to the cannons. They meant to deliver a point-blank broadside, then rush the *Perseus* as soon as the ships touched.

Rob would not allow them the opportunity. He rose and drew his sword, holding it aloft like a battle flag.

'At 'em, *Perseus*.'

His crew rose as one. The gap between the ships was too wide for a man to jump, but they had prepared for that. They had hung ropes from every spar the *Perseus* still carried, ready to swing across.

Rob led the way. He jumped on the rail, seized a rope end and kicked off hard, gripping the rope with his legs so that he could keep his sword hand free. For one weightless moment he was over the open water, as the *Rapace*'s side rushed towards him.

He let go of the rope before he had cleared her rail, letting his momentum carry him over it and onto her deck. He collided with a man and knocked him backwards, landed like a cat and brought up his sword in time to parry a cutlass coming at him.

The French crew were a shambles. They had thought the *Perseus* was already beaten, a prize awaiting the *coup de grace*. Half of them had not been looking at the British ship. They had been readying their guns for the last broadside, when the *Perseus*'s men came swinging at them.

The ships were still closing. Grappling irons sailed over the gap, bit into the gunwale and were hauled in, pulling the ships together. On the *Rapace*'s deck, the battle had already begun. The French crew had been surprised, but they were armed and not slow to react. Rob found himself surrounded. He barely had room to swing his sword. Instead, he wielded it like a short club, punching and parrying with the hilt.

A tremor went through the deck as the hulls collided. Rob kept his balance, but several of the men around him were thrown back. Rob drew a pistol and fired it indiscriminately at the mass of men in front of him, then followed with a flurry of sword strokes in the space that had been created. Steel rang on steel.

Behind him, the rest of the *Perseus*'s men clambered over the side, emptying her deck. Their momentum pushed the line of battle forwards, driving back the French defenders. Rob was carried into the press of men. It was hand to hand: shoulders, elbows and knees were almost more use than the weapons he carried.

An axe flashed beside him. Angus had arrived, swinging the outsize boarding axe with devastating abandon. He cut a swathe through the Frenchmen, making space for Rob to use his sword.

'Where is their captain?' Rob shouted.

Angus shrugged. Rob glanced towards the stern. On the quarterdeck, a man in a white uniform was duelling expertly with a gold-handled rapier. He ran a man through. One of Rob's crew – a Cornishman named Comstock – saw his chance for glory. He was behind the captain. He lunged forwards with his cutlass to cut the Frenchman down before he could free his blade.

Even with battle raging about him, the French captain somehow felt the danger. Faster than thought, he pulled his blade free of the man he had stabbed. In a single movement he pirouetted and brought up his sword to parry the cutlass. The cutlass was a heavy blade, but Étienne struck it so hard that it was knocked from Comstock's hand. The Cornishman was still gaping when the gold-handled sword sliced through his heart.

Rob moved towards the quarterdeck ladder. The fighting surged about him. Rob had never seen his crew fight with such ferocity. Battered and bloodied, outnumbered by an enemy that was fresh and ready, they still held their own. To his left, Angus laid into their foes with his boarding axe. On his right, Scipio spun and slashed his cutlass. They moved through the fray, three men fighting as one, carrying all before them.

Rob reached the foot of the ladder. A man stood above him, jabbing down with a sabre. Rob ducked out of harm's way, reached up and cut the man's Achilles tendon. As he crouched in agony, Rob grabbed his ankle and yanked him off the quarterdeck, throwing him down into the melee on the main deck.

In one bound, Rob was at the top of the ladder. He saw Étienne – and in the same moment, Étienne saw him. His instinct for danger was unerring. With a quick slash, he finished off the man he was fighting and turned to face Rob.

Space opened. Men seemed to shrink back. Étienne raised his rapier, his eyes examining Rob either side of the blade. In a split second he noted and analysed a hundred different angles: the way Rob stood, the way he moved, the way he held his sword. A smile curled the edge of his lip. This would be easy.

Quick as a snake, he moved in with a flurry of feints and then a lunge. Rob parried it: not a bad stroke, but against the quicksilver rapier it felt clumsy and slow.

The smile on Étienne's face broadened. Another time, he would have enjoyed toying with his opponent. He would have played him like a fish on a line, savouring the look in his eyes as hope turned to defeat. But that was self-indulgence. He needed to win this quickly.

Rob knew he was running out of time. It was obvious the Frenchman was a better sword fighter. The longer they fought, the more his superior skill would gain the advantage. But Rob's arms still had the strength he had developed as a topman, muscles honed climbing the rigging in every weather. Étienne had a slim, slight build.

Étienne advanced, the tip of his sword darting like a dragonfly. Rob took a more direct approach. He struck Étienne's blade with all his strength, beating it aside, then drove forwards.

Étienne stepped back, his arm shaking from the force of Rob's stroke. He had never encountered such ferocious power before, but he was not concerned. Sword fighting was a test of skill, not strength. Like a matador, he would draw the bull on to him and deliver the killing blow.

Rob was a brave fighter, but he had no guile. Étienne could read what he would do next as easily as if he had run up a signal flag. Étienne adjusted his guard, ready for what would come. In his mind's eye, he could already see the stroke, and how he would respond. He would dodge to his right, take a half pace forwards and skewer Rob through his throat.

All he needed was a little more space. He stepped back.

A boarding pike lay on the deck where a dead man had dropped it. Étienne didn't notice it until his left heel caught it. He stumbled. He planted his right foot to regain his balance, but the sole of his shoe landed in a pool of blood. His leg skidded from under him and pitched him backwards onto the deck. He threw out his arms to break his fall, letting go of his rapier.

He lay helpless on the deck. French and British alike paused their fighting to stare at the fallen captain.

Before Étienne could think of getting up, Rob drew the second pistol from his belt and levelled it at Étienne.

'Strike your ship,' he said. 'It is over.'

Étienne's face twisted in disbelief. How could this British rabble have taken the finest ship in the French navy? His hand scrabbled for his sword, but Rob planted his foot on the blade.

'You will have to kill me before I surrender my ship,' Étienne said.

'There is no shame in defeat with honour.'

'Only cowards believe there is such a thing as defeat with honour.'

'Very well,' said Rob.

A hush gripped the deck. He could feel eyes staring at him, British and French alike. Another man might have relented under the pressure. Rob's hand never wavered.

Étienne had fought without remorse. He would have slaughtered every man aboard the *Perseus* if he had to. Rob would feel no guilt for killing him.

'No!'

A woman's scream cut through the silence, as unexpected and extraordinary as if a mermaid had bobbed up beside the ship.

Sophie had appeared on deck. Rob did not know how she had arrived unnoticed, but suddenly she was there. Her uncle came behind her, holding her close to him. One arm was locked around her neck, while the other held a pistol against her forehead.

'Drop your sword,' Bracewell said to Rob. 'Or I will decorate the ship with my dear niece's brains.'

Rob stared at him in astonishment. He took two steps forwards. He wondered if it was a bluff, and if Sophie was complicit. But her eyes were flared open, her blood-red lips wide apart in genuine terror. She could not be acting. Nor was Bracewell, as his finger tightened around the trigger.

He would do it. Whatever blood ran in their family, it was a strain so cruel Rob could barely comprehend it. Sophie craved power, and Bracewell money: there was nothing else in the world either of them would not sacrifice.

'Please,' begged Sophie. 'Save me.'

Behind Rob, Angus growled, 'Let him do it. Or save him the bother and you put a bullet in the both of them. After what they've done, what she did to Phoebe – they both deserve it.'

Rob nodded slowly. The pistol in his hand was no good to him. It was pointing at Étienne. He could not fire it at Bracewell without risking hitting Sophie, and the moment he moved Étienne would come at him. What should he do?

Bracewell was a traitor and a monster. Sophie was not much better. How many slaves had died because of her cruelty? Would she waste one breath pleading for Rob's life if their positions were reversed? How could you weigh a woman's life against the lives of Rob's crew, and all the men who would die and suffer if Étienne and Bracewell gained dominion over the Caribbean.

Yet could Rob let her die? He would be as guilty as if he had pulled the trigger himself.

All those thoughts crossed Rob's mind in an instant. Yet before he reached his decision, he realised he had taken too long. Something touched his throat and he looked down. The shining point of Étienne's rapier flickered at his collar.

Étienne was on his feet again, his face shining with triumph. He nodded to Bracewell.

'An excellent ruse, *Monsieur*. You convinced me entirely.'

'Hah.' Bracewell's smirk said it had been no ruse.

He let Sophie go and she staggered to the rail, bent double as if she wanted to vomit.

'Now,' said Étienne to Rob. 'Your sword, please. What was it you said? There is no shame in defeat with honour.'

Thunder rumbled in the distance. With a sailor's instinct for any change in the weather, Rob looked up.

There was not a cloud in the sky. The only thing that marred the perfect blue sky was a puff of white smoke rising off the cliff.

It had not been thunder. It was cannon fire. Rob realised it a second before the balls smashed into the *Rapace*. There were only three of them, but the impact they had was like a broadside. Iron tore through the men on deck in a spray of blood and cartwheeling limbs. In an instant, all was bedlam. No one knew who was firing, or where the shots had come from. Men seemed to be dying as if an invisible god was tearing them apart.

'Kojo has got those guns working!' Rob cried.

The Maroon king had learned his trade well. The shots had all hit the *Rapace* amidships, in the narrow space where they would do most damage to the men on deck, and where most of the French crew had gathered.

'*Perseus!*' Rob shouted. 'To me! To me!'

His men surged onto the attack again. Some of the French crew had been killed, more panicked, and the rest were in such a state of disarray they could barely resist the British sailors.

But their captain had kept his cool. He stood on the quarter-deck, alone and aloof, and circled towards Rob.

As standard procedure, the *Rapace* had lowered her boats before she went into battle and put them out to be towed behind the ship.

Étienne was near the stern. He could have clambered over the rail and reached the boats without difficulty. But he did not move. He was immobilised by rage and disbelief. His beautiful ship had been overrun by the Englishmen it had been built to kill. He glared at the devastation – the overturned guns and splintered bulwarks, the corpses bleeding out into the scuppers. A vision of his mother appeared in his mind's eye: her white face and gold hair, her red mouth set with the disapproval he feared more than any blade or bullet. All his life, she had told him he was marked for greatness. He was special. Her favourite son. And he had failed her.

He should not have attacked the *Perseus*. He should have left her and pursued the convoy. That was his mission. He had held the outcome of the war in the palm of his hand. And he had thrown it away.

It was not his fault, he told himself. Three times he had gone into battle, and three times Robert Courtney had defied him. The man must be in league with the Devil. There he was now, wreathed in gunsmoke, striding across the quarterdeck.

Robert Courtney was the reason for all Étienne's misfortune. Killing him would make everything right. Étienne would recover his ship. He would capture the convoy. He would not let his mother down.

Étienne raised his sword. Rob gave a small nod. This time, there were no formalities, no salutes or *en garde*. Étienne went at Rob, so fast and hard that Rob had to leap away.

Their swords rang together, blade pressed against blade, faces inches apart.

'I will kill you,' hissed Étienne.

He drew back, rolled the blade around in his wrists and feinted to Rob's left. Rob was no fencer, but he was a good judge of his enemies. He saw the feint for what it was and did not chase it. Instead, he launched an attack of his own at Étienne's shoulder. Rob was fast, but Étienne recovered in an instant. Before Rob was halfway through his stroke, Étienne was in position and parried it easily. He riposted so quickly he almost overcame Rob's guard.

Even in the heat of battle, Rob was aware of the balletic artistry of Étienne's movements. They were so fluid, he could move from defence to attack in a heartbeat. Rob was on his own. Angus was in the waist of the ship, marshalling the *Perseus*'s men. Scipio had gone in pursuit of Bracewell.

Rob wondered if he was outmatched. His arms were weary from fighting, his legs leaden. Étienne was fresh and fired with a fury that made him lightning fast. His feet danced; his sword became an extension of his arm; his eyes burned with a rapturous flame. It was all Rob could do to fend off the nonstop barrage of thrusts and cuts and lunges coming at him. His arm became fractionally slower; Étienne's blade came closer to hitting its mark.

Rob was retreating, stepping over the wreckage and corpses on deck. He came up against the side of the ship, where the rail should have been – but the rail was gone. He teetered on the edge of the ship, rocking with its motion as waves surged around the hull below. He looked for a rope to grab, but there was nothing.

There were no last words. No final insult or crowing. Étienne was in a trance, a place beyond words. He lunged for the kill . . .

And nearly went over the side as his sword pierced thin air. He stumbled, catching himself on the stump of one of the rail posts. A six-inch splinter pierced his hand but he did not feel it. Where was his enemy? He looked into the foam below. Had the coward jumped into the water?

He shifted his gaze. Rob had jumped sideways onto the wooden channels that stuck out of the side of the ship to brace the rigging. Now he was running up the ratlines, going higher and higher – away from danger.

But he was unarmed. Rob had needed both hands to make his leap. The sword lay on the deck where he had dropped it.

Rage seized Étienne. Without thinking, he kicked off his shoes, ran to the shrouds and began to climb. Rob was as nimble as a wild monkey. He reached the mizzen top, scorning the lubber's hole, and carried on up to the topmast. Étienne followed. Rob had the advantage of height, but he could not climb forever.

At the crosstrees Rob ran out on the mizzen topsail yard, balanced on the thin timber like a leopard on a branch. The spar shook as Étienne stepped onto it.

The two men faced each other, swaying to keep their balance. A warm breeze blew around them. On deck, both crews watched their two captains. There was no question of surrender with honour now. Whoever lost would fall to the main deck and break his neck.

Both men took a moment to draw breath. Rob had more experience aloft, but Étienne had the poise of a dancer. And Rob was unarmed.

Étienne advanced, cutting the sword through the air. Rob was forced back. He was nearly at the end of the yardarm now, where the thin spar tapered to little more than a rope's thickness. He wobbled, thrusting out his arms for balance. Étienne gave a cold, mirthless smile. This would be too easy.

'Will you jump to your death,' he taunted Rob, 'or will you die like a man with a blade in your heart?'

'Will you kill an unarmed man?'

'*Oui.*' Étienne sliced the sword just in front of Rob's face, enjoying the way he flinched back. Another inch and he would have fallen off the end. The wind raced around them. 'Consider it justice for all the times you have defied me.'

He drew back his sword for the final strike.

A movement flashed in the corner of his vision. Probably just a scrap of canvas or a loose rope, but again his instinct warned him of danger. He glanced back.

A boy had appeared at the masthead, clinging to the rigging. His eyes were screwed almost shut, his face pale: he looked terrified. He must have climbed all the way up one-handed. His other hand held a bloodstained sword.

'Thomas!' Rob cried.

The boy grinned. 'Keep your eyes on the horizon,' he called.

He threw the sword – a perfect throw. Before Étienne could react, it sailed past him. Rob snatched it out of the air one-handed.

Now he could defend himself – but the movement had left him open. Étienne saw his opportunity. He lunged.

But he had underestimated Rob. With a topman's agility, Rob had regained his balance almost before Étienne started to move. His sword came into line. He parried Étienne's thrust with a dead hit, such an impact it nearly knocked both men off the beam.

Étienne retreated, steadying himself, adjusting to this new reality. The drop yawned on both sides. For all the thousands of hours Étienne had practised, nothing in the fencing salons of Paris had prepared him for this.

He blocked the thought from his mind and went on the attack again. Extend, parry, riposte. Keep on the balls of the feet, knees bent, back straight. Use the wrists. It was classical perfection.

Rob kept his eyes locked on Étienne's, reading his movements as best he could. Étienne gazed back with a supercilious hauteur. There was no emotion in those eyes, no passion or admiration for a worthy opponent. Only a cold certainty that he would win, because he was the better man.

Something erupted inside Rob. Instead of Étienne, he saw all the men he had learned to hate since he left Nativity Bay. Men like Lyall and Coyningham and Spinkley and Bracewell, with their fine breeding and empty hearts. Men who valued gold over friendship, ambition over loyalty, acquisition over kindness. Men who felt the world owed them everything, whatever the cost in human life.

The blades locked together again. Rob's heavy sword began to bend the slim rapier. Étienne had to spring back, almost losing his footing. His feet scrabbled for grip on the curved sides of the boom.

In that moment, Rob struck.

Forgetting everything he knew of swordplay, he gripped the weapon two-handed and swung it in a flat arc, just as he'd wielded the axe back at Nativity Bay felling timber. The move was not in any fencing manual. No true gentleman would ever have considered using it. But Rob was not a gentleman. He neither knew nor cared what the books or experts prescribed. He was a fighter, confronted with an enemy, and he knew by instinct what he had to do.

Étienne had not anticipated the move. He had never seen anything like it. Belatedly, he realised what Rob meant to do. He started bringing up the blade of his rapier to block it. It was a clumsy move, with none of the fluid elegance that he prided himself on. But his reflexes did not let him down. His blade came into position a fraction of a second before Rob's stroke would have reached his neck.

It made no difference. Rob's heavy sword hit the rapier with every ounce of his strength and dashed it out of Étienne's hand. He barely felt it give way. There was so much power in his stroke, it met as little resistance as if he had cut through paper. His sword never deviated. It carried through its arc, like a compass needle turning inexorably to north.

In the heightened awareness of battle, where a man feels every second as an eternity, Étienne saw his rapier falling away towards the deck. His mouth began to open, his hands began to move. Then Rob's sword struck.

It cut through Étienne's neck in a single, razor-sharp stroke. It split his vertebrae, severed his windpipe and his carotid artery. It continued its unyielding course, clean through the other side of the neck.

The cut was so precise, for a moment Étienne's head stayed in place. A thread of blood across his throat was the only sign of what had happened. His eyes widened, his mouth opened in a silent scream. The wind lifted his golden curls.

Then his head toppled off his shoulders and fell. The body followed after it with almost exaggerated slowness, raining blood over the men below. Étienne's body hit the deck. His head rolled away and came to a halt beside a shattered cannon. Blood pooled around it, staining the golden hair a sickly dark red.

Suddenly, all the strength left Rob. His legs buckled. He dropped to his knees, clinging on like a drowning man in a wreck. He was empty. The yard seemed a mile long, but somehow he found the strength to crawl back to the crosstrees. A halyard slapped against the mast, tugged by the fluttering of the huge white battle flag that streamed from the masthead.

Rob chopped through the halyard with his sword. The wind snagged the flag and carried it away. It soared for a moment, then drifted feather-light and settled on the waves. The last Rob saw of it was the golden fleurs-de-lis glimmering in a shaft of sunlight as the flag sank into the depths.

The men on deck cheered. The battle was won. But at the stern of the ship, there were still two men who had not given up the fight. Rob could see them almost directly below him. One was Scipio, bare-chested and bleeding but still holding his cutlass. The other was Bracewell.

He stood by the rail. Rob guessed he had been trying to escape to one of the boats trailing behind the frigate so he could reach the shore and his planter friends. In the confusion after the battle, it would have been easy to slip away unnoticed. But Scipio must have been waiting.

Rob saw what Scipio meant to do. He grabbed one of the stays and slid towards the deck.

'Stop!' he called.

He knew Scipio would ignore him. Scipio heard Rob, looked up and frowned. Before Rob was halfway to the deck, Scipio had grabbed Bracewell's shirt front. Bracewell shivered; his jowls trembled. He stared at Scipio's hand, at the colour of his skin, with something approaching horror.

'Let go of me, you black son-of-a-whore.'

'Wait,' said Rob as he landed on the planking. 'We will take him back to England to face justice.'

'This is justice.'

For a moment, Scipio held Bracewell's terrified gaze. Then he rammed the cutlass point-first into Bracewell's stomach.

The cutlass was an edged weapon, meant for hacking and slicing, not stabbing. But with Scipio's strength behind it, the blunt point punctured the skin. It sank through the vast fat of Bracewell's belly, deep into his guts.

Bracewell screamed. Blood poured over the blade. Scipio did not relax his grip. He twisted the sword around, opening a gaping hole in the belly, then jerked the blade upwards. Bracewell was slit open like a fish. His guts spilled out. He clutched his stomach to try and hold in his intestines, but Scipio grabbed them, pulled them out and threw them over the side.

Sharks had been circling, drawn by the blood running out of the frigate's scuppers. They surged eagerly towards the offal in the water, dark shapes snapping and twisting below the surface.

Bracewell was still alive. He screamed, staring at his bloodied hands. Scipio could have ended it with a stroke of his cutlass, but he did not. He stood, hands on his hips, watching Bracewell's torment.

There was only one way for Bracewell to end his agony. With a howl like his soul being torn out, a visceral cry of anguish and despair, he staggered backwards and threw himself over the side. Rob did not look. Once off Nativity Bay he had seen sharks stripping blubber from the carcass of a dead whale. This would be no different.

A breeze caught the sails, heeling the ship to starboard. A spent cannonball rolled across the deck from where it had come to rest. Without thinking, Rob put out his foot and stopped it. He picked it up, the smooth iron so heavy for its size.

It made him think of another cannonball, another ocean and another battle won. When he found the cannonball in Nativity

Bay, all those months ago, it had felt like a relic of a lost, heroic age. Now he had written his own chapter in the history of the Courtneys. And when he returned to Nativity Bay, he would not feel overawed by his ancestors.

But the story was not yet finished. There was work to do. He tossed the cannonball over the side and sought out Hargrave.

'Are there any cannon left intact?'

Hargrave nodded. His head was bandaged, but it had not wounded his ready smile.

'A few, sir.'

'Then fire a salute to the shore battery. They have earned our thanks today.'

By the time Cal reached the foot of the cliff, the longboat had pushed off. Not far: she was heavy laden, low in the water, and the panicked French gunners could barely manage her. But they were too far off for Cal to reach.

'Come back for me, damn you!' he cried.

A couple of the Frenchmen in the boat's stern heard him. They shot back furtive glances, then returned to their oars. The boat did not change direction. If anything, it started to move more purposefully as the men began to row in some semblance of unison.

Cal crawled to the water's edge and into the sea. Waves broke against his face and filled his throat with brine. They picked him up and flung him back down again, knocking his broken leg against the rocks on the seabed. He screamed, letting more salt water into his lungs.

He swam to deeper water, where he could float more freely. He splashed out, milling his one good arm and one good leg in a frenzied dog paddle. It was not enough. The longboat had reached the entrance to the bay and pulled out around the headland.

Treading water, Cal saw armed Negroes running down the cliff path behind. Some had muskets, but they did not fire at him. Perhaps they thought he was out of range. Perhaps they wanted to watch him drown.

Cal would not give them the satisfaction. He would not give up. If there was no way back, he would keep moving forwards. He swam on, teeth gritted with pain and determination. He would swim to Cuba if he had to. He was a survivor.

But he was not alone in the water.

Most of the sharks were feasting near the frigates, but not all. One had stayed closer to shore. Perhaps he liked the warmer waters, or had an ancient instinct for quarry. It was a bull shark, its grey body sleek and agile, searching for prey. Now, he smelled blood. His nostrils could detect it from half a mile away, and he was considerably closer to the floundering body than that. With a flick of his mighty tail, he turned towards Cal, following the scent to its source.

Cal had left the shelter of the bay. The waves were higher, while the current that flowed around the point made it almost impossible for his shattered body to gain any headway. Still he fought on. He imagined he saw Aidan before him, standing on the water, beckoning him on. *I will make you proud.*

Then he saw the dorsal fin.

With his first glimpse he wasn't sure. Perhaps it was a piece of flotsam, or a shadow on the water. The second time, he knew it for what it was. Sailing from South Carolina, he had watched the sharks that followed the ship. He had seen them swim alongside when one of the pigs on board had been butchered. Once, for the crew's amusement, Étienne had thrown a live chicken overboard. A shark had swallowed it whole.

Being captured by the Maroons would be better than the fate that was about to devour him. Cal turned around in the water, splashing frantically towards the shore. He forgot his pain, windmilling his wounded arm and kicking his broken leg as hard as he could. It made no difference. The current swept him on, so that however much he tried he never seemed to move. The bay was far away.

Long before he reached shore, the shark overtook him.

Rob learned many lessons that day. The one he remembered most was what came after the fight. In his grandfather's tales, sea battles had always ended with the victory, with the villain defeated and the hero triumphant. In reality, the hardest part came afterwards. There were the wounded to tend, repairs to be made – and only a battered, exhausted crew to carry them out. The thrill of battle quickly dissipated. Grief for fallen shipmates would come later. For now, it was endless chores.

Rob went below with Angus and Scipio to inspect his prize. The *Rapace* had suffered far less damage than the *Perseus*. Her hull was intact below the waterline, and she still had most of her canvas.

'At last you managed to take a ship and keep her,' said Angus.

'There were times I had my doubts,' Rob admitted.

Scipio bared his teeth in a smile. 'I, too.'

They made their way aft to the great cabin. The windows were shattered, and the walls bore marks of fresh repairs from when Rob had put cannonballs through it at Seabrook Bay. Étienne had been a man of sparse tastes. There was nothing extravagant or luxurious in his cabin. The only decoration on the wall was a cameo of an elegant woman, her golden hair piled up high and her dress cut low. Rob could not help staring at it for a moment. There was something bewitching in that face.

The floor creaked behind the dressing screen. Instantly, Scipio's knife was in his hand. Angus crossed to the screen and ripped it down. It fell to the ground with a crash as loud as a musket shot, and a high-pitched scream.

The three men stared. Sophie Bracewell appeared, wearing nothing but her corset and petticoats. Her long dark hair hung loose over her bare shoulders. With a cry, she flew at Rob and wrapped her arms around him.

'Thank God you are here,' she sobbed. 'I was terrified those sailors would find me and do unspeakable things.'

'Get away.' Rob tried to push her back, but she clung on. 'I love you, Rob,' she breathed. 'I know I did wrong. But all those things, I did them because my uncle forced me. He was a brute. You saw how he treated me on the quarterdeck.'

Rob hesitated. He remembered Bracewell holding the pistol to his niece's temple. He looked uncertainly into those imploring blue eyes. It would be easy to believe their innocence.

'I'm sorry, Sophie,' he said, 'but your uncle is dead.'

Sophie kept her poise; she didn't move an eyelid. Was there a tear forming in her eye? Was she grief-stricken inside but exercising supreme self-control, or was her heart made of stone? Rob couldn't fathom this extraordinary woman. She scared and excited him in equal measure.

But those eyes had not flinched when she watched Angus take four dozen lashes, nor when the *Perseus*'s officers raped the slave girls at Thebes Plantation. They had held his gaze while she tormented Phoebe at supper. A face as sweet as sugar – and steeped in blood and cruelty.

He tore her hands off him.

'Lock her in one of the officers' cabins,' he told Angus. 'See that no harm comes to her. We will put her ashore at Port Royal.'

'But what will become of me?' she cried. 'I will be destitute and alone. I have no friends in Port Royal.'

'I think you will make friends easily enough,' Rob told her. 'You have a talent for it.'

Angus dragged her away. Before they reached the door, Rob noticed she had a bag in her hand. She had picked it up unobtrusively, as stealthy as a Limehouse pickpocket. She held it wrapped in her skirts, but it was too large to hide completely. An oilskin packet of papers.

'Give me that,' Rob said.

Sophie clutched it closer, hugging it to her chest.

'Even you would not be so ungallant as to deprive me of this. These are only a few personal letters. All the property I have left in the world.'

With many other thoughts crowding his mind, and two ships to command, Rob might have believed her. But the word 'property' was like a Roman candle lighting up in his brain. He knew what people like Bracewell and Sophie meant when they talked of ownership. And he knew what was in that packet.

'Give it to me,' he said again. Without waiting, he ripped it from her hands. 'If there is anything of a personal nature here, you may have it later.'

Sophie's face contorted in a mask of rage, and suddenly she was not beautiful at all.

'You have ruined me!' she screamed. 'I am left with nothing.'

'I daresay you will inherit your uncle's estate,' said Rob. 'Unless a traitor's property is forfeit.'

'Without slaves to work it, the plantation is useless.'

'Then you will perhaps have to get your hands dirty yourself.' Sophie looked aghast. 'You will still have your freedom. That is more than you ever gave anyone else.'

Before she could argue, Angus bundled her out of the door. Rob heard her shouting curses as she disappeared down the passage.

'Give me your knife,' he said to Scipio.

He slit open the packet and pulled it apart. There were papers inside, bundles and bundles of them, neatly parcelled up with ribbons.

He read the writing on the topmost sheet.

This is to certify that a negro named Ulysses, aged now about 7 years, has been duly registered as the property of Hezekiah Bracewell.'

The brown ink on the papers was the colour of dried blood. Rob felt soiled simply touching them. These were instruments of torture no less than the chains and whips and branding irons on the estate. They were the tools that men like Bracewell used to keep their hands clean, to ape the guise of respectable men of business, while they profited from the most barbarous and bloodthirsty trade ever conceived. Each sheet of paper was a life, a human being who would be made to bleed and suffer, and die if necessary, for another man's profit.

Rob rummaged through the certificates until he found the one he was looking for. He passed it to Scipio.

Scipio stared at the certificate, a confusion of emotions on his face. Rob had expected him to be happy, or grateful. Instead, all he saw was hatred.

'Speak up,' said Angus, who had returned to the cabin. 'Captain Courtney has freed you.'

Scipio's face hardened. He balled the paper into a wad and threw it out of the shattered stern window into the sea.

'No,' he said firmly. 'I freed me.'

'Good men died so that you could walk free. Do they nae count for anything?'

Rob laid a hand on Angus's arm. He understood.

'That is not what Scipio means,' he said. 'A man is not less than a man because a piece of paper states it. He is a man by his actions.'

Scipio nodded. He clasped Rob's hand and looked him full in the face – not with gratitude or subservience, but as one warrior to another.

'You are my brother,' he said.

'You are mine.'

Angus grunted. 'I think that means I'm related to both of you.' He clapped Scipio on the back. 'Whatever battles are to come, we will fight them together, aye?'

'Aye.'

Rob gave Scipio the stack of papers.

'Go through these and find any that belong to people at Thebes, or those who fled. The rest, we will burn.'

There were more papers in the packet. Rob pulled them out and placed them on a side table. Like the other documents, their horror was in their ordinariness. Receipts, bills of sale, certificates of ownership, tallies of goods. They could have belonged to any purser or chandler – except that the goods in question were human beings.

But one paper caught his eye. A letter written in a scrawling hand, the paper torn by angry strokes of the quill as if a flock of crows had pecked at it. It was different from the anonymous clerks' hands that the slave papers were written in.

Rob picked it up, noticing the heavy seal stamped on it. His eyes went to the signature at the bottom, and he nearly dropped the paper in shock.

A knock sounded at the cabin door. Thomas's face appeared, white as chalk.

'What is it?' Rob asked.

'It's Mr Coyningham, sir.'

In the heat of battle, and the aftermath of victory, Rob had put Coyningham out of his mind, a problem to be dealt with later.

'What does he want now?'

Thomas swallowed. 'He's dead, sir.'

'Dead?'

'He killed himself.' Thomas trembled. He looked as if he was about to be sick. 'Blew his head off with a pistol. Terrible to see, sir. Sprayed his brains all over the inside of the brig.'

Angus crossed the cabin and put an arm around Thomas's shoulders, a split second before he would have fainted.

'Now, lad. You've had a shock. Let's get some grog into you.'

There was a brandy decanter on a shelf on the wall. Angus unstopped it and tipped a good measure down Thomas's throat. Colour returned to the boy's cheeks.

Scipio remained impassive. Rob gave him a sideways glance. It was a curious thing for Coyningham to have shot himself. He had been unarmed when he was taken to the brig, and his hands had been shackled. In the confusion after the battle, it would not have been hard for a man to slip below with a loaded pistol. Scipio, in particular, would have had reason. It was Coyningham who had turned him over to Bracewell after Tew was killed.

Rob shook off the thought. There were many men aboard the *Perseus* who bore grudges against Coyningham, and any one of them might have taken the opportunity. He would never know the truth, and it did not matter. Better men than Coyningham had died that day.

'Swab out the brig,' Rob ordered. 'Before his blood draws every rat on the ship.'

Thomas nodded and left. Rob took the decanter and swigged from it, barely feeling the burn of the alcohol.

'You are a dangerous man to cross, Robert Courtney,' said Angus. 'All your enemies are dead and defeated.'

Rob supposed it was true, though he took no satisfaction from the thought. He picked up the letter he had been looking at, wondering again at the signature.

'Not all of them.'

The President of the Board of Trade and Foreign Plantations occupied a sumptuous suite of rooms at the Palace of Westminster, as befitted the importance of his office. All the Empire's trade flowed under his gaze. The members of Parliament, who themselves profited handsomely from that trade, were profuse in their gratitude.

Christopher Courtney relished the power. His chambers were designed to project his authority and intimidate those who crossed his threshold. Any visitor had to make his way through three consecutive anterooms, each guarded by a more withering and formidable clerk, before being admitted to the biggest room of all. He had a desk as large as a bed, a high-backed chair that cast his face in shadow, and trophies of his far-flung dominions hanging from the wall. In pride of place hung his most recent and most precious acquisition, the trophy he valued more than everything else in the room.

The Neptune Sword.

It hung above a huge stone mantelpiece opposite Christopher's desk, so it was never out of his sight. It rested on velvet-lined brackets, with lamps mounted either side so that the gold glimmered and the sapphire in the pommel glowed like the sea on a summer's day.

It was mid-afternoon. Sunlight streamed through the high windows overlooking the Thames. Parliament was not in session, so the palace was hushed and empty. Christopher preferred it like this. It was easier to work without fools interrupting him with their obsequious requests and piffling queries, asking after the cost of sugar duties or why the war in America did not progress with more success.

He knew why the war in America was going badly. He, Christopher, had made it so. Everything had happened as he had dictated in this very office.

Yet he could not rest easy. These past weeks, he had been waiting for news from the colonies that the final action, the keystone of his design, had been achieved. Every letter, every messenger, sent him into paroxysms of hope and worry.

A clerk knocked on the door. He was a gaunt, hatchet-faced man who would not hesitate to kick out a cabinet minister like a stray dog if his master was busy. Yet now he looked uncertain.

'Yes,' snapped Christopher. Anxiety made him more short-tempered than usual.

'Lieutenant Hugo Lyall wishes to see you.'

Christopher banged his golden hand on the table.

'Send him in, damn you. What are you waiting for?'

A thought occurred to him.

'But Lyall is not an officer.'

The clerk shrugged. 'He is wearing a Royal Navy lieutenant's uniform.'

It was no doubt some affectation the young buck had picked up in the West Indies. Christopher was too impatient to give it any more thought.

'Send him in.'

The visitor stepped past the sour-faced clerk, jostling him as he did so. He did not apologise.

'Mr Lyall,' the clerk announced, then left the room.

He closed the door behind him. In his haste, he did not notice that the key which had been in the outer lock was no longer there.

Rob palmed the key and slipped it in the pocket of his uniform coat as the door closed. It was too hot for such heavy attire, and he had pulled his hat low on his head, but it helped explain the sword hanging from his belt.

'I have been expecting you these past three weeks,' snapped Christopher. It was months since he had seen Hugo Lyall, and he had little recollection of him. He did not trouble himself to remember such insignificant creatures. He had the feeling that the youth was taller and broader than he remembered, but perhaps he had grown on his travels. His face was hidden under the brim of his hat. 'What is the news from Jamaica?'

Rob didn't answer. He was staring at the Neptune sword.

'Well?' Christopher snapped. It had been the best part of fifty years since anyone ignored him, let alone a callow youth like Hugo. 'Answer me.'

Rob lifted the Neptune sword down from the wall. Christopher's face went scarlet. His eyes bulged; the vein on his neck throbbed against his collar. No one had ever dared such insolence in his presence.

'Put that back this instant.' Christopher's voice had become tremulous. 'Put it back before I summon my men and have you arrested.

Rob turned to the door. With a swift motion, he put the key in the lock and twisted it. Before Christopher could react, Rob strode to the centre of the room, still holding the Neptune sword, and pulled off his tricorne hat to reveal his face.

'Now,' he said, 'let me tell you the news from Jamaica.'

Rage and confusion threatened to tear Christopher apart.

'You are not Hugo Lyall.'

'He is dead. Bracewell is dead. The French are defeated. The West Indies are safe.'

'What? How?' The news came so fast Christopher could not get his words out. 'Who *are* you?'

Rob threw the hat into a corner and stood, bare-headed and defiant.

'I am Robert Courtney. Your great-nephew.'

Christopher could feel his ribs crushing against his heart. His collar seemed to be throttling him. Sweat trickled from his face. The room was too hot.

But he had confronted more terrifying enemies than this boy. They had died, and he had always emerged more powerful than before. He forced himself to breathe more slowly, to focus on the boy. There was not a man born who did not have a weakness, and not a man alive better at exploiting it than Christopher.

And he was not as helpless as he appeared.

'You have done our country a great service,' he said, rubbing his golden hand. 'I congratulate you on saving our sugar colonies from the French. I am sure I can arrange a suitable token of my gratitude.'

'*Our* country?' echoed Rob. 'You conspired with our enemies. You would have sold the colonies to the highest bidder. You deserve to have your head on a spike above London Bridge.'

'That is an outrageous slander.'

'I have proof.'

'Impossible.'

Rob raised the letter he carried. Even across the broad desk, the angry left-handed scrawl was vivid and unmistakable.

'How did you come by that?' Christopher asked. His heart began to accelerate again.

Concentrate. He would only have one chance.

He leaned over the desk, reaching like a beggar straining for alms.

'Give that to me.'

Rob held it out of his reach.

'If I make this public, they will hang you for treason.'

'Who would dare?' scoffed Christopher. 'Only Parliament can impeach me, and there is not a man in this house who is not in my debt.'

'Really?' said Rob. 'I have heard there is a group of men in Parliament united by their opposition to slavery. They would ensure you could not hide this.'

'Balderdash.'

'We are losing the war in America,' said Rob. 'The people demand scapegoats. If it became known that the President of the Board of Trade and Foreign Plantations had conspired with our enemies, you might find your friends are not as loyal as you think.'

Christopher steepled his fingers, gold against flesh. He was calmer, breathing more easily.

'Do you offer me an alternative?'

'These abolitionists I spoke of – they have proposed outlawing the slave trade in the whole of the British Empire.'

'They are lunatics,' said Christopher. 'That monstrous law will never pass the house. They could not muster half a dozen votes.'

'It would pass if you threw your influence behind it.'

Silence settled between them. Dust motes spun in the shafts of sunlight. Christopher gazed at the letter, at the sword, and at Rob's implacable face.

'That is your price?'

'That – and the Neptune sword.'

'And you will return that letter to me and speak of it to no one?'

'As soon as the King signs the law.'

Christopher nodded slowly. He stared down at his desk, as if in the throes of a great internal struggle. He rubbed his thumb against the side of his prosthetic hand.

He raised his head and looked Rob in the eye.

'I accept your terms.'

Rob was astonished. He had barely dared hope he might succeed, let alone that Christopher would surrender so meekly. He thought of the tens of thousands of Africans who would no longer suffer the torments men like Bracewell could inflict. He could hardly contain his joy. He had won.

Christopher gave an avuncular smile as he took in Rob's pleasure. He rose from his chair and extended his golden right hand.

'We are family, Robert. We should not be enemies.'

Rob hesitated. He did not trust Christopher, but he was elated by his success. More, he knew that the schism in the family had been his grandfather's greatest sorrow. Here at last was a chance to mend it.

And that, thought Christopher, as his thumb touched the invisible catch hidden in the golden hand, *is the boy's weakness. His fatal weakness. He cannot see past family.*

In India, Christopher had discovered a weapon called the *bagh nakh*, the tiger claw – a short, razor-sharp knife mounted on a spring and worn on the finger. It could be concealed in your hand, then opened at close range with lethal effect. Christopher had used it more than once. When he had his prosthetic made, he had commissioned the goldsmith to build a similar mechanism into the false hand. A spring-mounted blade, recessed under the nail of the index finger.

Rob rested the Neptune sword against the desk and grasped Christopher's hand. Christopher jerked his wrist. Inside the golden hand, a meticulously wound spring uncoiled in an instant. The blade stabbed forwards, cutting through Rob's unprotected flesh towards the arteries.

But Rob was not the innocent he had been the first time he arrived in London. He had not dropped his guard. He had seen the hunger in Christopher's face, the gleam of anticipation. He had felt the vibration of the mechanism unwinding. As the blade sprang out, he had begun to snatch his hand away, reaching for his sword.

Blood welled from his wrist. The blade had cut deep, but it had missed the artery. Christopher saw at once the wound had not been fatal. He reached into his desk drawer. Even in the Palace of Westminster, he always kept a pistol hidden, loaded and ready to fire.

Rob and Christopher brought up their weapons at the same moment, the Neptune sword and the pistol. They faced each other across the table.

Rob hesitated. Christopher did not. He pulled the trigger.

The gun was two feet from Rob's chest. Christopher could not miss. Rob felt the heat of the flames that spat from the muzzle, the sting as spent grains of gunpowder peppered his face. Almost at the same moment, he felt the impact against his chest.

Afterwards, the story would be told that in that fraction of a second, Rob had moved the Neptune sword to block the shot. The legend would grow that Rob was so fine a swordsman he could strike a bullet out of the air as easy as swatting a fly.

The truth was, Rob had no time to react, let alone to move. But whether through luck, or because Christopher's gaze was so fixed on the Neptune sword that it drew his aim, the sword was in the bullet's path. It hit the flat of the blade and ricocheted away harmlessly.

But it had done its damage. The steel blade that had survived a thousand fights was two hundred years old. It could not withstand the impact of a bullet at point-blank range. The sword broke in two. The upper half flew off and clattered to the floor, while the lower half – still fixed to the handle – bent back and smacked Rob's chest.

Rob gazed at the broken blade in horror. Christopher's shock was greater. His mouth was open as if in a scream, though no sound emerged. His skin was waxy white, his eyes bulging as he stared at the one thing in his life he had ever loved.

Rob did not wait for Christopher to recover. He did not want to find out what other weapons he had hidden about his office. He levelled the broken sword and lunged.

The fractured stump of the blade was almost as sharp as the tip. It had no difficulty cutting through Christopher's coat, his shirt and his skin. It slid between his ribs and plunged into the chest cavity.

Christopher brought up his hands and closed them around the hilt, though he made no effort to pull it free. He stared at his own image reflected in all the facets of the sapphire pommel. His eyes were still open as, with a sigh, he slumped over on his desk. Blood ran out and soaked into his papers.

Rob had no time to consider what he had done. A gunshot in the Palace of Westminster would not go unnoticed. On the other side of the door, the clerk was shouting and rattling the handle. Rob unwrapped Christopher's hands from the sword hilt and pulled it out of his chest, then retrieved the other half from the floor where it had fallen. He wrapped them both in a large map that Christopher had kept on a chart table.

He cut the sleeve off his shirt and tied it around his wrist to staunch the bleeding, then pulled his sleeve back down to hide it. The shouts outside the door had turned to the heavy thuds of someone trying to batter it down. It was lucky that Christopher, valuing his privacy, had insisted on a stout door.

Rob burst from it, flinging aside the clerk. Before the man could look in the room, Rob slammed the door shut and locked it.

'What has become of Baron Dartmouth?' said the clerk. 'I heard a shot.'

'It must have come from outside,' said Rob. It was not a convincing lie. Rob was covered in powder burns and blood, but he pushed past the clerk towards the outer door before the man could stop him. It would be assumed that Hugo Lyall was the last person to see Baron Dartmouth alive, and that would keep Rob safe for a time. Keeping his head down, he hurried out of the Palace of Westminster as quickly as he dared.

He did not breathe easily until he was safely away from Parliament and among the greenery of St James's Park. He slowed his pace along the gravelled walkway, trying not to draw attention.

Phoebe had been waiting for him. She ran to his side, taking in his injuries in an instant.

'You are bleeding,' she said.

'It is nothing.'

'And what is that?' She peered into the rolled-up map. 'The sword has broken. Oh, Rob.'

'Blades can be reforged, stronger than before.' He tapped the sword he wore at his waist. 'For now, I have my own weapon. The one I earned.'

It was not bravado. The horror he had felt at seeing the broken sword had subsided. Christopher was dead, and he was alive. Against that, what did gold and steel matter?

Phoebe took strength from his calm.

'You have blood on your new shirt,' she reproached him.

Rob laughed, grateful for the release of the tension.

'I was not made to strut about in pretty uniforms. I always get them dirty.'

'Then you will keep me busy, laundering them.'

Rob cupped her chin in his hand and looked her in the eyes.

'You will not need to do that. It does not become an officer's wife to sully her hands with menial jobs.'

Phoebe went still. Disbelief mingled on her face with a hope that would have been too painful to bear, if Rob did not know he could fulfil it.

'An officer's *wife?*'

'Yes.'

It was not a new or idle thought. He had pondered it all the way back from Jamaica. He would have done this sooner, but he knew he had to wait until he had confronted Christopher. Now, nothing stood in his way.

He dropped to one knee.

'Marry me, Phoebe.'

For a long time, she said nothing. Rob's heart seemed to stop. Had he misjudged her? Had he deluded himself?

'Can it be possible?' she breathed.

'My grandfather used to say, a man's destiny is what he writes for himself. And a woman's, too. If you want it, it is possible.'

Phoebe pulled Rob to his feet and threw her arms around him.

'Yes!' she exclaimed. 'Robert Courtney, I will be your wife forever.'

Their lips met – the sweetest kiss he had ever tasted. They stood in the park, pressed together, oblivious to the ladies and gentlemen who stared as they walked by. In the touch of her body against his, Rob could feel his future coming into being.

'Mr Courtney, sir?'

The sound of his name broke the moment. Rob pulled away from Phoebe, his hand instinctively moving to his sword. Had he been identified? Had Christopher's clerk sent men to catch him?

To murder a peer of the realm in the Palace of Westminster was to strike a blow at the very heart of the British establishment. No one would believe Rob if he claimed self-defence.

But it was not the Bow Street Runners or a company of Horse Guards. It was a young midshipman, barely thirteen, with a pimply face, wearing a coat that was at least two sizes too big for his scrawny frame.

'Mr Courtney?' he said again, looking uncertainly at Rob's battle-stained appearance.

'How did you know where to find me?'

'I did not. I was on my way to your lodgings. I recognised you by your . . . ah . . . lady.'

That was likely enough. There were not many naval officers squiring a black woman around St James's Park. Rob supposed he would have to get used to being singled out. How much worse would it be for Phoebe?

He realised the midshipman was waiting.

'Well? What is it?'

The midshipman pressed an oilskin packet into his hands.

'Your orders, sir. From the Admiralty.'

The wax seal on the packet was still warm. Rob split it open and read the orders. The Lords of the Admiralty recognised Rob's outstanding seamanship and courage, his heroism in capturing the *Rapace* and saving the convoy transporting supplies to the West Indies. In recognition of these endeavours, they required and directed Robert Courtney Esq to repair with all dispatch to the sloop-of-war *Viper*, and to take upon himself the charge of Master and Commander.

'They are giving me my own ship,' he said, hardly daring to believe it.

He read on. He was to join the Channel fleet, operating inshore on the French coast, gaining intelligence. It would be dangerous work – but that was not what made him pause.

'They want me to go to France,' he told Phoebe.

'You will go,' she said.

It was not a question. Still, Rob hesitated. An echo of something Bracewell had said ran through his minds, cruel words that cut all the more deeply for being true.

This whole war is paid for with sugar. Every button on your uniform, every grain of gunpowder, every stitch of canvas on every ship.

'How can I in good conscience defend an empire that is built on slavery?'

Phoebe nodded. For her, slavery was not an abstraction. It was years of her life, unnumbered and unspeakable atrocities that had been inflicted on her. Yet her voice was calm when she spoke.

'Britain is more than this. That is why Bracewell and your uncle turned against their own country. There are good men here, men who are fighting for justice, and they are already turning the tide. In England you and I can stand freely, and love and choose to marry. If it happens in England today, one day soon it will happen in the colonies. You must fight for that day, and against the nations which want to enslave men and women forever.'

Her words calmed Rob. Yet he was still unsure.

'I would be away at sea for months at a time. It would be a dangerous life. I would not be a good husband to you, or a good father to our children.'

'You would not be a good husband or father if you stayed on land, like a lion trapped in his den.' She stroked his face. 'I have watched you, Robert. The only time I have seen you truly happy is at sea with your men.'

'The only time I have been truly happy is waking in your arms,' said Rob, squeezing her waist. 'Also, you have only ever seen me on land when I was being chased by rebels or attacked by Frenchmen. Life is not always like that.'

Phoebe gave him a wry smile. 'I think for you, life is like that more often than for other men.'

The midshipman coughed. He had retreated to a discreet distance, but he was waiting awkwardly.

'Shall I take a reply to the Admiralty?'

Rob touched the hilt of his sword again, feeling its strength and power. Phoebe was right. This was the life he was born to lead.

'Tell their Lordships I will make for Portsmouth directly.'

The midshipman nodded and scampered away. Rob reread the commission, joy dawning on his face. *His own ship.*

'I will have to get used to calling you Captain Courtney,' said Phoebe.

'It has a good ring,' Rob admitted.

'Scipio and Angus are in Portsmouth already,' she said. 'They guessed where the Admiralty would send you.'

'As usual, I am the last to learn my own future,' Rob said in mock exasperation. 'I suppose they have already signed aboard the *Viper*?'

Phoebe lowered her eyes. 'You had better join them before they sow a mutiny.'

'I had,' Rob agreed. 'But I cannot leave without getting married.'

'You promised the Admiralty you would go straight to Portsmouth,' she reminded him.

'The Admiralty can wait a little longer.' He slid his hand around her waist and squeezed gently. 'And we will need time for a honeymoon.'

'This is not the best start to your command,' she teased him. 'You have been a captain five minutes and you are already disobeying orders.'

'It is the best possible start.'

He linked his arm in hers, and together they walked through the park and up the hill towards the bustle of Piccadilly. They attracted glances from the passers-by, but not as many as Rob had expected. Black people in London were a common sight. Thousands of them lived in the city, men and women who went about their lives just as any other. Who was to say who they should fall in love with?

That, after all, was freedom.

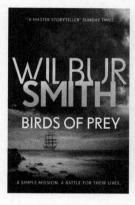 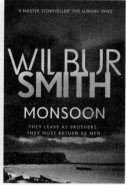 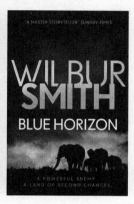

BETRAYED BY BLOOD. FREED BY FATE.

GHOST FIRE

Inseparable since birth, Theo and Connie Courtney are torn apart by the tragic death of their parents.

Theo, wracked with guilt, seeks salvation in combat, joining the British in the war against the French and Indian army. On a personal mission he meets the beautiful, innocent Abigail, with whom he falls madly in love. But when their tryst is discovered, Theo is left outcast in the wilderness, desperately fighting for his life. Determined to reclaim his honour and save Abigail, Theo does whatever it takes to survive.

Connie, believing herself abandoned by her brother, and abused and brutalised by a series of corrupt guardians, makes her way to France, where she is welcomed into high society. Here, she once again

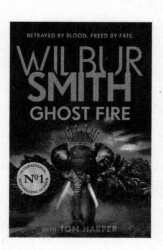

finds herself at the mercy of vicious men, whose appetite for war and glory lead her to the frontlines of the French battlefield in North America.

As the siblings find their destinies converging once more, they realise that the vengeance and redemption they both desperately seek could cost them their lives . . .

AVAILABLE NOW

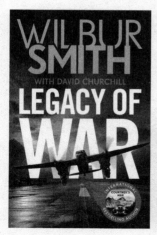
 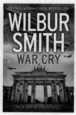 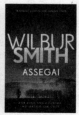

IN THE HEART OF EGYPT
A NEW POWER IS RISING

The New Kingdom is a brand-new Egyptian Series thriller by the master of adventure, Wilbur Smith.

Don't miss the rest of the Egyptian Series, *River God*, *The Seventh Scroll*, *Warlock*, *The Quest*, *Pharaoh* and *Desert God*.

AVAILABLE NOW

WILBUR SMITH

THE POWER OF ADVENTURE

Visit the brand-new Wilbur Smith website to find out more about all of Wilbur's books, read the latest news, and dive into Wilbur's adventure notebooks on everything from the Boer War to the Skeleton Coast.

And if you want to be the first to know about all the latest releases and announcements, make sure to **subscribe to the Readers' Club mailing list**. Sign up today and get a preview of the next epic Wilbur Smith adventure!

Join the adventure at

WWW.WILBURSMITHBOOKS.COM